# RIO

D0630375

Previous Books by Georgina Gentry

*Cheyenne Captive*
*Cheyenne Princess*
*Comanche Cowboy*
*Nevada Nights*
*Quicksilver Passion*
*Cheyenne Caress*
*Apache Caress*
*Christmas Rendezvous* (anthology)
*Sioux Slave*
*Half-Breed's Bride*
*Nevada Dawn*
*Cheyenne Splendor*
*Song of the Warrior*
*Timeless Warrior*
*Warrior's Prize*
*Cheyenne Song*
*Eternal Outlaw*
*Apache Tears*
*Warrior's Honor*
*Warrior's Heart*
*To Tame a Savage*
*To Tame a Texan*
*To Tame a Rebel*
*To Tempt a Texan*
*To Tease a Texan*
*My Heroes Have Always Been Cowboys* (anthology)
*To Love a Texan*
*To Wed a Texan*
*To Seduce a Texan*
*Diablo*: The Texans

Published by Kensington Publishing Corporation

# RIO
## The Texans

## Georgina Gentry

# ZEBRA BOOKS
## Kensington Publishing Corp.
http://www.kensingtonbooks.com

*This story is dedicated to the memory
of the six hundred men of the
Saint Patrick's Brigade
of the Mexican-American War
who went over to the other side.
Whether they were protectors of the faith
or traitors to the United States
is up to my readers and history to decide.*

# Prologue

Padraic Kelly looked around at the cactus and barren land, then chafed at the hemp rope around his neck that also tied his hands behind him. The oxcart he stood in creaked under his feet as the animal stamped its hooves in impatience and the smell of blood and gunpowder.

In the gray light of dawn, the roar of cannons and the screams of dying men echoed across the desert battleground.

Ah, but by Saint Mary's blood, the delay would not be long enough for the thirty condemned soldiers. Padraic turned his head and looked down the line of other men standing in oxcarts, ropes around their necks. Some of them seemed in shock, some had their eyes closed, praying to the saints for a miracle.

There'd be no miracles this morning, Padraic thought bitterly and wished he could reach his rosary, but it was tucked in the breast pocket of his uniform. It was ironic somehow that he had fled the starvation of Ireland to come to America and now his new country was going to execute him.

The colonel walked up and down the line of oxcarts, the early sun glinting off his brass buttons.

"Beggin' your pardon, sir," Padraic called, "for the love of mercy, could ye hand me my holy beads?"

The colonel sneered, his tiny mustache wiggling on his ruddy face. "Aw, you papist traitor! You'll not need your silly beads when the flag falls. We're sending all you Irish traitors to hell, where you belong."

He should have known better than to ask the Protestant officer for help. Hadn't he and most of the other officers treated all the new immigrants with disdain and bullying, which was the very reason some of the St. Patrick's battalion had gone over to the Mexican side? It hadn't seemed right, fighting fellow Catholics just because America had declared war on Mexico.

A curious crowd of peasants gathered, most with sympathetic faces, but the American soldiers held them back. There was nothing the unarmed peasants could do to rescue all these condemned men.

Padraic mouthed a silent prayer as he stared at the distant castle on the horizon. The early sun reflected off steel and gun barrels as the soldiers of both sides battled for control of the landmark. Smoke rose and men screamed and Padraic held his breath, watching the Mexican flag flying from the parapet.

"Yes, watch it!" The colonel glared up at him. "For when it falls and is replaced by the stars and stripes, you cowardly traitors will die!"

The Mexicans seemed determined to hold the castle as the hours passed and the sun moved across the sky with relentless heat, throwing shadows of the condemned men in long, distorted figures across the sand.

Padraic's legs ached from hours of standing in the cart and his mouth was so dry, he could hardly mouth prayers anymore. Behind him he heard others in the oxcarts begging for water. Padraic was proud; he would not beg, though he was faint from the heat and the sweat that drenched his blue uniform. He knew they would not give the condemned water anyway. Their guards did bring water to the oxen and Padraic tried not to watch the beasts drinking it.

In one of the carts, a man fainted and the colonel yelled for a soldier to throw water on him. "I don't want him to miss that flag coming down!" he yelled.

Padraic could only guess how many hours had passed from the way the sun slanted now in the west. The castle itself was cloaked in smoke and flames. He began to wish it would soon be over. Better to be dead than to stand here waiting all day in the hot sun for the hanging.

Sweat ran from his black hair and down the collar of his wool Mexican uniform. God, he would give his spot in Paradise for one sip of cool water. Well, his discomfort would soon be over. He didn't regret that he had fled the U.S. Army; he had done it because of his love for a Mexican girl. That love had transcended everything else. He did regret so many had followed him, some of them so young and barely off the boat. They had been escaping from the potato famine, but now they would die anyway.

The heat made dizzying waves across the barren landscape and he staggered a little and regained his footing. If he must die, he would go out like a man.

The crowd of sympathetic peasants was growing as word must have spread that the Americans were hanging their deserters. Padraic looked around for Conchita, hoping, yet dreading to see her. He did not want his love to see him die this way.

Hail Mary, Mother of God . . . He murmured the prayer automatically and he was once again a small boy at his mother's knee as they said their beads together. Now she would never know what happened to her son who had set off for the promise of America. It was just as well. He'd rather her think he was happy and successful than know he had been hanged like a common thief.

The riches of the new country had not been good, with so many Irish flooding in and everyone hating and sneering at the immigrants. If he could have found a job, he wouldn't have joined the army, but no one wanted to hire the Irish.

The fighting in the distance seemed to be slowing, though he choked on the acrid smell of cannon smoke and watched the castle burning in the distance. The Mexican flag flew bravely on the parapet but he could see the bright blue of the American uniforms like tiny ants as the invaders attacked the castle. It wouldn't be long now. The ropes bit into his wrists and he would give his soul for a sip of cold water, but he knew better than to ask. He closed his eyes and thought about the clear streams and the green pastures of County Kerry. He was a little boy again in ragged clothes, chasing the sheep toward the pens with no cares in the world save hoping for a brisk cup of tea and a big kettle of steaming potatoes as he ran toward the tumbledown stone cottage.

If only he could see Conchita once more. He smiled despite his misery and remembered the joy of the past three months. The pretty girl had been the one bright spot in his short, miserable life. He closed his eyes and imagined her in his arms again: her kisses, the warmth of her skin. He hoped she had not heard about the court-martial and the public hangings. He did not want her to see him die, swinging and choking at the end of a rope like a common criminal.

The rope rasped against his throat, the ox stamped its feet, and the cart creaked while Padraic struggled to maintain his balance. The colonel had stood them here all afternoon and now he almost wished the cart would pull ahead because he was so miserable, with his throat dry as the barren sand around him and his arms aching from being tied behind while his legs threatened to buckle under him.

*No,* he reminded himself, *you are going to die like a man, and a soldier. You just happen to be on the losing side.*

In the distance, he could see the blue uniforms climbing ladders up the sides of the castle as the fighting grew more intense. Screams of dying men mixed with the thunder of cannons and the victorious shrieks as the Americans charged forward, overrunning the castle now as the sun became a bloody ball of fire to the west.

The ruddy colonel grinned and nodded up at Padraic. "It won't be long now, you Mick trash. I knew I could never turn you Irish into soldiers."

"If ye'd treated us better, we wouldn't have gone over to the other side, maybe," Padraic murmured.

The colonel sneered. "And look what you get! We're hanging more than the thirty I've got here. General Scott asked President Polk to make an example of the Saint Patrick's battalion. If it'd been up to me, I'd have hung the whole lot, especially that John Riley that led you."

"Some of them would rather have been hung than to have been lashed and branded," Padraic snarled.

"It's better than being dead," the colonel said. Then he turned and yelled at the soldiers holding back the Mexican peasants. "Keep those brown bastards back. We don't want them close enough to interfere with the hanging."

Padraic watched the peasants. Some of them were on their knees, saying their rosaries, others looking up at them gratefully with tears making trails down their dusty brown faces.

"Paddy, dearest!" He turned his head to see Conchita attempting to fight her way past the soldiers.

"Hold that bitch back!" the colonel bellowed. "Don't let her through the lines."

"Get your filthy hands off her!" Padraic yelled and struggled to break free, although he knew it was useless. Conchita was so slim and small and her black hair had come loose and blew about her lovely face as she looked toward him and called his name.

There was too much roar of battle now as the Yankees overran the castle for her to hear him, but he mouthed the words, *I love you. You are the best thing that has happened to me since I crossed the Rio Grande.*

She nodded that she understood and her face was so sad that he looked away, knowing that to see her cry would make him cry, too, and he intended to die like a man.

A victorious roar went up from the American troops as they finally fought their way to the top of the distant tower. It would only be a few moments now.

"Take her away," Padraic begged his guards. "I don't want her to see this!"

The colonel only laughed. "No, we want all these Mexicans to see what happens to traitors. Why don't you beg, Kelly? Don't you want your little greasy sweetheart to see you beg for your life?"

In the distance, the American soldiers were taking down the ragged Mexican flag, but even as it came down, one of the young Mexican cadets grabbed it from the victors' hands and as they tried to retrieve it, he ran to the edge of the parapet and flung himself over the edge to the blood-soaked ground so far below. The Mexican peasants sent up a cheer, which the colonel could not silence with all his shouting. The cadet had died rather than surrender his country's flag to the enemy.

Now the American flag was going up, silhouetted against the setting sun. The peasants shouted a protest as soldiers climbed up on the oxcarts and checked the nooses. "No! No! Do not hang them!"

Conchita screamed again and tried to break through the line of solders holding back the crowd. "Paddy! My dear one!" She couldn't get to him, although she clawed and fought.

Padraic smiled at her and gave her an encouraging nod. If only things were different. He would have built a mud hut on this side of the Rio Grande and lived his life happily with this woman. If only he could hold her in his arms and kiss those lips once more.

Conchita looked up at him, her brave, tall man with his fair skin and wide shoulders. She made one more attempt to break through the guards, but they held her back. A roar of protests went up around her from the other peasants. He was her man and they were going to execute him and there was nothing she could do to stop it. She screamed his name and tried to tell him the secret, shouting that she carried his child, but in the noise of distant gunfire and the peasants yelling, she wasn't sure he understood, although he smiled and nodded at her and mouthed *I love you, too.*

"Your child!" she shrieked again. "I carry your child!"

At that precise moment, she heard the officer bark an order and all the oxcarts creaked forward. For just a split second, the condemned men swayed, struggling to keep their balance, and then the carts pulled out from under the long line of soldiers and their feet danced on air as they swung at the end of their ropes.

Conchita watched in frozen horror and tried to get to her Paddy as he fought for air, but the soldiers held her back. Her eyes filled with tears and the sight of the men hanging grew dim as they ceased to struggle.

"This is what the U.S. Army does to traitors and deserters!" the colonel announced to the crowd with satisfaction.

Conchita burst into sobs. She was in great pain as if her heart had just been torn from her breast. She did not want to live without her love, but she must, for his child's sake. She was not even sure he had heard her as she tried to tell him he would be a father. If it were a boy, she would raise that son and call him Rio Kelly for his father and the river that made a boundary between the two civilizations. And then she would go into a cloistered order and spend her life praying for the souls of her love and the other condemned men.

The soldiers were cutting the thirty bodies down now, and she broke through the line of guards and ran to her Paddy as he lay like a tattered bundle of rags on the sand. She threw herself on the body, weeping and kissing his face, but his soul had fled to his God and he could no longer feel her kisses and caresses.

Only now did she realize he had died smiling and so she knew he had heard her and knew he would have a child.

# Chapter 1

*On the outskirts of Austin, Texas, mid-April 1876*

Turquoise Sanchez knew she was in trouble when her mare began to limp. She dismounted and patted Silver Slippers's velvet muzzle. "Now what are we to do?" she murmured to the dapple-gray horse as she examined the loose shoe.

Silver Slippers nuzzled her owner and blew softly.

Turquoise looked around, assessing the situation. She was several miles from her downtown hotel and at least two miles from her friend Fern's ranch. In her tiny riding boots, with the midmorning sun getting hotter, walking and leading the mare didn't seem very appealing.

She sighed and took off her large-brimmed hat that shielded her face from the unforgiving sun and felt perspiration begin to break out under her turquoise, long-sleeved riding outfit. The turquoise and silver jewelry she wore now felt heavy on her small frame, and her long black hair was partially loose from its pins. She must look a mess.

Well, she'd gotten herself into this predicament. Most young women her age would never have gone riding alone, but then, Turquoise was more daring and resourceful than most young ladies.

"Silver Slippers, we'll just have to walk up this road a ways and see if we can find some help."

That wasn't likely to be forthcoming, she thought as she began to walk; this was a deserted dirt road without much traffic. At least Uncle Trace would become alarmed when she didn't meet him for luncheon at the hotel and would come looking for her. Except she hadn't left any messages as to where she was going. Sometimes it was not wise to be so independent.

Stubbornly, she set off walking up the road, leading the limping mare. Surely along this road somewhere she would run across a ranch or some chivalrous gentleman who would come to her aid. "Dammit," she muttered as she trudged forward, kicking at stones with her small riding boots. "What do I do now?"

She walked another quarter of a mile, perspiring and annoyed. She needed a cold drink of water and so did her mare. Turquoise rounded a curve in the road, and ahead she saw a small, rather run-down building with a rusty sign that read BLACKSMITH.

*Sometimes the good saints do answer prayers,* she thought. Without thinking, she crossed herself and walked faster. As she grew closer, she noticed a movement inside the big door and saw a man, and what a man.

He was tall, muscular, and very tan with a mop of unkempt black hair. He was naked to the waist and a silver cross gleamed on his sweating chest as he hammered on a piece of metal.

"Hello! Are you the blacksmith?" she called and he looked up, staring at her with big dark eyes. Mexican, she thought, or at least part Mexican.

"*Si,* senorita," he nodded as she approached. "How may I be of service?" He had a Mexican accent, as she expected, and a pleasing deep voice.

Rio Kelly watched the girl approaching him. She was a

small woman, smartly dressed, and everything about her spoke of wealth. She led a very fine dapple-gray horse, also of quality, just like the young lady.

She frowned as she walked up. "Some water for me and my horse," she snapped.

This was evidently a spoiled, high-class girl who was used to being waited on.

"You might at least say 'please.'" He pulled a handkerchief out of his back pocket and wiped the sweat from his dark face. Despite her ebony hair, she had light-colored eyes and very creamy white skin.

"I'm sorry," she apologized. "I'm hot and thirsty and, as you can see, in need of some help."

He stepped forward and took the reins from her hand and felt almost an electric shock as their two hands touched, although his was so much larger and stronger than hers. "There's a horse trough by my building and I've a well nearby. Let me get you a drink."

"*Gracias*—I mean, thanks," she blurted and he wondered again about this turquoise-eyed beauty. Her eyes were large and the color of a pale sky. "My mare has a loose shoe and I need to get back to town."

"Such a fine mare. She must have cost a fortune." He took in the wealth of silver and turquoise jewelry she wore and the fine leather boots.

The girl shrugged. "My guardian bought her for me two days ago."

"Does he buy you everything you want?" He was abruptly annoyed with the wealthy girl.

She blinked as if wondering why he was so short-tempered. "Not everything, but I wanted this mare."

He looked at her critically. "It's very warm to be wearing long sleeves and such a big hat."

"To protect myself against the sun," she said. "Ladies always protect themselves against the sun. It darkens the skin."

She had the lily-white skin of the rich gringos. He led the dapple gray over to the trough, where the horse drank gratefully. Rio tied the mare up and gestured toward the well. "Here, senorita—I mean, miss—let me get you a drink."

"'Senorita' is all right." She nodded. "I, too, am Mexican."

She didn't look Mexican, but he didn't say that. Instead, he led her around the building and down the lane a few yards to the well where he brought up a bucket of cold spring water, reached for the metal dipper, and offered it to her.

Even as she drank, he noted she was staring at his hand.

"A four-leaf clover?"

He glanced down at the small tattoo on the back of his right hand. "For my father. He was Irish. Allow me to introduce myself, senorita. I am Rio Kelly."

"Odd combination," she murmured and sipped the water again.

"I'm half-Irish, half-Mexican," he said by way of explanation and smiled at her in spite of himself.

"I am Turquoise Sanchez," she said, "and I need to get back to town to meet my uncle for lunch."

He nodded. "*Si.* As soon as I can heat my forge a little more, I'll get a new shoe on your horse."

"*Gracias,*" she said and took off her big hat, fanning herself with it.

She had the most luxurious long black hair and it was falling out of its pins and down on her shoulders. With her unusual turquoise eyes, he thought she was the most striking woman he had ever seen.

"Come then," he gestured and turned back to his shop. As they walked, she fanned herself with her big hat and looked around. "Lovely landscape. Do you own all this?"

He chuckled as he strode into the shed and she followed.

"Hardly, only fifty acres, this shop and that barn and house up there on the hill."

She turned and looked at a modest adobe ranch house and a red barn. "It's still very nice."

He shrugged and grabbed the bellows, blowing the fire still bigger. "There's five thousand acres next to me, but it's owned by some big New York company and I can never hope to earn enough to buy it."

She watched him as he grabbed his pliers and strode out to her mare, lifted the dainty hoof, and talked softly to Silver Slippers. "Ah, beautiful one, you'll let me change your shoe, no? Then you won't limp."

"Careful, she can be a little wild," Turquoise cautioned. "She has not been treated well."

He looked the mare over and scowled at Turquoise. "This mare has whip marks on her."

"I didn't put them there," she said, defending herself. "My guardian and I were out for a walk two days ago and I saw a well-dressed young drunk beating this horse. Before I thought, I ran out, took the whip from him, and struck him several times. Then my guardian knocked the man down and insisted he sell us the horse."

"Ah," the blacksmith said, nodding approval.

"So now she's my baby and I love her." Turquoise stroked the mare's velvet muzzle and the mare whickered and nuzzled back.

"I'd say the feeling is mutual," the man said and smiled, showing even white teeth in his dark face. He looked at Turquoise over his muscular shoulder, then returned to taking off the loose shoe as he reassured the mare. "Horses like me."

Silver Slippers barely blinked as he examined her hoof.

"Well," Turquoise said, surprised, "you really do have a way with horses."

He came back to the forge, picked up a new shoe, and held it in the fire. As it began to glow, he pounded and hammered it into shape. "And what are you doing in Austin, Senorita Sanchez?"

"I'm here for the big debutante ball tonight at the governor's mansion," she said. "Are you going?" Then she felt foolish as he paused in pounding the horseshoe and stared at her, a slight smile on his handsome face.

"Do I look like I fit in with Austin's fancy gringos?" he asked.

"I'm sorry," she murmured.

"Don't be." He shrugged his wide shoulders and examined the glowing horseshoe a long moment. "The Mexican population hardly knows what the gringos are doing and care less."

"Well, it's at the governor's home," she said. "Surely you have seen the governor's home?"

"Only from a distance," he said and, picking up the glowing shoe with his pliers, he carried it out to the horse trough and dunked it in, where it hissed and sent up steam as it cooled. "I'm sure, though, you will be the most beautiful lady there."

She felt herself flush at the bold way his dark eyes looked her over. "I doubt that. I'm sure there will be many of the most beautiful girls from the very best families."

He chuckled and she winced at the past memory. From the very best families. It had only been half a dozen years that her guardian had sent her away to the fine Houston school for upper-class Texas girls, most from Stephen Austin's original Three Hundred, the blue bloods of Texas founders. The girls had been so cruel to her that she had stayed only a week before fleeing back to the Durangos' ranch. She never told her guardian why she didn't like the private school. She was too proud to say that the gringa girls had taunted her about her Mexican name, teasing her with cruel words like "hot tamale" and "greasy Mexican girl."

"There, senorita." He held up the horseshoe, bringing her

out of her memories with a start as he walked with the horseshoe back out to her mare.

Turquoise watched him pick up the mare's hoof and gently and expertly pound the shoe on while the horse seemed unconcerned. "You are better than good with horses," she said.

*"Gracias."* He smiled at her. "Someday, I hope to make a living strictly as a vaquero and raise fine cattle and horses, but right now that's not possible."

"Well, I will pay you handsomely." She stepped forward, opening her small reticule.

"I did not mean to hint for more money." His expression turned cool.

"Oh, I intend to tip you for your trouble. After all, if you hadn't helped me—"

He backed away from her, holding out one big, calloused hand. "The charge is one dollar, miss, and I am not a lowly servant to be tipped by a rich lady."

"I only meant . . . ," she stammered as she realized she had humiliated him. "All right, one dollar." She put the silver in his palm and waited for him to assist her in mounting her mare.

"I'm sorry." He ducked his head. "You see how dirty my hands are and I wouldn't want to spoil your fine dress."

"Yes, of course." She realized then she had been looking forward to feeling the strength of this big man as he lifted her to her saddle. "I've been raised on a ranch and am perfectly capable of mounting myself." She swung up into her saddle and adjusted her hat so that it would protect her face from the sun. "Well, *adios.*"

He only nodded and she rode out at a brisk canter without looking back.

Rio Kelly stood holding the silver dollar and staring after the mysterious girl who was so obviously more white than Mexican, but had a Mexican name. This fine lady was far above him socially and not for the likes of a poor vaquero, but still, he knew he would think of her all the rest of the day.

Turquoise rode at a canter back to Austin and down Congress Avenue until she reined in in front of the Cattlemen's Hotel, the finest of its kind in all Texas.

The doorman hurried out to meet her and took the reins as she stepped down.

"What time is it?" she asked.

He pulled out a pocket watch. "Nearly noon, ma'am."

Turquoise heaved a sigh of relief as she turned to him.

"Please put my horse in your stable and give her a good rubdown and plenty of water. She's had a long ride."

"Yes, miss." He nodded with a smile, and she tossed him a coin.

That made her think of the haughty but poor blacksmith who had spurned her tip. Oh, well. She hurried inside and up the stairs to her suite of rooms.

Good, Uncle Trace wasn't here, which meant he was probably in the bar or in the lobby reading the papers.

She took off her hat and laid it on the dresser, looking in the mirror. She felt a fine layer of dust on her pale face and took off the long-sleeved riding outfit, then sighed as the cooler air touched her skin.

Walking to the bowl and pitcher, she poured a bowlful and proceeded to wash herself, especially her face. Then she sprayed herself with forget-me-not cologne.

Turquoise brushed her hair and put it up on her head with silver clips. Then she selected an expensive, pale pink lawn dress and tiny white slippers.

Now she picked up a lace, beribboned parasol that matched the dress and went down the stairs to lunch.

The maître d' met her at the dining room door and bowed. "Your uncle is already seated, miss."

"*Gracias*," she said and followed him across the crowded

dining room, ignoring the many men whose gazes seemed to follow her path.

"*Dios,* Turquoise, where have you been?" Trace Durango got up from his chair to greet her as the maître d' pulled out hers. "I was worried about you ridin' that new horse."

"It's a long story," she said, reaching for a linen napkin. "Silver Slippers is a wonderful mare, but she had a loose shoe and I was sort of stranded until I found a blacksmith."

His dark face frowned. "I've told you not to go ridin' alone. A girl could get into trouble in this big town, or get thrown by a spirited horse."

"Oh, stop fussing over me." She picked up her menu, noting that her half-Cheyenne, half-Spanish guardian was still handsome, although his black hair was graying at the temples as he approached forty. "I ride well. You should know. You taught me. By the way, we are going to shop for a ball gown after lunch, aren't we?"

He sighed heavily. "Now that's one chore I could do without. Reckon I could just sit in the buggy while you do it?"

"You are planning on coming tonight, aren't you?" she asked, looking over the menu.

"*Si,* but I'd rather be horsewhipped than get all dandied up and mix with these gringo city snobs. Honestly, Turquoise, I don't know why this means so much to you."

"Because all Texas girls of good family have to be presented as debutantes, or so the Austin papers say."

"Huh," he reminded her, "we sent you to mix with those snooty girls once at that fancy school, and you were home in a week."

She winced, not wanting to remember that painful time. However, she was grown now and her guardian would be with her. At the debutante ball was where she would meet the most eligible of Texas bachelors, rich, important, and influential, some handsome gringo who would protect her from slights and continual questions about her white complexion but Mexican name. "What looks good?" she asked.

"I'm having Mexican food, myself," he said, "with a cold mug of *cerveza* and plenty of chili peppers."

"If Cimarron were home, she'd be telling you you might get heartburn," Turquoise chided.

Trace grinned. "But she and the kids are gone 'til July to the big World's Fair thing."

"Philadelphia Centennial Exposition," she corrected. "And it's going to be a very educational experience for both your wife and the children, celebrating our country's one hundredth birthday."

"I don't understand why you passed up the chance to go with them," Trace grumbled and closed his menu.

"Because I wanted to be part of the debutante ball," she reminded him.

"I hope you enjoy it. It cost me enough to get you on the list. Besides being from the best gringo families, they must all be rich to pay that fee."

"And I can never thank you enough." She smiled at him and then nodded to the patient waiter. "I'll have the cold cucumber soup, those tiny chicken sandwiches, and a very tall glass of iced tea."

"What about dessert?" Trace asked as he gave his order to the waiter.

She sighed. "Maybe. That chocolate mousse looks excellent but so does the strawberry tart."

The waiter left and she sipped her water and thought. Somehow it was not as refreshing as that she'd had from the tin dipper at the blacksmith shop.

She felt the admiring gaze of many of the gentlemen, but she ignored them. A high-class white girl would only meet gentlemen on respectable terms, such as an introduction from a friend or relative or perhaps tonight at the debutante ball. That was what she yearned for, a gentleman who would

love her in spite of her Mexican name and questionable
blood, and who would protect her from all the hateful taunts
of mean-spirited gringa girls.

Tonight she would be the beautiful girl from the fairy
tale *Snow White,* and a handsome, rich, and successful
prince would fall in love with her and beg for her hand in
marriage.

She frowned. Yes, that had been her goal for some years
now. Then why did her mind keep returning to that dark,
muscular Mexican vaquero with the four-leaf clover tattoo
whom she had met this morning? He was everything she
did not want: poor, of no social standing, and yet, in her
mind, she saw that half-naked body gleaming with sweat
and her mouth wondered what it would be like to be kissed
by him. Uncle Trace stared at her. "What's the matter?
You're blushin'."

She felt guilty and flustered. "It's probably a touch of
sunburn, that's all."

She hid her face behind her napkin and coughed, annoyed with herself that she couldn't get the vaquero off
her mind.

# Chapter 2

After lunch, Trace ordered a rental buggy and Turquoise shielded herself from the sun with her parasol on the ride to the La Mode Dress Shoppe.

A middle-age, elegant lady approached them as they entered. "Hello, I am Mrs. Whittle. Welcome to my shop."

"Oh, yes," Turquoise said, "you're the one we sent the paperwork to."

"And all that money," Trace grumbled and took a chair.

"Well, sir"—Mrs. Whittle drew herself up proudly—"if we didn't keep the fees high, just anybody could take part and the society committee only wants the very best girls."

"That depends on who you're callin' the very best girls," Trace answered but Turquoise gave him a pleading look and he hushed. "Just sell my ward a proper gown."

Turquoise smiled and curtsied. "I am Turquoise Sanchez."

Turquoise noted Mrs. Whittle was now staring at her with a pronounced frown. "Sanchez?" asked Mrs. Whittle. "You don't look Mexican. I thought there might be some mistake in the paperwork and wrote it down as 'Sanders.'"

So here it was again—to be humiliated because she looked like a gringa but had a Mexican name. "I am

Mexican." Turquoise stuck her chin out stubbornly. "Does that make a difference?"

"Uh, well, it's just that we've never had one at our ball before."

"Well, now you do," Uncle Trace snapped and buried his nose in the newspaper.

Turquoise could almost feel the sudden coldness from the shop owner. She decided to ignore the glare because she was so excited and delighted with the shop. There were racks and racks of fine gowns, all fit for a fancy ball. Perhaps no one wore home-sewn dresses anymore.

Mrs. Whittle gave her a smile that didn't seem genuine and her voice dripped like ice water. "Now what did Mademoiselle have in mind?"

"I—I don't know," Turquoise stammered. "I have no idea what the other girls will be wearing."

"Umm, understandable."

Was she being insulted? She looked over at her guardian, but he was engrossed in the paper. Turquoise abruptly felt like an ignorant peasant, a Mexican girl who had grown up on a ranch in the Texas hill country. She certainly didn't want to make a fool of herself. She looked toward Trace but he had leaned back in his chair and was reading. He looked ill at ease in this most feminine of places.

"Now," said Mrs. Whittle, clasping her hands together, "let me help you pick out some gowns to try on. Does the senorita have a price in mind?"

"I—I don't know," Turquoise stammered.

"Give her anything she wants." Trace yawned.

The owner pulled a very bright, large-flowered dress from the rack. "Just perfect for a fiesta."

Turquoise blinked. Was that sarcasm in the lady's voice? "This isn't for a fiesta. I'm going to the debutante ball."

"The committee needs to be more careful," Mrs. Whittle murmured.

"What?"

"Nothing, my dear." Again the glib smile. "How about a bright color to go with your dark hair?" She began to pull dresses from the rack. There were many white and pastel ones, but the lady passed those by. "Here's a purple one, a red one, and a turquoise one in silk."

Turquoise looked at them. "They seem a little bright."

"You'll surely be noticed in any one of these gowns." Mrs. Whittle smiled at her.

They did seem a bit too much, but who was she to argue with a fashion expert like Mrs. Whittle? She wished she'd brought her friend Fern along, but after all, Fern had never been a debutante and wouldn't be much help. "I think I'll try these on. Are you sure this is what the other girls will be wearing?"

"Of course. My own daughter, Maude, is a debutante and most of the girls got their dresses here." Mrs. Whittle nodded. "Now I'll help you into them and you can decide."

Trace let out a soft moan. "I presume we'll be here all afternoon?"

"Well, after all"—the haughty lady drew herself up to her full height—"this is the social event of the season here in Austin. All the best people will be there."

It looked for a moment like Trace would say something again, but Turquoise gave him a pleading look and he sighed and returned to staring at the ceiling.

Turquoise took the dresses and went behind a screen. "Which one do you think?"

"What about the bright red one?" Mrs. Whittle suggested and reached for it.

"All right, if you think so." She took off her pink dress.

"Good choice!" The clerk helped bring the red dress up over her head. "You'll really stand out in this one."

Turquoise looked in the mirror while Mrs. Whittle buttoned up the dress. "I don't know. It seems so bright."

"I assure you, you'll cause a stir in this one."

She didn't want to cause a stir; she only wanted to be accepted by the gringas in spite of her Mexican name. Turquoise surveyed herself in the big cheval mirror. "No, this isn't it."

"What about the turquoise one?" Mrs. Whittle said. "Of course, it's a bit more expensive and if you think your gentleman friend would balk—"

"He's not my gentleman, he's my guardian," Turquoise corrected her as she began to pull off the scarlet dress.

"Of course, anything you say." The lady was smiling, but her voice was sarcastic.

Whatever was the matter with this clerk? Of course, Mrs. Whittle was used to dealing with snooty, upper-class patrons and maybe they all acted this way. Uncle Trace was now dozing in his chair. "I think the turquoise is the one. I can wear all my jewelry with it."

"Perfect," said the clerk and took the dress off the hanger.

Turquoise put the dress on and stared at herself in the mirror. It was a gorgeous dress that brought out the color of her eyes, but the bodice clung to her figure and was very low-cut, revealing a generous curve of breast. "I don't know. This one is a bit daring."

"Well, if it's too expensive for you, perhaps—"

"It's not the money," Turquoise protested. "It's just so— so bare."

"Of course." Again the woman's voice dripped sarcasm. "Of course, you could put a shawl around your shoulders. Let me get one." She disappeared and was back in a moment with a paisley silk scarf, which she draped around Turquoise.

"Oh, that does help." Turquoise smiled at herself in the mirror, knowing she looked very curvacious and feminine in the low-cut gown. "I don't know what Uncle Trace will think."

"Oh, just surprise him with it," the clerk urged her. "Shall I wrap it up?"

Turquoise nodded. "You really think I'll fit in at the ball? I don't want to do anything socially incorrect."

"Don't worry about it," Mrs. Whittle reassured her. She took the dress into the back room to box while Turquoise put on her pink frock and returned to the front area.

"Good." Uncle Trace yawned. "Can we go now?" He stood up. "You want to show it to me?"

"I want to surprise you," she said. She was already feeling uneasy that Uncle Trace would think the turquoise silk too daring. Maybe Fern would come by the hotel this afternoon and give her an opinion.

When they left the shop, her guardian carried the big box.

"Thank you, Uncle Trace."

"And I reckon I have to put on a monkey suit and escort you," he grumbled.

"Well, I guess I could go alone."

"In a town like Austin at night?" Trace snorted as he helped her into the buggy and she opened her parasol. "Not on your life."

"Uncle Trace, there'll be dancing and all the society people will be there."

"Sounds dull to me," Trace complained as he put the box in the back of the buggy and climbed in. "I don't want to dance with anyone but Cimarron, and society people are all dull snobs. I don't know where you get these high-falutin' ideas."

Tears came to Turquoise's eyes and she blinked them back. She had never asked Trace or any of the Durangos about her questionable birth except that she was certain old Sanchez, the ranch boss, was not really her father and with her parents both dead now, there was really no one to ask.

She was determined to reach a pinnacle of respectability so that no one would ever gossip about her again. A proper gentleman would give her security from the whispers.

They had barely returned to the hotel when her chubby, red-haired friend, Fern Lessup, showed up and the pair retreated to the bedroom to look over the dress while Trace left the hotel on business.

"Just look," Turquoise said conspiratorially as she unpacked the dress.

"Oh my word, it is beautiful!" Fern breathed and ran her hand over the turquoise silk with its sassy bustle. "It must have cost a fortune."

"It did, but the owner assured me I would be the best-dressed girl at the debutante ball, and that's important. Why, I might meet my future husband there."

"Imagine!" Fern gasped. "Just like Cinderella."

"Or some high-society Austin man. It is at the governor's mansion, you know."

"I know." Fern's brown eyes widened. "Except I'd rather go to a barn dance with Luke Jeffries. Neither of us would feel comfortable at a fancy shindig like this."

"Well, this is my first ball," Turquoise reminded her. "I've always dreamed of being married to an important man and no one sneering at me again and wondering if I'm really Mexican."

"Oh, Turquoise, half the people in Texas are part Mexican. They just don't talk about it."

"Well, I want to marry someone so important, no one would dare make rude remarks about me."

"You really want to marry some stuffy city man?" Fern asked.

For just a moment, she remembered the man she had met this morning, the sweaty sheen of his muscular brown body, the way his dark eyes had devoured her. She shook her head to clear it. "I've got to wash up. Then would you please help me with my hair?"

"Sure," Fern said. "I can hardly wait to see you in that dress. Get your curling iron and I'll get a lamp."

Turquoise washed and dried her long black hair while Fern put the curling iron over the oil lamp to heat. Then they curled her hair and put it up on her head in a mass of ebony curls with several turquoise and silver combs.

Next Turquoise put on a fine lace petticoat, a lace bodice, and long silk stockings under her lace drawers. "Do you think I dare put on makeup?"

Fern rolled her eyes. "You want to be taken for one of those girls on the street?"

"Good point. I'll just pinch my cheeks and bite my lips to give them some color."

"At least you don't freckle like I do," Fern said.

Turquoise looked in the mirror again. "I hope Uncle Trace doesn't forget and comes up in time to get dressed."

She took the dress out of its box and Fern helped her slip it on.

"My word!" Fern gasped as she surveyed the low bodice. "Your uncle let you buy this?"

"Well, actually, he didn't see it," Turquoise said defensively, "and I do have a shawl and some jewelry."

"Maybe you won't look so bare with the jewelry," Fern suggested.

She was having her doubts as she stared at her reflection in the mirror. The silk clung to her generous curves. She wasn't sure Uncle Trace would let her leave the hotel if he saw her in this dress. "It is the latest fashion, Mrs. Whittle assured me. She said I'd really fit in among the debutantes."

"I don't know about that," Fern said, still wide-eyed and doubtful.

Turquoise looked at the clock ticking on the bureau,

sprayed herself with forget-me-not perfume, and put on the fine turquoise and silver jewelry she owned.

Next door, she heard the key turning in the lock as Uncle Trace came into the adjoining room. "Hey darlin', are you about ready?" he yelled.

She looked at Fern and now she was spooked, too. "Actually, I'm ready, Uncle Trace. Why don't I go on ahead and you meet me there? I think there's supposed to be some kind of practice for the girls."

"Alone at night in a big city?"

"Stop worrying about me. I'll get a carriage and go directly to the ball."

"All right." He sounded uncertain. "It's at the governor's mansion, right?"

"*Si,*" she said and picked up her tiny reticule and her shawl. "Fern, walk down with me."

"Sure."

The two girls walked out into the hall and down the stairs. Turquoise had draped the shawl around her shoulders, but as they passed gentlemen, the men turned and gave Turquoise a wide-eyed look.

"My word," Fern whispered, "you are attracting attention, all right. I reckon I'm just too old-fashioned to keep up with high style."

Turquoise put her head in the air and walked proudly, as a society lady should, as she went to the desk and asked for a carriage.

The boy at the desk blinked and stared as he nodded.

Then the girls went outside to await the carriage. It was dusk and many people were coming and going.

"Well," Fern said, "I reckon I'd better be headed for home. Daddy will worry about me if I'm not home by dark."

"Come by the hotel tomorrow and I'll tell you all about it." Turquoise hugged her friend.

"Oh, I want to hear every word about all the dances and

the high-class gentlemen. Do you think they're that much different than cowboys?"

Again the vaquero from this morning came to Turquoise's mind. "I—I don't know. I'll tell you tomorrow."

About that time, her carriage arrived and Fern said goodbye and left as the driver helped Turquoise in.

"The governor's mansion," she said grandly and he nodded. Turquoise took a deep breath to quiet her nervous stomach. Maybe tonight there would be a Prince Charming at the ball who would fall in love with her and make her so respectable, no one would ever whisper about her again.

It was a warm dusk outside as the carriage moved down Congress Avenue. Turquoise was so nervous, she kept fiddling with her shawl. "Stop it," she warned herself. "You look as good as any of those gringa girls. Isn't Mrs. Whittle an authority on how to dress? Think about meeting the man of your dreams."

The man of her dreams. The Mexican vaquero came to her mind unbidden. He'd been so masculine and virile as he labored over Silver Slippers's hoof, and the way his dark eyes had looked into hers was bold and inquiring. Without thinking, she licked her lips, wondering what his kiss would have been like.

"We're here," the driver leaned down to announce as he stopped before a gigantic house with white pillars. Lights gleamed from every window and dozens of carriages were stopped out front.

"Oh, just look at all the carriages," she whispered to herself. "Why, half of Austin must be here." Her heart was beating hard as the driver came around to help her out. She must remember every detail to tell Fern tomorrow: what the inside looked like, what food was served, and how many gentlemen asked her to dance.

*Oh, suppose no one asks me to dance?* She imagined

herself standing by the wall, waiting. Well, at least Uncle Trace might dance with her.

The driver opened the door and held out his hand to assist her. Turquoise paused on the step and took a deep breath. This was something she had dreamed of for years, ever since she had read about the debutante ball in the newspapers.

*I am finally here,* she thought. She clutched her fan and glided across the porch and into the grand entrance. There was such a crowd that she could barely get through, although men stared at her and then stepped aside so she could enter.

"Girls! Girls!" Inside she could hear a shrill feminine voice and the sharp clap of hands. "I am Mrs. Van Hooten, and I am in charge here. Now all you debutantes gather up so I can tell you how we'll enter."

Turquoise pushed her way through to the ballroom where young ladies were gathering around the sharp-voiced, dumpy lady. Turquoise glided over to join them and they all turned to stare at her. Very slowly, it dawned on her that she was dressed completely wrong. She stared at all of them in horror and wanted to turn and run out, but there were too many people standing around in the doorway.

The other girls were all dressed in demure but expensive white gowns. They had little jewelry but wore long white gloves. She was the only debutante not wearing white. Mrs. Whittle had deliberately set her up to be humiliated. The tittering began and grew, then the whispering. The dowager in charge frowned at her. "Who are you?"

"I—I am Turquoise Sanchez," she managed to stammer.

"Sanchez? I've got a Turquoise Sanders on my list."

Tittering in the background.

"No, it's Sanchez." Turquoise bit her lip.

"Hmm, you don't look Mexican. We never had one before." The woman's lip seemed to curl.

The girls started to titter again and the older lady clapped her hands sharply, her gold and diamond rings glittering in the gas lights. "Behave yourselves, girls, and remember, tonight we are presenting the most eligible young ladies in the Lone Star State to the cream of Austin society. Now, each of you have your escorts? We will practice the presentations."

"Escort?" Turquoise asked. "My uncle will be here later—"

"No, no." The lady frowned and the girls giggled again. "Don't you know anything? You are supposed to have arranged for a young gentleman to escort you down from the stage."

"I—I'm afraid I don't have an escort," Turquoise said.

She heard whispering from the girls. "What do you expect from a Mexican girl?"

"Haven't you heard? She's the ward of the Durangos and he's got enough money to buy her way in."

Turquoise wanted to turn and run out but decided she would not let these vicious girls defeat her. She tried to stand straight and tall, as diminutive as she was.

"All right," Mrs. Van Hooten said with a sigh. "You girls, don't one of you have an extra brother or cousin here who might escort Senorita Sanchez in the ceremony?"

The silence was deafening. Turquoise felt like the lonely child who was always chosen last in games.

She heard a girl whisper, "She doesn't belong here. We don't have Mexicans at our balls."

The older lady clapped for silence again. "Doesn't any young man want to escort this young lady?"

What was she going to do? Turquoise felt her face burn with humiliation. It wasn't only the gaudy dress; now she was without an escort.

The silence seemed to echo and then, just as she was ready to turn and run out of the grand ballroom, a man's voice said, "I would consider myself lucky to be the escort of such a beautiful young lady."

She heard the shocked sighs and saw the faces of the girls before she turned to look behind her. A handsome, mature man stood there smiling at her. He was tall and elegant, with light hair turning slightly gray at the temples and eyes as pale as her own. He bowed before her, wearing the finest of evening clothes with a white rose in his buttonhole. "That is, if the young lady is willing."

He took her numb fingers in his and kissed the back of her hand. The way the girls were staring at him, they were in awe.

"Ah, Senator Forester," the older lady gushed, "we would be so honored to have a member of such a prominent family and our fair city's most eligible bachelor take part in our presenting of the debutantes tonight."

He stared into Turquoise's eyes, seemingly oblivious to the rest of the crowd. "No, it is I who is honored. What a pretty dress. May I ask where you bought it?"

The dress was all wrong and she knew it now, knew that Mrs. Whittle had deliberately sabotaged her. The girls snickered again, but she took a deep breath and stammered, "*Gracias,* sir. The dress came from La Mode."

He smiled at her. "It makes all the others look like hens beside a peacock," he murmured, but Turquoise noticed he said it loud enough for the other girls to hear and they all seemed to sigh as if the wind had been taken out of their sails. Then he lowered his voice and whispered, "I have been standing in the back, watching all the drama."

Turquoise could only nod gratefully.

"All right, let's get on with this," the lady said, obviously relieved that someone had stepped in to solve the problem. "The guests will be arriving soon. Now all of you go behind that curtain on the little stage and the young men will line up next to me on the podium. As I announce each girl, her escort will step forward, bow, hand her a rose, and then escort her out into the ballroom."

Senator Forester winked at her and let go of her hand. She walked toward the stage with the rest of the girls, but now they were crowding around her. "Why didn't you tell us you knew the Forester family?" one girl asked.

"I didn't know it mattered," Turquoise answered truthfully. Frankly, the Forester name sounded familiar, but she wasn't sure why.

"Why, Edwin Forester is the most eligible bachelor in Austin," another girl said. "They say he just can't find the girl of his dreams. He's certainly the catch of all Texas."

"Oh, of course." Turquoise smiled. "And he's escorting me tonight."

The other girls were looking at her as if she were Queen Victoria.

So her evening, which had started off to be such a disaster, was going to be a dream come true. Maybe Senator Forester was her Prince Charming. True, he looked to be in his late thirties, but many girls married older men, especially if they were handsome and rich. She fanned herself, hot with excitement, and suddenly an image of the vaquero came to her mind and she frowned. How dare he interrupt her thoughts? He was just a poor Mexican cowboy and could never give her the place in Texas society she hungered for.

They practiced and each time, the senator bowed low and kissed her hand as he handed her the rose. And each time, her heart hammered at his good looks and fine manners.

Once he whispered, "Are you of the El Paso Sanchez family? They own most of that county—"

"No." She shook her head and sighed at how dapper and sophisticated he was. She noticed how the other girls frowned at their callow young escorts. They were all boys but her escort was a man. She could sense the envy of the other girls. She noted with a start that the young man she had hit with the horse whip was escorting a plain, fat girl. He glared at Turquoise but didn't say anything. No doubt he, too, was awed by the senator.

To Edwin Forester, she whispered, "I didn't know I was supposed to arrange for an escort."

"Don't worry about it." He nodded. "You have one now and I daresay these other cruel little cats will shut up."

She was so grateful to him. "You are so kind."

"No." He shook his head and she thought again how handsome he was. "I was just lucky that you had no escort. I almost didn't come tonight. Debutante balls are such a bore, but maybe Fate took a hand so I could meet you after all these years of looking."

He was so well spoken and his voice purred. The most sought-after and most eligible bachelor in Texas and he had volunteered to escort her before all these rich and important people.

The ballroom was filling now with successful men in evening clothes and rich dowagers in fine gowns and jewels.

"The governor is here!" gasped one of the girls standing near her, and all heads turned.

*That must be him,* Turquoise thought, as an older, bearded gentleman moved through the crowd, stopping to shake hands. She saw him come up to Senator Forester and greet him heartily. The other men gathered around the senator, shaking his hand and talking to him. He must indeed be a big part of Austin society.

"Girls," Mrs. Van Hooten commanded in a sharp whisper, "let's all go behind the curtain now. The ceremony will be starting soon and then you'll make your grand entrance."

The flustered girls hurried backstage.

"I've been looking toward this night my whole life," one girl gushed.

"Yes," said another, "I might meet my future husband at this ball. After all, the best people in Austin are here."

Turquoise smiled to herself. Yes, this night was going to be like a fairy tale. She might be wearing the wrong dress and she might not fit in, but she was being escorted by Senator Edwin Forester of *the* Foresters. And then she remembered why the name had sounded so familiar: the Forester and Durango families had been enemies for generations— bitter enemies. What was going to happen when Uncle Trace saw her being escorted by a member of the Forester family? Would he make a scene? And what would happen when the handsome Edwin suddenly realized who she was? Tonight was shaping up to be a disaster after all. Maybe she could just drop dead backstage and avoid the whole terrible scene. Or maybe she could run out some back door and not take part at all.

But now the girls were lining up and the crowd seated at tables out front was being called to attention by the governor himself. It was too late to flee. She was about to create a major crisis and there was no way to avoid it unless the mansion suddenly burst into flames. She took a deep breath and wished she was back home on the Triple D or at the very least, Fern's father's ranch, sitting around playing checkers. Turquoise crossed herself and made ready to face the terrible scene that was bound to come.

# Chapter 3

From behind the curtain where she stood with the other fidgeting and giggling debutantes, Turquoise heard the pompous governor, Richard Coke, being introduced to polite applause. Then he spoke about how proud he was to be head of this "fair state and city."

All Turquoise could do was bite her lip and hope Uncle Trace came in late. She wasn't sure what he would do if he saw her being escorted across the stage by a longtime enemy.

Finally the governor finished and there was more polite applause. Then Mrs. Van Hooten spoke saying how proud she was to introduce this year's group of debutantes and how they represented some of Austin's finest and oldest families. Turquoise felt the other girls eyeing her and giggling. She wanted to shout at them that just because she looked white but had a Spanish last name, there was nothing questionable about her background, but she forced herself to remain quiet.

She felt beads of perspiration breaking out on her face, but she dared not wipe it as Mrs. Van Hooten was beginning to call the names of each debutante. Maybe Uncle Trace would be late. Maybe after the introductions she could excuse herself and Senator Forester need never find out she was part of an enemy family.

She peeked through the curtains. Miss Maude Whittle, plump in her white dress and gloves, was introduced and waddled out to polite applause, escorted offstage by the young man Turquoise had taken a whip to over Silver Slippers.

One after another, the girls' names were called and now it was her turn. Turquoise took a deep breath and stuck her chin out proudly. So she was Mexican in this Anglo crowd and she was dressed completely wrong, but she would show them what courage was.

"Turquoise Sanchez," sang out Mrs. Van Hooten and Turquoise stepped through the curtains, "escorted by Senator Edwin Forester."

The lights blinded her and she couldn't be sure if Uncle Trace was out in that crowd or not, but she heard the low murmur of voices, commenting and tittering on her gaudy dress and then awed comments as the handsome, suave bachelor stepped forward, smiling at her and bowing low as he extended a white rose. She took it blindly, a smile frozen on her lips as he took her arm and escorted her off the stage. "You are the most beautiful woman here tonight," he whispered and he sounded as if he meant it.

"Thank you. I'm so grateful you came to my rescue," she murmured and smiled up at him. Here at last was her handsome, respectable Prince Charming and all the other debutantes were looking at her with confusion and envy as they stood by their pimple-faced boy escorts.

"And to think, if I hadn't come tonight, I might never have met you." He looked down into her eyes, still holding her hand. "May I have the first dance, Miss Sanchez?"

She could only stare up at him and nod as the debutante introductions finished and the orchestra started to play a soft waltz. "But of course."

He took her in his arms and whirled her out onto the

dance floor. "I know no man is supposed to monopolize a deb's dances at this event," he murmured, "but I may just have to break that tradition because I don't want you dancing with anyone else."

Sure enough, other young men were crowding around her now as the music ended, but the senator shooed them all away. She looked around into the jealous faces of the other girls and heard Maude Whittle whisper, "How'd that Mexican country girl manage to snag the most eligible bachelor in the whole state?"

"Because she's the most beautiful girl in the state," the senator snapped at the plump and awkward Maude and whisked Turquoise out onto the dance floor again.

She was deliriously happy to be in his arms. The evening that had started out to be a disaster was now her triumph. How she wished Fern could be here to see it.

Why, Senator Forester was not only handsome and polished but at the top of the Lone Star State's social ladder. She had almost forgotten the Foresters were enemies until she saw Uncle Trace's angry face in the crowd along the wall. She could only hope he didn't create a scene.

But now he was striding toward them and then he tapped Edwin on the shoulder. "May I cut in?"

She held her breath, afraid the senator might object, and then he seemed to see the fury on the other man's face and nodded. Uncle Trace whirled her away and his words were bitten off and furious as he whispered, "What the hell are you doin'?"

"I—I didn't have an escort and you weren't here yet."

"The Foresters never do anything out of kindness. He's probably gloatin' that the Durangos were put in an embarrassin' situation."

"I didn't know who he was," Turquoise answered truthfully, "and he rescued me. I didn't have anyone to escort me from the stage."

"Damn it, I would have done it."

"You weren't here and it's supposed to be a bachelor."

"Edwin Forester is a bachelor all right, with the reputation of being a rake among the ladies."

"Oh." She was disappointed. She had felt his interest was genuine.

"Everyone in the crowd is whisperin' about the Durangos' ward being escorted by a family enemy."

"He doesn't know who I am."

"Are you sure he doesn't? Maybe he's just tryin' to make me look like a fool."

"I am sorry, Uncle Trace. I won't dance with him again and we'll leave soon."

"Fine. I'll be at the bar." The music ended and he escorted her to the sidelines, where young men crowded around, eager to sign her dance card. Trace strode away toward the bar.

And then elegant Edwin Forester was pushing through the crowd of boys. "Sorry, gentlemen, the lady promised the next dance to me."

Several boys protested, and Turquoise said, "I shouldn't—"

However, Edwin swept her into his arms as the music started and danced her out onto the floor. It seemed to Turquoise that every eye in the ballroom was on them. She was suddenly very uneasy to be so conspicuous. "Senator, there's something I need to tell you."

"All right." He smiled down at her and danced her through the open French doors and out onto the wide veranda. "It was hot in there anyway." He took both her small hands in his. "Now what is it, my dear?"

She licked her dry lips. "I—I presume you don't know who I am."

"You're the most beautiful girl at this ball," he declared.

"I'm also the ward of Trace Durango." Her words came in a rush.

He looked down at her a long moment, then he dropped her hands and laughed. "So that's what all the whispering was about in the crowd. I assumed it was because you were so beautiful."

"You didn't know?" She felt relief.

"No, although I sensed something was wrong when Trace Durango appeared. I'm glad I gave the staid citizens something to gossip about. We must be the Romeo and Juliet of Austin."

She turned away from him and looked out over the lawn. "Uncle Trace is not happy about it."

"I wondered why he looked so angry. He has a reputation as a gunfighter, you know."

"Aren't you upset with me?"

He put his manicured hands on her shoulders. "This isn't your fault, my dear, and it's a cruel joke on me. I finally find a girl who intrigues me and she's related to one of my family's bitter enemies."

She moved away from him. "I don't even know what the feud is about."

"Mostly I don't either," he admitted, standing next to her, leaning against the veranda railing. "I think it's been going on for three generations. I know there was conflict over business dealings between the grandfathers, and then what happened between my father and the old Don Durango." He sighed. "I was hardly more than a child when that occurred. I wish there were a way to end this feud so I might call on you."

She whirled, looking up at him. He was so tall and handsome, although his chin was a bit weak, but his eyes seemed so sincere. "We hardly know each other."

"I know, but just looking at you, it seems like you're the missing piece of the puzzle—why I have waited so long to marry. Will you be staying in Austin a few days?"

She nodded. "Uncle Trace is doing some business or something. We're at the Cattlemen's Hotel."

He took her hands in both of his. "Then perhaps we can see each other again. It's warm out here. Would you like some punch?"

"Please." She nodded and he turned and went back in, the music floating out to the veranda through the doors. Turquoise looked out over the manicured lawn, breathless with excitement.

Then she noticed a figure standing in the shadows of nearby bushes and started. "Who's there?"

"It's me, Rio Kelly." She caught the accent and the deep voice as he stepped out into the moonlight and she remembered how virile and masculine he was. He wore a short Mexican jacket adorned with silver conchos. He made a striking figure, although his jacket looked a bit threadbare.

"What are you doing here?"

He shrugged and motioned for her to come down the steps. She hesitated, then came down.

"You asked if I were coming, remember?"

"Well, I didn't think—"

"Of course I had to sneak over the back fence, but I wanted to see how you looked and how the other half lived."

"You're trespassing? You'd better leave or there'll be trouble."

He grinned at her and reached out and caught her hand with his strong right one. She noticed again the shamrock tattoo. "It might be worth it to dance with you once. You look beautiful."

"I'm dressed very inappropriately." She felt herself flush with humiliation.

"Oh? Says who? I think you look like the most beautiful girl in the world. I'll wager you made the other girls look pale and ugly."

The music started again and drifted faintly on the breeze.

"You'd better leave before Senator Forester returns."

"Ah." He grinned and raised one eyebrow in a mocking fashion. "So you have scored high, *si?* You may end up as the queen of Austin society yet, although he has a reputation in this town as a womanizer."

"I'm sure that's not true. Now you leave before he comes back and calls the guards."

"One dance and I'll leave." He took her in his arms and he was so much bigger and more masculine than Edwin.

"You promise?"

"I promise, senorita." He pulled her closer, holding her much too tightly to be respectable and dancing her slowly around the patio. His mouth was close to her ear and she could feel his warm breath and the hard muscle of him all the way down her body.

"This is too close," she objected but he paid no heed. She tried to pull away, but he held her closer still.

"Miss Sanchez?"

She heard the call from the veranda and looked back. Senator Forester stood there, silhouetted against the light from the ballroom with two punch cups in his hands.

"I—I'm coming." She tried to pull away from Rio but he took her hand and kissed it.

"Miss Sanchez, who is that out there with you?"

She could see Edwin peering into the darkness but the light behind him kept him from seeing clearly. "Let go of me," she muttered through clenched teeth, "or I'll scream."

"You wouldn't dare. It isn't something rich Anglo girls do." He kissed her hand again, mocking her.

"Just watch me!" She threw her head back with spirit and called, "Help, sir, there's an intruder!"

"Damn you, you little vixen!" Rio swore and turned loose, moving toward the shadows of the back fence.

However, Edwin Forester dropped the punch cups and

they shattered loudly on the veranda as he shouted, "Guards! Guards! We've got a trespasser!"

Three guards came running around the mansion and toward Rio.

"Good-bye, my sweet Mexican flower. You've got more spirit than I thought." The vaquero made a run for the back fence, but the guards caught him and they struggled.

Turquoise took a deep breath, praying he could get away. She regretted now that she had called for help out of spite.

Rio seemed to be holding his own in the brawl with the three guards while the senator watched from the veranda. Finally, one of the guards hit the Mexican on the head with a pistol and his legs folded under him. "We've got him, sir!"

"Good! I was worried about the young lady." Now Edwin came down off the veranda to stand by Turquoise as the guards hauled the half-conscious intruder to his feet. "Are you all right, Miss Turquoise?"

"Yes. I don't think he meant any harm. He only wanted to see the party."

Edwin scowled. "I was afraid the dirty rascal scared you or smudged your dress."

"I wasn't scared, Senator, and I wish you'd just forget this and let him go." She looked at Rio and was ashamed of her hasty actions. He had blood running down his face.

The senator did not look pleased. "Do you know this—this tramp?"

"He's the farrier who shod my horse," Turquoise said. "I'm sure he meant no harm. Please let him go."

Edwin Forester glared at the intruder down his fine, patrician nose. However, to Turquoise, he smiled and bowed. "Very well. For you, my lady . . ." He took her hand and led her back up on the veranda. "You just wait here, my dear, and I'll see that he's escorted out to the street and released."

"Thank you." She sighed with relief and watched Edwin

return to the three guards and the bloody vaquero. They all disappeared around the corner of the mansion.

Edwin made sure they were out of the girl's sight and then he said to the guards, "Toss this greasy bastard in jail for the night and don't be gentle about it."

"But I thought you told the young lady . . . ?" one of the guards protested.

"You heard me!" the senator snapped and turned on his heel to return to the veranda.

The stunning beauty still awaited him there. "He'll be fine, but he won't invade the governor's grounds again."

She took one last look at the lawn, ashamed that she had gotten Rio in trouble. Then Edwin took her arm and led her back toward the ballroom. She glanced over her shoulder, worried about the man who had been dragged out to be tossed in the street. "Thank you, Senator, for not making an issue of this."

He patted her hand with his free one. "If it hadn't been for your pity, I would have thrashed the young thug for being so familiar with an elegant lady."

"You are so gallant." And yet, he sounded arrogant. Besides, she remembered that he hadn't come running from the safety of the veranda until he was sure the three guards had subdued the trespasser. More than that, she had a feeling that if he had taken on Rio, the senator would have come out the worse for it.

They reentered the ballroom. Uncle Trace strode toward them, his face dark as thunder. Obviously everyone knew about the trouble between the families, because heads were turning to see what would happen. Turquoise had never felt so humiliated.

But there was no confrontation. Edwin abruptly excused himself and scurried away, leaving her to face her uncle alone.

"I think it is time we were leavin'," Trace snapped, his words bitten off.

"Of course." She ducked her head as he took her arm and led her out of the ballroom. She heard the buzz of conversation behind them.

The night air seemed cool as they waited on the steps for their carriage. Uncle Trace said nothing as he helped her in, nor did he speak until they were in their suite at the hotel.

"What a night!" He folded his arms behind his back and marched up and down the plush carpet. "The citizens of Austin will have something to talk about for months now."

"I'm sorry." She sat down on the edge of a chair. "I didn't know who he was and I don't think he knew who I was either. I had to tell him."

Trace paused before her. "What did he say to that?"

She bit her lip. "He seemed to shrug it off. Honestly, Uncle Trace, he came to my rescue. I didn't know I had to have a society bachelor walk me off the stage and no girl offered a relative."

He ground his teeth. "That's what you get for tryin' to move into snooty society." His tone was full of irony. "The gringos don't want anyone with Mexican blood—"

"But aren't you half-Spanish?"

He nodded. "It's nothin' to be ashamed of, as you seem to be. Your father must be turnin' over in his grave."

"That's the problem—my white face and my Mexican name." She'd never had the nerve to bring this up with any of the Durangos.

"Oh, to hell with the old gossips." Trace shrugged.

"And the dress"—she looked down at the gaudy turquoise silk—"I had no idea I would look such a fool. . . ."

"We were both ambushed," Uncle Trace snapped and ran his hand through his black hair. "That bitch who runs the La Mode Dress Shoppe must have recognized us as a pair of bumpkins who didn't know anything. You want me to deal with her?"

Turquoise shook her head. "I want to take care of that myself."

He flopped down on a chair and sighed. "I'm sick of this uppity town. Maybe we can go home early."

She flinched and walked to the window, looking out at the gas lights of the streets. She could still hear Edwin's voice and feel his embrace. She wasn't ready to go back to the ranch yet.

Uncle Trace loosened his collar. "And of all people for you to hook up with, Edwin Forester. You know we are enemies of that family."

"*Si,* but I don't know why, and he acts like he doesn't either."

Trace merely snorted.

She shook her head. "I know the two families are both rich and powerful and it's an ancient feud."

Trace pulled out a cigarillo and tapped it against the arm of the chair. "It goes back to our grandfathers. The Durangos have business principles, but the Foresters are ruthless and cutthroat. Why, they'd steal the milk from a baby calf's bucket."

She bit her lip, thinking maybe he exaggerated. "The senator didn't seem so terrible."

"Neither do tarantulas," Trace snapped, "but they sometimes bite. Remember the Foresters are notorious in that they are willin' to do anything, and I do mean anything to get what they want. How do you think he became a senator? And what were you doin' out on the veranda with him?"

That made her think of Rio and the way he had been treated. "We—we went out for a breath of air and—"

"Turquoise, I'm going to tell you something about the

Forester men. They've always had a bad reputation when it comes to women."

She looked into Trace's eyes. "You think because I am Mexican and obviously a simple country girl who showed up dressed inappropriately that he would try to take advantage of me?" She began to cry.

"I didn't say that." Trace put the cigarillo back in its silver case and walked over to pat her shoulder. "Frankly, I don't know what he is capable of and I don't want to have to kill him. His father—"

"Uncle Trace, times are changing. You can't just go around getting in a gunfight with every man you don't like."

"More's the pity," he snapped. "I just wish Cimarron were here. She'd know what to do."

"It's all right. It's over now." She straightened her shoulders, feeling guilty about the handsome farrier who had come at her offhand invitation. She didn't know what Uncle Trace would think about that.

"Good. Now we'll be here another day or two. I've got business, buyin' a few blooded horses and cattle. Why don't you forget about tonight and tomorrow, you go get Fern, and you two do some shoppin'? I have an account at all the stores. My wife has seen to that."

"That's what I'll do." She paused to kiss his cheek. "Thank you, Uncle Trace."

He mellowed. "Just forget about high society," Trace grumbled. "You've got the wealth and the power of the Durangos behind you. That should be enough."

But it wasn't enough, she thought. She wanted security—to be able to hold up her head in Texas society and never be laughed at or ridiculed again for her Anglo looks and her Mexican name.

"Good night," she whispered and went into her room and closed the door. Surely the Durangos and the Foresters could coexist in peace so she could realize her ambitions. It would be heady to be married to a man of power so that everyone, including those snooty gringa girls, would envy and look up to her with respect. Maybe tonight had been a disaster, but it hadn't killed her dreams. She wanted security, a big house, and an important husband. If she had all that, no one would dare whisper about her questionable background.

Edwin Forester. He could offer everything she hungered for and surely he couldn't be as bad as Uncle Trace said. However, when she tried to think about the elegant gentleman, the face that kept coming back to her was Rio Kelly's. She remembered the feel of his powerful arms around her, the virility of the man. But he was poor; poor and powerless. Yet she felt shame that she had caused him such humiliation.

As she drifted off to sleep, the lips that kissed hers were not the fine gentleman's but the hot, passionate mouth of Rio Kelly.

The next morning, she and Uncle Trace had breakfast together in the fancy dining room with all the silver, crystal, and snowy linen tablecloths. Today she wore a large white lace hat with aqua ribbons and an aqua, long-sleeved percale dress with a perky bustle. Last night seemed like a faraway dream. She looked around, smiling. "This is the way to live."

Trace shrugged. "*Si.* It's all right, but I prefer the patio at the ranch."

That was because he could look out over several hundred thousand acres the Durangos owned, she thought.

The waiter came to their table and she noticed how he snapped to attention, making sure the coffee, Spanish omelet, and sweet rolls were just to Senor Durango's liking.

Yes, this was the way she wanted to live permanently; waiters and salespeople hurrying to wait on her because she was also respectable and important.

They finished with little conversation.

Trace threw down his napkin and nodded to the waiter, who hovered in the background. "Excellent, as usual, Pierre. Charge it to my account."

The waiter rubbed his hands together. "*Merci,* sir." He pulled back Turquoise's chair as Trace got up and the pair walked outside into the cool spring morning.

She immediately opened her white lace parasol against the bright sun.

"Well, shall I call you a carriage?" Trace asked.

"No, I think I saw some interesting shops down from the hotel," she answered. "And I'll send a messenger to Fern to join me for an outdoor luncheon at that new tea shop on Congress Avenue."

"Fine. I may not be back until the middle of the afternoon." Trace nodded and looked toward the new horse-drawn streetcar moving down the street. "I think I'll try riding that. Austin is certainly up to date."

He tipped his Stetson to her and turned to run after the slow-moving vehicle. She watched him get aboard, then returned to the hotel lobby and hailed a bellboy to take a note to Fern. Yes, an outdoor lunch would be fun. All the best ladies would probably go there. Fern would want to hear about last night. Maybe Turquoise would leave out the most humiliating parts. Should she tell anyone about how Rio had taken her in his arms and held her so close? No. She shook her head. That would be too scandalous.

She turned and started down the sidewalk, twirling her parasol on her shoulder. There were at least two shops she'd like to see that were less than a block away, but first she decided to deal with Mrs. Whittle. She wasn't good at confrontation, except where a principle was at stake. She'd taken on the drunken lout who was whipping a horse and she could take on Mrs. Whittle.

She caught one of the slow-moving horsecars and rode to the La Mode Dress Shoppe. Turquoise marched inside, folding her parasol and laying it on the counter, behind which stood the arrogant Mrs. Whittle, studying her ledgers.

The lady looked up. "How may I—Oh, it's you."

"Did you not expect to see me again?"

Mrs. Whittle gave her an arrogant smile. "So how did you enjoy the debutante ball?"

"That was cruel of you"—Turquoise faced her—"knowing I did not know the proper thing to wear."

The lady sniffed. "Maude said you made a fool of yourself. That's what a Mexican wench gets for trying to get into white society. I hope you learned your lesson."

"Now I'm going to give you a lesson. Do you remember an old Texas saying that what goes around comes around and your sins will find you out?"

"Superstitious nonsense." Mrs. Whittle shrugged.

"Well, this isn't!" Turquoise slapped the sneering face and then grabbed her parasol and strode out, holding her head high. She had learned her lesson all right; she could only wish she was a high-class gringa girl who could demand respect. She burst into tears as she walked down the brick sidewalk. She was hurting inside and couldn't erase the humiliation she felt. Would she always be mistreated and scorned by white Texans for her Mexican name? She longed to have the money to buy that dress shop and fire the snooty owner.

After a few minutes' walk, she had calmed down and wiped her eyes. Of course it was childish to wish that. Mrs. Whittle wasn't worth the misery Turquoise was feeling.

After a block, a buggy pulled up next to her. It was the finest, with bright red wheels and pulled by a black horse of excellent quality in a new harness shining with silver. The driver took off his hat and bowed. "Miss Sanchez? I can't believe I ran into you. Do let me give you a ride to wherever you're going."

She blinked, looking at Edwin Forester's clothes. He was dressed in the latest fashion, boutonniere and all, and smiling down at her.

"I—I don't think I'd better—"

"Oh, nonsense! There's no use in your walking when you can ride."

He stepped down from the seat and bowed again, then took her hand and kissed it. "I can't forget what a wonderful time we had last night."

She knew she should protest, but she looked at that fine buggy and the elegant gentleman and let him help her up onto the seat. Uncle Trace would be so upset, but maybe he need never find out. She could only hope.

# Chapter 4

Edwin Forester climbed up beside her and snapped his little whip. The fine black horse started off at a smart gait.

"I'm just so pleased to run into you again. What were you doing in this area?" He gave her a dazzling smile.

She took a deep breath. He smelled of fine aftershave and he seemed so genuinely glad to see her. "I was confronting Mrs. Whittle at the La Mode Dress Shoppe for deliberately putting me in an embarrassing situation with the wrong dress last night."

He gave her a reassuring nod. "You were beautiful in it."

"But the proper dress for a debutante, as I now know, is simple white with long white gloves. I must have looked like a fool."

"I don't know what the others were wearing. You were so lovely, I never noticed them."

She chewed her lip. "That's kind of you to say, Senator, but—"

"Do call me Edwin." He reached to pat her hand.

"Well, Edwin, I really shouldn't be here with you. Uncle Trace—"

"Oh, yes." He gave her a mock frown. "I had forgotten about that little problem. I should sit down and have a talk with Senor Durango. I feel we should let bygones be bygones. This whole thing is senseless, especially since we are the two most powerful families in Texas. If we could partner up, we could control all of the Lone Star State."

She couldn't help but be dazzled by him. "But you're already a state senator."

"Oh, yes, but I want more. I've been thinking about running for governor and then, who knows? Maybe the United States Senate. Have you ever been in Washington, D.C., my dear?"

She shook her head, feeling like a yokel. She'd never been out of Texas and had only been to Austin a few times.

"Oh, you'd love it." He smiled down at her. "Fancy parties every night, balls at the White House."

"You've actually been to the White House?" Turquoise gasped.

"Oh, yes, the president and I are good friends. You'd love the grounds, such beautiful flowers, and the shops are wonderful. And I must say, as beautiful as you are, Washington would love you. You'd be on everyone's social list."

"Do you really think so?" He was so cosmopolitan and sophisticated.

"Of course. Why, you'd be the most popular hostess in the city, all the important people vying for invitations to your parties and the ladies all copying your gowns."

They were driving down bustling Congress Avenue toward the capitol.

"I'll show you the sights of Austin," he said grandly. "The capitol isn't much right now, but there's talk of a grand new building. Just imagine the parties I could have if I became governor."

She suddenly saw herself on his arm, leading the grand cotillion. She would be dressed in the latest fashion and as the governor's lady. No one would look down on her for her questionable background.

Edwin drove her around to see the sights and she was aware of women stopping on the street and giving her envious stares.

"I feel so conspicuous," she murmured. "You must know everyone in town."

"Well, I know all the best people," he said, "and I'm so happy that now I know you."

She felt herself flush and looked away. "I must have looked a fool in that bright, gaudy dress."

"That was not your fault." His voice was stern and cold. "Let's forget about that unfortunate incident, shall we? Just think, if it hadn't happened, I wouldn't have met you."

"You're being kind—too kind."

"No, I meant it." He reached out and patted her hand. His hands were pink and manicured—a gentleman's hands, not like Rio's big, strong, calloused hands.

"Let me show you the river," he said and snapped his little whip at the fine black horse, "beautiful clear water and very old trees."

She started to protest that she really should get back, but he had turned down a country lane and they were soon driving along the river. "It is beautiful," she admitted.

"They say that under those big live oaks over there is where gentlemen occasionally duel." He pointed to a shady dell as they passed.

"Duel? I didn't think men did that anymore."

He laughed. "Maybe in the rest of the country, but in Texas, it's still a way for gentlemen to settle their differences. We wink at the law. In fact, I own a set of exquisite dueling pistols myself."

"Have you ever shot anyone?" she blurted.

"Now that's not something for elegant young ladies to question." He smiled at her. "But I inherited the pistols. The Foresters go a long way back. Our family was part of Stephen Austin's original Three Hundred, you know."

He seemed quite proud of that fact and rightly so, she thought. "My goodness."

"Yes." He nodded. "When David Austin brought the first Anglo settlers to Texas, there were only three hundred of them; the blue bloods of Texas aristocracy. It's on both sides of my family."

She couldn't help but be impressed. Still, if Uncle Trace knew she had gone driving with him, there would be trouble. "I really should get back. I have a luncheon date."

He glanced sideways at her. "Not a young gentleman, I hope?"

"Oh, no." She laughed. "Just a girlfriend I don't get to see often."

"Good. I'd hate to think I have a rival. Here, we'll cross this low creek and go back to town."

"It looks a little deep," Turquoise protested as he drove into the water and abruptly, the buggy stopped. She heard him swear under his breath, then he applied the whip to the horse. "Get up there, you lazy nag!"

"Stop!" Turquoise protested. "The horse is doing all it can. We've hit some mud, that's all."

He sighed. "You're right. I'm sorry. Well, I guess I'll have to get my boots muddy." He made an expression of distaste and stepped down. The water was halfway up the fine leather. "And I just bought these boots, too."

"I'm so sorry," Turquoise said.

"It's not your fault," he replied, smiling up at her.

"Perhaps I'd better go for help but I don't want to leave you alone, my dear."

"If you'll just carry me over and set me under that tree, I'll be fine until you return."

"Of course, and I imagine you're light as a feather." He sluiced through the water back to her and she stepped off the carriage into his arms.

She knew immediately that this gentleman had no

muscle to him, because he took two steps backward and then went down, cursing. They were now both drenched and sitting in the cold water.

"Damn it! This is so embarrassing." Forester staggered to his feet as she scrambled to hers. "Excuse my language, Miss Turquoise, but this is a new coat besides the boots."

"Mr. Forester, I'll just go sit under the tree and you see if maybe you can drive the empty buggy out of the creek."

"Good idea." He reached up for the reins and the whip, but Turquoise protested again.

"It's not the horse's fault," she said.

He looked humiliated. "You're right. I'm sorry. I just hate to be inconvenienced and I've ruined your dress. I think we passed a farmhouse about a mile up the road. Maybe they'll have a team of work horses to get us out with. Will you be all right, my dear?"

"I'll be fine." She nodded and waded over to sit under the tree. "I don't think I care to walk that mile with you."

"Of course." He sounded grumpy as he started off up the road. Turquoise watched him until he was out of sight, then sighed. Her pale aqua dress was soggy and she was getting cold. She glanced up at the sun. It must be near time to meet Fern for lunch and her friend would be worried. Worse yet, if Uncle Trace came back and found Turquoise missing, there might be hell to pay. Why had she been stupid enough to come on this outing?

She knew why; she'd been dazzled by the influence and the power of this handsome, refined man and he seemed entranced by her. Edwin Forester was the most eligible bachelor in town and every well-bred girl in Austin had set her cap for him. If she could get past Uncle Trace's objections, what would it be like to snare the richest, most important man in Austin? She pulled her knees up and laid her arms on them. The black horse stood in the ankle-deep water and drank, flicking its tail at an occasional fly. It would be stupid to sit here and shiver and wait. Maybe she could get the buggy out of the creek herself. She was good with horses and Edwin didn't seem to be.

Turquoise took a deep breath and waded out into the creek. Feeling around the front wheel of the buggy, she found the boulder that was blocking the wheel. If she could only lift it out of the way . . .

She struggled to lift it, but it was too heavy. Behind her, she thought she heard a rider approaching, but she ignored it, pulling again on the rock. It was slick and it slipped out of her hands, and she sat down in the water with a big splash, her white lace hat falling off. "Damn, damn, damn." She watched her hat float down the creek.

"Well, hello, senorita, we meet again."

She looked up to see Rio Kelly mounted on a fine bay horse as he reined in on the other side of the creek and leaned on his saddlehorn. He watched her, an annoyed frown on his dark face.

She had never felt so foolish. "Well?"

"'Well' what?"

"A gentleman would help me." She kept her voice icy.

"After the trouble you caused me last night?"

"I'm sorry about that. Perhaps the senator overreacted."

He snorted. "I'd say so."

She tried to stand up, but her wet skirts threw her off balance and she plopped back down in the water. "Would you please help me?"

"I don't feel inclined."

She felt her temper rise. "Never mind. I'll get myself out."

"This should be amusing." He reached in his shirt pocket for "makins," then began to roll a cigarette.

"Are you just going to watch me?"

"*Si*. Oh, excuse me, Miss Sanchez. I know you are really white and don't speak Spanish, it means—"

"I known what it means," she snapped. Maybe she

should try another tack. "Look, I—I am sorry about last night. I didn't mean to embarrass you."

"Embarrass me? Ending up in jail overnight was a little more than that."

"The senator said he just had the guards throw you out in the street."

He glared at her. "Uh-huh. The senator is a liar."

"I don't believe you, and he's none of your business."

"You're right. None of this is my business." He leaned back in his saddle and smoked.

"Are you just going to leave me here?"

"*Si,* senorita. Let your fancy man get his boots wet."

"I've never been treated so—"

"No, I'll bet you haven't. You're spoiled and snooty, missy. It's about time you learned the whole world doesn't dance to your tune."

"I will have you thrashed by the senator." She was furious.

"Tell him to bring some help." He didn't smile as he smoked and watched her.

"I've never met anyone so rude." She staggered out of the water, her small shoes squishing as she walked up to him.

He shrugged, looking down at her. For an instant, they stared into each other's eyes. She thought for a split second he would reach down and lift her up on his horse. He was certainly strong enough to do that. What if he did and then tried to kiss her? If he did, how should she react? His lips looked full and soft and she had never been kissed before.

The buggy horse neighed behind them and the spell was broken. She stomped over and sat down under a tree.

Rio looked over the buggy critically. "Mighty fancy rig."

"Senator Forester offered me a ride this morning as I was going shopping."

"And there's so many shops out here on the creek?" He raised one dark eyebrow at her and grinned.

"I do not like what you are insinuating!" She was

furious, both with him and herself for getting into this situation.

"Senator Forester does not have a good reputation with women," he said. "Everyone in Austin knows that."

"That's just dirty gossip," she said, flaring. "He's been a perfect gentleman with me."

"Perhaps he is afraid of your guardian. Trace Durango has a reputation of being the best gunfighter in Texas."

"Senator Forester is refined. I can't imagine him brawling in the middle of the street or carrying a gun."

"Like the rest of us uncivilized Texans?" Now he stroked his horse's mane. "Well, I've got to go." He turned his bay stallion. "Come on, Peso."

She couldn't help but notice the way he handled the horse, so different from Edwin Forester. "I've got to get back to town. I'm meeting my friend Fern for lunch at about one o'clock."

Rio shaded his dark face with one big hand and looked at the sun. "I'd say you're late."

"Oh, goodness. If I don't show up, she'll go looking for Uncle Trace and there'll be trouble."

"Imagine that. I'd like to be there to see that."

"It may be awhile before the senator gets back. He's gone for help at a farmhouse about a mile up the road."

"I know the place. That's where I was headed to see if they had any horses that needed shoeing when I came across you."

She looked up at him. "Are you just going to leave me here?"

*"Si."* He pushed his black Stetson to the back of his dark hair. "You're not in any danger and since the senator is too stupid to get his own buggy out, I reckon he'll bring help."

"I'll pay you to give me a ride back to town." She kept her voice lofty as she leaned over and wrung some of the water out of the soggy aqua dress.

It was the wrong thing to say; she knew it immediately. "Senorita, I am not a paid servant. I was about to offer my help, but I can't be bought. Besides, don't you think you'll be embarrassed to come down Congress Avenue in a soaked dress, riding behind a lowly Mexican vaquero? What would people think?"

She drew herself up as proudly as she could, standing there in that wet dress and squishy shoes. "Never mind. I'll wait for Edwin to return."

His eyebrows went up. "Edwin? You call him Edwin?"

"What do you care? If I don't get back, Uncle Trace may find out and go gunning for the senator."

"Half the people in Austin would pay to see that little drama. Well, *adios,* Miss Sanchez. That means—"

"Damn it, I know what it means!" she shouted at him.

"*Hasta la vista* then." He tipped his hat with a smile and rode back the way he came.

She watched him with an incredulous stare as he rode away. "You come back here!" she yelled, but he didn't even turn his head. His stallion broke into a lope and the pair rode out of sight.

She had never been so angry in her life. People had always danced attendance on her every whim and here was a poor vaquero who had turned down her money, given her tit for tat and left her standing here. She was steaming, but there was nothing to do but sit down under a tree and wait for Edwin Forester to return. In the meantime, she waded down the creek and rescued her soggy lace hat.


Rio rode back to his blacksmith shop and slowly un-saddled his horse. He would have given that little spitfire a ride back to town, but then she had started ordering him about and offering to pay him like he was some errand boy. He didn't feel right about leaving a lady out on the road alone, but it was daylight and the senator was only a short distance away. Rio thought about spending the night in jail because of that pair and gritted his teeth. It served them both damned well if they had to deal with her overprotective guardian.

He put away his horse and was firing up his forge when his little spotted dog, Tip, began to bark. Rio looked out the open door. A man in a buggy was driving up and stepping down.

"Hello there, *hombre*," the man called. "We need to talk."

*"Buenas tardes."* Rio came out to meet him and noted the man was maybe close to forty, dark, and wearing a short, expensive Spanish jacket and flat western hat.

"I am Trace Durango." The man stuck out his hand.

Uh-oh. Rio shook it, thinking about the girl. "What brings you to my small place, senor?"

Trace looked around, then reached down to pat the small mongrel. "I looked at the job you did on my ward's mare yesterday. You did a good job, senor."

*"Gracias.* I do my best."

"I've got a lot of horses out at my ranch and my farrier has gone to Mexico City to visit relatives for a while. Might I persuade you to spend a week or two at the Triple D and do some shoein'?"

It would mean he could spend some time with the uppity beauty, but did he want to? She had treated him shabbily up to now. Maybe that was what intrigued him about her. He had plenty of women who were his for the asking, but the snooty girl who had had him thrown in jail was one he wanted to know better. "Senor, I might consider your offer. I have one vaquero who can keep my small ranch running for a while."

"Good." Trace Durango pushed his hat back and smiled.

"I like you, amigo. Would you consider havin' dinner with me tonight at Delmonico's?"

"Senor Durango"—he made a dismissing, embarrassed gesture—"I do not have the clothes for a fancy place like that."

"Nonsense. I have a private table in the back and the food is very good."

"I have heard." He was tempted. "Will we be alone?"

Trace shrugged. "No, my ward will join us, Turquoise Sanchez."

"Oh?" He didn't know for certain whether he wanted to face her sharp tongue. Suppose she told her uncle Trace about him abandoning her this afternoon? But the little vixen couldn't do that without relaying what and whom she'd been out there with.

"You sound hesitant." Trace grinned.

"She's—she's a great beauty." Rio looked away.

"She's that," Trace agreed, "but has the temper of a sidewinder."

"I agree." Rio nodded. "Some man needs to take over."

"No man so far has had the *cojones* to do so," Trace said.

Rio smiled. "Maybe no *hombre* has been *loco* enough to want to. It would be breaking a mustang filly."

Trace looked him over, nodding as if in approval. "*Si,* I think I would like to have you join us for dinner. It would be amusin'. Shall we say eight o'clock at Delmonico's?"

Rio nodded. "Thank you, senor. I look forward to meeting your ward again."

Trace turned back to his buggy. "Speakin' of which, she ought to be gettin' home from shoppin' and her luncheon about now. I should be gettin' back."

Rio ought to let the little rascal get into trouble, but somehow, he didn't want that to happen if she hadn't returned to town yet. "Please, senor, I know you have a lot of expertise when it comes to beef and horses. Could I get you to look around my little ranchero and see what you think?"

Trace shrugged. "You do me a great compliment, senor, but *si,* I would be happy to see your place, especially if there's some *cerveza* at the house."

Rio grinned. "Beer cold from hanging in the well." He nodded. "Let's go!"

With the little dog accompanying them, they headed for the barn farther up the road.

Edwin finally returned and the farmer's team pulled the buggy out of the mud. Edwin tipped the farmer handsomely. "There you are, my good man."

The old farmer shook his head and muttered to himself about "dudes" as Edwin helped the soggy Turquoise into the buggy, snapped the little whip, and headed back to town.

"I'm so sorry, my dear. It was just an accident."

Turquoise shaded her face with her limp, dripping hat. "I just hope my guardian isn't back at the hotel yet."

Edwin's pale face turned even paler. "I hope not, too."

They drove at a fast clip back to the hotel, Edwin looking very nervous as he reined in out front and rushed around to assist her. "Do you think your guardian will be upset?"

"Only if he finds out." She stepped down.

"I'd like to see you again." He took her hand.

"Send me a message," she said, turned, and hurried into the hotel lobby.

Fern was pacing the lobby and turned. "Oh, there you are! I was worried sick when you didn't meet me for lunch." She glanced down. "Is your dress wet? What . . . ?"

"Too much to tell. Have you seen my uncle?"

Fern shook her head. "Was that Senator Forester I saw helping you out of a buggy?"

Turquoise nodded with a conspiratorial grin. "Let's go upstairs so I can change and I'll tell you all about it."

"My word, this is just too exciting!" Fern scurried along behind her up the stairs. "I want to hear each tiny detail."

She'd have to let her friend in on everything and swear her to secrecy, Turquoise decided as she opened her door and they went in.

Fern flopped her chubby frame on the bed as Turquoise started to undress. "Now tell me what happened."

"Well, it started last night at the ball." Turquoise began to unbutton the wet dress. "Senator Forester actually asked if he could escort me from the stage."

"No!" Fern's mouth opened in astonishment. "Why, everyone says he's the catch of the town, but no girl has hooked him yet."

"You see," Turquoise went on, "I was supposed to have an escort and didn't know it, but Edwin is such a gentleman, he stepped in."

"Edwin?" Fern squeaked. "You call him Edwin?"

"You must cross your heart and not tell anyone, but I think he's wanting to court me."

"My word!" Fern breathed in awe as Turquoise changed. "But the Foresters and the Durangos are enemies. Everyone in Texas knows that."

"I know." Turquoise paused and smiled. "It's just like Romeo and Juliet, except I've got to bring peace between the two families before we could wed."

"Wed? Why, Turquoise, that would be the biggest wedding Austin ever saw."

"Of course, and he's planning on running for governor," Turquoise said as she changed. "Would you like to come to a party at the governor's mansion or maybe visit me in Washington if he runs for national office?"

"My word!" Fern said with a gasp. "I'm not sure what I'd wear."

"Well, just keep all this a secret for right now. My guardian would probably call him out if he knew."

"Oh, this is so romantic," Fern gushed. "It makes my and Luke's story seem so dull."

Turquoise frowned suddenly as she remembered the annoying vaquero. "There's just one problem, one person who might tell Uncle Trace."

Fern leaned closer. "Who?"

"Oh, never mind. I'm sorry we missed lunch."

Fern shrugged and got up off the bed. "Oh well, maybe I can lose a little weight before my wedding. I reckon I'd better get back to the ranch before Daddy and Luke start wondering where I am." The two girls hugged. "Honestly, Turquoise, you lead the most exciting life."

Turquoise shrugged. "Who knows what will happen next?"

"Well, keep me up on it. I promise I won't tell anyone."

Turquoise walked her to the door. "I think we'll be going back tomorrow or the next day. That sort of stops everything."

Fern paused in the door. "Love will find a way."

Turquoise sighed. "That's so romantic. The senator is such a gentleman, not like some men I've met." She frowned, remembering the vaquero.

Turquoise had barely put on a turquoise satin dressing gown and slippers, and sent the wet dress out to be cleaned when she heard Uncle Trace entering his room next door. She heaved a sigh of relief that she'd gotten back in time—no thanks to that arrogant hombre.

Now Edwin was everything she was looking for in a husband: important, prominent, a white member of the social scene. No one would dare whisper about her background if she were wed to him.

But what annoyed her was that the other man kept popping into her imagination; the big, primitive vaquero with the dark, haunting eyes and the shamrock tattoo on the back of his hand.

Uncle Trace knocked on their adjoining doors. "Turquoise?"

"Yes, Uncle?"

"Don't make any plans for the night. I'm takin' you to a new place."

"Oh? How exciting." Maybe it was the kind of place where the society people might eat.

"Did you enjoy your shoppin'?"

"Uh, yes."

"Good. I'm going to take a little nap before dinner, so you occupy yourself."

"I'll read a book," she called back. She bathed and began to wash her hair. She had just wrapped it in a towel and was drying it when there was a light tap at her door. She opened it a crack to a bellboy. "Miss Sanchez?"

"Yes?"

He handed her a note. "I was told to give this to you."

She tipped him and closed the door quietly before opening the envelope. On monogrammed paper in refined handwriting, the note read:

*Dear Miss Sanchez:*
   *I apologize humbly for this morning's mishap. I beg you to forgive me and hope to see you again soon.*

             *Your most humble and adoring servant,*
             *Edwin Forester*

She smiled as she sat back down and reread the note before tearing it up in tiny bits. So she had Edwin interested in her. What should she do now? Obviously her guardian was not going to allow this enemy to call on his ward because of this silly family feud. She knew they were returning to the ranch tomorrow. In the meantime, she laid out one of her most beautiful turquoise dresses, put her hair up in elaborate curls, and dusted herself with forget-me-not-scented talcum powder and perfume.

Now how could she get a note to Edwin? He was probably still in his office at the capitol. She sat down at the little desk and reached for note paper. She was uncertain what to say. She didn't want to sound too eager, but on the other hand, she didn't want to discourage such a suitable beau who offered everything a girl could dream of. No, she decided there just wasn't any way to get a note to Edwin without someone on the hotel staff alerting her uncle. She sighed, picked up a book, and tried to read.

It was a romance, but she couldn't keep her mind on the pages. She could possibly snare the most sought-after bachelor in Austin. Wouldn't that be a feather in her cap? All those girls from last night's ball would be so envious and wouldn't dare insult or demean Turquoise again.

Finally, she gave up on the book about the time she heard her guardian stirring around in his room. With a sigh, she began to dress. Supper at a fine restaurant would have been an exciting treat before, but now dinner with her uncle sounded dull. It was the kind of thing old maids did—go out to eat with relatives. Well, it was getting late. If she did manage to reach Edwin, he probably already had plans, an important meeting or something.

It occurred to her that if they had a quick bite in the hotel dining room, Uncle Trace might want to go to bed early. In that case, she might manage to sneak out and meet Edwin if she could get a message to him.

She could hear Uncle Trace moving about in his room now and she knocked on the door.

"Come in," he said.

She opened the door, watching him comb his graying

hair. "Uncle Trace, maybe we could have just a quick bite in our rooms."

"On our last night in town?" He snorted. "That surprises me, Turquoise. Since we may not be back in Austin for months, I thought you'd like to see how the other half lives."

"Well, yes. Is it a really fancy place?"

*"Sí."* He nodded with a grin.

If it were a fancy place, Edwin might be there. That was all she could hope for now unless she feigned a headache and returned to the hotel early. Then it might be too late.

"Don't look so glum," Trace said as he began to button his shirt. "I've invited someone to join us for dinner." He started through the connecting door of the suite.

"Oh. Who?"

"Never mind. Just get your wrap and I'll meet you in the hall in ten minutes."

She closed the door, intrigued. Maybe it was some eligible young man, she thought as she surveyed herself in the mirror. Her dress was turquoise-colored tulle with a full skirt and a small, perky bustle. She put silver and turquoise combs in her black hair and looked again. The dress was more modest than the other one. She bit her lips and pinched her cheeks to give them a rosy glow.

"Turquoise, are you comin'?" Trace's impatient voice from the hall.

No, there was no way to get a note to Edwin now or make any plans to meet him later. She grabbed a cashmere shawl. "I'm on my way."

She went into the hall and took his arm. He wore an expensive dark, short Spanish jacket and handmade black boots. *"Dios.* You look like a goddess." He grinned and winked. "All the young men will be watchin' you tonight."

They started down the hall.

"So who's joining us for dinner? Some dull old rancher who'll want to talk about shipping cows to market?"

"Don't laugh, young lady. That's what puts money in the bank to pay for those fine dresses you always want."

"I don't want to seem ungrateful," she said quickly and gave him her most fetching smile.

"Don't worry about it. We're glad to have you on the Triple D. What would we do without you to teach all our vaqueros' children?"

"It's little enough for everything you've done for me," she said as they went out on the street and Trace hailed a carriage.

"Delmonico's," Trace said to the driver as he helped them in.

"Delmonico's?" Turquoise almost squealed with delight. "Isn't that supposed to be the finest supper club in Austin?"

Trace grinned. "I figured you'd like it. Probably horribly dull with a bunch of stuffed shirts having dinner, but I hear the food is good."

She leaned back in the seat, happy now. She'd always dreamed of eating at Austin's best restaurant. According to Fern's gossip, it was the place to be seen.

It was dark when the cab drew up in front of a bustling establishment with many fine carriages out front. Her heart was beating with excitement as her guardian escorted her inside. It was spacious with fine carpets and many candelabra lighting the walls with a soft glow.

A snooty head waiter came up to them. "You have reservations?"

"I am Trace Durango and yes, there's a gentleman waitin' for us."

Turquoise looked around. In the candlelit room, there were crowds of expensively dressed people. She glanced about as the head waiter led them across the fine carpet toward the back. At the same time, she saw two men sitting at separate tables alone. One of them was Edwin Forester and the other was Rio Kelly.

# Chapter 5

Turquoise hoped beyond hope they were walking toward Edwin's table, but of course they walked right past it to another where Rio Kelly sat. He stood up awkwardly, wearing a rather frayed Spanish short jacket with silver conchos. "*Buenas noches,* senorita, senor."

Trace waved him back down. "Don't be so nervous, Rio. We're just havin' dinner, after all. I think you two have met because of Silver Slippers."

"Hello, senorita."

She nodded to the vaquero and felt a bit sorry for him. There was sweat on his dark face and he looked as awkward and out of place as she had felt last night. He was cleaned up and she had to admit he was handsome, but his suit was out of fashion and frayed on the lapels. Trace pulled out a chair for her and, forcing herself to smile, she sat down in such a way that she could see Edwin. "Good evening, Senor Kelly."

She stole a glance at Edwin. He was dressed in a fine suit with a red boutonniere. Could he possibly have known she would be here? Just as she wondered that, a gorgeous blond girl and two older women joined him for dinner. The elegant blonde seemed familiar somehow. His whole party looked much at ease in the elegant café.

Rio cleared his throat. "You look very beautiful tonight, senorita."

"Oh, please." Trace snorted. "Stop fillin' her head with compliments. She's difficult enough to live with."

She felt herself flush and was so angry at her guardian, she gritted her teeth. "Thank you for the compliment, senor."

She picked up her menu and ground her teeth at the thought of the aristocratic blonde at Edwin's table. Now she remembered why the girl looked familiar. The beauty had been one of the debutantes.

Trace turned to see what Turquoise was staring at and frowned. "Oh, Edwin Forester and his mother, the Iron Lady."

The older woman did look imposing with her stern face, dove-gray, severe dress, and gray braids piled across her head.

"Who are the others?" Turquoise tried to sound off-handed.

"Hmm." Trace shrugged. "I believe that's banker Turner's wife and his daughter. Now, what about drinks before dinner?" Trace returned to his menu.

"I—I'll have some sherry and chicken Kiev," Turquoise said. She wasn't a bit hungry and kept stealing looks at Edwin. She wasn't sure if he had noticed her or not.

Rio seemed to be struggling with the menu as the waiter came to their table.

"*Mezcal* or *cerveza?*" Trace asked and the other man nodded.

*Mezcal.* That was a drink for the lowest class of Mexicans. Turquoise pretended not to hear, but her face burned with humiliation.

Rio looked at the fancy menu, then at Trace and shrugged, evidently bewildered.

"Never mind, senor." Trace grinned. "What about a big steak and some potatoes and hot rolls?"

"That sounds *muy bueno,*" the other man said and handed his menu to the waiter, evidently relieved.

"How do you like your steak, Rio?" Trace asked.

"Rare."

"I'll have mine well done, and the lady will have chicken Kiev, whatever the hell that is," Trace grumbled.

"Very well, sir." The waiter took the menus and left.

"Uncle Trace, don't be so unsophisticated," Turquoise scolded.

"I'm just a Texas cattleman," Trace said, "and I like my food plain and hot."

At Edwin's table, she could hear him ordering from the wine list in French while the waiter scribbled on his pad and said, "Yes, monsieur. Yes, we have some rare wines in our cellars. I'll send our wine steward over to you."

In the meantime, the *mezcal* and the sherry were delivered to the Durango table.

"You're quiet as a tree stump tonight, Turquoise," Trace complained. "Usually, you're as talky as a magpie."

She sipped her sherry, miserable to be there. "I just don't have much to say." She looked down at her plate.

Rio fiddled with his napkin. "I'm afraid the young lady finds the company dull."

Trace frowned at her. "I'm sure that's not it." He nudged her hard under the table.

"Hmm? Oh, no." She wasn't even sure what was being discussed.

"She's usually bright and entertainin'," Trace said and he looked annoyed. Then he began a discussion about hay and whether Rio thought alfalfa was better for horses than prairie hay.

At Edwin's table, they were discussing Carolyn Turner's grand tour of Europe and what she thought of the art galleries of Italy with Edwin telling witty tales of his year at Oxford.

Turquoise ducked her head and looked at her plate, listening to the laughter at the other table. Next to Miss Turner, she felt stupid and homely; a country bumpkin who had never been out of Texas. Of course, if she could wed into the Forester family, she would have the chance to travel and learn sophistication.

Their food came and it was hot and delicious. Miserable at watching Edwin dining with the beautiful Carolyn, Turquoise ordered another sherry.

Trace frowned at her. "This isn't like you, and you've hardly eaten a thing."

"I'm fine," she snapped and sipped her drink, barely touching her chicken while Trace and Rio made short work of the steak and potatoes.

The waiter returned to the table. "Dessert, senor?"

Trace nodded and wiped his mouth. "I'll have apple pie with vanilla ice cream if you've got it. What about you, Rio? Turquoise?"

She shook her head and sipped her sherry. "Nothing more for me, thanks."

"Rio?"

"Do you suppose they have flan?" Rio asked.

Turquoise frowned. "This is a fancy place. I doubt they serve Mexican stuff."

Trace glared at her. "I'll ask. If not, what do you want?"

"Chocolate cake and coffee."

Trace grinned. "Sounds good. You have flan?" he asked the waiter.

The waiter's lip curled ever so slightly. "No, sir, but we do have the cake."

"Good, and coffee." Trace nodded.

Turquoise looked over at the Forester table. A waiter carried some flaming dessert in a silver dish to Edwin's table, causing admiring looks from the other diners.

Turquoise fiddled with her sherry and sulked. What was the point in begging off with a headache if she was just going to be stuck in the hotel while Edwin dined with the beautiful blond daughter of a rich banker?

She watched the two men at her table enjoy their desserts and wished she'd ordered something. Then the men pushed back their dessert plates and sipped their coffee.

"Well," Trace said, "it looks like the orchestra is about to start. Rio, I'm sure my ward would love to dance."

The orchestra began a waltz.

Rio asked, "Miss Turquoise, would you care to—"

"I don't think so," Turquoise said and then saw Edwin leading the gorgeous blonde out on the dance floor. "No, wait, I've changed my mind."

Rio pulled out her chair and took her hand, leading her onto the dance floor. Once again she was enveloped in his big arms and she remembered how strong and masculine he was. His coat might be old and frayed, but he waltzed beautifully. She could feel his warm breath against her hair and tried to put more distance between them. "You waltz well, senor."

"*Gracias.* Some of the cantina girls taught me." He grinned down at her.

She felt herself flush. "I'm sorry. I did not mean to pry."

"Then you shouldn't have asked." He grinned. "You think I do not notice you watching the senator dance with the banker's daughter?"

Was it so obvious?

"I didn't mean to be rude," she murmured.

"You have been nothing but arrogant and rude to me since the first time we met." He whirled her around the floor and held her closer. She seemed to fit right into the embrace of his muscular arms. "Senorita, if I had any pride, I'd abandon you on the dance floor and walk out."

She looked up at him. "And make a laughing fool out of me? You wouldn't dare."

"Don't tempt me, Turquoise," he whispered against her ear. "I've already taken more off you than any woman I ever met."

"If you're afraid of what my uncle might—"

"I am afraid only of God and the devil. Now be quiet and pretend you are enjoying dancing with me."

She saw Edwin whirl by and saw he was trying to catch her attention, but there was nothing she could do about meeting him, so she ignored it. The blonde must have recognized her, though, because the girl said something loudly about a "gaudy turquoise dress" and laughed cruelly.

Turquoise's face burned but she stuck her nose in the air and pretended she had not heard. She'd looked like a fool, she knew, at the debutante ball and now here she was dancing with this vaquero in his frayed jacket. Then she realized women were giving Rio admiring glances and trying to catch his eye, but Rio seemed to ignore them all.

It was a long evening. Uncle Trace danced with her once, then complained he was tired and retreated to the bar. Rio danced with her over and over. Once Edwin passed their table and paused. "Would you save me a dance, Miss Sanchez?"

Before she could answer, Rio snapped, "The lady is with me, senor." His tone left no room for argument.

Edwin scowled and walked away.

Turquoise seethed. "You might have let me decide that."

"Your guardian left you with me for safekeeping and he would not be happy to return and find you in the arms of that shady skunk."

"Edwin Forester is very high class," Turquoise said, miffed.

"And white?" Rio suggested.

She felt tears come to her eyes. "Can't you understand what it's like to have a Mexican name, but look white? People whisper behind my back about who fathered me."

"People whisper about my father, too," Rio said softly and took her hand.

"But it's worse for women, and the senator treated me with great respect."

"Maybe so, but I hear he dallies with all the pretty servants at his mansion."

"I'm sure that's just idle gossip," she said, defending him.

At the senator's table, the group was getting up to leave, Edwin being very solicitous of the three ladies.

Turquoise watched them go.

Rio said, "Forget him, Turquoise. He'll marry some society gringa of his mother's choosing. Besides, he must be almost twice your age."

"Oh, shut up. He's worldly, handsome, and sophisticated."

"All the things I'm not."

"You said it, not me. You know," Turquoise said, "I think I'm getting a headache. Why don't you join Uncle Trace in the bar and I'll get a carriage home?"

He smiled at her. "Senorita, a real man would never allow a lady to go home alone after dark in a big city such as this."

She heaved a sigh. "I am well able to take care of myself. Like any ranch girl, I can handle a rifle."

"Ah," he smiled," and do you have one with you?"

She flushed with annoyance. "I—well, no, I don't."

"Then your uncle and I will escort you home. Now if you really have a headache, perhaps the waiter can bring you some bitters—"

"I'm feeling much better," she snarled.

"Good. Then shall we dance again?"

"I don't think—"

But he was already pulling her to her feet and holding her close, much too close, as they waltzed. She tried to pull back but he held her tightly, his breath warm against her hair, her breasts pressing into his chest. She had to look up to see his face and she didn't like that, nor did she like the way her small hand fitted into his big, calloused one. She remembered Edwin's hands, so soft and manicured; a gentleman's hands. Rio smelled like a man, a little cigarillo smoke, a touch of liquor, the male, salty, sunburned scent of a cowboy. His eyes were dark brown where Edwin's were pale. Edwin had a soft, pink face and graying light hair. He also wore expensive cologne and the finest of fashions.

She tried not to, but she enjoyed the dance. And now the orchestra struck up "Good Night, Ladies" as they danced, and she saw Uncle Trace come out of the bar.

"Oh," she said, "it's time to go."

"Let me get your wrap," Rio said.

"I can do that myself."

He ignored her protest and led her back to the table and put the soft cashmere shawl around her shoulders, his hands lingering just a moment longer than needed. She could feel his breath next to her ear and for a moment, she thought he would kiss her ear. Did she want him to? No, of course not, she scolded herself. She had never been kissed before and when she allowed some man to be the first, she wanted it to be a man she wanted to marry, not a Mexican cowboy.

Uncle Trace joined them just then. "Well, it looks like you two have had a good time."

"I did," Rio answered. "I'm not sure about the young lady."

"It was very nice, Senor Kelly," she said in a cold, polite tone.

"Good." Uncle Trace grinned. "Otherwise it would be a long train ride home."

"What?" Turquoise blinked.

"Oh, didn't I tell you?" Trace said as they started to leave the restaurant. "I need a bunch of horses shod. Rio is goin' back to the ranch with us."

Oh hell. She didn't know whether to be angry or just annoyed. She wouldn't be returning to Austin for months. That would probably mean the end to any possible romance with Edwin Forester. By then, he'd probably be engaged to some snooty rich girl like Carolyn Turner.

The next evening, her friend Fern came to see her off.

"My word," she said with a giggle, her freckled nose wrinkling, "I see you have a handsome man accompanying you home."

Turquoise turned and looked toward Rio standing and talking to her guardian on the platform. "Oh, that's just the farrier. Uncle Trace hired him to come shoe a bunch of horses."

"He's mighty handsome anyway," Fern said. "Any girl would enjoy a trip with him."

"I don't think so," Turquoise answered and looked around, hoping against hope that Edwin Forester might come to the train to see her off. But of course he didn't know she was leaving today and wouldn't want to face Uncle Trace anyway.

The train whistle tooted a warning and the conductor yelled, "All aboard!"

Fern and Turquoise hugged each other.

"Now remember," Turquoise said, "you promised to take good care of Silver Slippers. I need a horse to ride when I come back to town and I hope that's soon."

"I promise I'll move her to our best pasture," Fern

whispered. "I can hardly wait for the next chapter of your romance."

"Remember, you're sworn to secrecy," Turquoise reminded her. "I don't know how I can keep in touch with Edwin."

Fern grinned and wrinkled her freckled nose. "Come back and visit me soon. You know we need to work on my wedding plans."

Turquoise started for the train. "That's an idea. I'll try to get back." She waved to her friend, wondering if Edwin would forget her before she ever returned to Austin. There was nothing she could do about that now. She saw Uncle Trace and Rio striding toward the train as the whistle tooted again.

Fern waved a hankie and Turquoise waved back as the two men swung up on the train. Then the train shuddered and chugged, beginning to move out of the station.

"Well," Trace said with a smile, "I'm surprised you left that new mare behind. I thought you'd want to bring her home."

Turquoise said, "Fern promised to look after her so I'll have a horse to ride when I get back to Austin to help plan her wedding."

"Sounds logical." Uncle Trace grinned. "They should be servin' in the dining car soon. Or shall we go into the club car for a drink first?"

"I don't think I'm hungry," Turquoise said, pointedly ignoring the tall Rio.

"Good. Then the men can have a drink." Trace clapped the other man on the back. "Come on, amigo, we'll have a couple of drinks and talk."

"*Sí.*" The other grinned and nodded.

The men started through the car and Turquoise frowned. The two liked each other too much. On the other hand, they

were a lot alike, and neither was the polished gentleman
Edwin Forester was.

She took a seat on the scarlet horsehair cushions of their
private car and waited for the black waiter in a white jacket
to come through the car striking his small gong. "Ladies
and gentlemen, first call for supper, first call."

Impulsively, Turquoise decided she would go ahead and
eat. That way, she wouldn't have to share a table and conversation with Rio Kelly. She hurried to the dining car and
stood swaying in the entry, looking down a long line of
crisp white tablecloths.

"Ma'am?" The black waiter came to her. "Will you be
dining alone?"

"My uncle and his employee might join me later, but I'll
eat now."

He led her to a table and pulled out the chair. Outside the
window, the scenery flew by as the train chugged deeper
into the hill country. Purple shadows of dusk settled over
the landscape and outside, bluebonnets and scarlet Indian
paintbrush dotted the landscape of grazing cattle and
horses. She ordered a sherry and decided on beef pie in a
crispy crust. She sipped the wine and enjoyed the scenery
as the car filled with diners.

The beef pie was excellent; hot and filled with a creamy
burgundy sauce. There were also small new potatoes floating in melted butter and fresh asparagus. She topped it off
with excellent coffee and an orange creme cake. Turquoise
was just finishing as Trace and Rio joined her.

Uncle Trace said, "I thought you weren't hungry."

"I changed my mind."

"*Buenas noches,* senorita." Rio nodded politely

She gave him a curt nod. "If you gentlemen don't mind,
I think I'll go out on the platform." She stood up abruptly
as Rio tried to pull her chair out for her.

Trace covered a yawn. "Myself, I think I'll catch a quick nap after we eat. We'll get in late, Rio."

*"Si."* He sat down and Turquoise headed through the dining car, grabbing onto chairs to keep from losing her balance on the swaying train. Behind her, she could hear the two men discussing horses.

It was dark outside now as she went out on the back platform and watched the shadowy landscape they chugged past. The scent of wildflowers and cedar trees drifted to her as they passed through the hills. Soon she would be home and she would return to teaching the small children of the ranch employees. She loved children, but with Senora Durango and her children gone to Philadelphia, things would settle back down into the humdrum of ranch life, broken only by an occasional visit to the tiny village on the edge of the Triple D.

And back in Austin, there would be glittering parties and elegant dinners, talk of politics and money, important people traveling to Washington, D.C., and New York City. Well, maybe there was no future for her except the ranch, after all. And yet, she wanted so much more; she yearned for glamour and respectability.

After a while, she heard the door open behind her and a man cleared his throat. She didn't turn around. It was surely Uncle Trace coming out for a final smoke and maybe to scold her for being curt with the other man.

Then a deep voice with a Mexican accent said, *"Perdone,* senorita, would you mind if I joined you?"

Rio.

She didn't turn around. "I don't own this train. You're certainly entitled to come out here." She kept her voice icy.

A long silence, then "Do you mind if I smoke?"

She merely shrugged. She heard the strike of a match and then the pleasing scent of burning tobacco.

"Senorita, if I may be so bold, if I have done anything to offend you, I offer a thousand apologies."

She felt herself cringe. She was the one who had been rude. "You have done nothing except leave me in the middle of a creek without coming to my aid."

"Are you still angry about that?"

"Yes. It was thoughtless of you."

He laughed, a low chuckle. "I would have aided you, but you began to treat me like a lowly servant. I'm not used to that from women and I may be poor, but I am proud, missy."

"Perhaps I was a bit uppity," she admitted.

"A bit?" He snorted and she wanted to give him a good whack, but she had a feeling this wasn't a man to take that. He was just a little wild and uncivilized and she was used to men humbling themselves over her beauty.

"I'm just disappointed to be returning to the ranch so soon, that's all."

"I hear it is the biggest in Texas. I could only hope to own such a spread someday. You are very lucky to have such a benefactor."

She turned slightly to look up at him. He was so big and powerful, looming over her with those dark eyes and the silver cross reflecting the moonlight. "You just don't understand, I like ranch life, but I've always hungered for something more and a half-Mexican girl can't—well, never mind." She turned back to watch the tracks under them slipping by.

He came closer and threw his smoke away. She saw it hit the tracks behind them with a shower of sparks. "Oh, senorita, I do understand. How do you think a poor, fatherless boy who's also half Mexican survives but by his wits in a city like Austin?"

"What happened to your father?"

"That's a rude question for a young lady," he said. "But

since you're nosy, my father was an Irish soldier in the Mexican-American War who fell in love with a local girl."

"I'm sorry. I didn't mean to pry." So he was much like her, she thought; half-Mexican bastard.

The train lurched on uneven track and she stumbled, grabbing for the rail. The man behind her reached out and caught her, pulling her back. "Senorita, are you all right?" His hands were strong and powerful, not the hands of a gentleman at all.

"I—I'm fine. I think I should go in now." She turned abruptly and was looking up into his rugged face, their bodies almost touching.

He stared down into her eyes and she saw passion and need there, but he stepped back and bowed low. "After you, Miss Turquoise."

They returned inside and settled down in the Durango private car where Trace was already dozing over a ranch magazine. Rio leaned back against the cushions and slept, but she could not sleep. She had had one chance maybe to meet the important people and mingle with them and now she was headed back to her schoolroom.

Finally, the train stopped at the tiny village station in late night. A buggy driven by the ranch foreman, Pedro, was waiting and they all piled in, Rio putting his hands on her slim waist and helping her up into the buggy where he sat next to her.

"Hey, Pedro." Trace shook his hand. "Anything much been happenin' while we been gone?"

"Not much, boss." The two men got in the front of the buggy and they started off.

"I've bought some new blooded cattle," Trace said. "They'll be shipped in here soon. Otherwise, it was a pretty dull trip."

Dull trip? How could he say that? Turquoise thought as she tried to scoot farther away from Rio, but the seat wasn't that wide. It had been the most exciting time of her life.

It was ten miles back to the ranch and sometime in that monotonous buggy ride, Turquoise fell asleep in spite of herself. When the buggy finally pulled up before the big white hacienda with the fountain in the front patio, she was leaning against the big man and he had put his arm around her, cradling her against him.

She sat bolt upright.

"I was keeping you from falling," he explained.

Trace was already stepping down. "*Gracias,* Pedro. Take Rio over and find him a place in the bunkhouse. He'll be with us a few weeks shoein' horses."

Pedro's white teeth gleamed in his dark face. "Ah, good, amigo. You'll be here for Cinco de Mayo then?"

*"Sí."* Rio nodded. "I'm looking forward to it." He stepped down and helped Turquoise from the buggy, then stood looking down at her. "Good to see you again, senorita."

"Yes," she said and walked into the house, Trace right behind her with the luggage. She looked back and saw the buggy headed toward the bunkhouse.

"Ah, good to be home," Trace said with a sigh as they entered. "Now if Cimarron and the kids were only here. I hope they get enough of Philadelphia to last a lifetime."

"I wish now I'd gone with them," Turquoise said as they entered the front parlor.

"Well, you were bound and determined to be a debutante," Trace griped. "Damned foolishness."

She'd been humiliated, that was true, but because of it, she'd met Edwin Forester, who was everything she dreamed of in a husband. Problem was, he was now more than fifty miles away and in this isolated ranch country, it might as well have been the distance to the moon.

She awakened the next morning thinking of all she had to do with her little class today, then realized suddenly it was Saturday. She dressed in a plain blue denim dress and went downstairs where old Maria was serving steak, eggs, and tortillas, washed down by strong black coffee.

"Well, good mornin', sleepyhead. It's eight o'clock. The day's half gone." Trace grinned at her and Pedro jumped to his feet as she entered the big dining room. "We've already been layin' out work for the day."

*"Buenos dias."* Pedro grinned at her with his gold front tooth.

*"Buenos dias,"* she said with a yawn.

Trace pulled her chair out and the men sat back down. Maria entered and poured her some coffee.

"Ah, little one, you have a good time in the big city, *si?*" Maria patted Turquoise's head, as she had always done.

"It was fun." Turquoise smiled at her. "I'll give you all the details later, lots of shopping."

Trace groaned. "Well, that's not something I'm eager to hear about again. Come on, Pedro, let's go over to the bunkhouse and get that new man started."

Rio. She frowned at the thought. There was something about him that both annoyed and excited her. She sipped her coffee and waited for the two men to go out.

"Are the children all right?" she asked.

Maria nodded, a big smile on her face. "They hope you brought them something, senorita."

Turquoise grinned. "I did. Candy and some books. Oh, and I brought a beautiful shawl for you."

"For me? Oh, you shouldn't have, senorita."

"But of course I did. You have been like a mother to me since my own was killed." That sobered Turquoise and she tried to remember her mother, Rosa. All she remembered was that she had been beautiful and stormy, but had died a heroine saving Trace and his woman, Cimarron. Her father had loved her the most, she knew, but there'd always been a rumor that he was not really her father, that the old don or one of his white friends had fathered her and pressured old Sanchez into marrying the fiery servant girl to cover up the scandal.

She did not want to think about that now. She ate with gusto the scrambled eggs with hot chili peppers, cured ham, and some warm tortillas, covered with honey and butter. Then she shared some of the ham with the tiny brown chihuahua, Tequila, that had hopped up on the nearest chair, begging and whining.

Maria clucked with disapproval. "You shouldn't spoil the dog so."

"Oh, everyone does," Turquoise answered. "Has there always been a chihuahua here at the Triple D?"

"Always." Maria smiled. "And most of them named Tequila. Remember the one that is buried at the old don's feet?"

Turquoise nodded. And right next to the old don in the family graveyard was his faithful foreman, Sanchez, the only father she'd ever known.

After she ate and drank more coffee, she brought out the silk shawl she had brought the cook, who oohed and aahed over it and kissed and hugged her.

"Now I think I'll go out and find the children," she said as she started for the front door. "They'll be expecting to see me."

Tequila, the little chihuahua, trotted along behind her.

Turquoise gathered up her gifts and went out to find the ranch children. They were all waiting in front of the little schoolhouse near the blacksmith shop. "*Buenos dias.* Did you miss me?"

"*Si,* senorita!" All the children gathered around her, some shy, some more bold. She looked down into all the little brown faces and dark eyes, loving them all. "I brought candy and books and toys for all of you." She sat down on the schoolhouse step and began to pass them out.

Seventeen-year-old Juanita joined them. "Ah, senorita, we are all so glad to have you back."

Turquoise paused in handing out the gifts. "And I brought you some pretty earrings."

The girl smiled with pleasure. "All I want is to be able to teach school like you."

She accepted the earrings and Turquoise finished handing out the gifts. After visiting with the children awhile, Turquoise walked away, near the horseshoeing shed.

Rio leaned against the door smoking a cigarillo. He wore no shirt and his muscular brown body gleamed with sweat. The sunlight reflected on the small cross hanging against his broad chest. "*Buenos dias,* senorita."

She gave him a curt nod and started to walk past.

"You are a nicer person than I had thought," he said, "bringing gifts to all the children."

She was drawn to him, even though he was not the man she had planned for. "If that's supposed to be a compliment—"

"I did not mean it as an insult." His voice was cold.

"I hope you will be leaving soon," she snapped and strode past him.

"I'll be here at least until after Cinco de Mayo," he called after her. "I wouldn't want to miss the celebration."

So that meant he would be here at least another week. She could hardly wait to have him gone. He annoyed her in a way she couldn't understand. She shook her head, trying to shake the image of the big, virile male from her mind. How in the world was she going to ever make a connection with Edwin Forester again? She wished Cimarron were home. Maybe she could reason with her stubborn husband.

The night of the big celebration, the children had been let out of school to help Turquoise and the ranch hands string the crepe paper and lanterns around the big front patio. It was a major Mexican holiday, celebrating the fifth of May, when Mexican soldiers had defeated the French invaders and run them out of Mexico. She had always enjoyed and helped with the festivities. The whole ranch had been given the day off and there was much tequila and wine flowing. A small band showed up at sunset and Turquoise helped old Maria and Juanita set up tables full of good food while the cowhands had a whole cow and a pig turning on a spit over the glowing fire nearby.

Then she went in and put on a bright flowered dress with all the jewels that matched it. When she came out, it was warm and dark outside with all the people in a happy mood, visiting and dancing.

Uncle Trace lounged against the rim of the big fountain in the courtyard, smiling as he sipped his drink and watched the crowd. "It is a very big celebration this year. I only wish Cimarron and the children could be here."

Turquoise smiled and nodded. "The ranch crowd, with all the neighbors, seems to get bigger every year." She wondered what kind of festivities were happening in Austin. Certainly the upper-class Anglos like Edwin wouldn't take part. She felt a bit of guilt because she enjoyed these festivals so much.

"Well"—Trace turned his head—"look who's comin' to the party."

She turned to look.

Rio Kelly, all washed and scrubbed and dressed in his short Mexican jacket and best boots, came toward them, smiling. "Ah, senor, such a great party." He shook hands with Trace and then bowed low to Turquoise. "Senorita."

Now he was probably going to ask her to dance and she wondered how to say no without annoying Uncle Trace.

Instead, Rio looked across the courtyard. "Excuse me, please."

As Turquoise watched in disbelief, he strode across the courtyard and bowed before Juanita. The girl looked dazzled and thrilled as he led her out onto the courtyard and they joined in the Mexican folk dance.

"Well." Uncle Trace grinned. "You should see your face, Turquoise. Evidently, you were expectin' him to ask you."

She felt her face burn with humiliation. "Of course not. I don't even like the man. He's just a vaquero."

"But a mighty handsome one," Trace said, pointing out the obvious and sipped his drink.

The dance ended and Rio walked over to another girl and bowed, then led her out onto the courtyard as the music began again.

Turquoise felt awkward standing here, watching him dance. "Maybe we should start serving the food."

"The beef isn't ready yet," Trace said as three little boys ran past them, chasing each other as they circled the fountain. "Turquoise, if you really want to dance, I—"

"No, I'm fine," she snapped. How would it look if no one except her uncle asked her to dance? "I can help old Maria set out the plates." She went over to help at the tables, all lit with torches, and watched Rio out of the corner of her eye. Sure enough, he was dancing with yet another girl and seemed to be having a wonderful time, throwing back his head and laughing while the girl smiled up at him, obviously smitten.

How insulting. The least he could do was ask his hostess for a dance. The more she thought about it, the more annoyed she became. She covered it by pretending to be engrossed in helping with the plates.

Abruptly, there was a man at her elbow. "Senorita, would you care to dance?"

It was him.

"I don't think so," she snapped. "I'm very busy."

"Fine," he said and whirled her around, took her in his arms, and began to dance.

"Didn't you hear me? I said—"

"Be quiet, missy. You sound like a chattering squirrel."

"Of all the nerve!" She tried to pull away from him, but he was strong and she didn't want to make a scene.

Now what was she going to do?

# Chapter 6

"Let go of me," Turquoise threatened, "or I'll scream."

"I don't think so." He looked down into her eyes and didn't loosen his grip. "You've been waiting for me to ask you to dance all evening."

"I have not."

"Then why have you been sneaking looks at me?"

She felt her face flush. "I was worried that some of our naive young girls might be taken in by your roguish charm."

"It certainly doesn't seem to work on you." He held her even tighter.

"If Edwin could see what you're doing, he would thrash you within an inch of your life."

"I doubt that the sissy boy has ever been in a barroom brawl."

"And I'm sure you have."

"Quite a few." He nodded.

About that time, Pedro rang the big bell on a post outside the ranch house. "Food is ready, amigos!"

Immediately, the band stopped playing and the crowd began lining up. Turquoise pulled out of Rio's arms and went over to help serve. When she looked back, Rio had a pretty girl on each arm, escorting them to the dinner.

Two of the cowboys lifted the roasted steer off the spit and began carving it.

Turquoise dished up the pinto beans and the tortillas. There was Mexican and American food, pies and cakes, and casseroles, each woman striving to outdo the others.

Uncle Trace mingled with the crowd, shaking hands, hugging babies, patting little ones on the head.

Turquoise stationed herself behind the table, dishing up food to the long line of people, pretending she did not see Rio as he came through the line with two plates. "You must be very hungry, hombre." She snorted.

He grinned back. "Oh, I'm getting plates for the senoritas." He nodded over his shoulder toward the pretty Mexican girls sitting on a bench across the courtyard.

She didn't know why she felt so annoyed, but she almost slammed the cole slaw and the beans onto his plates. Then she waited for him to say something, but he seemed oblivious to her mood as he grinned again and swaggered across the courtyard to the girls who were waiting for him. Turquoise stared at them. That trio was having entirely too much fun.

"Turquoise? Turquoise?" Uncle Trace reached out and tapped her on the arm.

"What?" She jumped, startled.

"How about givin' me some of those beans?" Uncle Trace said. "You've brought the line to a complete stop."

She looked around into all those waiting patiently to be served. "Oh, I'm sorry." Now she did a slow burn while she continued serving.

Rio came back for a plate for himself and she slammed food into it so hard, he almost dropped it.

"Enjoy!" she snapped.

"Oh, I will." He sauntered back to his senoritas.

She tried not to watch him while she served others. She hoped he choked on the beans. But instead, Rio and the pretty girls had finished and were laughing together.

Turquoise finally got herself a plate, but she wasn't hungry. She stood near the table, toying with her food.

About that time, Rio came back to the table. "Ah, senorita, now I'll take some pie. Everything looks so good."

"Including the local girls?"

"*Si,* especially the local girls." He grinned.

"Get your own pie."

"Which one did you make? Lemon?"

She couldn't think of a sassy answer while he picked out a big plate of pie and sauntered away again.

She watched his broad back as he strode to the giggling senoritas. He seemed to be enjoying the food immensely. Now one of the girls had taken his fork and was feeding him. Turquoise would like to feed him. She'd ram that fork down his gullet.

She stayed by the table, trying to eat, but the food seemed to stick in her throat. When she glanced up, she thought he might be watching her.

Now he strolled over to the table. "Ah, Miss Sanchez, the food was *muy bueno.*"

"I'm glad you liked it." She kept her voice cold. Out of the corner of her eye, she could see the band setting up to play. Now this annoying hombre would ask her to dance and she would flip her hair, turn up her nose, and refuse.

Instead, he looked over the food again. "I wonder if the young ladies and I might have some more pie?"

"Pie?" He wasn't asking her to dance; he wanted pie.

"There it is. Cut it yourself," she growled and turned away while he surveyed all the pies as if trying to decide among them.

She strode to one side and sat down on a hay bale with her plate, pretending to eat, but she sneaked looks at Rio carrying the pie back over to the pretty girls and they seemed to be enjoying it. She hoped the pie made the girls fat.

The *mezcal,* tequila, and beer were flowing freely now and the band began to play a Mexican folk tune. Turquoise put down her plate and watched. Under the glow of the lanterns, it seemed Rio was dancing with every woman at the festival, everyone but her.

Now Uncle Trace helped the little boys set off fireworks. Sky rockets made bright trails against the dark May night and exploded into a rainbow of colors.

Okay, so Rio wasn't going to ask her to dance. Well, she didn't want to dance with him anyway. She wanted an elegant, successful gentleman who wore boutonnieres and this vaquero certainly wasn't that. She returned to the table and began covering the bowls and wrapping the leftovers. The party seemed to be getting louder as beer and wine flowed, the laughter rose, and the band played louder. She tried to look very busy so no one would notice she wasn't dancing.

Then she was startled as Rio came over to the table. "If you want some more pie—"

"No, senorita, I want to dance with you." He bowed low.

"Have you run out of senoritas?" she snapped.

"Maybe I was saving the best for last."

"I don't think I care to—"

"Sometimes a lady needs to know when to close her mouth and smile." He came around the table and took her hand, then half led, half dragged her out onto the courtyard.

"Are you telling me to shut up?" She resisted, but masterfully, he took her in his arms. She tried to protest that she didn't want to dance, especially not with him, but his strong arms enveloped her and her face brushed against the fabric of his jacket as they danced. His jacket held the male, woodsy scent of a man who spent his time in the wind and sun. She told herself she must not make a scene, so she shut up and let herself press against his big chest. She could lay her head against his shoulder, he was that tall, but she tried not to do that. His powerful hand was warm on her small waist and the other grasped her delicate fingers firmly. He had big, square hands from roping cattle and shoeing horses, strong capable hands that could caress a woman, subdue a wild mustang, or hold his own in a fistfight.

She felt molded against his lithe muscles, his thighs pressing against her body. He was holding her too close. Uncle Trace wouldn't like that at all, but she looked over and saw Trace was occupied with the fireworks. She tried to pull back, but Rio held her firmly and whispered against her ear in soft Spanish. "Don't."

How dare he? After dancing with every woman at the festival, he was getting a little too forward with her. What should she do? She started to protest and he whispered, "Hush."

The music ended and she pulled back and looked up at him. "I'll have you know I am a modern woman and I am not used to being ordered about by a man, especially an employee of my uncle's."

He looked stung and stepped back. "You're every bit as snobby as everyone says you are."

"I beg your pardon!" She brought back her hand to slap him, but he caught her hand and held it, grinning down at her. "Or maybe like a blooded filly, you just need the right man to gentle you."

For a split second, she thought he might pull her to him and kiss her, and without thinking, she leaned toward him. Instead, he shook his head and walked away.

She found she was holding her breath, wondering what it would be like to be kissed by this big Texan. Then she was furious with herself. Of course this wasn't the kind of man she wanted to kiss her. She wanted a civilized, high-class man like Edwin Forester. Then why did she find herself feeling disappointed?

Turquoise looked around to see if anyone had witnessed the scene and was relieved to see no one paying the slightest bit of attention. Rio had disappeared into the shadows and she wondered if he had taken both senoritas out into the shadows of the night with him. He was surely enough man to satisfy two women. Well, let him play the stallion with some of the other girls. She tried to push the images from her mind of him kissing a nubile girl as she clung to him, his dark face hot against her breasts while she whispered, "Oh, Rio, do that again. Oh, Rio . . ."

Damn Rio. She hoped he got his bare butt mosquito bit out there in the grass.

The band stopped playing and the party began breaking up, people gathering children and yelling good-naturedly to each other as they straggled away. Maria started wrapping up leftovers and Uncle Trace came over to Turquoise.

"Well, I reckon it was a very good Cinco de Mayo. We've never had such a big crowd before."

"It was very nice," she said, not looking at him. "Maria, let's save this leftover cole slaw."

Uncle Trace yawned. "I'm sorry you didn't get to dance. I should have invited more cowboys over from some of the surroundin' spreads."

"I was too busy to dance," she said, relieved that he must not have seen her dancing with Rio. "Besides, none of the cowboys are marriage material and as your hostess, I was too busy seeing everyone got fed."

"Good girl," he said and yawned again. "Well, let Maria put away things and let's go to bed."

From the distance came low laughter and a man's voice, murmuring in Spanish. Was that Rio? She pricked her ears, but couldn't be sure.

Uncle Trace laughed. "I reckon some of these couples

are findin' other ways to celebrate now that the dancin' is over."

"I'm sure I wouldn't know about that," she snapped and felt her face burn. Had Rio taken one or both of those girls out onto the soft grass with him? Of course she didn't care; he was only an arrogant vaquero, after all.

However, when she lay in bed with her upstairs windows open, she smelled the scent of wildflowers on the night breeze and pictured all the couples out in the grass, making love, and had never felt so alone in her life. In her mind, she was in Rio's arms and he was kissing her and holding her close.

She took a deep breath, shuddering and feeling a deep wanting within herself. Her thighs felt warm and she imagined him stroking them and then caressing her breasts.

What was she thinking? She sat bolt upright in bed, shocked at herself. She was not some chambermaid, rolling around in the grass with some randy male. She intended to give herself only to the kind of man who could offer her respectability and social position. But that man was at least fifty miles away in Austin. She must find a way to get back there before Edwin forgot about her.

That settled, she dropped off into a troubled sleep in which Rio told her to hush and then kissed her protesting lips until she stopped protesting and clung to him, wanting more, much more.

It was late afternoon the next day and Rio was about to quit work. He was still a bit groggy from last night's festivities as he leaned against the forge. He reached for his denim shirt and took a deep breath. At that moment, he smelled the scent of forget-me-nots blending with the scent of hay and hot iron. He turned to see Turquoise enter the shed. She looked as haughty and beautiful as ever in a leather split skirt, vest, and boots, with a western-style hat whose brim protected her lovely face from the sun. He felt his insides clench. He had wanted this woman from the first time he had seen her, so elegant and so unattainable for a lowly nobody like himself. "*Buenas tardes,* senorita."

He saw her look him up and down and realized he was smeared with sweat and smudge from the forge.

"Oh, you." She played with her leather riding gloves. "I did not realize you were still working. I am finished teaching for the day and was merely looking for a hired hand to saddle a horse for me."

"*Si,* I can do that, senorita, but you might say 'please.'" He leaned against the forge and wiped the sweat from his dark face.

"Never mind." Her pert nose went up in the air. "I'll do it myself and I'll tell Uncle Trace you were rude and impertinent and he should fire you." She whirled to leave.

He grabbed her arm with one big hand, wanting to pull her to him and kiss her until that arrogant frown left her face. "Are there no cowboys over at the barn?"

"Probably." She jerked out of his grasp and for a moment, he thought she considered hitting him with her gloves, then maybe thought better of it.

"Then why do you go out of your way to order me about?"

She seemed speechless, then whirled again to leave. "You got my sleeve dirty, and besides, you are impossible."

"But you already knew that, senorita." He grinned. "Wait and I'll saddle horses for both of us."

She drew herself up proudly. "I don't remember asking you to accompany me, hombre."

"Then I'll ride in another direction. I've finished my work for the day."

"Very well." She shrugged and with head high, she

strode out of the shed, Rio following easily with his long steps.

"Remember not to go into that pasture over there." She pointed as she walked. "There's some blooded bulls there that are dangerous."

He laughed, catching up with her. "Did I tell you that in Mexico, I tried my hand at bullfighting?"

"Were you any good?" She looked over at him with new interest, imagining him in a suit of lights, striding into the arena in tight pants.

"Well, I'm still alive, so I reckon I was okay, but I never cared for it. It seemed weighted against the poor bull— not sporting."

They went into the barn. It was a big barn with many stalls, each holding a fine horse. The horses nickered at them and she took in the scent of hay and the good smell of leather and horses.

He looked around. "So many good horses. I could only dream of such."

"Take your choice," she said grandly, reaching for a bridle. "I left Silver Slippers in Austin with my friend Fern, so I'll ride this blood bay mare."

He looked up and down the row of horses. "How about this black one? He looks spirited."

She made a sound of dismay. "Oh no, not Night Spirit. He's a dangerous horse. No man is brave enough to ride him except Uncle Trace."

"Ah, is he related to the famous Night Wind?"

She nodded. "But he has a bad temper."

"Worse than yours?" Rio grinned and reached for a saddle. "In that case, I'll ride him."

"Worse than mine." She gritted her teeth and smiled without mirth. "Don't say I didn't warn you." She led the blood bay out.

"Wait, senorita. I will saddle her for you. Isn't that why you came to the shed?"

She coughed. "Yes, of course. I needed a hired hand to help me." She wasn't certain why she had gone to the shed. Now she wished she hadn't. "Since you're an employee, you might as well earn your keep." She sat down on a bale of hay and watched him bridle her horse.

"You are rude and impudent," he said as he saddled the bay. "Someday, some man will turn you over his knee and paddle you until you show good manners."

"You wouldn't dare!"

"I didn't say me, senorita, I said some man, maybe your future husband."

She sniffed and frowned. "The kind of man I marry will be civilized and cultured. He wouldn't think of spanking a woman."

"Someone like Edwin Forester?" He paused and gave her a direct look.

"Perhaps." She looked away. "Please do not mention that name to my uncle. He does not like the Foresters."

"And with good reason." Rio finished saddling the mare and handed the reins to Turquoise. "The Mexicans whisper that he takes advantage of every pretty maid that works in that big house and his mother fires them or has them shipped back across the Rio Bravo if they dare complain."

"That's dirty gossip!" She was more than annoyed. She grabbed the reins, swung up on her horse, and nudged her into a gallop and out of the barn.

"Hey, senorita, wait for me!" Rio called after her, but she ignored him and took off across the field.

She grinned to herself as she rode. The farrier would have a very difficult time getting Night Spirit saddled and even if he did, she would be gone out of sight so he could not catch up with her. The Durangos owned most of three counties and she could ride all day without reaching their boundaries.

Turquoise dropped back into a leisurely canter and rode through the cedars and rolling hills. She hated to admit she liked ranch life; it conflicted with the fact that she also yearned for a sophisticated life in a big city where no one would dare whisper about her past because they feared her husband's power.

She wondered how Rio was doing on saddling that devil horse. She smiled to herself as she rode. He couldn't say she hadn't warned him. Maybe she should have stayed to witness the fun.

Damn that girl. Rio watched her gallop away. He didn't know what to make of her. Sometimes she acted like she hated him, then she went out of her way to seek him out to tease and tantalize him. He knew he could never have her, not with her high and mighty goals, and yet he had never met a woman he desired so much.

Rio led Night Spirit out. The stallion was flighty, laying his ears back and dancing about. "Ho, boy." Rio stroked the black muzzle. "Hombre, you behave yourself and we'll go follow that beautiful mare and the girl on her, *si?*"

He had a way with horses, and the stallion quieted and let Rio saddle him. Rio talked soft Spanish to the stud for a moment as he led him out of the barn and mounted up. The black horse stepped sideways and snorted, jerking against the bit. "So you want to run, hombre?" Rio murmured. He looked around for the girl and saw just a bit of her long black hair flying in the breeze before her horse disappeared over the far horizon.

Rio gave the stallion his head and Night Spirit responded, taking off like a bullet across the pasture. This was indeed a fine horse, Rio thought as they galloped after the blood bay. After a few minutes they caught up with Turquoise and she seemed surprised. "I thought Night Spirit would dump you in the manure of the barn floor."

"Horses are like women," he said in his soft Mexican accent. "They respond to someone who knows how to handle them with a firm hand and a little gentleness."

She felt herself flush and took off at a gallop, Rio right behind her. They rode in silence for a long time before she drew in on a bluff.

"You handle the horse well." Her voice held grudging praise. "Very few can ride him."

"We understand each other," Rio said. "We should get down and walk awhile, cool the horses."

Before she could dismount, he swung down, came around to her, and helped her dismount.

She had such a tiny waist, he thought as he put his big hands on her and eased her down. For just a moment, he held her, looking into her face. She was looking up at him and her lips were pink and soft and he wanted to kiss them over and over, pull her down on the soft grass and make love to her. Even though she cared nothing for him, he would have done anything for her, climbed a mountain, killed a man, stolen a fortune. But he was just a poor vaquero and she was a haughty, spoiled girl and way above him. He would not give her a chance to rebuff him.

For a moment, she looked up at him as if she felt the magnetism, too, then she pulled out of his arms and they began to walk along the ridge. He felt himself shaking from having her in his embrace, even for a moment. He had made love to many women, but none he wanted as much as this one. It occurred to him that they were far from anyone and that he could take her now, as he had wanted to do since the first moment he saw her, but he did not want her that way. He wanted her to come willingly into his arms, needing him as he needed her. "This is a beautiful ranch," he finally managed to say.

"You have a ranch," she answered.

"Only a few poor acres," he conceded. "What you have seen is the big spread next to mine."

"Why don't you try to buy it?"

He laughed. "It doesn't occur to a rich girl that I might not have the *dinero?* Besides, it belongs to some big New York company. I tried to track the owners down one time, but it was impossible. I couldn't afford it anyway. It's almost five thousand acres."

"And close to Austin, where someday it might be very valuable," she noted.

"I don't believe in wasting my time dreaming about that which I can never have." He looked at her, adoring her, wanting her, knowing he lied.

"I have dreams, too," she admitted, her big turquoise eyes soft now. "I would like to have a man who could protect me from the whispers."

They paused and looked at the sun low on the horizon. "What do they whisper about?" he asked.

She shrugged. "That I am a bastard, that Sanchez was not really my father."

"Why don't you ask Trace Durango?"

"I—I'm afraid to know, I think. Perhaps Trace doesn't know, either. The old don and Sanchez are both dead. Gossip says Sanchez married my mother, who was a housemaid at the ranchero, to keep scandal down. Some say I was fathered by maybe the old don himself or one of his friends."

"Your mother never told you?"

Turquoise shook her head. "Rosa was a wild beauty. I barely remember her. She died when I was very young."

There was a long silence. "I'm sorry," he said.

"It doesn't matter. She wasn't much of a mother or a

wife," Turquoise admitted. "Senora Cimarron has raised me and educated me. I pay her back by teaching the other children on the ranch."

"I would say Juanita is old enough to take over the school," Rio said.

"You noticed her, did you?" There was a trace of jealousy in her voice.

He laughed. "How could a man not? But she's a bit young for my taste."

"I dare say Austin is full of lusty senoritas waiting eagerly for your return."

"A few." He didn't want to think about all those Mexican girls in the taverns, the ones with full breasts who clawed his back and had sweaty, passionate sex with him. He only yearned for the girl standing near him now, but he did not say that. If he did, she might laugh.

"And what is your story?" Turquoise asked as they paused and looked at the sunset. "All I know is that you have a four-leaf clover tattoo and that your father was Irish."

"My story might be the same as yours," he answered so softly that his voice was a whisper. "He never married my mother and she lives now in the cloistered Convent of the Little Sisters. I send as much money as I can so she can pray unceasingly for his soul and other sinners."

"He did not love her?"

He shook his head. "He loved her very much."

"Then why—?"

"The army hanged him for a traitor," he snapped. "Now don't ask me any more. I should not have told you that. I've never told anyone."

He looked away, angry with himself that he had let this unobtainable girl get inside him as no woman ever had.

"It's all right. Perhaps I, as no one else could, understand." He felt her touch his arm and her voice was gentle.

He had not seen this part of her before, the girl inside who could be a kindred soul. He did not know what to make of this, knowing her only as the snooty, ambitious ward of a rich rancher. He did not like feeling vulnerable, especially to this beauty.

"We should be getting back." Turquoise looked over at his anguished face. His background was as scandalous as she thought hers to be.

"All right, Miss Turquoise." He came around as she started to mount and put his hands on her waist.

She paused, looking up at him. Again, there was that split second that she thought he might kiss her and she saw the uncertainty in his dark eyes that was mirrored in her own soul. Would she want him to? How should she react? Should she return the kiss or slap him for his impudence? She never got the chance to find out because abruptly, he took a deep breath and stepped back, barely helping her up into her saddle before mounting up himself. They rode back to the ranch quietly and without speaking.

Trace came out to greet them as they reined in before the barn. "Oh, there you are. I was beginnin' to worry."

"I was fine, Uncle Trace." She dismounted.

"I knew you were all right if you were with Rio. I was worried about him when I realized he had taken the stud. Night Spirit is a very dangerous horse."

Rio grinned and dismounted. "Night Spirit and I understand each other. He is a very fine stallion, Senor Durango."

Trace nodded. "You're the only one besides me who's ever ridden him, so you must be a born vaquero."

Rio scuffed his worn boot in the dust. "I was only riding to protect the senorita," he answered modestly.

"I can look after myself," she snapped.

Trace frowned at her, then said, "Put the horses away, will you, Rio? And you, young lady, come on in. Maria has been holdin' supper for you. Oh, I got a wire from Cimarron. She and the children are havin' a wonderful time."

She tried not to glance backward as she accompanied Trace into the ranch house. There was something about the Irish-Mexican hombre that drew her; maybe it was that she sensed he could be as wild and untamed as Night Spirit.

That night she lay sleepless, remembering that moment when she thought Rio would kiss her. The thought made her feel hot and restless. She wondered what it would have felt like. Would it have been savage, his tongue forcing itself between her lips as he held her so tightly, she could feel his muscular chest hard against her soft breasts? She tried to wipe out that thought and concentrate instead on Edwin Forester. Yes, Edwin was the kind of man she had always planned on marrying, and some poor vaquero wasn't about to change her ambitions even though she struggled to get him out of her mind. That made her angry with him for interfering with her dreams.

Yes, she didn't know how, but she must find an excuse to journey to Austin again. School would not be out for a couple of weeks; perhaps she could take the children to the capitol to see the sights. Trace Durango must certainly approve if it were an educational trip.

That was it. The legislature was still in session. She would take the children on a tour of the state capitol and maybe there she would see Senator Forester. It was worth a shot. She wondered what his kisses would be like. She could only imagine what heat Rio's kisses must generate. Surely one man's kisses must be much like another's and she was not going to change her plans just because her addled brain kept thinking of a virile vaquero's strong arms.

Yet when she drifted off to sleep, it was not Edwin she dreamed of; she was safe in the embrace of Rio, who held her close, made passionate love to her, and dared anyone to hurt her or gossip about her. She was his to love and protect. When she awakened suddenly, she was drenched with perspiration and gasping for air. More than that, she was angry with the lowly hombre for invading her dreams and upsetting her life. More than ever, she was determined to put Rio out of her thoughts and her future.

# Chapter 7

Rio lay on his narrow bed in the bunkhouse listening to the other cowboys snore. He couldn't sleep, thinking about Turquoise. Finally he got up, pulled on his pants and boots, and went outside into the dark. The night was warm now that it was May, and the breeze seemed to kiss his bare chest. He imagined it was Turquoise kissing his skin and pulling her blouse low to touch her nipples against his hot flesh.

That threw him into a need that almost drove him into a frenzy. There was an outdoor swing near the side of the ranch house and he sat down, staring up at her window. She was up there, maybe lying sleepless herself. She might be wearing some flimsy bit of silk that outlined the womanliness of her and he had an urge to tear down the door, race up the stairs to her bed, and claim her. Would she open her arms and her warm thighs to him? He wanted to love and protect and hold her, make her his in the ultimate way a man can make a woman his own, give her his seed, and keep her with him forever.

He laughed and leaned back in the creaking swing. He knew he had no chance with this haughty girl who wanted more from life than love. She wanted social position and money, and of that, he had neither.

He heard a noise and was instantly on alert. Then a pretty Mexican girl came out of the shadows. "Hello, amigo, may I join you?"

He didn't want any company with his fantasies, but he shrugged. "It's not my swing. Senorita, why are you not in bed?"

She laughed and sat down in the swing, leaning toward him. "I might ask you the same question."

He wished she would go away. "I couldn't sleep."

"Me either. I have been thinking about you, hombre, since the night of Cinco de Mayo."

He tried to remember the girl, but she was just an average pretty senorita whom he now recalled staring at him during the festival. "Your family will be looking for you."

"My family is fast asleep," she whispered against his ear, "and I would like to know you better."

He started to protest, but when he opened his mouth, she slid up against him and kissed him, the kiss deepening as she rubbed her generous breasts against him. She wasn't the girl he loved, but his maleness took over and in his need, he returned the kiss as she pawed at him, and pressed him back against the swing. He closed his eyes and pretended she was Turquoise, kissing her like he yearned to kiss the haughty, unattainable girl.

"Let's go into the barn," the girl whispered, "and finish this."

"I don't think—" he protested but she cut off his words with her lips.

About that time, he heard a slight noise and looked up. Turquoise stood at her open window, looking down at them. Her long black hair hung loose over her shoulders and her white silk nightgown clung to her soft curves and round breasts.

Rio jumped from the swing, dumping the sultry girl on the grass. He looked up, wanting to call to his love, tell her he was sorry, that he hadn't meant to kiss the voluptuous girl at all, but Turquoise gave him a furious glare and slammed her window shut, drew the curtains, and disappeared.

Mother of God. Well, if he had ever had even the slightest chance with Turquoise, it was ruined now.

The lusty girl stood up, her blouse falling off one shoulder, showing a generous expanse of breast. "Ah, amigo, don't mind her. Let's go into the barn and I will pleasure you."

His manhood was aching for relief and this passionate girl was so willing. It was tempting because Turquoise had already jumped to the conclusion that he was making love to the other girl. Yet he found himself saying, "No, senorita. I'm going back to the bunkhouse now."

She clung to him, promising him all sorts of wild ecstasy, but he only shook his head. "No."

"You are a fool!" she hissed and flipped her skirts, exposing long, slender legs. "I see what you want, but you'll never get her, you hear? You aim too high for a poor vaquero."

"I know." He shook his head gently. "But she's the only one I want."

"Then you're stupid because you'll never be the one in her bed. You hear me? You can't buy the silk sheets to lay her on or the fine perfume to spray on her tits."

"Go home." Rio shrugged and returned to the bunkhouse. Everything the girl had just said was true and it was hopeless. He realized now he had come to the ranch, not for the handsome salary Trace Durango had offered, but to be close to the haughty, cold girl he hungered for.

He did not get any sleep that night, but as he twisted and

turned, he decided that he should give up and go back to Austin as soon as possible.

Turquoise lay sleepless as well. In spite of his attentions to her, it appeared he was ready to take any randy girl who offered him her body. She decided she would never speak to him again and she stayed with her vow for several days. Yet late one afternoon, she found herself drawn back to the blacksmith's shed. He labored over a glowing forge, naked to the waist, his virile body drenched with sweat, the crucifix gleaming in the light.

Now he looked up and frowned at this princess in white organza. It reminded him of the night she had stood in her window in sheer white silk. "I wasn't expecting to see you again."

She felt foolish, not even sure herself why she had come. "I—I wanted to make sure you had fixed the wheel on my buggy."

"Done," he snapped and returned to his work.

She watched his hard, dark muscles as he worked and the four-leaf clover tattoo on his right hand. "Will you be leaving soon?"

He hesitated. "*Si.* Probably tomorrow. I've got most of the horses shod and my own ranch needs me."

"Oh." She didn't know what to say. She stood there awkwardly, thinking she ought to turn and go. "It—it's been nice having you here. The children like you."

"I like them, too."

"Perhaps I can come to Austin sometime and bring the children."

He shrugged as if he was indifferent and went on hammering a horseshoe.

"Rio"—she moved closer—"I didn't mean to seem so snobbish."

He looked up at her with those hot, dark eyes. "I understand, senorita. You want to better your place in life. I can't fault you for that."

"Yes." She stood on one foot and then the other. "Well, I guess it's good-bye then."

He swore in Spanish. "Then say it and get out of my life!" His dark eyes flashed with anger. "Why do you keep coming near me, tantalizing me, making me want you—?"

He reached out suddenly, wrapped his muscular arm around her tiny waist, and dragged her to him. She stared up at him, feeling the heat of his virile body through her thin organza dress, torn about whether to protest. And then he kissed her.

She put her hands on his bare shoulders to push him away and then hesitated as the kiss deepened. His mouth seemed as hot as a branding iron. In spite of herself, she found herself clinging to him as he molded her against his tall frame, feeling the heat and the power of his maleness through her thin clothing as he embraced her. His mouth dominated hers, forcing her lips apart as he kissed her. She tasted his mouth, salty and warm and demanding, and let the kiss grow hotter, not pulling back as he buried one hand in her mane of black hair and murmured sweet things against her lips.

It was he who finally pulled away, breathing hard as he stepped back, apologizing profusely. "Senorita, I'm sorry. I did not mean disrespect. . . ."

She was speechless for a long moment, not sure how she should react. She had been kissed without her permission by a poor vaquero and it was the first time she had ever been kissed on the mouth by a man—a passionate man who surely wanted more. His hot lips invading hers had sent shock waves of need through her body that she had not known could exist. It shook her to her very core and she didn't like not being in control of her emotions.

"You—you are impudent indeed," she snapped and, in a swirl of thin white organza and black curls, fled the shed.

He sighed, staring after her. If she told her guardian, Trace Durango might come after him with a pistol, and he couldn't blame him. A woman's innocence was the most valuable thing she owned, and yet, Rio had almost thrown her down on the dirt floor of the shed and taken her, so great was his need for only this one woman. Indeed it was time he returned to Austin.

That evening, he went to call on the master as Trace settled himself in a comfortable leather chair before the big stone fireplace. "Ah, Rio, come in. Would you like a cigarillo and a brandy?"

"No, sir. I have come to tell you I need to return to Austin tomorrow."

"So soon?" Trace raised his eyebrows.

*"Si."* Rio nodded. "I hear your own blacksmith is due back anytime and I have my small ranch to attend to."

"I see." Trace's dark eyes seemed to burn into him as smoke encircled his head. "Your sudden leavin' wouldn't have anything to do with Turquoise, now would it?"

He squared his shoulders, ready to take his punishment like a man should. "So she told you."

Trace looked baffled. "Told me what? She was quiet as a mouse all through dinner and then scurried away to her room. Is there something I should know?"

Rio rubbed his chin. "Well, sir, then I will tell you. This afternoon, she came to the shed where I was working."

Trace grinned. "She does seem to end up wherever you are."

"She is so beautiful. I—I forgot that she is a well-brought-up lady and I am just a vaquero."

Now Trace frowned at him. "And?"

"She came so close, almost taunting me, and I forgot myself and kissed her."

Trace leaned back in his chair and seemed to relax. "Nothin' more?"

"I swear to you by the Virgin Mary that nothing else happened."

Trace seemed to smile then and took a sip of his drink. "And did my arrogant ward slap you?"

Rio shook his head. "She just looked startled and then she ran."

Trace chuckled. "Then she must have liked it."

Rio shook his head. "I don't think so. I apologized and she said I was impudent, whatever that means, and she ran away."

Trace's eyes seemed to drill into him. "And are you in love with Turquoise?"

Rio sighed and nodded. "Hopelessly, but she sets her sights higher. She wants money and social position." He decided he would not get her into trouble with her guardian by mentioning Edwin Forester.

Trace seemed to consider a long moment. "My ward is a foolish, spoiled girl who does not know a good man when she sees one. Would you like my permission to court her?"

Rio gasped. "I couldn't hope for that. I only own fifty acres and could not provide for her as she is accustomed to."

Trace shrugged. "If you are willin' to work hard, you could rise in the world."

"She won't have me." Rio shook his head. "That's why I'm leaving early. I can't see her every day and know she will never be mine. It's torture."

Trace sighed and stood up, shaking hands with Rio. "I understand. I felt the same way about my wife, but through sheer determination, I claimed her."

Rio turned to go. "I'm afraid, Senor Durango, that is not the case with Turquoise."

Trace clapped him on the shoulder. "Maybe when

you are gone, she will realize that she cares for you, too. Absence makes the heart grow fonder, they say. I'd like her to forget all this foolishness about debutante balls and Austin society. Most of those gringos are foolish and dull."

"I wish Turquoise felt that way." Rio nodded to him and started out the door.

"I will send your earnin's to you in the mornin' before you catch your train. Maybe I might ask Turquoise to drive you." He smiled and winked.

"I think she'd rather drive the devil to hell," Rio mused aloud and then was gone.

The next morning, Turquoise knew she looked a fright at breakfast.

She felt Uncle Trace staring at her. He said, "You don't look like you slept well. Is something botherin' you?"

"Not at all." She kept her gaze in the depths of her coffee cup. In truth, she had dreamed over and over that Rio Kelly was kissing her and kissing her. His mouth on her throat and then moving lower still as she begged him to take her. She had awakened in a cold sweat with her bed covers tangled from her twisting and turning all night.

"Oh, Rio Kelly is leavin' this mornin'," Uncle Trace said and cut his breakfast steak.

"Who?"

"You know, the visitin' farrier."

"Oh, him." She shrugged indifferently and returned to her Mexican omelet, but it tasted like cotton in her mouth.

"I thought you might want to drive him to the train."

She snorted and sipped her coffee. "I have a school to teach. Let one of the hands do it."

"Today is Saturday," her uncle reminded her as he drank

his coffee, "and I thought you might have errands to run in the village."

"I don't think so." She kept her voice cold. "Anyway, I don't care for the man. He's rude and arrogant."

"Oh? He seemed very polite to me."

"You just don't know him well—" And then she stopped. She should tell Uncle Trace about the kiss in the shed, but her guardian might take a horse whip to the man. That was all Rio Kelly deserved, but somehow, the kiss was very personal and she did not want to share the event with anyone. Besides, she did not really want to get Rio in trouble. Actually, now that she thought of it, she was a bit flattered that the man had wanted her so badly, he had lost control. Now if she could just get that kind of reaction from Edwin Forester.

"All right then," Uncle Trace shrugged and stood up. "I'll get one of the hands to drive him—"

"On second thought"—she hadn't even realized she was going to say it—"I need thread and things from the village. I guess it won't be too much trouble to drop that farrier off at the train station."

"Good. I'll go pay him and see if he's ready to leave." Trace left the dining room.

"Uncle Trace, I've changed my mind—" She got up and hurried after him, but he was already gone, striding across the big paved courtyard toward the bunkhouse. Oh, hell. She gritted her teeth. Why had she said she would drive him? She did need a few things from the village store, but not badly enough to spend time with that arrogant cowboy. Suppose he tried to kiss her again. She felt her anger rise at his impudence and then remembered the kiss. No wonder girls giggled and talked about being kissed. It had been a heart-pounding, almost indescribable thrill.

In a few minutes, Uncle Trace came back in. "I told Rio you'd drive him. He didn't seem pleased."

"He didn't?" She bristled. "Well, we do seem to clash with each other."

"Like flint and steel?" Uncle Trace suggested as he walked away.

"More like a dog and a cat!" she yelled after him, but he didn't turn around. Now what?

She didn't relish an awkward ten-mile buggy ride with a man who didn't want her to drive him any more than she wanted to ride next to him, their bodies almost touching.

She thought about it a long moment, then smiled. She would invite a bunch of the children to go along for the ride. She hurried away to the workers' little houses.

When Rio came out of the bunkhouse, the wagon was waiting. Turquoise sat on the seat, dressed in a leather riding skirt and boots, plus a western hat to shield her fair skin from the sun. He smiled in spite of himself. "*Buenos dias,* Senorita Turquoise." It would be torture, but sweet torture.

Then five little brown faces popped up out of the back of the wagon. "*Buenos dias,* Senor Rio."

He must have looked surprised, because the girl smiled in a mocking way. "I hope you don't mind. The *ninos* and *ninas* wanted to go along for the ride."

"Of course not." He shook his head and climbed up on the seat beside her. He loved children, but he wasn't sure whether he was happy to have them along. It would keep anything questionable from happening in case he weakened and wanted to kiss her again. One look at her stern face told him that was why she had brought the children along.

He reached for the reins.

She shook her head and clucked to the team, starting off with a jingle of harness. "I'm driving."

"It is generally the man who drives," he said.

"Not in this case." She put her pert little nose in the air and pulled out on the dirt road leading to the village.

He didn't know whether to admire her for her obstinacy or turn her over his knee and then take the reins away from her.

"I feel foolish, having a woman drive me," he muttered.

"I've been raised on a ranch. I drive well." She laughed and did not give up the reins.

In the back of the wagon, the children were singing a folk tune, not well, but loudly.

It was going to be a long, long trip, he thought and decided he could do nothing but let her drive. Their bodies were almost touching and he seemed to feel the electricity from her warm thigh against his and again, he remembered the kiss. That made his manhood swell and he twisted in his seat, uncomfortable.

"My guardian said you didn't want me to drive you to the train."

"I didn't think you'd want to."

"I don't," she snapped, "but I needed to go to the village on errands, so he demanded I go."

"Hmm." He wished the ride were over. He had no chance with this girl and it was torture to sit on this wagon seat, their thighs almost touching. He could smell the faint scent of forget-me-nots on her skin and her hair shone black as ink, pulled back under her western hat. He must break this spell she held over him. When he got back to Austin, the first thing he must do is go to his favorite saloon and make love to one of their voluptuous whores. Or maybe two or three, he thought, changing positions on the seat again. It might take three girls to end this need in him.

They did not speak the rest of the trip as the wagon bumped along. The children sang and laughed in the back, oblivious to the tension on the front seat.

Turquoise had never felt so uncomfortable in her whole life. The ride had seemed the length of Texas and she was angry with her uncle for putting her in this awkward position, then remembered she had volunteered on impulse. She'd been too aware the whole ride of Rio's closeness, of the way his thigh touched hers when the wagon hit a rough spot in the old road.

They started down the only street in the small village. She heard the train coming in the distance, its whistle echoing across the hilly terrain.

"The train! The train!" The children jumped up and down with excitement.

Rio looked back over his shoulder and grinned. "Have you little ones never ridden a train before?"

"No, senor," came a chorus of voices.

He looked into Turquoise's pale eyes. "Perhaps the senorita will bring you to Austin someday to see the sights."

"Perhaps I will," she said and she did not smile and looked away as she reined up before the station hitching post.

The sound of the train chugged closer and the children chortled with excitement. Rio climbed down, then reached up and lifted each little one from the wagon. "Now don't get on the tracks."

He turned and looked up at Turquoise. "You will get down, senorita?"

"Why not?" she said and started to step to the ground, but he reached and put his strong hands on her waist and helped her down to the road.

For a moment, he looked down into her face, still holding on to her. He might kiss her, she thought, which would be disgraceful in public. It horrified her to think she wanted him to. *Don't be a fool,* she scolded herself as she pulled away from him. One man's kisses must be like another's and Edwin Forester was the man she intended to hold and kiss her.

"Don't forget your bags," she reminded him and strode

across the boards of the platform to where the children were gathered, waiting for the train to chug into the station.

She turned to watch him grab his bags out of the back of the wagon and stride over to the children. "*Hasta la vista,* kids." He grinned. "Maybe I will see you again."

"We'll miss you, senor." They all chortled, gathering around for a last hug.

"I hope you'll miss me, too." He turned to Turquoise.

"Not likely." She kept her expression and her voice cold. She must not get involved with this man. He could offer her nothing, and yet . . . no, she reminded herself again, she must not, could not love this vaquero.

The train pulled into the station with a grinding of wheels, the smell of smoke, and a shower of coal dust.

Rio held out his hand to her. "*Vaya con Dios,* senorita." Go with God.

She did not take his hand. "Good-bye, senor. Have a safe trip home."

"If you're ever in Austin—"

She shook her head before he could continue. She did not want this to go any further and yet . . . she reminded herself again that she had higher ambitions than a small ranch and a bare existence.

"All aboard!" the conductor yelled. Rio stepped aboard as the porter grabbed his bags.

The children set up a chorus of farewells, waving at Rio, but Turquoise forced herself to stand and nod as if she were seeing any employee of the ranch off on a trip.

"Come on, children. The train is leaving now." She herded them away from the platform but couldn't stop herself from glancing back.

Rio still stood in the train door, staring after her. He smiled as she looked back and she turned away quickly, annoyed with herself. She told herself she was glad to see him gone as the train blew its whistle, then chugged slowly out of the little village. They all stood and watched it until it was only a black speck in the distance and a lingering bit of smoke.

"All right, children, now we'll go to the general store, and I'll buy each of you a peppermint stick."

Little Juan turned dark eyes up to her. "Are we going to Austin to see Senor Kelly?"

The others set up a howl. "Let's go see Senor Kelly!"

Even the children were aligned against her. "I don't know, I don't think so, maybe." She turned and looked one last time as the train disappeared over the horizon. Now she wasn't certain whether she was happy or sad that he was gone out of this town and out of her life.

She wanted to go to Austin, all right, she decided as the little group walked toward the store, but not to see Rio. She needed an opportunity to see Edwin Forester and give him another chance to court her. She intended to become Mrs. Edwin Forester and to reign as the queen of Austin society.

# Chapter 8

Rio sat at the train car's window, his face pressed against the glass for a long time, looking back at Turquoise and the children until he could no longer see them. He knew he could never have the turquoise-eyed beauty, but that didn't stop him from wanting her, needing her as a man needs a woman. No, more than that. He wanted to keep her with him always, hold her and protect her from anything or anyone who might hurt her, put his seed deep within her and give her his son. Yet she was not his to love and cherish, and would never be.

He slumped back on the scarlet horsehair cushions and tried to think of something else on the trip back to Austin, but she dominated his every thought.

That night after he returned to Austin, he went to the local cantina where he knew all the girls. It was a busy night, with vaqueros drinking *cerveza* and *mezcal,* women dancing and laughing to the guitar music in the background. Rio sighed and ordered a drink, then another. This place used to be amusing; tonight it seemed dirty, dim, and sad.

He spotted a whore he used to like, a beauty with big breasts. "Hey, Margarita, you want a customer?"

*"Si."* She paused and gave him a sultry look. "But for you, Rio, it is free. You know how to give a woman much pleasure."

His manhood rose at the thought of lying between a woman's warm thighs. "Then at least let me buy you a drink." She came over to the bar and leaned against it, humming to the guitar music in the background. "Tequila," she said to the mustachioed barkeep who wiped the scarred counter with an old rag.

"And another one for me." When the drinks arrived, Rio held his up. "Here's to pleasure." He smiled at her.

"I know you'll give me that," she purred, sipping her drink, then leaned against him so that he got a good look at her full breasts in the low-cut blouse.

He was a little drunk now and he inhaled the scent of stale beer and cigar smoke, cheap perfume and tortillas. "What's new around Austin since I've been gone?"

She shrugged and took his hand. "Nothing much. A big fire downtown, a few fights, and a stabbing in our alley, that's all. Come with me now."

He let her lead him through a door to a dimly lit hallway and down that hallway to her room. She closed the door and turned to him, smiling as she pulled her blouse off. She wore nothing underneath it and her breasts were large and full. He felt his manhood pulse hard as stone and he thought, *Si, I could take three women tonight, my need is so great.*

She began to unbutton his shirt and rubbed her big breasts against his bare chest as she nuzzled there. "I'll make you forget about any other woman."

Turquoise. Abruptly her face and big, turquoise eyes came to his mind even as he embraced Margarita. Damn her. Why must the elegant beauty invade his mind? Even though he fought against it, he felt his manhood fading and he pulled away from Margarita.

"What's the matter, honey?"

"Nothing. I—I changed my mind, that's all." He backed away from her, feeling foolish and unable to perform. That was loco, he told himself; he had been pleasuring women since he was fifteen. He had a reputation for satisfying women that was widespread among the senoritas.

She moved toward him, rubbing her big breasts against him. "Come on, Rio, you know I want you."

But he didn't want her. With a horrible, sinking feeling, he realized his body was not going to cooperate with his intentions. "No, I must leave now."

"What?" She clung to him, rubbing against him, kissing his face. "No, you must finish this. Rio, I want you."

He knew he couldn't complete the act if he tried. Still a little drunk and angry with himself, he turned and fled the room with her calling after him.

Quickly he left the cantina and rode back to his small ranch. There he put away Peso and sat out on his porch watching the lights of the nearby city and feeling the cool breeze on his face. Damn that arrogant Turquoise. She had spoiled him for any other woman. Margarita would tell the other girls what had happened and there would be whispering that perhaps he had lost his manhood and was no longer capable of pleasuring a woman.

He was capable all right, but the only woman he wanted to lie with was the one he could never have. He sat on the porch a long time, smoking and remembering that one kiss and imagining kissing her all over, her writhing under him and begging him for his caresses as she spread her long legs and he took her in the ultimate embrace. The thought made him sweat and breathe heavily.

Angrily, he ground out his smoke and went into his small house and went to bed, but she would not let him sleep. She was like a fever in his blood and he knew he would never want another woman except the one he could not have.

The next morning, he finally awoke, tired and irritable. He could not spend his life mooning over the uppity girl; he had work to do. He called to his hand and they fed horses and cattle, and then he opened up his blacksmith shop for the day's business.

Back at the Durango ranch, Turquoise plotted to take the children into Austin. And too, there was a question she had always wanted answered and had never had the nerve to ask. Steeling her courage, she caught Uncle Trace sitting on the veranda one evening two days after Rio had left.

She watched the big fountain out front as she leaned against a pillar. The little brown chihuahua trotted up and jumped into Trace's lap. "Uncle Trace, I have a question I have wanted to ask a long time." She played with the lace on her blouse.

He grinned and sipped his tequila. "Ask away."

How could she ask this and get a straight answer? "I—I have heard whispers about my origins all my life."

He immediately looked uncomfortable. "Who dares spread idle gossip? I'll have them fired—"

"No, no. It's everywhere, even in Austin. They say my papa was not really my father. He was so dark-skinned, as was my mother. Just looking in a mirror, it's evident I'm not all Mexican. I wonder—"

"I really don't know much about it." He avoided her gaze and patted the little dog. "I think you shouldn't try to open that Pandora's box."

"I thought the old Don Diego might have told you something before he died—"

"No." Trace shook his head. "I had gone out into the hall with the priest when my father died. Maybe he told the priest something in his final moments. I don't know, but you know the priest would not be willin' to discuss that."

"Old Don Diego was Castilian Spanish, wasn't he? And light-skinned?"

Her guardian frowned at her. "What are you implyin'?"

"So many masters take servant girls into their beds—"

Trace swore aloud. "I can assure you, the old don loved no one but my Cheyenne mother. He would not have stooped to such a low thing."

She bit her lip, knowing she had handled this badly. "But many Anglos came to the ranch, friends and cattle buyers. Perhaps—?"

"I don't know." He shook his head, evidently still angry. "And even if I knew, I would not tell you. I say let the dead past stay buried," Trace said and sipped his drink. "Old Sanchez was a good father to you, wasn't he?"

She nodded. "The only father I ever knew."

"Well, then, that should be enough."

The finality of his tone told her he knew no more or if he did, he would not tell it. There was a long silence as darkness settled over the hacienda and the cicadas began their rhythmic hum. She sighed and decided to change the subject. "Have you heard from your wife and when she will be home?"

His face lit up and she knew he adored his woman. "Probably around the Fourth of July. There's just too many things to see in Philadelphia. She says some man has invented something called a telephone. It works like a telegraph only you can hear real voices."

"No!"

Trace nodded. "With the country now almost a hundred years old, there's no tellin' what will be invented next. Why, they're even talkin' about horseless carriages, maybe run by steam."

She shook her head. "They can't replace good horses."

"That's what I think, too."

"Uncle Trace"—she gave him her most winsome smile—

"I've been thinking. When I took some of the children to the train, they got all excited. They've never been on a train before or even seen the Texas capitol."

"*Si,* I'm sure that's true." He seemed relieved to be off the subject of her origins.

"Don't you think now that May is almost over, I could take them on a trip and maybe show them around Austin? It would be very educational."

"I don't know, Turquoise, I don't have time to take off right now with all the brandin' and besides, we just got back from Austin."

"Oh, you wouldn't have to go." She turned toward him, pleading. "Fern could meet us with her buggy and we might stay with her. Just think how educational it would be and such a treat for the children."

Trace rubbed his chin. "Well, *si,* I reckon it would be educational."

"And didn't I hear that the old don was once a member of the legislature? I could show them the capitol building and tell them about Texas history."

Trace seemed to consider a long moment while she held her breath. Suppose he figured out she was hoping to meet up with Edwin Forester again?

"Turquoise, you aren't hopin' to rendezvous with a man there, are you?"

She felt her heart stop. "I—I don't know what you mean."

He laughed and winked at her. "You aren't a very good liar. Well, *si,* of course you can go and take the children. And by the way, tell Rio I said hello."

She felt herself flush all the way to her toes. "Rio? Oh, yes, certainly." She turned and fled before he could ask more questions. So he thought she might be meeting with Rio. Trace Durango had no idea that her target was the high-born senator, an old enemy of his family's. If she did become engaged to Edwin, how would she broach it with Uncle Trace? As hot-headed as he was, perhaps she would wait until his wife returned.

Rio. His dark, brooding face came to her mind and she tried to brush it away, but she couldn't brush away the memory of his kiss. It had started her heart pounding in a way that made her want to cling to him and return that kiss in a most unladylike way. She shook her head, trying to wipe out the touch and scent and feel of the big, muscular male. A poor half-Mexican vaquero did not fit into her plans.

Three days later, she loaded up the five small children and took the train to Austin. She had worried that Juanita would want to go, and then would tattle on Turquoise, but Juanita came down with a bad cold and stayed at the ranch.

Turquoise felt almost guilty as she stepped off the train in Austin with the excited children. She wasn't good at such underhanded plots.

Her chubby friend Fern was waiting on the platform and ran to hug her. "I'm so glad to see you again. I'm hoping you can stay long enough to help me with my wedding."

Turquoise laughed and hugged her. "Of course. How's Silver Slippers?"

"Galloping up and down our biggest pasture and eating grass. She's a beautiful mare."

"I can hardly wait to see her," Turquoise said, "but first help me corral all these *ninos* and *ninas* before they get lost in the station."

She and Fern herded all the excited, laughing children out to where Fern had a buggy waiting. They helped them in and climbed up in the front. Fern picked up the reins and they were off.

"So, Fern, anything exciting happen while I've been gone?"

Fern shrugged. "Not much. Austin in the late spring is rather sleepy. Oh, there was a big fire. You know that La Mode Dress Shoppe? It burned down."

"Oh? I wish I could say I was sorry, but that Mrs. Whittle caused me a lot of humiliation. Did she get out all right?"

"Just barely. They say it was arson, deliberately set."

"Oh? Now who would do such a thing? Maybe she did it herself for the insurance."

They drove around town pointing out the sights to the children: the homes, the river, the capitol.

"Fern, these kids all look tired and hungry. I think we'd better call it a day."

"Sure, we'll go back to the ranch. I want you to meet my intended."

Turquoise laughed. "I think I've met him. When's the wedding?"

"Sometime late in August, but we haven't set the exact date yet. You are going to be my maid of honor, aren't you?"

Turquoise was touched. "Why, I'd be honored."

They drove a moment in silence as the children settled down in the back of the buggy and dropped off to sleep. Turquoise tried to sound casual. "Is the legislature still in session?"

Fern nodded. "For another day or two, I think. They're arguing over taxes."

"So what else is new?" Turquoise smiled. She was already making plans. She would take the children to the capitol and hope to run into Senator Forester. Then it would be all up to him.

The road to Fern's ranch led past the blacksmith shop and Turquoise didn't know whether to look as they passed, but she couldn't stop herself.

Rio stood at the open forge pounding out a horseshoe. Sweat ran down his brown, muscular body and the sunlight reflected off the crucifix around his sinewy neck. He looked up and stared at them as they passed, but he made no sign of recognition.

"My word!" Fern giggled after they passed. "I'd call that a hunk of prime beef!"

Turquoise forced herself not to look behind her, but she could feel his gaze penetrating her back as they drove on up the road. "Oh, Fern, you're awful."

"Still, that man could almost make me forget about Luke. I wonder what it would be like to be in his arms?"

Turquoise didn't answer. She closed her eyes, remembering how Rio had jerked her to him, kissing her with passion and heat. She ran her tongue over her lips, tasting his hot mouth again.

"Are you okay, Turquoise?" Fern looked over at her, anxiety on her freckled face.

"What?" Turquoise jerked out of her revelry. "Oh, I'm fine, just tired, that's all."

They rode the rest of the way in silence, with Turquoise trying to put Rio out of her mind and think about Senator Forester and all his social position and prestige.

That night, she ran out to see her horse and rode Silver Slippers until dark. When this intrigue was all over, she intended to take the beautiful gray mare home.

The next morning, she washed and scrubbed the children and after breakfast, she and Fern loaded them into the buggy and headed for the capitol.

"We'd rather go swimming," little Pedro complained.

*"Si!"* Juan yelled.

"Maybe we'll do that tomorrow," Turquoise admonished him. "I told Senor Trace I would educate you and teach you some Texas history, so you must see our capitol."

The three little girls chortled with delight. "Will there be sweets?"

"Maybe afterward," Turquoise assured them all.

Fern gave her a knowing look but didn't say anything. For that, she was relieved. With the children in tow, she and Fern walked into the state capitol.

Fern looked around, awestruck. "My, it is big, isn't it?"

Turquoise nodded, thinking how important Edwin Forester must be to be part of all this. "I think we should introduce the children to a real legislator."

They walked up and down the halls until she found the door she wanted. "Look, children, here's Senator Forester's office. I danced with him once at the debutante ball. Perhaps we can meet him."

She and Fern herded the children into the outer office and a prim young man with eyeglasses and a pimply face looked up from his desk. "Yes?"

"We would like to introduce the children to the senator," Turquoise said. "I'm Turquoise Sanchez and this is my friend Fern Lessup."

The young man frowned. "He's much too busy right now. He's giving an important speech later this morning to the Senate."

"Oh." Turquoise turned to leave.

Just then, a voice called through the door. "Elmer? Who is here?"

The young man jumped up like his pants were full of red ants and went into the next room, then he returned, smiling and bowing. "Why didn't you tell me you were good friends of the senator? Come right in." He preceded them, opening the door.

Edwin Forester stood up from his big mahogany desk and came around, smiling and holding out both hands. "Ah, Miss Sanchez. I'm so glad you came to see me." He took both her hands in his, looking down at her.

He was every bit as handsome and dignified as she remembered with his graying blond hair, although his chin was a bit weak. As usual, he was dressed in the height of fashion with a yellow rosebud in his buttonhole.

"Senator, this is my friend Fern and some of the children from the Triple D ranch."

"Ah, Miss Fern"—he bowed to her and she looked like her knees had turned to jelly as he gave her a warm smile— "I'm so glad to meet you and all these little future voters."

He shook hands with all the children as Turquoise said, "Now, children, this is a very important man. You will remember the day you met him."

"As important as Senor Durango?" Pedro piped up and Edwin frowned.

"Yes, of course." Turquoise gulped.

Edwin pulled out his gold pocket watch from his vest. "The Senate will be gathering in less than fifteen minutes and I'm due to make a speech. Why don't you take seats in the Senate gallery and listen?"

Turquoise and Fern both sighed. "That would be so exciting. Will they let us in?"

Edwin's chest puffed up. "I'll see to it personally," he said grandly, "and in the meantime, how would you all like to have lunch today with me at my home in Tarrytown?"

"Tarrytown?" Fern gasped.

Turquoise had no idea what that was, but judging from Fern's reaction, it must be impressive. "Oh, Senator, we couldn't impose—"

"Nonsense." He shook his head. "I'll send a messenger to Mother to set places out on the patio for seven more."

She was going to eat dinner with an important senator in the best part of town. The girls who had ridiculed her should see her now. "If you're sure it won't be any trouble—"

"Of course not. It's settled." He cleared his throat and made a grand gesture. "Now let me get you seated in the

Senate gallery and I'll send a message home. I'm looking forward to showing all of you more of Austin."

Turquoise realized he was staring at her and she blushed. He was rich and important and that meant everything to her. Rio crossed her mind, but she brushed it away. His kisses might be unforgettable, but he could not give her the security and social significance that she craved.

The children whined and wiggled in their seats but as the Senate quieted and Edwin arose from his chair, his big voice rang out. "Gentlemen and fellow senators, I'd like to introduce some special ladies and little future voters, Senorita Sanchez, Miss Fern Lessup, and the children from the Triple D ranch who are here today visiting and learning Texas history."

Turquoise and Fern stood up and nodded as the senators applauded. So this was what it was like to be in the spotlight and be admired and respected. It was a giddy feeling.

Then Edwin cleared his throat and began to speak on the subject of taxes, the future of Texas and the city of Austin. He even mentioned patriotism and the yellow rose of Texas and how every senator who was a true Texan should vote his way on this bill. The children wiggled and twisted during the senator's speech but Turquoise was mesmerized. *This is an important man,* she thought, looking down on him from the balcony. He walked up and down the Senate floor, waving his fist in the air and making statements that resonated throughout the big room.

Afterward, the audience in the gallery applauded and other senators crowded around Edwin, shaking his hand, clapping him on the back. He looked up at her and smiled grandly, so handsome with his light hair that was just graying at the temples.

He met them out in front of the capitol. "Well, what did you think?"

"Magnificent!" Turquoise exclaimed and nudged little Pedro, who nodded and smiled.

"Yes," Fern said, obviously impressed. "Just brilliant."

Edwin's chest puffed out and he looked a bit pompous. "We'll vote this afternoon and I'm sure my bill will pass."

"Is it good for Texas?" Turquoise asked.

He frowned at her. "Well, ahem, yes, it's good for certain people and it will give Forester Industries a wonderful tax advantage."

Fern looked like she was about to ask a question, but the senator said, "Let me call for a carriage to take Miss Fern and the children to my home. Senorita Turquoise, why don't you ride with me and I'll show you the sights of Austin along the way?"

She took a deep breath, knowing Uncle Trace would not approve, but thinking how grand it would be to be seen along Congress Avenue in the senator's buggy. "Fern, can you manage?"

Fern didn't look too happy. "Of course."

Turquoise supervised Fern and the children into a carriage and once she saw them off, the senator escorted her to his fancy buggy. "I usually have a big carriage and a driver, but it's a nice day and I feel like driving myself."

He took her hand and helped her up into the buggy. The way his eyes fastened on hers sent a chill of excitement through her. "Senator, I haven't had such an exciting time since the night of the debutante ball."

"You flatter me, my dear, and you must call me Edwin." He climbed up beside her and snapped the reins at the fine black horse that pulled the rig. "I never had a real chance to apologize about the buggy getting stuck in the creek."

"Oh, think nothing of it." She remembered that night with him escorting the beautiful blonde.

"I also didn't get a chance to explain about dinner at Delmonico's that night."

She bit her lip. "You don't owe me an explanation, Senator."

"Oh, but I wouldn't want you to think I wouldn't rather have taken you to dinner. My mother has been pushing me to marry and her candidate is Banker Turner's daughter—beautiful, but so dull."

That made Turquoise feel much better. "I never really got a chance to thank you for rescuing me at the debutante ball. I was so mortified in that gaudy dress."

"I enjoyed it." He nodded and smiled. "I hear that shop burned down later. It was all Mrs. Whittle deserved."

"It wasn't important." She shrugged. "I do feel sorry for her. I hope she was insured."

He shrugged. "I don't feel a bit sorry for her after the cruel way she treated you. Anyway, if it hadn't been for that ball, I might not have met you."

She tried to be coy. "That's true. Actually, we still hardly know each other."

"But I'm hoping to know you better, a lot better." He turned and smiled at her and he was so polished and educated, her heart fluttered.

She didn't know what to say. She thought herself fairly well educated and well read, but just what did one say to an important state senator who held such power and prestige?

"You're awfully quiet, my dear," he said as they drove along at a fast clip.

"I'm just drinking in what a big city this is."

"That's the truth, and the Foresters own a lot of it and intend to own more."

"Aren't you rich enough?"

He laughed. "No one is rich enough, especially if they want to buy mansions and jewels for lovely ladies."

She didn't know what he expected her to say. She felt very young and stupid with such a prestigious man.

He smiled at her. "As a matter of fact, I'm trying to buy

up land now in one of Austin's worst Mexican slums. Some of them are hesitating."

"I can understand that," Turquoise said. "What you consider a slum, they may consider their homes."

"Well, I guess it is better than what they had in Mexico, but it would improve the looks of Austin, you see."

Turquoise felt her face flush scarlet and the senator coughed and said, "A thousand pardons, my dear. I didn't mean people like you, a lady of charm and class. I meant the low-class, uneducated peons."

"But Senator, weren't the Mexicans here first?"

"Now what does that matter? Texas belongs to the Anglos now."

She was getting angry. "Do the Mexicans know you feel that way about them?"

He laughed. "Of course not. I need the rich ones' votes, so I go to their celebrations and eat their tamales and talk about how Texas depends on them."

She didn't like him quite as well as she had before, but she told herself that maybe most Anglos in Austin felt that way.

"We're almost there, my dear," he said as the horses clopped along. "What do you think of Tarrytown?"

She looked around. The houses were grand places with perfect lawns that made her sigh at their beauty. "This is the most beautiful neighborhood I've ever seen."

"It's considered the place to live in Austin," he said grandly. "Of course, my parents were among the first residents."

He drove the buggy up the brick driveway of a very large and imposing brick mansion, complete with white columns.

A big man on a ladder painting a window turned and stared at her. She noticed a jagged scar across his chin.

"Luther," the senator yelled at him, "don't forget the

trim." Then he turned to Turquoise with an exasperated sigh. "You just can't get good help these days."

About that time, a Mexican butler came out to meet them. The man took the horses by the bridle as the senator stepped down and came around to assist Turquoise. "My dear, you are about to meet my mother, Harriet. You saw her the other night."

She remembered the hatchet-faced woman in the dove-gray dress with gray hair piled in braids on her head. She had looked snooty and imposing. "Yes, I saw her."

"Some call her the 'Iron Lady,' but let me tell you, she is the undisputed queen of Austin society."

Turquoise took a deep breath. Was she going to measure up? She really dreaded this meeting and now she wished she had not accepted the invitation. However, it was too late. A Mexican maid in a white apron and cap was opening the big door and escorting them inside.

# Chapter 9

Turquoise took a deep breath and held her head high as she entered the huge mansion. The inside was dark and smelled of rot, mildew, beeswax polish, and dusty velvet drapes. From the entry hall, she could see a huge library off to one side and a dim parlor full of ornate Victorian furniture to the other.

Edwin scowled at the meek little maid. "Where's Mother?"

"Ah, senor, she's out in the garden with the other guests."

"Good." Edwin turned and smiled at Turquoise. "Looks like the kiddies got here before us. You'll like our garden. Mother prides herself on her flowers."

From upstairs came a strange, haunting laughter.

Edwin sighed. "Anna, couldn't you keep Miss Emily in her room today 'til the guests leave?"

"We try," the maid whispered, "but you know how she escapes and wanders the halls."

Turquoise gave him a questioning look.

"I have a sister who . . . she is sometimes not well." Edwin looked shame-faced, as if he were reluctant to talk about her. "She was carried off by the Indians some years ago and when she was recaptured, her mind was affected."

Turquoise felt a great deal of sympathy for him and patted his arm. "Never mind. I understand."

He gave her a pleading look and wiped his eyes. "We try to keep her hidden, and not many in Austin know about her."

"It's all right, Edwin," Turquoise said gently.

"It's such a load off my heart that you understand." He looked almost ready to weep as he squeezed her hand.

She felt so terribly sorry for him. "I understand. I won't tell anyone."

"Thank you. You're so kind." Now he breathed a deep breath. "Let's forget this sadness and go out into the garden and see what Mama has planned for lunch."

He took her arm and escorted Turquoise down the hall and through French doors out into a beautiful garden with a small fountain and fish pond and tables set up under the shade of china berry trees. Fern and the children were already seated. They shouted greetings.

Turquoise recognized the older lady with gray hair done up in braids and a dove-gray dress. Her face was stern as she came to meet them.

"Ah, Mama, this is Miss Turquoise Sanchez and you've already met her friends."

Harriet Forester came forward, giving Turquoise the briefest nod of acknowledgment and hugged Edwin. She gave him a cold peck on the cheek, then stared at Turquoise again, seeming to bore into her with eyes as pale as Edwin's own. "Sonny, you know our house is always open to your constituents. How do you do, Miss Sanchez?"

Turquoise curtsied. "Very well, thank you. Your son made a grand speech on the Senate floor this morning."

A rare smile seemed to cross the woman's thin lips. "He's a born politician like his father and grandfather before him. You know he's planning on running for governor?"

"Now, Mama"—Edwin grinned and reddened slightly—"you know that's not decided for sure."

"But of course it is!" she snapped. "And after that, the United States Senate in Washington and maybe, who knows? The country could use a Texan for president."

"Oh, Mama, you embarrass me." But he looked happy and ran his hand through his graying blond hair in confusion.

He was more ambitious and important than Turquoise had realized. "I think you would make a great governor," she said with enthusiasm and Edwin looked pleased.

"Now," commanded Harriet Forester, "let's have lunch. I have a cold gazpacho soup, a baby greens salad, and some roasted quail, plus iced tea and chilled sangria, and a wonderful French chocolate mousse I thought the children might enjoy." She signaled to a Mexican houseboy in a white jacket who hovered in the background. "Jose, as soon as we are all seated, you may begin serving."

The children and Fern waved to her from their table as she and Edwin crossed the patio. She could only hope the children remembered their table manners as Edwin seated her at a small, separate table under a giant rosebush that dropped pink petals on them as Edwin sat across from her. "Like the place, my dear?"

"It's breathtaking!" She inhaled the scent of the pink roses, thankful that the Iron Lady had joined Fern and the children for lunch instead of her and Edwin.

"Someday it will all be mine." He took one of her hands in his well-manicured ones. "Of course the governor's mansion is finer, but this is the best house in Tarrytown."

"I'm sure it is," she agreed, looking about. "Any woman could be happy being the mistress here."

"Unfortunately, all these years I've been looking for just the right lady." He looked deep into her eyes. "But none has ever really touched my heart."

She felt her own jump as he squeezed her hand. "I'm sure you are the most eligible bachelor in Austin, if not all Texas."

He smiled. "Perhaps. I know I have had a reputation as a ladies' man, but that's because I never found one I wanted to settle down with, or one Mama approved of."

She nodded, not sure what to say. The others were being served and concentrating on their food, although Fern sneaked a wink at her.

In contrast, Mama seemed to notice the pair holding hands and her stern face clouded up like thunder. Jose served the cold soup and salad just then and that gave her an excuse to pull her hands away and begin to eat with the heavy, monogrammed silver. "Hasn't your mother been choosing women for you to meet?"

He paused with his spoon halfway to his lips. "Yes, for years, but they're always so dull or homely."

"The banker's daughter wasn't homely," she said.

"No, but she was dull. You know, if I do run for governor, people would be much more trusting of a married man than a bachelor."

What was he getting at? She dare not hope as Jose took the fine china bowl away and replaced it with a crisp, browned quail. It was delicious and she ate in silence for a long minute and sipped the chilled sangria wine. It had sprigs of mint floating in it and slices of lemon and orange on the rim of the crystal.

"I realize, Miss Turquoise, I am a few years older than you. I'm almost thirty-seven."

She gave him a winsome smile. "Sometimes a mature, thoughtful older man makes a much better husband."

"I'm glad you feel that way."

She actually wasn't quite sure how she felt. This was all moving too fast. She decided to change the subject. "Edwin, this is the best food I've ever eaten."

He smiled at her over his roasted quail. "We are more civilized here in the big city than out on a ranch. I imagine the food there is pretty plain."

"Well, yes, but it's good." She spoke out loyally for Maria.

"We have a French cook and plenty of household staff," Edwin said, "but it takes a good hostess and manager to run a place this large. My mother is getting elderly and hopes to give up the reins someday to a daughter-in-law."

Turquoise glanced at the poker-faced woman who kept glaring at her. The Iron Lady didn't appear to be ready to give up the reins to anyone. "Do you have other brothers and sisters?"

He nodded. "But they are off at school, except Emily, and none of them are interested in politics or the family businesses. Since I am the oldest son, Mama expects me to carry on the family name."

She didn't answer, suddenly not sure how she felt about Edwin. There was something about him that fascinated her, maybe because of his influence and prestige. No one would whisper about her behind her back anymore if they had to deal with one of the wealthiest, most powerful men in the state.

She imagined her wedding night with Edwin and abruptly, her mind went to the muscular brown body of Rio. How dare the cowboy interfere with her plans?

Jose took away the plates and replaced them with crystal dishes of chocolate mousse that got a chorus of approval from the nearby children.

Edwin paused with a spoonful of the delectable dessert halfway to his mouth. "A penny for your thoughts?"

"What?" She came back with a start from the memory of Rio's hot mouth and muscular body against hers.

"You seemed far away." He smiled and then continued eating.

"I—I was simply enjoying the moment." She sipped her sangria. The scarlet drink was sweet and cold. "This is such a beautiful home and garden, Edwin."

"Good. I'm glad you like it." He beamed at her. "I can almost imagine you standing at the door in some gorgeous dress just the color of your splendid eyes, greeting guests at one of my many parties. We have a lot of parties and balls here."

"I love parties and balls." She smiled at him and dipped her ornate silver spoon into the creamy dessert.

"Somehow I just knew that. We seem so much alike." He gave her a warm, intimate look that was almost like a kiss.

"My uncle would have a fit if he knew I were here," she said.

Edwin frowned. "You know, this silly feud has gone on far too long. I think we need to sit down together and talk. Surely we could find some common ground and live in peace."

"Oh, Edwin, that sounds so good. I don't even know how this trouble all started."

He frowned. "I know a little of it that best be forgotten. Some of it dates back to my grandfather and the original Durango—business dealings, I think. And my father and Trace Durango's father . . ." He paused, frowning. "But I'd be willing to call a truce. I'm not sure about Mama."

Turquoise glanced at formidable Mama. She decided it would be easier to fight a cougar. "If only the two families could live in harmony."

He grinned at her. "That gives me some hope. I'll work on it."

They finished lunch with Turquoise in a daze. Marry Edwin? He hadn't asked her yet, but he had certainly been hinting. What would Uncle Trace say? She wished Cimarron would get home so she could give Turquoise some advice. After all, Cimarron was the only one who could deal with Trace Durango's temper because he adored her so, but she wouldn't be home for weeks.

Now Edwin smiled at her and took the wilting yellow rose from his buttonhole. "This rallied the senators this morning and put them in the mind to vote my way this afternoon, but now I think my favorite flower will always be pink roses."

He reached up and broke off a pink rosebud from the bush that shaded their table and put it in his buttonhole. "Pink roses will always remind me of you, my dear."

She smiled at him, genuinely flattered. "That's sweet."

"Not as sweet as you, dear Turquoise." He pulled out his big gold pocket watch. "My, how times flies when you're with a charming lady. I must be getting back to the capitol."

Just then, Mrs. Forester clapped her hands and stood up. "It's been wonderful, entertaining Edwin's guests, but I know he has important business to attend to." She led everyone out onto the front drive. "I do so enjoy meeting some of Edwin's constituents," she said and smiled, but her cold eyes didn't smile. "Edwin, you will be home for dinner, won't you, dear?"

He kissed her on the cheek. "Of course, Mama, but now I must get back to the Senate and push through that vote. The people's business, you know."

The carriage that had brought Fern and the children was waiting out front.

"Miss Turquoise," Edwin said, bowing low, "I would return you myself, but I must get back."

"Oh, don't trouble yourself," Turquoise said quickly. "I'll ride with the others."

Mrs. Forester said her good-byes and started back into the house.

Edwin caught Turquoise's hand. "Could we meet for lunch tomorrow?" he whispered.

"Well, I guess," she said. "The children would like it."

"No, I meant just the two of us," he whispered. "I have to be at the farmers' market to make a late morning speech to a bunch of cattlemen. There's an outdoor café that is quite good. Could you be there at noon?"

This was all moving too fast. "I—I suppose I could," she said as she turned toward the carriage. "But Edwin, I don't think your mother liked—"

"Oh, she loved you. That's just her manner. When you get to know her, you'll see."

Mrs. Forester had paused at the front door and was looking back, glaring at her.

Turquoise had a feeling the old lady saw her as a threat and would never like her.

"Noon at the farmers' market, the little café," Edwin said hurriedly and helped her into the carriage.

She nodded, looking down at him, thinking he was afraid of his mother. "All right, I'll be there." Then she instantly regretted it.

The carriage pulled away and Fern leaned toward her, whispering, "My word! This is so exciting! I think the senator is very interested in you."

"Oh, I don't know. Maybe." Turquoise shook her head, confused about her own feelings.

"Why, half the girls in the social set have set their caps for him, but none of them have had any luck," said Fern.

"But he's almost thirty-seven," Turquoise said, "and I'm barely twenty."

"So? My father is fifteen years older than my mother," Fern reminded her. "You know older men often marry younger girls. Just think what it would be like to be the governor's wife or even go to Washington, D.C. Have you ever been to Washington?"

Turquoise shook her head. "No, but I've always wanted to. Just imagine the parties and balls and fine homes, getting your name in the newspapers every time you gave a tea."

She settled back against the cushions and looked around at the children. Most of them were full of food and nodding off. At the end of the week, she had to return to the ranch. A lot might happen before then. She wondered if the senator's kisses would be as hot and passionate as Rio's. Then she chided herself. No, of course the senator was an educated, civilized Anglo, not some wild, hot-blooded vaquero who seemed eager to take her down on the nearest grass and rip her blouse away, kissing her breasts with a hot, wet, greedy mouth and then his lips would move lower still. . . .

She blushed at the thought and shrugged it off. All Rio could offer was fierce, wild mating like two untamed mustangs, while with the senator, she would have satin sheets, power, and prestige. But most important, no one would ever question or ridicule her background again.

That evening, Edwin came home from the Senate to find his mother waiting for him in the library. He sighed and poured himself a whiskey. This time, he would stand up to the Iron Lady; it meant that much to him.

"Well, Edwin, did the bill pass?"

He nodded and sat down behind his desk. "Of course. My speech this morning was very persuasive."

"I knew it!" Her eyes glowed with triumph. "You are just like your father and grandfather and you will be governor next election. My other children may have disappointed me, but not you, Edwin."

He sipped his whiskey and sighed. "Yes, of course. And after that, the U.S. Senate. I know it's important to you."

"It should be important to you, too," she scolded and paced the floor in her gray silk dress. "Now all you need is a wife. Voters feel more confidence in a married man.

Now, you met all those girls at the debutante ball, and that lovely Turner girl. Surely one of them—"

"Mama, I have chosen my wife already." He glared back at her, determined to stand his ground. "You met her at lunch today, the beauty with the pretty eyes and black hair. She is the most enchanting thing I have ever met and somehow, it just seems we are meant to be together." He took the pink rosebud from his lapel and sniffed its fragrance, remembering that luncheon and the girl.

"That one? Surely you jest, son." His mother threw back her head and laughed but there was no humor in it. "Who is she, anyway? I've heard what a fool she made of herself at the debutante ball. My social circle is still laughing about it."

"That wasn't her fault." He frowned as he thought about Mrs. Whittle. He had paid her back by having her dress shop torched. "If you must know"—he took a deep breath—"she's the ward of one of the most powerful, richest families in Texas—besides ours, of course."

She blinked. "Who? I know all the best families—"

"The Durangos." He closed his eyes and waited for the explosion.

For a moment, he heard her choke and gasp, then she strode over to the crystal decanter and poured herself a drink, gulped it, coughing before she took a deep breath and turned on him. "You wouldn't dare! You wouldn't dare marry into our most bitter—"

"Mama"—it was like facing a fire-breathing dragon—"maybe after all these years, it's time to make peace with them. Do you realize what an asset it would be to unite the two most powerful families in Texas? Why, we could control everything."

She put down her drink and wrung her hands, still pacing. "Now I know how Jesus must have felt when he was betrayed by Judas. We have been enemies for three generations and you know how your father died—"

"My father was a fool and a woman-chaser, but he shouldn't have tried to seduce that one," he said without thinking. "Everyone knew—"

"You ingrate! You whelp! You dare say that to me?" Her voice rose to the screaming point. "Never! I say never! And I'm sure the Durangos feel the same way." She turned on him. "Does the present don even know you are seeing his ward?"

She had struck home. He tucked the wilting rosebud into his pocket for safekeeping and poured himself another drink. "I don't think so, but I'm planning on talking to him."

"I will have a heart attack and be in my grave before I will allow this wedding."

"Mama," he said, taking a deep breath, "I have always been a dutiful son and done whatever you wanted, but on this one thing, I will not be moved. I will marry this beauty and you will swallow it and be all smiles at the wedding so there will be no gossip in our social circle."

"I will die first!" she wailed. "Edwin, come to your senses! Pick a girl from your own crowd, one with a good background, social prestige, and wealth of her own."

"Like my father did?" He glared at her.

She nodded. "All right, like your father did. It might not have been a love match, but we were well suited for each other. Your father knew what was important and my father was rich. Together, we built a very successful empire."

"Mama, you don't understand. I don't want a business merger, with affairs on the side. I want a marriage, love, and children—"

"Oh, sonny, spare me the flowery poetry. Haven't you tupped half the women in Texas, besides most of our housemaids? I've lost count of those I've fired without references or had sent back over the border."

"They say the apple doesn't fall far from the tree." He shrugged and got up from his desk, walking over to pour another drink. "Yes." He nodded. "I'll admit it. Since I was hardly more than a boy, I've been a rake. I felt it was my right, like helping myself to candy because it was there and my family was privileged, but I've changed. I've found the girl I want to marry and I intend to ask her."

"Edwin, your father would turn over in his grave." She took a deep breath. "All right, so you're hot for her. Keep her a few weeks and sleep with her until you get your fill, but promise me you will not marry that Mexican tart—"

"Don't call her that." He seethed. "She's a special lady and I will have her by my side as I climb the political ladder. I will marry her or I will die trying, and damned be anyone who gets in my way."

His mother's stern face went white. "I do believe you mean it."

"I do. Turquoise Sanchez will be Mrs. Edwin Forester."

His mother clutched her chest. "I can't believe you would buck me this way, Edwin. There's dozens of society girls, rich, beautiful girls throughout Texas who would be thrilled to marry you."

He shook his head. "I will have no one but her and I will stomp or step over anyone who tries to stop me."

Harriet took a deep breath. "All right then. Perhaps she won't have you."

"Are you joking?" He chortled. "She is young, naive, intoxicated with my power and success. There is one small problem."

He walked over and stood staring out the window at the elegant house down the street.

"What could be worse than a Mexican nobody marrying into this blue-blooded family?" She was weeping now.

"Dry those crocodile tears, Mama. I'm not going to listen this time. This beauty, this ward of our family's worst enemies, will carry my name and give you grandchildren."

"Mexican grandchildren?" Her voice seethed with sarcasm.

"May I remind you she doesn't look Mexican and anyway, I don't care about her background. You will respect her because I am determined to make her mine, whatever it takes." He was damned if he would back down, no matter how much his mother cried and protested. It was time he took control of this household, as was his right.

She was sobbing now. "Your father wouldn't have approved of this girl either."

"I don't give a damn," Edwin snapped. "The old man is in his grave and I'm alive. Alive, do you hear me? You are going to act pleased if it chokes you and help with the biggest wedding Austin ever saw. We'll invite the whole city, maybe have the reception in the city park, and all those people will be so flattered, they'll vote for me in the next election."

"But what if the Durangos object and won't allow it?"

Edina thought a minute. He wanted Turquoise with a passion that passed all common sense and reason and he would have her in his bed or die trying. "I might seduce her. You know I'm good with women and she's very naive and impressionable. If she were with child, the Durangos would consent to the marriage rather than be humiliated."

He smiled, imagining making love to the beauty. He had lured many women into his bed, maybe even forced a few, but he looked forward to taking Turquoise's virginity as he had never lusted after another woman. He would do anything, anything to possess her, even if he had to lock up his mother in a nursing home and assassinate Trace Durango. "I am meeting her for lunch again tomorrow."

"So soon?" His mother sobbed. "Edwin, I beg you to think about this—"

"Mama, damn it! I have been thinking about marriage for more than ten years while I played the stud and waited for you to pick out a suitable wife for me. Well, this time, I'm doing the picking. Now you will shut up and act pleased or you will find yourself confined to your room with a maid to look after you because I will tell everyone you are losing your mind like poor Emily."

"You wouldn't dare!" Again her face turned pale.

"Don't try me, Mama. Now this is the end of the discussion." He slammed the library door as he exited and from upstairs, he heard the haunting laughter of his crazy sister.

Nothing was going to spoil his happiness with his future bride—nothing. Before the wedding, he would have Emily carted off to the asylum and if need be, imprison Mama in her room. As governor, he could do almost anything and no one would question it.

Turquoise, Fern, and the children had returned to Fern's ranch and while the children went outside to play, Fern was still breathless with excitement. "My word! Did you ever see such a mansion, and to think we all had lunch with the senator."

Turquoise smiled dreamily. "Yes, it was rather grand, wasn't it? And the way he introduced us on the Senate floor. I felt so important."

"And the way he looked at you." Fern was still babbling with her memories. "I believe that man might ask to court you."

Turquoise frowned. "Well, you know what my guardian would think of that. Maybe we shouldn't mention this to anyone."

Fern whirled around the room. "It's like Romeo and Juliet: two families who are enemies. And he's so handsome and rich."

"Uh-huh." Turquoise felt troubled. Yes, she had been excited and thrilled to be singled out in the Senate gallery and invited to Edwin's mansion, but his mother had glared at her, evidently not pleased at all. The Iron Lady would be a formidable, maybe an impossible mother-in-law. Worse than that, Turquoise's mind kept returning to a certain vaquero and the way Rio's kisses had tasted.

*Don't be a fool,* she scolded herself. *You have always hungered for respectability. As Senator Forester's bride, you would have that.* And yet . . .

She spent a sleepless night, now not looking forward to joining Edwin for lunch. Would he ask permission to court her? Did she want him to? Of course she did, she chided herself as she put on an especially charming dress, daffodil yellow and springlike. She added a large white lace hat with yellow ribbons.

"That looks good with your dark hair," Fern exclaimed. "When you get back, you must tell me everything that happened."

"Of course." Turquoise looked at herself in the mirror and smiled. Yes, she did look fetching. "You'll take the children to Barton Springs for a swim?"

"Yes, Luke will go along." Fern nodded. "We'll have a good time."

"You know, Fern, you are a dear friend." Turquoise hugged her. "Maybe we should keep all this just between us."

"Of course." Fern's freckled nose wrinkled as she smiled and lowered her voice to a whisper. "I'm sure my father or even Luke might not approve of all this. If the senator asks you to be his bride, it will be big news across all of Texas."

"And I'll need time to bring my guardian around,"

Turquoise said. "You know what the Durangos think of the Foresters."

"But love will conquer all," Fern squealed and whirled again. "I wish my romance were half so exciting!"

Turquoise didn't answer. She had a feeling she was getting into something too big for her to handle. She had a heavy weight in her stomach as she borrowed a buggy and set off for the farmers' market to meet with Forester.

# Chapter 10

Edwin was waiting as she drew up in her buggy. He hurried to meet her and tied up her horse, then brought her down from the seat. He wore a light summer suit with a pink rosebud as a boutonniere. When he saw that she noticed it, he smiled and said, "I told you pink rosebuds would always be my favorite from now on."

"I thought you would forget," she answered.

"Never! And yes, you are as beautiful as I remember. You look like a summer day in all that yellow."

She blushed and took his arm, twirling her lace parasol with its yellow ribbons. "Senator, you embarrass me. I'm sure you have known many women, some much lovelier than I."

He looked at her seriously as they walked. "It is true, I have known many women. I'll not lie to you, my dear, I have been known as a womanizer for years, as my father and grandfather were, and in all that time, I had never found a woman who interested me for more than a week or two."

She felt awkward under his adoring gaze. "Perhaps I will only interest you for a week or two."

He smiled down at her. "I thought that at first, the night

I first saw you, but then, there was something about you that seemed to call out to my lonely heart, as if we were soul mates or had known each other in another time or place. Do you believe in reincarnation, my dear?"

"I—I don't know. I don't know much about it." She wasn't as well read as she wished, and he was so educated and well traveled.

"I'll take you to Europe and to the Orient," he said. "We'll have so much fun. My life was so dull until you came along."

He patted her hand as he led her to a table. It was a small café away from the road where the cattle came up as the cowboys drove them into the marketing pens. There were bright umbrellas over the tables on the flagstone-paved patio and there were flowers in bright-colored pots all around.

"Why, this is charming," Turquoise said as he pulled out a chair for her.

"A charming luncheon for a charming lady." He smiled and sat down across from her. "I just got through speaking to a bunch of cattlemen, so I thought it was the only time today I would have for you and I wanted to see you again."

"Did you really?" She smiled back into his adoring eyes. He might be older, but he was so distinguished, with his graying hair and fine clothes.

"Don't be coy. You surely knew that." He reached, took her hand, and smiled again. "I have never been so happy as I have been lately. It's almost as if you complete me, as if I've been looking for you forever. Of course, you must know how I feel."

She felt herself blush again under his direct gaze. "I suppose I had guessed, but I was afraid I might be wrong and just another one of your silly conquests. I hear half the women in Texas are scheming to be your wife."

"No." He shook his head and a light curl fell across his

forehead. "You are not wrong. From the first moment I saw
you, I felt a connection that I have never felt with any other
woman and believe me, I have met most of the most beautiful and accomplished women in Texas."

She didn't know what to say.

The waiter came and Edwin ordered a pitcher of sangria,
the red wine with slices of orange and lemon floating
among the ice. "Also, we'll have chilled fruit salad," he ordered with a tone of authority, "and perhaps some cold
roast beef sandwiches if it suits the lady."

"It does." Turquoise noticed the deferential way the
waiter bowed and nodded. Yes, Edwin Forester was an important and powerful man. As his wife, she would be
treated with the same respect and deference.

Turquoise turned to watch the cowboys a few hundred
yards away driving the cattle into the pens. "This is so
quaint."

He shrugged. "It's just business, my dear. What I really
want to talk about is us—you."

"Yes?" She wasn't certain now if she wanted to know.

"I will just say it, Turquoise. I know I am almost old
enough to be your father and our families have been enemies for several generations."

"I don't think of you as older. I think of you as mature.
And as for the families, I was certain yesterday that your
mother did not approve of me."

He shrugged and frowned. "My mother is getting senile
and I am gradually taking charge of the family businesses.
I can deal with her, but it is true, the family feud could
create problems."

"My guardian might come around if he thought I was
really loved and provided for."

He leaned closer. "No woman would ever be as loved and
adored as you would be, my dear." He kissed her hand. "You

will have everything you ever dreamed of: money, jewels, travel. Whatever your wish is will be my command."

"Oh, Edwin, I—I don't know what to say." She had a sudden feeling that she was getting into something she didn't want and was angry with herself. Hadn't she dreamed of a marriage like this since she was a very young girl?

He took both her hands in his and kissed them. "Just say you will let me court you. I will go to Trace Durango and beg on my knees if I must, humble myself before an old enemy, for a chance to win your heart. Then I will beg on my knees to you."

A powerful, influential senator on his knees, begging for her hand in marriage. All she had to do now was say yes and all her dreams would be fulfilled. She would wed a man so rich and handsome, half the women in Texas would envy her. No one would ever whisper about her questionable parentage again. And yet, she hesitated. "I—I need to think about this."

"Of course you are overwhelmed, but while you are thinking, I am going to shower you with so many gifts, spoil you so much, you won't dare say no."

"Oh, Edwin, you are too good to me."

"I love you, my darling, and I will spend the rest of my life proving it to you. There is nothing I wouldn't do to win you."

The food and the drinks came just then and the wine was cold and the fruit salad chilled. The tiny cold roast beef sandwiches were excellent.

"My," she said as she wiped her lips on a linen napkin, "I had no idea there was such a good café out here. I guess Uncle Trace must not know about it. At least, he hasn't mentioned it."

He laughed. "I'm pleased you like it. It's one of Austin's little secrets. The wealthy cattle barons like a good meal when they come out for the auctions." He pushed back his plate and surveyed her as she finished her food and the waiter took the dishes away.

"Edwin, you look amused. What are you thinking?"

He laughed. "I'm truly happy, maybe for the first time in my life. All these years, I've been looking for something that my money and power could not buy and finally, I've found it. I'm trying to decide whether I should buy you a string of pearls or maybe diamonds." He stared into her eyes. "No, it must be turquoise, just the color of your eyes, and maybe surrounded by diamonds."

She looked down at her hands modestly. "Edwin, I do think you are trying to sway me with gifts."

He laughed. "Of course I am. You are playing with me, my darling. I'm sure there's no other man who can offer you what I can."

"No, of course there isn't." Rio crossed her mind. He was a poor rancher with as questionable a background as her own. She had always dreamed of just what Edwin Forester was now suggesting, but all she could think of was that moment in Rio's arms when he had kissed her in a way that made her pulse pound and she had felt weak and help-less in his embrace. That angered her, that the vaquero came unbidden to her mind at this exact moment, which should be the happiest and most triumphant of her life.

Edwin frowned. "Oh, here come the poor Mexicans' few cattle."

"What?" She turned to look at the road.

"The Mexican ranchers get together and throw a few cattle into the sale now and then, but they don't bring much. They can't afford the fine bloodlines the Anglo ranchers offer. Now there's a horse I'd like to own."

Through the dust, abruptly she recognized Rio on his fine bay stallion, driving a small herd ahead of him. He wore faded denim, but also a concho belt and a flat, black Spanish-style hat.

Edwin said, "I'd like to buy that stallion, but that stubborn Mexican probably wouldn't sell him. Say, isn't that the one who showed up at the ball?"

Turquoise didn't answer. Her gaze was fastened on Rio and now he had noticed her and glared back.

Abruptly a great black bull from the herd broke loose and, bawling loudly, rushed across the grass toward the diners on the flagstones. Men screamed and tables were overturned as the diners fled from danger.

Rio immediately wheeled his stallion and took off after the bull, but the tables and flowerpots kept him from maneuvering.

Edwin scrambled to the top of their table. "Look out, my dear!" He reached a hand to lift Turquoise to the tabletop, but she caught her heel in her chair and went down, even as the bull gored a waiter on one of its curved horns and threw him across the flagstones.

It all happened so fast: Edwin shouting a warning from the safety of the tabletop and Rio throwing himself off his horse and grabbing a red tablecloth. "Stay still, Turquoise!"

She couldn't move, entangled as she was in her yellow skirts and the fallen chair. She could only lie there in the dust in horror, staring at the huge black bull that pawed the flagstones. Around her, people still screamed and ran.

The bull's one horn dripped red from goring the waiter and she lay there paralyzed with fear, watching the scarlet blood drip into the dust. Abruptly Rio was between her and the bull, waving the tablecloth at him like a matador's cape. "Ho, *toro,* here, *toro!*"

The bull paused, his eyes red with rage as he pawed the ground. Rio did not move, he only waved the tablecloth to get the animal's attention. She glanced up and saw Edwin shaking with fear, but he did not come off the table to protect her. Only Rio stood between her and the maddened animal and now he played the bull like a matador. "Ho, *toro,* come, *toro!*"

The beast ran at him and he flipped the tablecloth so that the animal thundered past, coming dangerously close to Rio's muscular body. But unlike a matador, Rio held no sword to defend himself. Even as she and the others watched, Rio teased the bull into chasing him, gradually, leading it off the patio until two vaqueros rode up with ropes to lasso the foaming, pawing bull.

Rio turned to her now, touching the edge of his hat with the tips of his fingers. "Senorita." Then he turned to walk toward his horse.

"Wait!" Edwin yelled and climbed down off the table. "Let me offer you a reward for saving us, and I'd like to buy your horse."

Rio gave him a cold, dismissive look with his dark eyes. "I did not do it for you, senor, and my horse is not for sale." He gave Turquoise a scornful look, then wheeled and mounted his horse, rejoining the vaqueros who were herding the cattle down the lane into the market pens.

"Well, he's an arrogant one, isn't he?" Edwin sniffed, holding out his hand to Turquoise, who took it and stood up, dusting her skirt off.

"Maybe he was insulted to be offered money for something any heroic Texan would have done." She rethought how Edwin had scrambled to safety, leaving her to fend for herself.

Edwin merely snorted. "Trying to make an impression on the ladies, no doubt. Cheap heroics. Are you all right, my dear?"

She nodded. "It was exciting."

He smiled. "Well, it will make good press."

"What?"

"Never mind." He pulled out his big gold watch. "Well,

my darling, I must be off to deal with business. I think you would find it dull, so why don't I take you back to your buggy and you can go shopping or something?"

"All right." She had really wanted to see Rio again, to thank him. She thought Edwin's actions had been humiliating.

"I'll send a message and we'll meet again tonight. I know of an elegant place for dining and dancing. All the best people frequent it."

"All right." She didn't look at him. He might have money, power, and social prestige, but a little nagging worry nibbled at Turquoise's mind.

He led her back to her buggy, helped her up, and kissed her hand. "Until tonight then."

She nodded and drove away. When she looked back, he was staring after her with a possessive, passionate expression.

Instead of going shopping, she returned to Fern's ranch. She didn't quite know what to do with herself. Fern and her fiancé and the children were still at the swimming hole and Turquoise couldn't seem to settle down. Instead, she paced and thought. She was supposed to meet Edwin at some swanky place for dinner and dancing, but suddenly, she didn't want to go. However, she didn't want to return to the Triple D ranch either. She wasn't sure what she wanted.

Late that afternoon, a messenger came with an enormous bouquet of pink roses and a note of where she was to meet Edwin.

Toward evening as she washed and dressed, Fern came back in with yelling, excited children. "Oh, it was so much fun!" Fern said.

The children joined the chorus. "*Si,* it was fun."

Little Pedro said, "I dived off the bank and Susanna learned to swim."

"I'm glad you all had a good time, because we'll probably be going home tomorrow," Turquoise said, avoiding Fern's surprised gaze.

While the ranch cook fed the children, Fern followed her into her room. "What do you mean, 'go home tomorrow'?"

"I just think maybe we've been gone long enough." Turquoise kept her voice vague as she began to brush her hair.

"My word! I saw that gigantic bouquet in the living room," Fern said. "It obviously cost a lot of money."

"Obviously." Turquoise pinned her ebony hair up and looked in the mirror.

"Well, out with it. Is the senator courting you?"

"Yes, he is." She continued to work on her hair.

"Aren't you going to give me the details?" Fern leaned on the dresser and waited.

Turquoise shrugged. "He wants me to meet him for dining and dancing this evening. Oh, and a bull got loose at the market and caused some excitement before it was recaptured."

"Is that all?" Fern sounded disappointed.

"For the moment." Turquoise looked through her dresses, trying to decide what she owned that was fine enough to go dining and dancing with Edwin Forester. "I don't really own anything suitable," she thought aloud.

"If you marry him, you can buy out the stores," Fern said with a grin. "Of course, the best one, the La Mode, has burned, but there's lots of others."

"Uh-huh," Turquoise finally said. "I'm having second thoughts about marrying Edwin Forester."

"Are you thinking about what a fit your guardian will throw?" Fern asked.

"That's part of it." Turquoise put on the finest lace lingerie she owned.

"What else?" Her plump friend seemed to be hanging on every word.

"I—I'm not sure." She turned on Fern irritably. "I really don't want to talk about it until I think it over."

"But this is everything you dreamed of. . . ."

"I know, but it's complicated. Please, Fern"—she patted her friend by the shoulder—"I—I've got some thinking to do. A lot of things have happened and now I'm not sure what I think."

Fern looked puzzled. "Okay."

"I'll tell you when I decide, all right?"

Fern sighed. "All right. I hope you know what you're doing." And she left the room.

No, she did not know what she was doing. She was beginning to feel she might be playing with blasting powder. Here she was, getting dressed to meet with a man who had declared his love and who wanted to shower her with luxuries. Her heart ought to be singing, but if it were, it was a sad song. She was angry with herself and not sure why.

It was almost dusk outside. Turquoise sprayed herself with forget-me-not perfume and put on the bright turquoise dress she had bought for the debutante ball. It might not have been appropriate for the ball, but it would be just right for elegant dining and dancing. Then with a heavy heart, she walked out into the living room. Fern was reading the children a story and got up, coming over. "The buggy is waiting for you outside."

"Thank you, my dear friend." She hugged Fern. "Don't wait up. I'm not sure I'll have an answer for you tonight."

"Maybe I'd better pray for you," Fern said.

"I think you might." Turquoise smiled and went out the front door in a whirl of silk skirts.

She drove into town as night fell across Austin. On a street corner, a scruffy newsboy yelled, "Read all about it! Heroic Senator Saves Crowd!"

She reined in and called to the boy. "Please, I'd like a paper."

"Hot off the press, miss. Just came out a few minutes ago." The scruffy boy came over to the buggy and handed her a paper. She tossed him a dime. "Gee, thanks, miss." He tipped his cap to her.

It was difficult to read the paper in the glow of the gas streetlights and she squinted to see the headline.

"Heroic Senator Saves Crowd. Senator Edwin Forester, scion of the well-known family, behaved in an exemplary fashion today as he stood off an escaped and dangerous bull at the stockyards. The lovely lady accompanying him fainted in the excitement and he had to help her to her feet after he ordered the vaqueros to take away the dangerous animal. Senator Forester is at the moment trying to pass a bill that will give the livestock raisers a better tax situation, and after today's heroic action, no doubt . . ."

"No doubt he was a pompous fool." Turquoise threw back her head and chuckled to herself. Of course only a handful of people would know the truth. Everyone else in Austin would believe the newspaper story. Well, when she met Edwin tonight, she wouldn't mention the article.

Abruptly she wondered if Rio had seen this. He probably didn't take the paper, so he needn't know that he had been omitted from his own heroic tale. Not that he would care. He hadn't taken on that bull for the senator or anyone else in the crowd, he had done it for her and her alone. She knew that from the way his penetrating gaze had glared back at her as he rode away.

At the very least, she ought to thank him profusely and apologize for Edwin's abrupt rudeness. It wouldn't take very long and Edwin would think she was being fashionably late.

She turned and drove toward Rio's small spread.

She pulled up at the hitching post and little Tip began to bark. There was a dim light on in the crude adobe and for a moment, she wondered what she was doing here and if he would harshly rebuff her. Perhaps she was a fool. She almost turned the buggy and drove away but about that time, Rio came out on the porch. He was naked to the waist and stood there silhouetted against the light, the crucifix gleaming in the moonlight. He had a rifle in one hand. "Who's there?"

"It's me, Turquoise Sanchez."

"What do you want?" His voice was hostile.

"Can't I at least get down?"

A long moment of silence while he seemed to think it over. Then he yelled at the spotted dog and Tip stopped barking. Rio laid his rifle in the porch swing and walked slowly out to the buggy. "Yes?"

She looked down into his dark eyes and saw the anger and the need there. "Can't I at least come in?"

He shrugged. "It makes no difference to me. You are dressed fancy, senorita. I take it this is not for a trip to my humble ranch?"

She felt her face flush as she tied her reins over her dashboard. "You might at least help me down."

"Excuse me, I forget my manners toward a lady." He bowed and she was not sure if he was mocking her or not. Then he stepped up and held out his hands to her. Big, strong, honest hands, she thought, remembering Edwin's fine, gentleman's hands.

She let Rio lift her and his hands almost spanned her waist. He set her slowly on the ground but he did not turn her loose. His dark skin rippled over hard muscle and he smelled of smoke and horses and tequila.

His rugged face looked down into hers. "You are dressed very fine. Where do you go tonight?"

"None of your business," she said, not looking at him. "Aren't you going to invite me in?"

"You want to lower yourself by coming into my small house, senorita?"

"Stop it," she raged. "I am trying to be nice."

He glared at her. "Ah, and do you come to offer the poor vaquero a reward, too? Maybe a few pesos for saving you and your companion from *el toro?*"

She started to turn away. "Damn it, now I'm not sure why I came. I certainly didn't expect this kind of response."

He caught her arm. "*Perdone.* I don't know what to think. Senator Forester would not be pleased if his lady was seen at a Mexican bastard's poor ranch after dark."

She began to weep. "Must you treat me so cruelly? I came to apologize for his arrogant behavior and to thank you for saving my life."

He didn't let go. "And after you have apologized and thanked me, you can go with a clear conscience back to the senator, who is waiting with gold and diamonds to lure you into his bed?"

She looked up at him, in a rage. "He has been very honorable. He wants to marry me—"

"He wants you in his bed," Rio growled and jerked her up against his broad chest. "I saw the look in his eyes, the hunger for you. Do you not think I feel the same hunger?"

Then before she could react, he pulled her to him so hard that she could not breathe, bent his head, and kissed her savagely.

# Chapter 11

For just a moment, she was helpless in his arms and then she began to fight him, but he did not let her go. Gradually the kiss deepened and she could deny her own need no longer. She clung to him, returning his kiss with all the banked fires within her. His mouth dominated hers and she surrendered, opening her lips while he thrust his tongue deep within, caressing the velvet of her mouth in a manner that said: you are mine, only mine, and I will take you and no other man will.

She moaned aloud and opened her lips still more, sucking his tongue deep into her throat, entwining her tongue with his and then letting him suck her tongue into his mouth.

His strong arms imprisoned her and yet it was her own need that would not let her struggle. He reached down and pulled the low-cut turquoise lace away from her bosom so he could enclose her breast with one big hand as if he owned it, and she could not object. She could only gasp at his touch on her nipple.

He whispered against her mouth. "The senator may buy you, but by damn, I'll take you first and let him have my leavings."

The time was now to object, to tear away from him and run for her buggy, but she did not want to run. She did not want to leave his embrace.

He pulled back and looked down at her with a question in his dark eyes. She hung arched over his arm in surrender and her eyes must have given him the answer he wanted. He swung her up into his arms, carrying her lightly as he strode through the night to where red oleanders dropped their perfumed blossoms near the hacienda and he laid her on the soft grass. He stood over her, breathing heavily, sweat gleaming on his dark, muscled frame. "You still have time to go," he warned, "if you want to join the senator for dinner."

She didn't want the senator's money or jewels, she wanted something much deeper, much more primitive. In surrender, she held her arms up to her conqueror.

He glared down at her. "If you stay, you know I will take that for which he is willing to offer you a kingdom."

"I don't care," she breathed. "This is tonight, and tonight I only want to quell this hunger inside me that seems to be burning like a flame."

He fell to his knees, looking down at her. "This is not the way it should be, taking you like the lowest whore out on the grass."

"Would it be any better on satin sheets?" she whispered and looked up at him.

"Turquoise, you torture me, and you do it wantonly again and again," he gasped and then reached down and ripped the front of her dress away. She lay there in the moonlight as he stared at her generous breasts, so pale in the dim light.

Her first impulse was to cover her nakedness with her hands, but she was hypnotized by the raw hunger in his dark eyes that seemed to caress her bare breasts, and she lay there, letting him look his fill.

He lay down next to her and then he stroked and caressed her breasts into peaks of desire and she could feel the pulsating hardness of his manhood against her thigh. She sensed he was right, remembering festivals where she knew vaqueros took girls out into the night for hours of hot rutting and yet she could not, would not, get up and leave.

Instead she whispered, "Teach me. I know nothing of this. Teach me and make me your own."

He needed no further urging as he bent his head and kissed each breast, then flicked his tongue around the dark circle of her nipple until she was arching her back, wanting him to taste even more. Rio fastened his hot mouth on her breast and she felt the touch of his rugged face gently across her skin. She put both hands on each side of his dark head and pulled him down, urging—no, demanding—that he suck both her breasts until her nipples were swollen and aching.

She reached to touch his manhood and he gasped and pulsated against her hand. "Unbutton my pants," he breathed. "Touch me, hold me, my dear one."

And she needed no urging. She fumbled with his buttons as he continued to suck her breasts. His manhood came out, big and swollen, wet with his own need. She abruptly was reminded of watching the great stallions back at the ranch, rubbing against a mare in heat as she teased and fidgeted about while the stud's maleness hung heavy and slamming against his belly as he danced before he grabbed the mare by the back of the neck with his teeth and reared up on her hindquarters, plunging into her again and again as they mated.

She stroked Rio's manhood and he grew more agitated, kissing her face, her eyes, her lips. Then his hand reached under her skirt and pulled it up, tearing away her lace drawers so that his fingers could roam her, tease her until she was wet with desire. "I want you," she gasped. "I need you!"

"I intend to take you," he answered. "And if I have nothing but tonight, tomorrow the senator can have my leavings."

"Is that all I am to you? A conquest?" she whispered against his lips.

He cursed. "I am under your spell and I will have your body tonight if it costs me my life!"

"Then take me and welcome." She let her silken thighs fall apart and his fingers touched her, caressed her. She reached to touch his throbbing maleness and it was wet with his own desire.

He came over her, holding up most of his weight with his elbows. She could feel the tip of his manhood hard against her mound. He hesitated almost as if giving her one last chance to say no and roll out from under him, but she wanted this as badly as he did. "Now, my sweet one, I will make you mine in a way no man ever can again."

They were like two wild mustangs in the moonlight as he plunged deep into her and muffled her cry with his kiss. And he began to ride her, deeply, slowly.

Her excitement grew with each hard stroke and her hands went around him, clawing his lithe back with her need to pull him closer, deeper. "More, more, and more!"

She was arching her back, meeting him thrust for thrust, her long, slim legs wrapped around his dark body so that he could not escape even if he wanted to. If this was love, no wonder people were willing to die for it, she thought. Nothing could feel any better than this: a man who desired her beyond reason, mating with her under an oleander bush while carmine petals dropped on them both and in the background, the moon shining bright and yellow across the new summer grass.

He came down hard into her again and her insides tried to clutch him, not wanting to lose him, but he pulled back and then came into her hard again. She tilted her hips up to meet him, flesh slapping hard against bare flesh, wanting him deep, deep inside of her. She knew she was clawing his back with her need but she couldn't stop herself and he rammed into her, faster and faster, while she moaned aloud with each thrust, wanting more and more and more. Her whole body seemed to be afire, and his thrusts only seemed to add fuel to her flame as she dug her nails into his hard hips, urging him deeper still.

Then abruptly, he gasped and came into her one more time and she could feel his throbbing maleness jerk and then begin to give up his seed. She tilted up so that she could take—no, demand—every single precious drop. The excitement built until she could stand it no more and she shuddered and her body arched against his for a long moment, and they clung together in the age-old embrace of mating.

She knew nothing for a long moment of blackness and then gradually she came back into this world. Rio was kissing her face and brushing her damp hair from her forehead. "Did I hurt you?"

"I don't know, maybe a little, but I couldn't stop."

"I couldn't either." His voice was regretful and he sat up. "I've ruined you. You will hate me tomorrow."

"No, I never will. Not after that." She sat up and reached up to hold his dear face in both her hands.

He pulled away from her. "I am sorry I did this. I wanted you so much, I seemed to go loco."

"I liked it. Do it again to me." She reached out and brushed her lips across his bare chest.

"Don't do that, Turquoise. It drives me wild. You should go home, clean up, and go to your senator. He need never know where you have been."

"But I'd be so late." She brushed her tongue across his nipple.

"Make up an excuse," he gasped. "He'd believe anything

you tell him. You can still have that big house and all his money."

"All I want at the moment is to be in your arms again," she whispered against his chest. He cursed softly and pulled her to him, and they made passionate love again and again.

It was toward dawn that she awoke in his arms and smiled. She had never felt so beloved and safe as she did at this moment. She kissed the side of his face, and his dark eyes flickered open and he frowned. "I thought I had dreamed you here," he whispered and kissed her again.

She took a deep breath, content and her need no longer burning like a prairie fire. "It'll be dawn soon," she noted.

At that he sighed and sat up. "I have behaved badly. Turquoise, you know I have nothing to offer you. You have sold your virginity too cheap. The senator would have given all he owned for it."

"It is mine to give away and to the man I choose." She shrugged.

"Look at you. Your dress is in shreds and you smell of me," he said. "People will whisper and ridicule you if they find out."

"You know, for the first time, I'm not sure I care what people think." She yawned and pulled her shredded dress up on her white shoulders. "All of a sudden, I am not worried about people whispering about my background or my need for security and respectability. I feel so safe with you."

He kissed the tip of her nose. "I would kill to protect you," he whispered. "You know that, don't you?"

She nodded and laid her face against his bare chest so that he put his arms around her and held her close. She felt safe for the first time in her life, knowing this man would love and protect her because she was truly his woman.

Then he sighed. "But I know I am doing you an injustice by claiming you. The senator may have been looking for you all night. He may have telegraphed your guardian or had the whole of the Austin police force out."

"Oh, I hadn't thought of that. I guess I'd better meet with him today."

Rio nodded as he pulled her to her feet. "Yes, clean yourself up and go to him. It's not too late for you to accept his proposal. I saw the way he looked at you. He's so blindly in love with you, he'll believe anything you tell him."

She blinked. "Are you saying I should pretend that last night never happened, go ahead with my life and marry him?"

He stared into her eyes. "I told you last night I wanted you and then I lost my senses and took that which I could never hope to own. I have nothing to offer you except a small ranch. I cannot imagine you married to a poor vaquero who blacksmiths on the side to keep tortillas on the table."

"So you don't intend to make an honest woman of me?" She was growing angry now.

"Turquoise." He made a helpless gesture. "You don't understand—"

"I understand all right. Now that you have satisfied your lust rutting around on me all night like a stallion on a mare in heat, you are ready to toss me to him so you won't have to bother with me anymore." She began to cry.

He sighed heavily. "Cut it any way you like. I did not offer you anything except sex and you wanted it as badly as I did. Now go on with your ambitions and I'll go back to my forge."

She swung at him but he shied away and caught her hand, then he pulled her to him and kissed her as if he would never let her go. "Good-bye, senorita. *Vaya con Dios.*" Go with God.

"God damn you, you—you dirty Mexican. I hate you!" She pulled her torn turquoise dress up, trying to make it less tattered. Then she stalked away, eyes blinded with tears. She swung up in her buggy, trying to rearrange her torn and wrinkled skirts as the sun began to peek over the eastern horizon. "You are a cad and a dirty bastard!" She snapped the whip at the dozing horse and the buggy took off at a fast clip.

Rio stared after her long after she was out of sight. So she hated him even though he adored her. He could not hold onto her because he did not meet her dreams and she would soon grow tired of living in poverty. However, he had last night to remember her by and maybe, many years from now when she was married to a rich man and had children and all the luxuries she desired, once in a while in the dead of night, she might remember this night, smile in the darkness, and think of him with kindness.

Turquoise was lucky enough to return to Fern's ranch and get inside, hide the torn dress, and slip into her bed just before the ranch began to awaken. What was she to do? Now that she was away from Rio, she was uncertain again. He evidently had only wanted a quick romp and she had behaved like some drunken *puta,* a whore, humping in the grass with a vaquero. She was ashamed and humiliated, but when she remembered those moments in his arms, she knew she wanted to do it again and again. She tried to think of sleeping in Edwin's arms, with his fine, soft hands on her body, and winced. But of course, if she married him, he would have that right. What was she to do?

She finally got up, cleaned up, and dressed, thankful that no one seemed to realize she had been gone all night. At breakfast, she only toyed with her eggs and finally said to Fern, "I think the children and I should go home on this afternoon's train."

"My word, I hoped you might change your mind," Fern said.

The children moaned. "Aw, senorita, can't we stay another day or two?"

"No." She didn't look anyone in the eye. "I think we have been gone long enough. Senor Trace will be missing us."

Fern pursed her lips and gave her a searching look. "Well, if you insist. I was hoping you would stay around and help me plan my wedding."

"Oh, I can come back for that," Turquoise answered. Right now, she just wanted to escape and think things over. Yet she knew she owed Edwin an explanation and she dreaded that meeting.

So after breakfast, while Fern took all the children down to the barn to play in the hay, Turquoise dressed herself in a white dress of dotted Swiss, complete with a big lace hat and umbrella. Both the hat and her waist had a band of turquoise satin. She borrowed the buggy once again and with a sense of dread, drove herself out to the capitol. The building looked deserted, most of the legislators gone home now that this year's session was over.

What was she to tell him? With her heart beating hard, she marched into his outer office and faced the pimply faced clerk. "I'm here to see Edwin, I mean, Senator Forester."

Elmer gave her a piercing stare. "I'll see if he is accepting visitors, Miss Sanchez." The young man disappeared into the inner office and then returned. "The senator says he will see you now."

She followed the clerk into the office and Edwin looked up from his paperwork. "Elmer, you may go to lunch early."

Elmer seemed reluctant to leave. "Are you sure, sir?"

"Go to lunch!" the senator thundered.

"Yes, sir, but don't forget that important meeting you

have this afternoon." Elmer scurried away like a frightened mouse.

Edwin stood up, looking at her coldly. "May I offer you a chair, my dear?"

She took it, determined, but her throat went dry. She had finally decided what she was going to do and it went against everything she had always dreamed of. "Edwin, I'm sorry about last night."

He sat back in his leather chair, looking at her with an icy gaze. "I sat there for three hours, watching my big bouquet of pink roses wilt, waiting and wondering if something terrible had happened to you."

Should she lie? She wasn't good at it. "I—I was detained."

He steepled his fingers and looked at her. "I drove out to the Lessup ranch and they told me you had left in plenty of time to meet me."

Oh dear, Fern had forgotten to tell her that. "Edwin, I'm really sorry, but—"

"And then I talked to a man on the street who had seen a pretty dark-haired girl wearing a turquoise dress, and driving a buggy, heading away from downtown."

"What do you want me to say?" She stared at her hands folded in her lap.

"I have never been so humiliated." He took out a small velvet box, opened it, and flung the diamond necklace across the desk where it slid and landed on the floor at her feet. She looked down. It sparkled in the sunlight. "I had bought you this expensive bauble and was planning on asking you to marry me last night."

"I know. I'm sorry I disappointed you."

"Is that all you've got to say? To keep telling me you're sorry?" His voice rose. "Turquoise, I've been a great womanizer. That's no secret. And finally when I'm ready to give my heart to the woman I have fallen madly in love with, she doesn't bother to show up."

She chewed her lip, not wanting to say "I'm sorry" yet again.

"Of course." He lowered his voice and smiled at her. "I know you are so much younger than I am, and maybe only a silly girl, not yet mature enough for marriage, but I would be willing to forgive and forget—"

"Edwin, I'm so sorry, but I've decided I can't marry you." She leaned forward, pleading for understanding with her eyes. Gazing into his, she saw the immense love there and was truly saddened that she had caused him pain.

He leaned back in his chair and sighed. "So what has happened that brought about this great change from yesterday noon to today?"

She couldn't tell him about searing-hot love under crimson oleander bushes or the fact that she no longer cared about respectability and gossip about her heritage. "I—I just decided that we were wrong for each other, that's all."

"Wrong for each other?" He almost seemed to explode. "Do you realize in your silly foolishness what you are walking away from? I am a very rich and powerful man who can buy you anything you want. You'll have travel, servants, jewels by the bucketful, a mansion, maybe even the governor's mansion. It might not stop there. Can you imagine yourself on my arm as we attend a cotillion in Washington when I become a United States senator? Maybe I might even aim higher than that. A thousand women would answer yes if I proposed, and why in the hell only you obsess me, I'll never know! Only you seem to complete me!"

She listened to his harangue and couldn't be cross with him. Instead she felt deep pity for him. "Yesterday, all that was important to me. Today, it doesn't seem to matter."

He stood up and paced, stopping to look down at her.

"It's your guardian, right? You dread facing him and telling him you want to wed a bitter enemy. I would face him for you gladly, if you would only be mine."

She shook her head and looked away. "No, I think I have the courage to face the Durangos, but—"

"Then in God's name, what is it?"

She paused, unsure how to tell him without hurting him badly.

"There's another man." He paused before her and glared down at her. "Yes, that's it. You've found someone with more money and power and trinkets than I have. Who in hell can offer you more than Senator Edwin Forester?"

She shook her head and looked at the floor. The valuable diamond necklace reflected the light. Last night had probably been only a one-night fling for Rio Kelly and tonight, he might be back in the arms of some sultry girl from the cantina. "I'm so sorry I've hurt you, Edwin. I'll be returning to the Triple D this afternoon."

He paused, dropped to one knee, and tried to take her hand, almost pleading. "Turquoise, my darling, give me one more chance. I will shower you with so much attention and love and gifts that you could not possibly refuse me."

She pulled away from his moist, soft hand. "I'm really sorry, Edwin, but no. I've changed somehow, and my priorities have changed. That's all I can tell you. I must go now, and you have a meeting to attend."

"To hell with the meeting!" he swore and stood up. She thought she saw just a hint of madness in his eyes. Edwin Forester had always gotten everything he wanted and he could not, would not, accept the fact that he could not have her. She was suddenly a little frightened of him.

She stood up and he tried to take her in his arms, but she pulled away from him. "Your mother will probably be relieved. I could tell she saw me as a threat to her plans."

"To hell with her, too," he growled. "If she offends you, I could put her in a nursing home without a second thought."

"Edwin!" She was genuinely shocked at his ruthlessness. She had underestimated this man; there was nothing he would not do to get what he wanted.

"Oh, don't act so shocked. I would do anything for you, anything to possess you. I did not really live until I met you and I cannot, will not live, without you."

"You are saying that out of hurt and anger," she reproached him gently. "After all, you've only known me a little while."

He shook his head, tears in his eyes. "Turquoise, my darling, I'm begging you. Don't leave me."

"I'm sorry, Edwin, I just don't love you."

Now his expression turned threatening. "I want you to think this over before you refuse me. I always get what I want and I want you for my wife."

"Not this time, Edwin. I'm sorry if I hurt you. I must be going now." She was becoming a little alarmed at his rage. She hurried out the door and down the hall, listening to the mixed curses and pleadings that echoed after her.

Edwin reached over to pick up the priceless necklace off the floor and slammed it against the wall before he flopped back down in his chair and stared at the photo of his illustrious grandfather at the convention when Texas became a nation.

It was unthinkable that any woman, especially one who was part Mexican, would spurn anyone as important as Edwin Forester. And it was ironic that after all the women he had seduced, the one he loved, he could not have. What was the old Texas saying? What goes around comes around and . . .

There had to be a man involved. He gritted his teeth in

rage. Yes, that was it, some man with more money and power than even Edwin Forester. Last night, she had rendezvoused with some lover, but who? The thought of her lying naked in another man's arms made him clench his fists and want to kill this stranger. He wished his father were here now to give him advice, but Father had been killed in a duel more than twenty years ago. The fine dueling pistols still resided in the bottom drawer of Edwin's desk.

He didn't know how much time had passed, but finally he heard Elmer moving around in the outer office and yelled at him, "Elmer, get in here!"

"Yes, sir!" The pimply faced clerk dashed in, breathless.

"I'm not going to make that business meeting—"

"But, sir—" Elmer protested.

"Damn it, don't argue with me. I've got something more important to do."

With that, he stood up and strode out of his office. Yes, there had to be another man and Edwin was not a good loser. If that man were dead or bribed to leave the state, the silly young girl would soon forget him and return to Edwin.

"I will have her yet," he vowed to himself as he stormed out of the capitol and to his waiting buggy. "First I must track down this man and deal with him. I will possess Turquoise body and soul, no matter what it takes!"

# Chapter 12

Leaving Silver Slippers in the good care of her friend Fern, Turquoise loaded onto the train with the children and returned to the Triple D ranch. She was determined to put the happenings in Austin behind her. However, on the hot June nights, she found herself sleepless, staring out the window and when she did sleep, she relived that passionate night in Rio's arms and woke up trembling with a sheen of perspiration on her skin.

One morning at breakfast, Trace looked at her and his brow furrowed. "I've been meanin' to ask what's wrong with you. You've been mopin' around ever since you got back from Austin."

Was it that apparent? "Nothing. It's just hot and school's out, so there's nothing much to do."

"Your friend Fern is gettin' married in August. I reckon you're excited about that."

She nodded. "I'm glad for her. I still need to pick out the fabric for my dress for the wedding."

Trace sipped his coffee and winked at her. "You wouldn't be a little sad that you don't have a fella of your own?"

"Of course not," she snapped and tried not to remember Rio's kisses.

"I kinda thought you might be a little sweet on that blacksmith who worked for me for a couple of weeks."

"Him? Why, I don't even remember his name." She looked at her plate to avoid Trace's piercing gaze.

"Uh-huh." He nodded knowingly. "You know, he kinda hinted he'd like to court you, but he admitted he didn't have much to offer."

Much to offer. His kisses seemed to burn her lips again. Passion and love like that were worth more than gold and mansions, but she had realized that too late.

Trace leaned back in his chair. "Didn't see him while you were in Austin?"

She felt the blood rush to her face. "No. I mean, maybe I saw him in the market or something."

"You don't lie very well." Trace laughed and stood up. "I wouldn't mind havin' him in the family. He's a solid, honest hombre and he evidently is very smitten with you."

"No." She shook her head and looked away. She didn't want her guardian guessing any more than he already knew. "I don't think it could work out."

"Well, that's a shame." He reached for his hat and turned to go outside. "At least Cimarron and the kids will be back at the end of the month and maybe you two can do some shopping or plan your dresses for the wedding. Remember, we'll all go into Austin to meet her train. She'll probably have gifts for everyone, so that's something for you to look forward to." He left the dining room.

Turquoise stared after him. Had her moodiness been so apparent? She must do a better job of covering up and forget about Rio. She left the table and went to find Juanita. She was going to let the girl start helping teach in their little school in September and she needed to work with her.

A week passed and then another. One morning in

mid-June she got a letter from Fern and read it with excitement as she sat down to dinner.

"Well," Trace said, "that's the first time I've seen you smile in ages. What's up?"

"Oh, it's Fern. She wants me to come back to Austin to help her with wedding plans."

"You want to go?" He signaled for old Maria to serve the steak and potatoes.

"Of course. It will be fun."

Trace shook his head as he cut his big steak. "Beats me why women get so excited and spend so much time on a wedding. Men would just as soon step up in front of the *padre* and get it over with."

"Don't tell me that," she chided and helped herself to the hot rolls. "I understand that when you married Cimarron, it was the biggest party the county had ever seen and she had a dress fit for a queen."

"Well, *si.*" He nodded chagrined. "I gotta admit I did it because I was so happy to get her."

"Well, Luke is happy to get Fern, too, and they'll be expecting all of us to turn up for the ceremony."

"Oh, you know we wouldn't miss it. She's no beauty and I understand her dad is so relieved she finally got a man that he's going to roast a whole cow and there'll be barrels of beer."

"Men." She snorted and dug into her salad.

"You wouldn't be going to see a certain vaquero while you're in Austin, would you?" he teased.

"Probably not." She sighed. "We just don't seem to fit together." She dared not mention Edwin Forester. Her guardian had never suspected anything, so there was no use in him finding out now.

"Okay, have it your way. You can catch the train tomorrow and you and Fern can spend days lookin' at fabric samples and flowers—all the stuff men hate."

* * *

She arrived back in Austin the next night. As she stepped off the train and walked through the station, she thought she saw a man she recognized, a pimply faced little rat of a man. She froze, staring at him, and he looked back, but then she glanced away and he was gone. She took a deep breath. The man had looked like that Elmer who worked for Senator Forester. Well, maybe not.

"Turquoise, you are being silly," she scolded herself. "Even if it were him, what difference does it make? He was probably here to meet someone for the senator or take a trip himself. You know, since you told Edwin you wouldn't marry him, he's probably moved on and is courting someone else by now."

Fern waddled up just then and threw her ample arms around Turquoise. "My word! You look like you've seen a ghost."

"Oh, it was nothing." She brushed it off. "I'm glad to see you."

They hugged each other again while Fern rattled on. "I've been waiting for you to arrive." She was breathless with excitement. "I just can't get Luke interested at all in choosing boutonnieres."

Boutonnieres. That made her think of Edwin and his pink rosebuds, but the thought was crowded out by the image of crimson oleanders. "That's just men." Turquoise laughed. "All they want is to get the bride into bed."

"Turquoise!" Fern's freckled face blotched red with embarrassment and she giggled. "Why, I haven't even thought about that."

Turquoise didn't answer as they got into Fern's buggy and drove back to the ranch. She had thought about nothing else, she realized, since she'd left Rio's arms last time.

"Have you seen anything of that farrier, what's-his-name?"

"Who?" Fern looked puzzled. "Oh, him. No, I haven't seen him, but the senator has been very visible in the papers and making speeches everywhere. I wonder why?"

"He wants to run for governor," Turquoise said and then was upset that she'd spoken.

"Well, now, how do you know that?" Fern asked as they drove. "He's even told the papers he's not sure about his political future."

"I'm just guessing." Turquoise gulped. "I mean, anytime a politician begins to appear everywhere and make speeches, you can bet he's up to something."

She lapsed into silence, remembering the scene in Edwin's office where he had let her know he wanted her to be the next governor's lady and offered her wealth and privilege for sharing his bed. Had she made a bad mistake by turning him down? No, she thought, her priorities had changed and besides, there was something a little unbalanced and scary about Edwin Forester.

Elmer returned to the senator's office and stuck his head in the inner office. "Sir, I was just down at the depot to get those dispatches off to Washington and guess who came in on the afternoon train?"

"I'm not into guessing games," Edwin snapped.

"That lovely young lady with the black hair and turquoise eyes."

Edwin immediately looked up. "Oh, where was she headed?"

Elmer adjusted his wire-rimmed glasses. "I don't know."

"That's interesting, but I've got work to do." The senator feigned a yawn. "Now I've got a meeting to attend, so you get back to work and I'll return later."

Edwin went outside the capitol building and looked around. He had spies around town and they would tell him what he needed to know. Maybe Turquoise was coming to see him. He could only hope she was in town to tell Edwin she had changed her mind and was eager to have him court her. He smiled at the thought.

The next morning, Turquoise and Fern went to a dozen fabric shops in Austin, choosing the fabric for the bride's gown and hers as the maid of honor, which of course, was a pale turquoise lace to match her eyes.

When they finally got back to the ranch, Fern sighed. "I've got to meet with the seamstress late this afternoon. You can go shopping or rest."

"I am tired," Turquoise admitted. "Maybe I'll take you up on that."

However, while Fern was meeting with the seamstress in her room, Turquoise changed into a riding outfit, saddled up Silver Slippers, and started out for a ride. It was a comfortable day for late June. Where should she ride to? She didn't mean to, but like a magnet, her path seemed to lead to the blacksmith shop.

The little spotted dog met her at the gate, wagging its tail and leading her toward the shop.

Rio was working at his forge as she rode up and before he looked up and saw her, she watched his dark, muscular body shine with sweat as he worked and remembered how it had felt to be embraced by those muscular arms. He still wore the little cross and she watched the tattoo on his hand as he worked.

He looked up and he did not smile. "What is it you want?"

She felt like a fool. "I—my mare may have a loose shoe.

I thought you might look at it." She started to dismount but he waved his hand to halt her.

"You can stay in the saddle." He strode over, picked up Silver's hoof, and examined it.

She looked down at his tousled black hair and had a terrible urge to reach down and run her hand through it, but of course she held back.

He stared up at her, standing so close she could have reached out and touched his rugged, dark face. "I don't find anything wrong with your mare's shoe."

She sighed. This was so difficult for her. "I don't suppose you'd like to take the rest of the afternoon off and maybe go riding with me?"

He did not smile. "You forget I am a poor man. To take off costs me money."

Without thinking, she blurted, "I will pay for your time."

And now he scowled at her. "Oh, *si,* I forget. You are used to having money and you think money can buy anything. I am sorry, senorita, it cannot buy me." He turned and walked away, back to his forge.

Tears came to her eyes and she struggled to hold them in. "Please, I—I need to talk to you."

He frowned coldly. "About what?"

"I don't know—about us, about what happened that night."

"I am a gentleman," he said with great dignity. "If you are worried that I will talk, I would not destroy a lady's reputation. I have apologized to you and regret it ever happened. As far as I and the world are concerned, nothing occurred that night."

She slid off her horse and stood there holding the reins. "How can you say that?"

He shrugged and picked up his hammer. "I'm surprised to see you again, senorita. I figured that by now you would be engaged to the senator. Did he not ask you?"

"He begged on his knees."

Rio snorted. "That should give you much satisfaction, two men making fools of themselves for you. How many diamonds and fine homes did he trade for you?"

She hated him for his sarcasm, yet loved him still. "I said no."

"That really surprises me." He gave her a searching look with his dark eyes.

"After that night in your arms, why would it? After that night, how could you think I could allow another man to make love to me?"

He shrugged. "Because money and social position were so important to you."

"Maybe I was a fool. Maybe I've changed."

He seemed nonchalant as he picked up a horseshoe. "The girls at the cantina were glad to see me again."

She winced, imagining him in another woman's arms. "I don't doubt that. I don't have any other experience, but I think you must be very good at what you do."

"So this is it?" he snapped. "The privileged girl is in town and would like to be provided stud service to entertain her for an afternoon?"

She stepped to him and slapped him; slapped him so hard, she left fingerprints on his face and his head snapped back. Then she whirled to walk away, but he ran after her and grabbed her.

"Let me go, you heartless bastard!" She struggled to break his grip while he whirled her around and held onto her as she fought him.

"Wait, don't go, my sweet one," he whispered. "I deserved that."

She was weeping now and trying to pull away from him, but he was too strong for her.

"Oh, Turquoise, my only love." He buried his dark face against her hair. "You will be the death of me yet. We are not meant to be together, and yet you are in my blood, roaring through my brain when we are not together. I lied, I've touched no other woman, wanted no other woman but you." He jerked her up against his bare, brawny chest and kissed her hard.

For a split second, she struggled and felt the heat of his sweat and the raw power of his sinewy muscle and then she surrendered and returned his kiss with all the passion that was in her.

"If you only want stud service," he whispered, "I am your lowly slave and will be content to amuse you for the afternoon, though it breaks my heart I do not mean more to you."

She was weeping now and clinging to him. "That's not why I came. I—I don't know why I came."

"You came for this," and he kissed her deeply, thoroughly, as she clung to him and let him caress and embrace her.

After a moment, he pulled away from her and wiped the tears off her cheeks with the tip of his finger and smiled. "You have soot on you now, pretty one, and on your fine clothes, too."

"I don't care."

"Of course not. Your rich guardian can buy you more."

"Will you stop that!" she raged and jerked away from him, starting for her horse.

"Wait one momento!" he commanded and she paused by her horse. "Let me close up here and get a saddle. We'll ride."

She turned and looked back at him as he grabbed a rag and wiped himself off, then reached for a faded denim shirt. "I don't know why I came."

"It doesn't matter." He smiled ever so slightly. "I'm glad you did." He came over and lifted her up into her saddle and she followed him down to the barn, where he saddled his fine bay quarterhorse and mounted.

"You have some good horses," she said.

"*Si*, but not many. Someday if I work hard, maybe I can add to my herd and buy more land." He rode up beside her and they started off at a walk, Tip running ahead of them, sniffing at the grass and barking at an occasional rabbit.

"Where are we going?" she asked.

"I want to show you my ranch," he said, glancing over at her. "It's only fifty acres, but there's some good pasture and a nice small lake back there in the hills."

She looked toward the rolling grass on the other side of the fence. "Whose is that?"

"Not mine." He shook his head. "Some New York company and even if it were for sale, I can't afford it."

"Well, fifty acres is a good start and can raise a few good horses and cattle."

They rode past his small adobe house and she stared at the scarlet oleanders and remembered.

He must have misinterpreted her stare, because he said, "I'm afraid it's not much, but it's big enough for me and my one ranch hand."

She looked at him as they passed. "It looks cozy. I imagine a little paint and some curtains and any woman could be happy there."

"It's not a mansion, Turquoise," he reminded her.

"Sometimes mansions can be cold and lonely," she said, remembering the big, dark house of the Foresters.

They rode for a few minutes in silence. The wind whispered through the dry grass and the desert willows that bloomed now all pink and white.

"This is really a fine ranch," Turquoise said, enjoying her ride across the prairie.

He didn't say anything until they reached the edge of a clear, small lake. They let their horses drink and then he dismounted and came around to her, looking up at her. "If you only came to be pleasured, I wish you'd be honest with me. Don't let me hope it might be something more."

She blushed, wanting his body now that she knew the skill with which it performed. "Stop saying that. I—I'm not really sure why I came."

"Maybe you want to turn around and ride back to your friend's ranch? It's late afternoon. You would be back before dark and no one ever need know where you'd been."

"I don't think I'm ready to go yet," she decided and held out her arms to him.

He reached up and eased her down from her horse, but he didn't release her from his embrace. "This is loco," he whispered and then let go of her and led the two horses under a tree and tied them, where the two grazed peacefully. She stood and watched him, wanting to run her hands through that black mop of hair.

"There's a shady place over near the lake's edge," he said and gestured. Then they walked there together and sat down on the grass. Tip lay down near them, panting from all his rabbit chasing. Rio offered her his canteen. "Are you thirsty?"

She nodded and took it with a smile. It seemed such an intimate gesture, drinking from his canteen.

"I don't know what you're doing here, senorita. Every time I see you, it just tears me up inside but it's such pleasant torture."

"I can't forget that night," she confessed. "And I wanted to experience it again."

He nodded. "I've gotten you all smudgy," he said. "I need to wash up, if you don't mind."

"Go ahead."

He stood up and pulled off his boots, then walked down to the water's edge. He hesitated only a moment before he peeled off his pants and stepped into the water. He wore nothing but the cross around his sinewy neck. She got a quick glimpse of long, lean thighs and a hard butt, but what she noticed most was the big manhood between his thighs. Yes, this was a stallion of a man. He swam and dived, coming up like a seal and blowing water into the air while she laughed. She reached into her sleeve and pulled out a lace hankie, wiping the perspiration from her face.

He stood waist deep, watching her. "Come on in, the water's fine."

She shook her head and laughed. "No, thanks. You come out."

He came out then, water dripping off his dark body He reached up and wiped his ebony hair back from his rugged face. He stood looking down at her and she looked over his naked body boldly.

"I don't want to get you wet," he said and flopped down on the grass next to her. "You'd have some explaining to do then."

She reached out and put her hand on his shoulder. "I'm not sure I care."

He turned his head and kissed that hand. "I care. I can't ruin a lady's reputation where no gentleman would have her and high society would gossip about her. That's what you've been trying to escape all your life, isn't it?"

"I was wrong," she whispered and leaned over and kissed him. "I came for this and you know it."

"I knew it before you did." Immediately, he seemed to forget his caution. He pulled her to him in a tight embrace and returned that kiss. Her western hat fell off as he reached to untie her hair. She could feel the water from his lithe body soaking through her clothing and she reached up and ran her hand through his wet hair and clung to him, wanting what he had to give.

"Turquoise," he whispered against her lips, "don't make a fool of me. I'm vulnerable to you like I have never been to another woman, and you can hurt me bad."

"I can't promise you anything," she gasped. "I only knew that I had to come, had to feel your arms around me again."

He kissed her again and then with a low moan, kissed her face and eyes and then her lips again, his cold face wet against her warm one. "I'm getting you soaked," he whispered.

She looked around. It was dusk. "You're right, maybe I need to take this outfit off and hang it over a limb. It'll dry in the breeze."

"Are you sure you want to do that?"

"Unbutton the back of my blouse," she said, pulling off her leather vest as she turned.

She felt his fingers on her back as he unbuttoned her blouse and then he leaned and kissed along her backbone, which sent goose bumps up her spine. Then she stood up and pulled the split skirt and blouse off, hanging them over a low tree branch.

"You are beautiful in your underwear. It must be expensive," he said, looking her up and down.

"Imported lace," she answered and began to unbutton her bodice until her breasts were bare.

"Oh, such breasts!" He stood up and put his hands under her bottom, lifting her to him so that his lips could caress and lick and kiss those breasts.

"You're still getting me wet," she gasped as she arched against his mouth.

"You should have thought of that before you came looking for me."

She watched him, suddenly feeling bold in the growing darkness. "Is anyone liable to see us?"

"Not likely. My cowhand is gone down to San Antonio tonight to visit relatives." He stood there in the twilight, naked and proud.

She couldn't keep her gaze off him as she pulled off her lace bodice, then sat down to pull off her boots. "You mean, the house is empty?"

He nodded. "Would you rather go there?"

She shook her head as she stood up and put her fingers on the tops of her lace drawers, then unbuttoned them. "No, I think I like it here on the lake bank. It's wild and uninhibited somehow." She let her drawers fall to her ankles, knowing he was watching her, caressing her body with his dark gaze. Then she stepped toward him and he grabbed for her and pulled her hard against his wet, naked body. He was all power and manhood. She could feel it throbbing hard and big against her belly.

A coyote howled in the distance somewhere and Tip came alert and growled.

She stiffened and looked up at Rio.

"Don't worry," he whispered against her ear. "I have my rifle with me."

"Don't you carry a pistol like Trace does?"

He shook his head and kissed her face. "I'm no good with a handgun. I'm not a gunfighter. You know a rancher only really needs a rifle."

"Then make love to me, my vaquero," she demanded. "I command you, make love to me like I have dreamed of you doing ever since that time under the scarlet oleanders."

He seemed to need no further urging. He swung her up in his arms and she arched her back so that he could kiss her breasts, and then he lay her on the soft grass in the early darkness and lay down next to her.

She took his big right hand in her own and kissed the shamrock tattoo on the back of it. "I don't care who your father was or your mother either. I have never felt like this about any man before."

He pulled her hand up to his mouth and kissed it. "I have had many women, Turquoise, I won't lie to you about that, but since I made love to you, I think no other one will ever satisfy me again." He bent and kissed her breasts and then caressed them with his strong, suntanned hands, molding them up into peaks so his hot tongue could lick her nipples and make her squirm and moan.

His hand went to explore her, touching her, teasing her with his fingertips while she spread wide, wanting him to touch deeper still. She was panting and dewy wet now, wanting him, needing him.

"Do what you did before," she begged against his mouth. "Make me one with you, mount me, take me. . . ."

He needed no further urging. He pushed her knees up on each side of her black hair that spread under her in the grass like spilled ink. He knelt between her thighs and she could see his maleness, all hard and erect and throbbing. Past his shoulder, the sky seemed to be alight with stars and she felt like a wild, primitive thing, ready to mate with her male in the darkness under the trees.

He came into her slowly, making her grab onto his waist and try to pull him down into her. "You torture me," she gasped. "Come deeper still."

"Make it last, pretty one," he whispered and came down relentlessly, gradually, while she bucked under him, wanting it all, urging him with her own fierce need. He rode her slowly, rhythmically, while she dug her nails into his hard hips and begged him to ride harder, faster until he succumbed to her wishes and rode her hard, pulling almost out and then slamming into her with a loud slapping of flesh on flesh. She grunted each time he came full into her and she locked her long legs around his waist so that he could not escape until he had given her what she hungered for. She was using him for her pleasure and she felt no shame in it.

One last second as he plunged into her and climaxed hard, she dug her nails into his hips so that he could not escape and they clung together under the stars and reached the pinnacle of pleasure together.

She did not know how long it lasted or when she gradually returned to consciousness. Her eager body kept convulsing, holding onto his, not wanting to let him go until she had squeezed out every drop of seed he had to give, and then she wept softly while he kissed her mouth ever so gently.

"My little love," he whispered, "what am I to do with you except pleasure you when you beckon me like a lowly servant? We are so unsuitable for each other."

"You can make love to me again and again," she murmured against his mouth.

"And this is my future? You will marry some prominent, rich man and then sneak over to see me now and then so that I can satisfy your greedy body?" He shook his head and pulled away from her. "No, that hurts me. It makes me no more human than a well-hung stallion."

"It's more than that. I think I love you." She sat up, protesting.

He reached out and cupped one of her generous breasts, stroking and teasing it until she was gasping for air. "Let's not talk about it anymore. I can settle for that if I must. Why don't we swim?"

She laughed. "Why don't we?"

They dove naked into the cool water, swimming and splashing like two children playing hookey. He caught her in the water and kissed her all over, then lifted her up in his arms and kissed below her belly.

"Oh," she gasped, "you've got me wanting you again."

"I said I would service you whenever you wanted, my lady," he promised and carried her over, lay her in the shallow water so that more than half of her was exposed to the night air. Now he lay on top of her and rode her with a passion as if he had never had her before, and she thought if he made love to her all night, she still wouldn't be satisfied.

"It's getting late," he finally said regretfully. "Let's wash up and dress. I've got some chili at the house and some enchiladas."

"I'll wager they're not as good as I make," she said,

splashing in the water and then standing up, letting the warm night wind dry her naked body.

"You can cook, too?" He laughed and smacked her bare bottom.

She nodded. "I didn't get enough of you. Can you keep this up all night?"

He winked at her in the moonlight. "I'm probably only good for half a dozen times, but tonight, I'd better get you back to Fern's ranch before someone starts looking for us." They began to dress slowly. She didn't want to leave him, but of course she must. She had been lucky the last time to get home before the Lessup family discovered she'd been out all night. Of course Fern probably knew, but she wouldn't tattle. Tip had come awake and now stood looking toward the south and growling.

As they dressed, Rio sniffed the south wind. "Do you smell smoke?"

She shook her head and pulled on her boots. "I don't smell anything."

"It would be bad if we got a prairie fire going with this wind," he said and sniffed again.

She took a deep breath. "You know, now that you mention it, I think I do smell smoke." Tip began to bark and then the little dog took off at a run for the house and barn over the hill.

Rio's rugged face turned abruptly serious. "Mount up. We'd better check."

She needed no further urging. They both swung into their saddles and started toward the ranch at a lope. When they topped the hill, they heard little Tip barking frantically and could see the house and the barn and the farrier's shed. The flames lit up the sky like a torch.

*"Dios!"* Rio swore. "The barn's on fire! Let's go!"

# Chapter 13

They rode back toward the barn at a gallop. Even at this distance, they could hear horses neighing in panic, see the flames scarlet against the dark sky and riders with torches galloping around the barn.

"What the hell?" Rio swore and Turquoise saw him reach for the rifle in the boot of his saddle. The quartet of attackers seemed to see them approaching and took off at a gallop, little Tip barking and nipping at their horses' hooves.

Rio put the rifle to his shoulder and fired. One of the riders fell from his saddle and went end over end across the ground. The other three took off down the road past the blacksmith shed and away.

Turquoise was breathless with fear and excitement as she shouted, "Who were they?"

Rio shook his head. "I don't know. We've got to save the horses!" Even as he yelled, he was off his horse with Peso still running.

The flames from the barn rose higher and Turquoise could hear the neighing and stamping of frightened stock. She reined in sharply and dismounted. Silver Slippers, like the well-trained horse she was, slid to a halt.

"You stay here!" Rio ordered as he ran toward the burning building.

"You need help!" she protested and ran into the barn right behind him. The acrid smoke choked and blinded her, but she heard terrified horses and cattle trying to break free from their stalls. The flames were hot against her skin but she did not retreat. Rio grabbed a saddle blanket, wrapped it around a horse's head, and led it out of its stall and toward the open barn door.

The black smoke swirled around her as she ran through the barn, opening stall doors, but the panicked horses refused to budge, choosing instead to rear and neigh. Turquoise knew a frightened horse might not move, so she pulled off her blouse and ran into a stall. The gray mare inside reared and neighed. Turquoise took a deep breath and grabbed the mare's halter. "Whoa, girl, I'm going to get you out." She wrapped her blouse around the mare's head and patted her muzzle. "Come on, girl, come with me."

The mare quieted and Turquoise led her through the flames and out into the yard. She was choking and coughing as she turned loose of the horse and it ran toward the lake.

"You little fool!" Rio yelled. "You could get trampled trying to help me! Stay out!" Then he ran back into the barn.

She wasn't going to let animals burn to death if she could help it. The scarlet flames now roared against the black sky, sending showers of sparks into the air, but Turquoise took a deep breath of fresh air. Grabbing up her blouse, she ran back inside. The flames had built as they caught the dry timbers. All around her seemed to be the fires of hell. The black, acrid smoke blinded her, so that she couldn't see Rio anymore. She felt her way along the stall doors, where she saw a terrified black colt trying to kick down the gate to his stall.

"Take it easy, boy," she said, attempting to soothe him.

"I'll get you out. Trust me." The colt reared and struck out at her with his front hooves, but she got the blindfold over his eyes, opened the gate, and led him out.

Rio was ahead of her with another horse. "Stay out!" he ordered her. "The whole thing is liable to collapse at any moment!"

"Not as long as there's animals in there!" she shouted back and ran after him into the fiery barn. The heat seemed to blister her tender skin and she choked and coughed on the thick air. The whole barn was afire now. There was no chance of saving it, but she was determined to save the animals. This time she led out two mooing calves while ahead of her, Rio brought out another horse.

The whole barn looked like a giant funeral pyre against the black night, but they both ran in again to save horses. Inside, she was gasping for air and unable to see. Flaming timbers crashed down around her, showering her with sparks that burned her skin, but she ran blindly down the row of stalls until she found another terrified horse that reared, striking at Turquoise with its hooves. "Whoa, boy, I'm here to help," she yelled and grabbed the horse's halter, dodging the flaying hooves.

She couldn't see anything and wasn't certain which way was out. Then she felt cool air blowing against her face from the outside. This time, she only made it to the barn door and couldn't go any farther. She let go of the horse as she fell to the ground just inside the barn and it galloped past her and outside into the night.

"Turquoise! Turquoise, where are you?"

Vaguely she heard Rio's voice and managed to raise up off the smoldering hay on the floor, but didn't have the strength to stumble to her feet and run outside. She was going to die here, she thought in a daze, only a few feet from the life-giving air outside. Well, maybe she'd be unconscious and wouldn't feel the pain.

And then Tip nuzzled her with his wet nose and barked and barked. "Get out," she gasped to the little dog. "Don't die here with me."

However, the terrier continued to bark and in moments, she felt strong arms lifting her. "Turquoise, you little fool! I told you to stay outside! If Tip hadn't led me to you, you'd have roasted alive in there!"

She didn't say anything as Rio carried her out of the barn and across the yard. He set her down by the water pump, pumped a little into his hands, and splashed it on her face. "Are you all right?"

The cold water revived her and she turned her face toward the flaming barn. "Did—did we get them all out?"

He nodded and as she watched, the barn collapsed into a pile of burning timbers and glowing ashes. "Lost a bunch of hay and saddles. Didn't have a chance of saving the barn without anyone here to help carry water buckets."

"I did the best I could," she gasped.

"I know you did." He took her smudged face gently between his two big hands and knelt and looked down into her eyes. "You've got more spunk than I gave you credit for."

She looked back up at him, grinning. "I was raised on a ranch, remember?"

He kissed the tip of her nose. "Well, at least we saved all the animals. I'd better go look at the hombre I shot and see if I know him."

Turquoise stumbled to her feet. "And you'll have to send for the sheriff."

"*Si,* you're right."

With Tip following them, they walked around to the man who had fallen from his horse. He was dead all right, Turquoise thought. Rio was good with a rifle.

Rio flipped the big man over on his back and shook his head. "No, I never saw him before. Don't know why he'd want to set my barn on fire."

Turquoise squatted and looked down at the dead man. The light from the burning barn lighted his features eerily. She gasped as she saw the jagged scar across his chin. It was Edwin Forester's handyman, Luther.

Rio didn't seem to notice her reaction; he was already looking down the road after the disappearing raiders. He shrugged. "Maybe they just hate Mexicans. Anyway, pretty one, you'd better get back to Fern's ranch before they start looking for you."

Thank God he hadn't asked her if she recognized the dead man. "Yes, I guess I'd better." She walked toward her horse.

"With all that's going on, you might not be safe on the road," Rio said. "I'd better escort you home."

"You've got plenty to do here," she protested.

"Don't argue with me," he snapped. "I'm escorting you home. The dead man isn't going anywhere and the barn is beyond saving."

"What about all the animals we just got out of the barn?"

"I can close the gate down at the road and they won't get out. Now mount up, but better put your blouse on first. Tip, you stay here and make sure the stock doesn't get out."

There was no point in arguing with this man, she thought and obediently, she dressed and swung up on her horse. He mounted his and they rode away from the barn that was burning down to a pile of embers. Little Tip obediently stayed with the livestock.

"I can't imagine why they picked my barn," Rio mused as they rode. "I didn't think I had any enemies."

Turquoise didn't say anything. The dead man was Senator Forester's handyman. She remembered seeing Luther at the Forester mansion. Did the senator know anything about this? If so, why would he bother with a small rancher like Rio Kelly? *Oh my God,* she thought, *is this because of me? Did Edwin find out about Rio and me?*

"You're awfully quiet," Rio said as they rode through the darkness to Fern's ranch.

"I'm just tired," she lied, her mind busy. Tomorrow, she would confront Edwin and find out if he knew anything about this. Surely the prestigious senator wouldn't get mixed up in something as lowdown as burning out a small rancher.

They rode to Fern's place in silence. The ranch dogs began to bark as the pair rode up and Fern and her lanky old father came outside.

Fern's freckled face wore a frown as they dismounted. "Where have you been? We were worried."

Turquoise said, "This is Rio Kelly, a friend of mine. We ran into some trouble."

Rio nodded as he shook hands with Mr. Lessup. "Someone set fire to my barn, but we saved all the livestock."

Fern's father frowned. "Any hombre who would burn a barn is as lowdown a skunk as a horse thief. Any idea who done it?"

Turquoise didn't say anything and Rio shook his head. "I got to go for the sheriff. I shot one of the hombres. The other three got away."

Fern's eyes widened. "Turquoise, you're all smudged and dirty."

"But we saved all the livestock," Turquoise said.

"She's got a lot of grit," Rio added and she saw the admiration in his dark eyes.

Old Mr. Lessup looked to Rio. "You need any help?"

Rio shook his head as he swung up on his horse. "No. The barn is gone, didn't have a chance of saving it. I'll just ride into town and get the law to come out and take a look at the dead man, but much obliged anyway. *Buenos noches,* ladies." He touched the brim of his hat, wheeled his horse, and rode away.

Turquoise looked after him as he rode away. To the

Lessups, she said, "It's been an exciting night. I just wish we could have saved his barn."

"I'll talk to some of the other ranchers," the old man grunted. "Maybe everyone can donate some hay and grain for his stock 'til he gets back on his feet."

"I'm sure he'd appreciate that," Turquoise said.

"You look like you could use a bath," Fern noted. "My word, I wouldn't have been brave enough to run into a burning barn."

Turquoise shrugged. "I heard those terrified horses and the calves bawling and I didn't even think about danger. I just knew we had to save them."


Rio rode into town and found the sheriff. "You'd better come out and have a look. Some coyotes tried to burn me out and I shot one of them."

The fat sheriff looked grumpy as he sucked on a toothpick. It was clear he wasn't too happy about having to ride out to a ranch this late. "Was it just some of you Mexicans drinkin' tequila and it got out of hand?"

Rio frowned. "No. I told you, four hombres set fire to my barn and I killed one of them. You'd better come have a look."

"Oh hell, okay." He got up out of his chair and grabbed his hat. As they went out the door, he yelled at two deputies lounging against the hitching post. "Hey, you, Joe and Bill, come along with us. This Mexican says some bastard burned his barn."

The two men didn't look happy to have to mount up. "Can't it wait?"

The sheriff shook his head as he swung into the saddle. "Nope. The Mex says he killed someone."

That seemed to make it a little more interesting. The other two mounted up and the four of them rode back to

Rio's ranch. By now the barn was only a pile of glowing coals with thin wisps of smoke drifting in the breeze and the rescued animals were peacefully grazing across the pasture. Tip came running, wagging his short tail.

All four men dismounted and stood looking down at the dead man.

The sheriff pushed his Stetson back. "Yep, he's dead, all right." He squatted down and stared. "Hey, that looks like—"

"Who?" asked Rio. "I don't recognize the hombre."

"Whoa." The sheriff glanced up and frowned at him. "This man's been shot in the back."

Rio frowned. "*Sí*. They were escaping and I took a shot at them."

"But shootin' a man in the back?" one of the deputies asked.

"Look"—Rio gestured—"the bastard was burning down my barn—"

"Says you," snapped the sheriff, sucking on his toothpick. "Maybe he was just riding by or something. You got any witnesses?"

Rio hesitated. He didn't want to get a lady mixed up in this dirty business. "No. But I didn't have any reason to kill some stranger except he set fire to my barn."

The sheriff shrugged. "We got a dead man who was shot in the back and no witnesses. We better take you in, Mex."

"Me?" Rio touched his chest in surprise. "Holy Mother of God, I swear I didn't do anything except try to protect my property. Why don't you look for the other outlaws instead?"

The sheriff pulled out his pistol. "Put your hands up, hombre. Bill, you handcuff him, and Joe, throw that dead man over a horse and let's take him back to town."

"Now wait a minute," Rio protested, but Bill snapped the handcuffs on him. "If I'd been guilty, I wouldn't have brought you out here. I'd have buried him in an unmarked grave and kept my mouth shut."

"Or maybe you just wanted us to think you was innocent," the sheriff opined. "Everybody mount up. Let's get back to town."

"You're holding me for murder?" Rio asked.

"You bet. I got a man shot in the back and only your word to back it up, no witnesses."

"I got nothin' to hide," Rio protested.

"Then let's get ridin'," the sheriff ordered. "It'll be dawn purty soon and I'd like some breakfast."

The deputies threw the dead man across his horse and they all rode back to the courthouse.

As the sheriff locked Rio in a cell, he asked, "You got anyone you'd like to have notified?"

Rio shook his head. Most of his friends wouldn't have enough money to bail him out even if he could be bailed out and he certainly didn't want to drag a lady like Turquoise Sanchez into this mess. He had to protect her and her reputation at all costs.

"No, nobody."


As soon as Sheriff Barnes had had some breakfast, he headed over to the state capitol. Senator Forester was just arriving at his office when the sheriff walked up, doffing his Stetson and chewing a toothpick. "Senator, I've got something I need to talk to you about."

The senator looked out of sorts. "Can't it wait? I'm running late this morning."

"I think we'd better talk," the sheriff said, picking his teeth.

"All right, come in." The senator gestured and to the little pipsqueak at the desk, he barked, "Elmer, get us some coffee, will you?"

The sheriff was humble as he followed the senator into the office and accepted a fine cigar. He waited until the senator sat down and gestured toward a chair before he took a seat. "Senator, I'm here on a rather delicate matter."

"Yes? You need to sell tickets to the law officers' ball, or—?"

"No, of great importance to you." The sheriff sniffed the fine cigar, then put it in his shirt pocket for future use. "It has to do with—"

The senator gestured him to silence as the pimply faced Elmer returned with a tray and mugs of coffee.

He put down the tray and looked at the senator. "Would you like me to serve—?"

"Never mind, we'll do it ourselves. Now get out." He gestured impatiently.

"Very well, sir." The younger man fled the scene.

Senator Forester took a cup and gestured that Sheriff Barnes should do so. "Now you were saying . . . ?"

"Is your handyman, Luther, missin'?" The sheriff sipped his coffee.

"Is that all? How should I know?" The senator looked annoyed. "Even my damned driver was late this morning. I can't keep up with all the worthless help."

"Maybe you should find out." Barnes sipped the coffee and sucked his teeth.

"Why do you want to know?" The senator raised one eyebrow.

"Well, your handyman's been shot graveyard dead," the sheriff said, "something to do with a barn."

"A barn?" the senator snapped. "You bother me over a barn? I've got important matters—"

"Luther was shot in the back," the sheriff said and added importantly, "I arrested the man."

"Now I guess the county wants me to pay for the funeral?" The senator sipped his coffee. "Killed in a bar fight?"

The sheriff shook his head. "Naw. His killer says Luther was burnin' down his barn."

"Now why would Luther do that?" The senator pulled out his watch. "Any witnesses?"

The sheriff shook his head. "No. He says he shot him in the back because Luther and his friends were burnin' his barn. But you know them Mexicans, no tellin' what really happened."

"Mexican?"

"Yeah." The sheriff nodded. "Rio Kelly, a small rancher. I got him in jail."

"I hope you keep him there," the senator said with a nod. "Damned Mexicans just taking over this town. You can't trust them, Sheriff, and who knows what Luther and his friends were doing last night, maybe having a little innocent fun and some greasy bastard killed him for it. We need more law and order in this city."

Sheriff Barnes puffed his chest out, but his big belly got in the way. "That's just what I always say, sir."

"You're going to keep him in jail until trial?"

The sheriff grinned. "Yes, sir. I doubt he can make bail or hire a good lawyer. It's pretty cut and dried. He shot a man in the back, so he'll go to prison or hang."

The senator leaned back in his chair and smiled. "You're a good man, Sheriff. We need more men like you. Damn, I'll have to find a new handyman now."

"Yep, that's too bad." Sheriff Barnes stood up. "I just wanted to make sure you didn't have any idea why Luther was out there."

"Now why would I?" the senator scoffed. "I don't have much to do with Mexican peasants. By the way, Sheriff, I'll make sure you have enough money to run your campaign next time. You just remind me." He stood up and offered his hand and the sheriff shook it.

"Why, thank you, Senator."

The senator escorted him to the door. "Think nothing of it . . ."

"Barnes, sir, Pete Barnes."

"Like I said, Barnes, we need more tough lawmen like you. We've got to stop mollycoddling these killers."

"I reckon we're both in agreement on that," the sheriff said and went out. The senator was a very good man. Pete hummed to himself and grinned all the way back to the jail.

Back at Fern's ranch, Turquoise slept little, wondering why anyone would want to burn out Rio's small, struggling ranch. Because she had recognized the dead man, she felt she had to find out if Edwin knew anything.

Come morning, she washed up and dressed in a blue dotted Swiss frock that was perfect for the hot weather, got a lace parasol, and borrowed Fern's buggy. As she rolled into town, grubby newsboys on corners were holding up papers and yelling "Read all about it! Custer killed at Little Bighorn!"

People began to gather on the sidewalks to talk and grab papers.

She stopped her buggy and gestured one of the boys to her side, and held out some change. "Here. What's this you say?"

"General Custer was killed at the Little Bighorn River several days ago," the boy shouted as he took her money and handed her a paper.

She stared at the article. "General Custer, who was once assigned to Austin right after the War, has been wiped out with his entire command in Montana by a huge force of Cheyenne and Sioux."

She lay the paper on her buggy seat. The news was sad and exciting, but she had something more important on her mind. She snapped the reins at the paint horse.

She drew up before the capitol and stepped down, tying up her horse. Then she went into the capitol building and up to Senator Forester's office. The same little man was outside at his desk. "Elmer, is the senator in?"

The pimply faced secretary jumped to his feet. "I'll see, ma'am." He disappeared inside. In a moment, he stuck his head out. "Yes, the senator will see you, miss."

He acted like he might want to hang around and eavesdrop, but instead, he went back to his desk, watching her.

Turquoise went past his desk and into Edwin's office, and carefully closed the door behind her.

He stood up and with a big smile, rushed forward to meet her. He had a pink rosebud in the buttonhole of his expensive suit. "Well, my dear, this is a surprise. I am so glad to see you. Since you've changed your mind, perhaps we can have lunch—"

"Edwin, I'm not here on a visit," she said. "There's something that's happened."

"Oh, you mean about General Custer? Sad. I had dinner with him several times when he was assigned to Austin. We've got to wipe those savages out, teach them a lesson."

"No, something else."

He looked baffled, but then he smiled. "Well, anything you need, I'm ready to help. You know that, my dear. You see by the rosebud I haven't given up hope."

She winced. "I wish you wouldn't bring that up. Anyway, have you heard there was a barn burned last night?"

He gestured her to a chair. "A barn? You're bothered over a silly barn? What has that to do with me?"

"Edwin, one of the raiders was killed. I saw him and recognized him as that scar-faced handyman of yours."

He stared at her, eyes wide with surprise. "Luther? Luther is dead? Oh my, I doubt the poor chap has any relatives, but I'll give him a funeral. That's the least I can do for the man. But why would he burn someone's barn? You just never can tell about people, can you? Sherry?" He walked to the sideboard and poured himself a drink.

She shook her head. "Luther was helping three other riders burn a barn when he was shot and killed."

"Hmm." He paused and sipped his drink. "Do tell. Now just how do you know this?" He gave her a searching look.

She glanced away. "I—I just happened to be visiting the owner. Your Luther and the other three were evidently burning the barn and the owner interfered."

"Oh, now, do we know that for sure?" He seemed to be patronizing her. "Maybe the men just happened to be riding by and the owner shot Luther by mistake?"

"By mistake?" She couldn't keep her voice from rising in frustration. "Honestly, Edwin, I saw the whole thing. They were burning the barn and the owner shot him."

"If you say so. Why would you think I knew anything about it?" Edwin sounded testy. "When you came in, I had hoped you might be reconsidering my offer—"

"Oh, I can't think about that right now." She made a dismissive gesture. "The man who shot your handyman is a friend of mine. He might get into some trouble over this."

Edwin turned away to look out the window. "I see. So you would like me to use my influence to help him?"

"I would so appreciate it."

He turned around. "It's always possible I might not be able to do anything." She gave him her most appealing smile. "I've heard you often have more influence than the governor."

"Oh, my dear, you flatter me." He smiled modestly. "Of course, I do hold sway in certain circles. However, we don't know if your friend is in trouble yet."

She came to him and he took one of her small hands between his two well-manicured ones. "But I can count on you if I need to, Edwin?"

"Of course, my dear." He kissed her hands. "I would do anything in the world for you. You know that."

The way he was looking into her eyes and kissing her fingers made her uneasy. She disengaged her hands. "Thank you, Edwin." She turned and walked to the door, pausing. "You are kinder to me than I deserve."

"I don't hold a grudge," he assured her. "And I would do anything for you. I've told you that. I'm upset any of my employees might be involved in anything underhanded. Are you sure your friend is telling the truth?"

She nodded. "I was there, Edwin, and I saw what happened, and even if I hadn't been, I would stake my life on this man's innocence." She went out the door, feeling better about everything.

Edwin stared after her, cursing softly. What a mess. Turquoise was so innocent and naive and that was the reason he'd had her followed and had sent the four out to burn down the barn and kill all the vaquero's livestock. He had had them nose about the hacienda to make sure no one was at the house before they fired the barn. But Turquoise had been there and with that low-life Mexican. He tried not to picture her in that vaquero's arms, his dirty mouth on hers, his big hands on her pale white body. Edwin's jealousy sent him into a rage and he paced his office.

He hadn't expected Turquoise to turn up as a witness. That stupid Luther; getting himself killed might throw suspicion on Edwin. Now the question was how to get rid of that Mexican bastard while letting Turquoise think Edwin was trying to help him.

Surely she was not involved with that penniless hombre. Edwin gritted his teeth at the thought. His hope was not dead yet and maybe Edwin might still end up with the beauty. He'd like to see that Mexican hanged, but that wouldn't win Edwin the fair maiden. Maybe Edwin could pretend to help and then get rid of his rival by having

Sheriff Barnes stage a fake jail break. The Mex would be shot and killed as he tried to escape. That's what the sheriff would swear to.

Turquoise rode out to Rio's ranch and couldn't find him anywhere. Puzzled, she went back to Fern's ranch.

"Hey," Fern said, "where have you been? A boy just brought a telegram that Mrs. Durango will be home in a few days and Senor Trace will be catching a train here to Austin to meet her."

"That's good," Turquoise said, still deep in thought. "We can all journey back to the ranch together."

"Who was the handsome vaquero with you last night? I thought you were being courted by Senator Forester."

"It's very complicated." Turquoise shrugged.

"You look upset," Fern said.

Turquoise sighed. "I just went out to his ranch but Rio's not there."

"So you've definitely decided it's the vaquero instead of the senator?"

Turquoise nodded. "I never thought I'd say that, but I've decided that love matters more than security and respectability."

Fern smiled. "I could have told you that."

"I just wish I knew where Rio was. I might take the buggy and go into Austin and look around for him."

Fern shook her head. "Some of those places men frequent are no place for a lady."

Her father came in just then. "What's this about?"

Fern explained.

Mr. Lessup said, "Why don't I ride into town and make a few inquiries? You girls stay here."

So he rode out and the girls tried to work on the wedding plans, but Turquoise couldn't think of anything but what had happened to Rio.

* * *

That afternoon, Fern's father returned and he looked grim as he walked into the ranch house. "The news isn't good. They've got Rio in jail. They're gonna try him for murder, since the man was shot in the back."

"Murder?" Turquoise gasped. "No, it wasn't—"

"It doesn't matter." The old man's face was grim. "He's a nobody, a Mexican. I wouldn't be surprised if they sent him to prison in Huntsville for years or even hung him."

Turquoise cried out in dismay and Fern said, "Daddy, did you have to say it out loud like that?"

"Sorry," the old man muttered.

"Do you think they'll let me see him?" Turquoise blinked back tears.

The old man shook his head. "That jail isn't a place for a young lady. I didn't even see him myself."

Turquoise didn't answer, but her mind was working hard. Trace would be in town in a couple of days and he was rich and powerful; maybe he could help. However, she knew someone who had influence and power and who had offered to help her if she needed him. Edwin Forester. She was going to have to visit him again and beg for a favor.

# Chapter 14

Early the next morning, Turquoise dressed, borrowed Fern's horse and buggy, and drove into town to the jail. The yawning deputy on duty didn't want to let her see Rio, but she persisted and finally he led her down a short row of dingy, smelly cells.

"Somebody to see you, Mex." The deputy smirked and left. Rio came to the cell bars. "What are you doing here? I don't want you in this dump."

"You know I would come anyway." She looked at him. He was dirty and unkempt and there were dark bruises on his face. "I'm going to get you out on bail."

He shook his head. "They say I'm at risk for fleeing to Mexico. The bail is so high, I can't make it, and even all my friends together couldn't raise that much: ten thousand."

"I know several people who can," she said. She wanted to reach through the bars and stroke his black, tousled hair, but she knew he was embarrassed for her to see him like this.

"Go home, Turquoise." He turned away from her. "This was never meant to be. You wanted more than a poor cowboy will ever have, and I reckon I'm gonna hang. Maybe Edwin Forester is the right choice for you."

"No," she pleaded. "Rio, it's you I love."

"Well, maybe I don't care about you. Maybe you were just a plaything for me." He didn't look at her.

"I don't believe that." Tears came to her eyes. "I'm going to get you out and then you can decide whether we're meant to be together."

"You're wastin' your time." He strode over and flung himself down on his narrow cot, closing his eyes. "Don't come back here. I'll tell the jailer not to let you in."

She winced at his grim tone. "I will come back," she promised.

He did not answer and she sighed as she turned and went down the dim hall. Somehow, she would help him and then if he didn't want her, that was his decision to make.

She left the jail and drove directly to the capitol building, tied up the buggy out front, and went inside and down the hall to Edwin's office. To the weasel of a secretary, she said "I need to see the senator."

He looked her over with just a hint of curiosity. "I'll see if he's in to visitors, senorita."

He disappeared into the big door and in moments returned. "The senator will see you now."

He led the way and opened the door for her. She stood there, making sure she heard his footsteps echoing away before she came over to the desk. She did not want Elmer eavesdropping on her conversation.

Edwin stood up from his desk and came over, taking both her small hands in his clammy, soft ones. "Ah, my dear, so good to see you again. I think about you all the time. See? I still wear a pink rosebud in my lapel."

She forced herself not to pull away from him; after all, she needed a favor. "Senator Forester—"

"Edwin, remember?" He squeezed her hands and looked down at her with tearful eyes.

She managed a smile. "Yes, Edwin. Well, I need a favor and it involves a lot of money."

"My dear, you know I would give you my whole fortune. What is it your little heart desires?"

"Oh, it isn't for me. It's for a friend."

"A friend?" He seemed instantly on his guard.

"Yes, a friend is in jail and the bail is ten thousand dollars. I was hoping you would lend me the money to get him out. I can go to my guardian, but he won't be in town for several days and I need it immediately."

His jaw went tense and she saw the muscles working there. "Who is it?"

"The vaquero who's accused of killing Luther."

His hands tightened on hers so hard, she winced and pulled away. "Let me get this straight," he said. "You want me to provide the money to get that greasy Mexican cowboy out of jail? The man who killed my dear friend?"

She knew by his expression he did not, would not, give her one penny to help Rio. "He didn't murder him and I want to help him."

He gave her a wounded look. "My dear girl, I don't even know this man except the gossip I've heard in the last few hours. I don't know . . ."

"Then why was your handyman involved in burning down his barn?"

"Surely you don't think I had anything to do with this." He went into a spasm of coughing and turned away, hurrying over to pour himself a drink. "I swear to you, my dear, that I have no idea what my hired help does on their own time. No jury would believe that a rich, prominent man like me would have any reason to burn down some poor Mexican's barn."

She took a deep breath for courage. "I think we both know that isn't true."

Edwin didn't answer. "I don't know what you're insinuating, my dear, but I'll excuse it since you're so upset and hysterical."

"Edwin," she said in a cold voice, "I am not hysterical. I merely need to borrow some money immediately."

He clasped his hands behind his back and walked over to stare out the window. "Did this poor galoot send you to beg for bail?"

"He did not!" she snapped. "In fact, he said I should not come to the jail again and to forget about him."

"Very good advice." He turned and looked at her. "Obviously he'll be hanged or sent to prison for a long, long time. You'd be an old lady by the time he got out."

"But Edwin," she pleaded, "you have power and influence. You're a lawyer, and I hear, a great one. I'm sure you could get him acquitted."

He sighed deeply and turned to her. "I guess I must now tell you what I only found out a few minutes ago."

She felt a chill of foreboding. "Tell me."

He paced up and down. "The sheriff has now found the other three men and they are all respectable citizens. They all are ready to swear in court that the four of them were merely riding by, saw the fire, and were attempting to put it out when this Mexican came riding and shooting out of nowhere and killed poor Luther before he could explain."

She grabbed the back of a chair, shaken. "Edwin, that isn't true. I was there."

He gave her an earnest look. "My dear, I want to believe you would not lie just to save your friend, but these three men are respectable citizens. Why, one of them is even a church deacon."

"I'll testify in court," she said.

"And ruin your reputation? Oh no, my dear, you can't do that. Besides, the jury might not take the word of a woman against three solid citizens and business owners."

"But Edwin, with your help and position, you could—"

"And why should I?" he snapped. "I'm afraid to even guess what you were doing there that night. In fact, I won't let my mind dwell on it. Yes, I could probably fix things, all right, but I don't see why I should Unless . . ."

"Yes?" She walked up to him, looking into his face.

He put his hands on her shoulders. "You know I love you. I never thought I would stoop to admitting I would be willing to take some low vaquero's leavings, but in spite of all that, I still want you more than anything I've ever wanted in my life. And with all your beauty and charm, you would make a wonderful senator and then a governor's wife."

She looked up into his eyes and saw the pain and the need there. "I'm sorry, Edwin, I don't feel the same way about you. Once I thought I might, but then—"

"That Mexican cowboy came along?" His face turned an angry red. "Would you not marry me even to save him?"

She pulled away from him, blinking in disbelief. "Why, that's blackmail."

"No, it's a business deal." He seemed to regain control of himself. "I will save your cowboy and have him deported to Mexico, provided you marry me. After I shower you with adoration, jewels, and everything a woman could want, you'll learn to love me. A poor cowboy's life isn't the life for a beauty like you."

She shook her head and backed away. "No, Edwin. I would be cheating you because I could never forget him. As long as Rio lived, he would be in my heart and mind."

He ground his teeth. "Then come to the hanging, my darling Turquoise, and watch your greasy Mexican swing, knowing you could have saved him."

"You are an evil man." Turquoise gasped and backed toward the door. "And to think I was once so enamored, so charmed by you."

"Turquoise, wait, I'm sorry. Can't we talk?" He came

toward her, but she had found the door and fled through it, running down the hall past the surprised Elmer.

Now what was she to do? She knew she could get money from her guardian, but he didn't have the influence over the courts and the important people of Austin that Edwin Forester would have. She went directly to the telegraph station and sent Trace a wire:

DEAR UNCLE TRACE. STOP. NEED TEN
THOUSAND DOLLARS IMMEDIATELY FOR
RIO'S BAIL. STOP. CAN YOU GET IT FOR ME?
STOP. DETAILS WHEN YOU ARRIVE. STOP.
LOVE, TURQUOISE.

She returned to Fern's ranch and the next morning, a wire was delivered to Fern's ranch.

DEAR TURQUOISE. STOP. I HAVE WIRED MY
BANKER AT AUSTIN FIRST NATIONAL TO
GIVE YOU THE MONEY. STOP. I'LL BE THERE
FRIDAY. STOP. FAMILY DUE IN LATE
MONDAY. STOP. LOVE, UNCLE TRACE.

Turquoise sat down in a chair and heaved a sigh of relief. "I'll get Rio out this morning."

Fern's father said, "That jail is no place for a lady. Why don't you let me handle this?"

Turquoise shook her head. "No, I want to be the one to meet him when he gets out." She turned and went into her room to dress, her heart beating hard. Rio might not want to feel obligated to the Durangos, but she was afraid to leave him in jail any longer. She had seen the black bruises and cuts on his face that the jailers had surely put there.

She met with the banker and the lawyer who would take

care of the paperwork. By afternoon, she was standing in front of the courthouse as Rio walked out.

She ran to meet him. "Oh, darling, I've been so worried."

He took her in his arms and looked down at her. "How did you manage this? Was it the senator?"

She shook her head and kissed his face. "No, Trace Durango put the money up. He'll be in town Friday because his wife is coming in from Philadelphia Monday. That will give us a chance to talk to his lawyer and mount a defense."

He held her to him. "I don't like being beholden to anyone."

"I know." She took his hand and they walked toward her buggy. "You're proud, but everyone needs help now and then. It's all going to work out. You'll see."

He helped her up into the buggy, got in, and took the reins. "I don't see how it can, Turquoise. I'm poorer than I was, with the loss of the barn and all that hay and tack."

They started down the road. "It doesn't matter," she said and smiled. "We'll make it somehow."

"Easy for you to say," he muttered. "I can't ask Trace for your hand now, not with me being so poor and a murder charge hanging over my head. The gringos are determined to hang me."

She sighed. He was so stubborn. "So what do you intend to do?"

He shrugged and stared straight ahead as he drove. "I reckon I'll work twice as hard as a blacksmith to try to pay Senor Durango back. I can't think any further ahead than that."

"Oh." She fell silent, realizing just how serious this was going to be. Rio was a proud man. She looked at his big, strong hands on the reins and thought the four-leaf clover tattoo hadn't brought him much luck.

They drove in silence back to his ranch. The farrier's shed looked pretty small, she thought, and so did the house.

The barn was now only a pile of ashes. The Mexican hired man came off the porch and started walking toward them, grinning. Tip came running and barking, his stubby tail wagging.

Rio sighed. "This is the worst part," he said to Turquoise. "I'll have to let my hired hand go."

"I still love you," she whispered and put her hand on his arm as he stepped down from the buggy.

He turned and looked up at her. "And damn it, I still love you. I can't help it." He reached up and pulled her face down in a passionate embrace, kissing her fiercely.

She looked into his eyes. "We'll make it work somehow."

He shook his head. "I'm afraid it's too much for us, sweet one. Now go back to Fern's house and wait for Trace to arrive day after tomorrow."

"We might run away to Mexico, where the law can't get you," she suggested.

"So you could live in a mud hut and eat tortillas and beans?" He shook his head. "I love you too much to do that to you. Besides, I'm an honest man and I've got to pay your guardian back."

The hired man was almost to them now, grinning with snaggled teeth. "Hey, amigo, I missed you."

Turquoise nodded to them and turned her buggy, starting back to Fern's house. She felt helpless, not sure what to do next. Maybe she should have told Rio she had recognized the dead man, but that would only cause Rio to go after the senator and make things worse. She had to do something to help, but what?

Late that afternoon, a well-known local grocer, Clegg, showed up at Edwin's office.

"You fool!" Edwin snapped. "Didn't I tell you and

the others not to come here? I don't want anyone to connect us."

"Please, Senator, I'm begging you," the balding, mild-mannered man said. "You forced me to help burn that barn because I owe you money I can't pay, but I didn't realize there'd be a killing."

Edwin shrugged. "What about the other two?"

The man looked like he might weep. "We're all upstanding citizens and we never would have gotten involved if we hadn't been blackmailed or had our notes called by you. Now, if anyone finds out who we are—"

"They won't."

"Nelson is so upset, he's thinking about confessing to his congregation."

"What?" Edwin lit a fine cigar. "Tell him if he does, I'll tell them about his arrest back in Des Moines twenty-five years ago."

"His wife would leave him over that."

"Then tell him to keep his prayers and his confessions to himself."

"If word gets out Watson was involved, he'll probably lose his dry-goods business."

Edwin sighed. "Tell him to remember that."

"But we didn't know anyone would get killed and now it looks like we'll have to testify in court. Commit perjury."

Edwin smiled. "I don't think it'll ever come to trial. Knowing that stupid vaquero, he'll probably try to escape and head for Mexico."

"You think so?" The balding man looked relieved.

Edwin nodded and stood up. "Now get out of here and you three keep your mouths shut."

The other licked his dry lips. "I'm worried. You know that old Texas saying: 'What goes around comes around and your sins will find you out.'"

Edwin cursed, then threw back his head and laughed.

"Nonsense. Surely you aren't naive enough to believe that some old bearded guy who calls himself God is going to come down from the sky to mete out justice? That's superstitious hogwash."

"I don't know about that. Sometimes—"

"Now get out of here and you three take a nice vacation to Dallas or Kansas City. There's not going to be any trouble as long as you stick by your stories."

"All right." The man seemed uncertain, but he left.

"Damn all these weak people and their consciences." Edwin took one more puff and tossed the fine cigar in the brass spittoon. No, he couldn't have anyone testifying; he might not be able to depend on them. What he would do was have the sheriff arrange a fake jail break, and wouldn't it be too bad if that Mexican got shot as he escaped? That would wrap everything up neatly.

About that time, there was a knock at the door and Elmer stuck his head in.

"What is it you want?" Edwin sat down behind his big desk.

"Sheriff Barnes came by while you were in conference. He said you might like to know that Mexican got bailed out."

"What? Who? Never mind, I can guess. Now get out of here, I'm busy," Edwin snapped.

He stared out the window and tried to plan. So the Durangos must have come through with the bail money. But the Durangos didn't have the legal power here in Austin that Edwin did. That still involved a trial. Damn it.

Now where would that Mexican bastard go after he got out of jail? Back to his ranch, of course.


Late that afternoon, Edwin drove to the Boxing Ring, a seedy saloon in the worst part of town, and entered through the side door. The unshaven, scarred owner nodded to him and quickly ushered him into a back room. "I'm honored, Senator, to—"

"Shut up, Hamilton." Edwin frowned. "I need some really tough hombres."

The other nodded. "I got 'em: Brown and Gilbert."

"I'll pay good and in cash."

"Okay. What do you want us to do?"

He leaned toward the muscular man. "You used to be a boxer, didn't you?"

"Yep. Fifty fights, almost got a crack at the big time. They called me 'the Hammer.'"

Edwin pulled out a wad of cash from his wallet and laid it on the scarred table. "I want you to get Brown and Gilbert and pay a call on an hombre for me."

The unshaven one didn't blink, only gathered up the money, whistling at the amount. "For this, you want we should kill him?"

"No, that might bring too much notice. I just want your mugs to pay him a little visit and encourage him to leave Austin, go back to Mexico where he belongs, but first I'm going to offer him a bribe. If that doesn't work, I'll let you know and you boys can deal with him." Quickly he told of his plan and the other man nodded.

Then Edwin slipped out of the saloon, went by his bank, and took out twenty-five thousand dollars in gold, then returned to his office, vastly pleased with himself. If the vaquero left town suddenly, the girl would think he didn't care about her and Edwin might have another chance.

Turquoise wouldn't be the first woman to be swayed by luxury and gifts. She could learn to love him, Edwin thought, and anyway, he wanted her enough for both of them. A May-December marriage could work out and he would smother her with gifts and adoration; anything to get her in his bed, to be his possession so that he could caress her, make love to her every night. There would be children and he would make her so happy that this poor Mexican cowboy would become only a faint memory, and eventually, she would forget about that vaquero completely.

Edwin stood up and smiled. Yes, this evening he would call on the Mexican himself, and if that didn't work, the toughs could deal with him.

Edwin pulled out his gold watch and looked at the time.

Elmer stuck his head in the door. "Can I leave now, Senator?"

"Sure. I'm ready to go home anyway. I think Mama is planning one of her soirees and she'll expect me to show up for that, dull as they are."

Edwin waited a few minutes, then walked down the empty halls and out to his buggy. It was growing dark as he drove out to the small ranch. A dog began to bark as he pulled up the road past the burned barn and the small horseshoeing shed and reined in in front of the adobe house.

"Who's there?" A big man with a rifle came out on the porch, accompanied by a little terrier, barking frantically.

"Call off the dog," Edwin called. "It's a friendly visit."

"Show your hands." He didn't put down the rifle, but he told the little mutt to hush and it lay down obediently.

Edwin picked up the carpet bag and stepped down, holding up both hands and smiling. "I don't carry a gun. I'm a law-abiding citizen."

He stepped toward Rio and the Mexican scowled. "Oh, it's you, Senator. What is it you want?"

"Where's your hired hands?" Edwin looked around.

"Only had one and I couldn't afford to keep him."

"Aren't you going to invite me in?" Edwin didn't want to make any fast moves. Most ranchers were good with a rifle.

"I reckon." The other man grudgingly lowered the gun. "What is it you want?"

Edwin walked up on the porch, still carrying the carpet bag. "I've come to do you a favor."

"When a politician says he's going to do me a favor, I've learned he's probably going to raise my taxes or steal something." He opened the door and gestured Edwin to come in.

"I resent that," Edwin said, but he came into the humble house anyway and looked around. It was cozy and clean, but so small and humble, it depressed him. He tried to imagine his darling Turquoise here, but winced. She deserved a fine house and plenty of servants, which he intended to give her. He took a chair and waited for the other man to sit down.

Rio frowned at him, still holding the rifle. The little dog growled at him even though Edwin snapped his fingers at it. He really hated dogs.

"What is it you want?"

Edwin tried to smile like he did to the voters. "I heard you were having problems and since you're one of my constituents, I thought I'd try to help you."

"I voted for your opponent," Rio said and didn't smile.

"That's okay. I'm very well-off, so they say, and I heard you had financial difficulties and thought I might help you out."

"Why?" Rio didn't smile and rested the rifle against the wall next to him.

"I thought you might want to make a fresh start and get away to Mexico while you still can."

"You mean, jump bail, turn tail, and run?"

"Well, if you want to put it that way," Edwin stuttered. "Surely, man, you know you haven't got much of a chance with an Anglo jury. I'm prepared to give you enough money to live comfortably down in Mexico. I brought it with me."

He shrank back under Rio's cold stare. "And you would do this why?"

"Because I'm soft-hearted and I don't want to see you hang."

"I don't believe you," Rio snapped.

"Look." Edwin opened the carpet bag. "I've got the money to prove it. All you have to do is take it, pack up, and be gone by morning and not tell anyone you're leaving. You'll get a whole new life over the border, plenty of beer and cantina whores."

Rio shook his head and stood up. "Sorry, there's a woman who holds me here in Texas. Besides, I'm not one to run from trouble."

Now Edwin was angry and he stood up, too. "Look, let's call a spade a spade. I'm in love with Turquoise Sanchez and I can offer her everything you can't: a life of luxury and privilege. Why, she'll probably end up as first lady of Texas."

Rio didn't say anything for a long moment, slowly nodding. "So that's it. You want to pay me to leave so you can have her."

"You must admit it would be better for both of you." Edwin was pleading now. "It would save you from hanging and she would gradually forget you and marry me. You don't have anything to offer her."

"You're right about that." Rio looked sad. "It's selfish of me to want her. I have nothing to offer but my undying love and devotion. You can give her all those things she craved since she was small: social status, respectability, a big house."

"So you'll do it?" Edwin held out the carpet bag.

Rio smiled without mirth and shook his head. "In the first place, Senator, if I jump bail, Trace Durango, who trusts me, will lose ten thousand dollars and I'm too honorable to do that to him."

"There's enough here to pay him back and still enough

for you to live like a king down in Mexico." He held out the carpet bag.

Rio stared at the bag but he didn't take it. "True, you can give her more than I can, but if you'll remember, Senator, we just fought a war over whether one man can buy and sell other people. I can't be bought and I'm not sure Turquoise can be bought, either."

"Of course she can!" Edwin's voice raised. "All women can be bought with wealth and trinkets. She'd be mine if you left town."

"I think you underestimate her, Senator. I would bet my life that Turquoise has changed and that you can't buy her. Now get out of my house and take your suitcase full of money with you." He opened the door and glared at the shorter man. "You heard me, get out!"

"You'll regret this," Edwin growled, clutching his bag of gold coins. He didn't quite understand this cowboy. Rio was poor, but he was refusing money. Honor was something a poor cowboy couldn't afford. He brushed past the big man and strode across the porch to his buggy.

"Get off my ranch before I shoot you," Rio yelled behind him and Edwin hurried his steps, hopped into his buggy, whipped up the startled black horse, and took off down the road at a fast pace.

When Edwin looked back, Rio stood on the porch glaring after him, rifle in hand, little spotted dog by his side.

"All right," Edwin grumbled under his breath as he drove away, "I gave you a chance to clear out, but no, you were too stubborn. Now I'll make you wish you had taken my deal."

When his henchmen got through with that Mexican, Rio would wish he'd never been born.


Rio spent a sleepless night trying to figure out what to do. He awoke early, made some strong coffee, and dressed.

No matter what happened, he needed to earn some money. He walked down to his little blacksmith shop and built up the forge fire, began to work. He had broken wheels and plows to mend, horses coming in later to be shod. Besides, working kept his mind off his problems.

Rio worked hard all day, delighting in the toil that kept his body and his mind busy. As twilight came on, he lit a lantern and continued to pound hot iron and shape it. He half-hoped, half-dreaded the fact that Turquoise might come by. The situation had not changed except that he was out on bail and could hold her and make love to her now. The thought of her warm embrace and soft mouth came to him and he sighed. She had ruined him for all other women.

He was intent on his work when he thought he heard a horse whinny. It didn't sound like one of his. Tip had been asleep on the dirt floor next to him and now the dog raised its head and growled. Rio stared out into the blackness of the night past his dim lantern glow, finally deciding it was just a passing buggy.

"Go back to sleep, Tip," he told the little dog and returned to his work, the sound of his hammer cloaking any other sounds.

Abruptly Tip was up and barking frantically even as a man's voice behind him said, "Drop that hammer and don't turn around."

Instinctively, Rio turned, bringing the hammer up as a weapon, but now there were several men and one of them cracked him across the head with a rifle butt. Dizzy and half-blinded, he stumbled and fought as Tip barked and barked and then heard the dog yip as someone kicked it.

"My dog! Damn you! Don't hurt my dog!" He staggered, but in the darkness, he couldn't see his attackers except he knew they were big. One hit him again and the hammer dropped from his limp hand. When he came to, they were tying him up. He tried to get a look at their faces, but one voice said, "Put a gunnysack over his head quick, you idiots!"

He was so dizzy, he thought he would pass out. He couldn't see Tip anywhere and he tried to break free, but the men's sheer weight took him to his knees. He fought as hard as he could but they tied his hands to his sides and now a sack over his head blocked out his sight. The sack smelled of dust and old grain and his head ached. He could feel something warm running down his forehead and wondered if it were blood. "What do you bastards want? I don't have any money."

That man laughed and said, "That's not what we're after." To the others, he snapped, "Spill the coal oil on everything. We'll set fire to the place after I'm finished with him."

"No!" Rio tried to fight again, but they had his legs tied together. This business and his house were all he had left and he'd fight to the death to protect them.

He could smell the coal oil now being splashed around the shop. "Why are you doing this? I got no quarrel with—"

The men only laughed and one man said, "Stand him on his feet and drag him to the anvil. I've got my orders. Untie his right hand and put it up there—yes, that one with the clover tattoo. We'll see how lucky it is for him."

Rio cursed and fought, but they forced his hand up on the anvil, spreading it out.

"Now," said the rough voice, "before you burn to death, I have a personal message for you."

What? Who hated him this much? Even as he thought that, he heard the swish of a hammer coming down full force on his hand and the agony of the blow. He couldn't stop himself from crying out.

"That's good," said his attacker with a laugh. "It's broken. He'll be crippled for life, or at least the few minutes he has left. Let's get out of here, men."

They let go of him and Rio collapsed on the dirt floor of the shoeing shed. His hand must be broken because it felt on fire and his bloody head throbbed. He lay there, only half-conscious, and heard someone strike a match.

"Let's go!" the man yelled and Rio heard the sound of running feet and the rush of flames followed by the sound of horses' hooves as they galloped away.

He smelled smoke and heard the crackle of fire. He knew he had to get out of here or burn to death. He rolled over on his belly and tried to crawl, but his broken hand shrieked with pain every time he put it out in front of him. He wasn't even sure which way to go. Rio felt the heat of the blaze as the shed began to burn, but he managed to reach up and jerk the sack off his head. The shed was lit only by the flames licking up the walls. With his broken hand, he tried to untie his legs and it sent shots of pain up his arm. He thought for a moment he might faint, but he knew if he did, he would certainly burn to death.

His legs were only partly untied, his broken hand already swelling and turning black. He gritted his teeth and dragged himself toward the open shed door, choking and coughing on the black, acrid smoke that made him dizzy. "Holy Mary, Mother of God," he prayed, "is this the way I must die?"

And abruptly cool air seemed to blow toward him, reviving him and giving him a new will to live along the dirt floor toward the open door. Every inch was agony, pulling himself with his swollen hand and his encumbered legs. Above him, the roof was on fire now and he knew that any minute, the roof would cave in, burying him in a pile of fiery boards that would roast him alive.

Then a wet nose brushed his face and a wet tongue licked his face. "Tip! They didn't kill you after all. We've got to get out of here, boy."

He began to crawl again toward the life-giving air, the dog whimpering and running around him.

Then from outside, he heard a woman screaming, "Rio, Rio, are you in there?"

It must be an angel's voice. Maybe he was already dead and didn't realize it.

"Rio? Where are you?" No, it was Turquoise's voice. He crawled toward it. Then she was beside him, grabbing his arm and pulling him toward the door.

"For God's sake, get out of here!" he shouted at her. "The roof's about to go!"

"Not without you!" she shrieked and pulled even harder.

She was going to die, too, unless he managed to get out. That gave him renewed strength and he dug his nails into the dirt and crawled even though his broken hand sent waves of agony up his arm and through his whole body as he did so.

"Come on," Turquoise urged, "it's only a little bit farther."

Half dragging, half crawling, he moved toward the open door. The air around them both was as hot as the breath of hell. Behind them, part of the roof collapsed.

"Get out, Turquoise. Take Tip with you!"

She ignored him and kept dragging his big body toward the door.

He had to get out; he had to keep her from dying with him. He gritted his teeth, ignored his hurting hand, and crawled. Rio took a gulp of cool air just as the rest of the roof began to collapse behind him. "Look out!" he shouted and managed to stumble to his feet. With the dog running ahead of them, the two of them fell out the door and onto the grass as the roof crashed down with a roar and a shower of sparks.

Between them, they stumbled away from the burning building and Rio collapsed on the cool grass, Tip whimpering and licking his cheek. Turquoise ran to the pump, came back with a dipper of cold water to splash on his blistered face, and then brought another for him to drink. He shared it with Tip, who didn't seem to be hurt. Rio sighed, lying on the ground watching the shed burn, lighting up the dark night. Finally he sat up and she untied his legs.

Turquoise ran back to get another dipper of water, put it in his right hand, and he cried out and dropped it.

"Oh, dear God, what's happened to you?"

"Night riders," he gasped, "attacked me and set a fire."

"Don't talk," she commanded as she ran back to the pump for another dipper of water and held it to his lips. He drank deeply. "Why? Why would they do this?"

He shook his aching head. "I have no idea, but I reckon I can guess."

"Who?"

He shook his head again. He wasn't about to tell her who he thought was responsible. It would only add to the problems. "I—I think there were three of them. I don't know what they wanted."

Abruptly she seemed to see his right hand. "Oh my Lord, Rio, your hand—"

He looked down at it. It was swollen and purple. He tried to flex it and had to bite his lip to keep from screaming in pain. It might be doubtful if he could ever use it again. "One of them took a hammer to it."

"What beasts!" Turquoise cried. "How cruel."

He shook his head. "You think you can help me get up to the house?"

"Lean on me." She helped him to his feet and he put his arm around her shoulders. "I'll take care of you."

They hobbled through the cool night to the house, Tip running after them. Rio's head still throbbed and his hand felt like it was on fire. "I'm lucky you decided to come by," he admitted, "after I told you to stay away from me."

"I couldn't do that. I love you," she whispered.

"But nothing's changed," he gasped as they went up the steps and into the little house. "I'm still going to be tried for murder and now I'm maimed, maybe for life. I won't be able to work."

"You don't know that. I'm sure Trace Durango will help you. He's due in town soon."

She sat him down in a chair and he leaned back and sighed, then looked at his injured hand. "Couldn't just kill me, had to break my hand. I'm worse than poor, Turquoise, now I'm crippled."

She took his swollen hand between her two small ones and kissed it tenderly. "You can still sit on a horse and run a ranch," she said, "and I still love you."

There was no point in trying to send her away. His soul wasn't strong enough to do that even though it would be best for her.

"Here," she said, "I'm going to soak your hand in cold water. Maybe that will bring the swelling down. Then I'll put some liniment on it and wrap it."

Even as she fussed over him, he leaned over and kissed the top of her head.

She looked up at him. "I knew you didn't mean it."

"God help me, I should," he gasped. "This is not the life for you."

"Let me decide that." She reached to kiss him and he put his one good arm around her, pulling her close. "You need to get some rest."

"Rest?" he snapped. "How can I rest? All I can think of is revenge." He started to get up, but she pulled him down.

"You're no good tonight with a bloody head and a busted hand. I'm going to put you to bed and you've got to let that hand heal. Besides, you said you couldn't identify them."

"I've got to do something." He looked at his throbbing hand as she wrapped it. "They might come back."

"I'll stand watch."

"Can you shoot?"

She hesitated. "A rifle, maybe. I've shot a rifle a few times, but never a pistol."

"I don't even own a pistol." He stifled a moan. "I'm no good to you, Turquoise. I can't even take care of you."

"I don't care. I love you anyway. Now let me put you to bed." She pulled him to his feet and led him to the bedroom.

He sat down heavily on the edge of the bed and she pulled his boots off. "Now lie down."

"My hand's throbbing like hell," he complained.

"I'll get you some whiskey. Then I'll raise your hand up on a pillow and maybe it won't hurt so much."

"What if they come back?" he muttered.

She found the whiskey and held the bottle to his lips. "I doubt they'll return tonight, knowing the fire might bring some curious onlookers."

He seemed to be drifting off to sleep. "I can't protect you if they return."

"I'll stand guard," she said and got his rifle from where it leaned in a corner. "I think I can shoot well enough to scare them off."

"Blow out the lamp," he murmured. "You don't want to be a target."

She blew out the lamp and sat down on the bed, leaning the rifle against the post. She stroked his forehead. "Just relax," she whispered. "Everything will be all right."

"If you stay here all night," he said, "Fern's father will tell your guardian—"

"I told Fern to cover for me," she said, snuggling down against him. "I just knew you were in some kind of trouble."

He leaned over and kissed her cheek. "You're the damnedest woman I ever met."

"That's why you like me," she said with a grin.

He stared into her pale eyes in the moonlight that filtered

through the window. He hadn't told her about Edwin Forester's visit, when he'd offered a bribe to get Rio to go to Mexico. "I—I suspect the senator might be involved."

"Tonight?" She shook her head. "Why, he came by the Lessup place this evening, brought me some flowers, and stayed a couple of hours to visit, even though I had told him we were finished. He's not one to take no for an answer."

Rio leaned back and closed his eyes, not saying anything. He was almost certain the senator was behind the night raid. Forester's visit to the Lessup ranch might have been to establish an alibi. Tomorrow Rio intended to confront him. "Turquoise, listen to Tip. He'll let you know if there's anyone lurking about."

"Stop worrying," she whispered and reached to brush his black hair away from his smudged face. "Tip and I can take care of things. You get some sleep."

She could see he was trying to keep his eyes open, but soon, he dropped off into a fitful slumber.

With Rio asleep, she felt alone and scared. She took the rifle and moved to a window where she could watch the front of the adobe house. Tip lay down next to her and she patted the dog's ears. If anything moved out there, she intended to kill it. She would do anything to protect the man she loved.

# Chapter 15

As soon as Turquoise drove away at dawn, Rio attempted to clean himself up. He felt groggy and sick and his swollen hand throbbed like a drum. When he looked in the little mirror over the wash bowl, he had dark circles under his eyes and purple bruises and cuts on his rugged face. As he washed with his one good hand, he mused about last night and thought about who could have planned the attack. Only one answer came to him: Senator Edwin Forester.

When he had failed to bribe Rio to flee to Mexico, Forester had called in henchmen to try to maim and kill him. The longer Rio thought about it, the more angry he became. It was time for a showdown.

Turquoise had fried some ham and eggs for him and made a pot of strong coffee. She had also admonished him to stay in bed and rest today and she would check on him later.

Well, that wasn't going to happen. He managed to pull on his clothes and stumble out to saddle Peso. It was difficult with one hand bandaged, but Rio was a stubborn man. He rode into town, down Congress Avenue to the state capitol. As he was tying his horse to the hitching post, he saw Edwin Forester coming down the capitol steps, surrounded by newsmen. Rio listened a split second. The interest seemed to have something to do with some bill the senator was going to present to the legislators next session.

Rio took the steps two at a time and pushed through the crowd. "Forester, we need to talk."

The senator waved airily, not even looking at him. "Do make an appointment with my secretary for Wednesday. That's when I see my constituents."

Rio caught his arm. "No, we need to talk now."

The other men, seeming to hear the anger in his voice, melted back away from the senator.

Edwin Forester really looked at him this time, staring in disbelief with his cold eyes. "I doubt we have anything to discuss." He shouldered his way past Rio. "Now if you'll excuse me—"

"Damn it! You will talk to me!" Rio grabbed Forester's shoulder with his good hand and spun the man around as the others watched in wide-eyed shock. "I ought to kill you for everything you've done to me!"

The senator stumbled backward. "My good man, you must be mistaken—"

"No, I'm not!" Rio roared. "We're going to have this out."

In the background, he heard someone whisper, "Better call the law."

Forester blinked. "Am I to understand you want to do me bodily harm?"

"You damn betcha!" Without thinking, Rio swung with his swollen right hand, clipping the senator across the face. The senator managed to keep his balance, but blood trickled out of the corner of his mouth and the blow reverberated all the way up Rio's arm. For a moment, he staggered and clenched his teeth at the pain.

The crowd gasped but the senator kept his cool demeanor and faced Rio with a thin smile. "I'm not even sure who you are."

"The hell you aren't!" Rio moved in closer. Two reporters grabbed him and held him back.

Very slowly, the senator pulled out a monogrammed handkerchief and wiped the blood from his thin lips. "Are you challenging me to a duel?"

"A duel?" Rio hesitated, dizzy with pain. "*Si,* I reckon I am."

Edwin Forester drew himself up proudly, looked around, and addressed the crowd. "You all are witnesses. This crazed person has challenged me to a duel."

One of the reporters said, "Surely you aren't serious, sir? Dueling has been outlawed for forty years."

"Why don't you just let the sheriff jail him for assault and battery?" suggested another.

"No." Forester shook his head. "My honor has been impugned as a man and as a Texan. We all know dueling is against the law, but Texans still fight them occasionally." He faced Rio. "As the challenged party, I get to choose the weapons and I own a fine set of dueling pistols."

"Dueling pistols?" Rio felt as confused as the crowd looking at him.

"Are you a yellow-bellied coward?" The other man wiped his bloody mouth again. "If so, you should apologize and—"

"Damned if I will!" Rio shouted. "Pistols suit me!"

The reporters pressed forward, intent on the new drama. "Senator, you're going to fight a duel? Don't you remember that your father—"

"Of course I remember." Edwin smiled without humor. "I'm sure none of you will tell the law, because you'll want to attend." A murmur of agreement from the crowd and a whisper went around the circle that the senator was more of a man than most of them had given him credit for.

Rio glared at him. "Just tell me where and when."

The senator sniffed disdainfully. "Our seconds can set that up."

"Our what?"

"I really shouldn't be dueling a social inferior," the senator said. "By custom, I am supposed to thrash you with my cane."

At that, Rio went for him again. Two men caught him and pulled him away as he shouted, "This society bastard sent men to burn down my barn and business and busted my hand. Look at it!" He held up the swollen, bandaged hand.

The senator scowled. "You Mexican trash. How dare you accuse me of something so vile? I could sue you for libel, but instead, we'll duel."

"I told you to tell me when and where."

"Very well. Since you don't even seem to know what a second is, I'll set this up. Under the big oaks down by the river Monday evening at dusk. Tuesday is July Fourth and there'll be so many firecrackers and rockets going off the day before, no one will notice if they hear pistol shots."

This was Thursday. Rio realized abruptly that he had four days to learn about dueling. "I'll be there."

"Fine." The senator stuck a fine cigar in his mouth. "I'll bring the pistols."

Rio turned to leave, striding down the capitol steps. Behind him, he heard the newsmen peppering the politician with questions about the duel.

One newsman ran to catch up with him. "Mister, are you loco?"

"I don't think so. Why?"

"You don't know that Senator Forester is considered an extraordinary pistol shot?"

So of course that was why Forester had chosen pistols, Rio thought. Rio was pretty good with a rifle, but he'd never even seen a dueling pistol. "I can take care of myself," he muttered and strode back to his horse, then rode out. His broken hand throbbed, but he rode to Fern's ranch anyhow and dismounted as dogs ran out, barking a greeting.

"Hello. Anyone home?"

The front door opened and Fern and Turquoise came through the door.

Turquoise looked anxious. "How are you?"

"Fine, I reckon."

Fern looked him over curiously. "That hand looks bad, worse than Turquoise said."

Turquoise turned to Fern. "I think maybe Rio and I need to talk."

Apparently reluctant, Fern returned to the house.

Rio tied up his horse. "I've got to tell you something." He had to fight the urge to take her in his arms, but he must not think of that now.

Turquoise looked up at him. She waited for him to hold out his arms to her, waited for him to say that he'd been wrong and they could make a go of it. Otherwise, why had he come? "You haven't come to say good-bye, have you?"

He shook his head. "I'm not leaving town, if that's what you think."

Gently, she took his bandaged hand between her two small ones. "Whoever did this may burn your house next." She stepped closer, looking up at him, seeing the pain in his dark eyes and the sadness.

"By God, I'll go down fighting. I'm certain Edwin Forester is behind all this."

"Edwin? I can't imagine he'd have the nerve to—"

"He hired bullies to do his dirty work."

"The trouble is, you can't prove it." She sighed. "And he's got important friends."

"And he's determined to have you." Rio's voice was bitter.

"Must we discuss this again?" Her voice rose. "I told you, I've made my choice."

"Can we find a place to sit and talk?" Rio looked toward the house.

She turned and saw Fern's curious face peeking out from behind the curtains. "Sure. There's a small grove of trees with a swing over to the left of the house."

They walked there slowly and sat down in the swing. The silence was awkward, no sound except the creak of the swing.

"How's your hand?"

He shrugged. "I reckon it's broken. I'll probably never have full use of it again."

"Have you seen a doctor?"

He hesitated, not wanting to tell her he didn't have the money. "There's not much that can be done except bandage it up and wait to see."

"Doesn't it hurt?"

He lied, shaking his head. "No, it's all right. But I'll admit I had a hard time getting dressed and saddling my horse."

She smiled up at him. "You're as independent as a hog on ice. You'll manage."

"A one-handed vaquero," he said ruefully. "Yeah, I'll manage to run a ranch, all right."

"You could with some help," she said.

Rio shook his head. "He said I was Mexican trash and I reckon he's right."

"Who said that?" she demanded.

"Senator Forester. We had a run-in on the capitol steps less than an hour ago."

Her lovely face went ashen. "Oh God. What happened?"

"I went after him, just wanting to knock that superior grin off his face, and it's turned into a duel."

"A duel?" She looked incredulous. "No one fights duels anymore."

"Apparently in upper society, they still do. It's pistols at sundown."

"Oh my God, when?" She buried her face in her hands.

"Monday, under the big oaks by the river."

There were tears in her eyes that she couldn't hold back as she slowly raised her head. "I hear Edwin is a good shot with a pistol."

He shook his head. "I can't help that and I sure wasn't gonna back down."

"Your pride's going to kill you," she gasped.

"Look, Turquoise, I'm a Texan and a proud one." He put his hand on her shoulder. "I couldn't knuckle under, and even if I was a good shot, I'd be in a spot with my right hand broken."

She began to cry. "That clever rascal has set you up to kill you in front of witnesses."

"I reckon he has."

"Isn't there anything that can be done? Why don't you just not show up?" she implored him.

"And let him think I'm a coward? Turquoise, no man can call himself a man if he turns tail and runs when another man challenges him—especially a Texan."

"Men and their damned pride." She laid her face against his chest without thinking and he stroked her hair.

"Maybe I'll get lucky. Maybe he'll have an off day."

"You think Edwin would have accepted the challenge if he'd thought he couldn't win?"

"I've still got four days to learn."

She looked up suddenly. "I know someone who's the best in Texas with a pistol, Trace Durango, and he's due in on the train tomorrow morning. Maybe he can teach you."

"Not fast enough." Rio shook his head. "Well, maybe he'll at least be my second. That's what the senator says we both need. I'm not sure what they're supposed to do."

"This is a nightmare," Turquoise said, sobbing. "I just can't stand by and watch Edwin coldly shoot you down."

He pulled her close. "Turquoise, you are not to come to this."

"You can't keep me from it. I'm my own woman."

"You're my woman and I'm ordering you not to come. If I'm killed, I don't want you to be there. If I live, I'll see you Monday night and then we'll celebrate the Fourth together."

She looked up at him, tears running down her face. "I've got to do something. I can't just wait for you to get shot down."

"You can wish me luck." He took her small face in both his hands and kissed her lips very gently.

She clung to him. "So that's it? I just wait for you to go honorably to your death?"

"You don't have much faith in my shooting."

"You told me yourself you were good with a rifle, but not with a handgun. And this time, you'll have to shoot left-handed."

"I've got to go." He pulled her close. "What time does Trace's train get in tomorrow?"

"Early. That doesn't give him much time to teach you. His wife is due in on the train from Philadelphia late Monday afternoon."

"Good, then you can meet her train and give yourself something to do until this is over."

"You think I can go have tea and cookies and make small talk while you two are trying to kill each other down by the river?" She was almost hysterical.

He kissed the tears from her eyes. "Please don't cry. I warned you I'd bring you nothing but unhappiness and misery and that we didn't have a chance at a future."

"Let me decide that." She reached up to kiss him and his mouth was hot and seeking the depths of hers as his good hand went to stroke her breasts, making her breathless with her own need. She clung to him a long moment. "Rio, I love you so."

"You'll get over me if you must." He shook his head. "You need to find someone better, Turquoise, some hombre who can give you social position, all that respectability you crave."

"You're all I crave," she insisted. "When I'm away from you, I think of nothing else but being in your arms, having your hot kisses on my bare skin."

"Forget me." He stood up. "My four-leaf clover hasn't brought me any luck. I'm doomed to die early like my father. Maybe the senator is right: I'm just a half-Mexican bastard who doesn't deserve happiness."

"That's not true."

"If the senator wins the duel, he'll beg to marry you and you can end up as first lady of all Texas."

"Marry him with your blood on his hands? Damn it, no! I'd rather be your woman and live in an adobe hut than be Forester's first lady."

He kissed the tip of her nose. "I'll meet Trace's train and see if he can teach me anything. You stay away from me until this is over. You distract me too much." He turned and strode away.

She started to call after him, but what good would it do? He was determined to fight this duel, even though he had almost no chance of winning. Men and their damned honor.

She watched him leave and then she took a deep breath and wiped her eyes. She must not let the Lessup family know what was going on. She didn't know if Fern's father might try to stop the duel, but the coming together of these two stallions in battle was inevitable and if it weren't

Monday night, it would be some other time. It was point-
less to interfere. And yet, she must do something.

She went inside and did not answer much to Fern's curiosity. Her night was sleepless. The next day, she put on
her best turquoise dress with a wide-brimmed hat, perfumed herself, borrowed Fern's buggy, and drove out to the
capitol.

Rio had told her not to interfere, but she had to try. She
couldn't let her lover be shot down in cold blood. With her
heart beating hard, she tied up her buggy and walked
toward the senator's office.

Elmer looked over his spectacles in surprise.

She pasted a smile on her face. "Tell the senator Miss
Sanchez is here to see him."

The secretary nodded and disappeared into the inner
office. In a moment, he returned. "The senator will see you."

What was she going to do? Beg Edwin to call off the
duel? Ask him not to show up? Ask him to deliberately
miss when he took his shot? She wasn't sure herself.

As she entered the office, the senator rose and rushed
toward her. "Turquoise, my dear, to what do I have the
honor of this unexpected visit?"

As always, he wore an expensive suit and a flower in his
buttonhole. It was a pink rosebud. That meant he was still
thinking of her.

She let him take her hands. "I—I have been rethinking
things, Edwin."

He smiled. "I knew you would come to your senses.
With me, you would live like a queen."

She sighed and turned away. "Well, not if you get killed
in some silly duel I hear you're involved in."

"Oh, you've heard about that?" Now his voice was
guarded. "If you're worried about my safety, my dear, don't.
I am an excellent shot."

She turned back toward him. "But isn't this sort of thing bad for your reputation? I mean, isn't it against the law?"

He laughed. "Maybe, but you know Texans. They'll vote for the kind of real man who'd go toe to toe in a shootout."

She winced at the thought. "Edwin, I don't think I could marry a man who would coldly shoot down another this way."

"Oh, I see." His voice was cold. "So is your concern for me or for the other man?"

She looked at him directly. "What difference does it make if I'm willing to end up in your bed?"

"Hmmm." He nodded. "I don't know whether to call you a shrewd businesswoman or a scheming little slut."

"Again, what difference does it make if I end up in your bed?"

He seemed to be picturing that in his mind. "You tempt me. You know how much I want you. There's just something about you, Turquoise, something I can't seem to put my finger on that draws me to you. You're enchanting, bewitching."

"Then you'll forgo this duel?"

"Does that greasy Mexican vaquero really mean that much to you?"

"I—I don't want any blood spilled, that's all."

"So if I call off this duel, you'll marry me?"

She didn't look at him, imagining herself naked in his arms, letting him kiss and caress her naked body in his grand, silk-sheeted bed. "Yes. We'll have to elope, of course, because you know my guardian won't stand for it."

He laughed wickedly. "If we're already married in the church and the marriage is consummated, there's not much he can do about it."

She walked to the window and looked out at Congress Avenue. "Your mother will not be pleased if she can't have a gigantic social wedding."

Edwin walked up behind her and put his hands on her shoulders and kissed the back of her neck. "So she can put on the biggest reception this town ever saw. That will make her happy."

She felt his clammy fingers on her shoulders through her thin turquoise dress and tried not to shudder. Worse yet was the thought of moving into the Forester mansion with the Iron Lady as her mother-in-law. "I'd better go. You probably have work to do."

"Don't you want me to take you out and buy you the biggest diamond ring in Texas?"

"Not today." She shook her head. "We'll talk later."

"All right, my dear."

She turned around and he tried to take her in his arms and kiss her, but she pulled back, turning her cheek, and he kissed her there. "I can hardly wait for our wedding night," he gasped.

"Please, Edwin, you embarrass me."

He laughed. "You are a prim little thing after all."

Prim? What would he have thought if he had seen her with Rio, clawing his back and bucking under him? Even now, her body ached for the virile vaquero, but she would do anything, even let this man mount her and enjoy her nubile body, to save Rio's life.

"Look, my darling, I can't promise to call off the duel," he said. "To do so would cause me to lose face with all the voters, especially after a dozen or so heard me accept his challenge on the courthouse steps."

"Then what—"

"Maybe I could miss or fix the pistols so they misfire. A man doesn't actually have to kill the other in a duel. He only has to go through the motions to show his bravery."

"But suppose something goes wrong?" she asked.

"Let me show you." He walked over to his desk and opened the bottom drawer, then brought out a leather case.

"See? I own the finest pair of dueling pistols in the country. In fact, my father was killed with them." He scowled at the memory.

"In a duel?"

Edwin nodded. "It was a long time ago. I was a boy."

She looked at the pistols. They were beautiful; burnished brass and walnut grips, obviously very, very old. "Could you really fake this?"

He nodded. "For you, my love, I'll do it. I promise on my honor as a gentleman."

She sighed with relief. "Then as far as I'm concerned, you can make wedding plans. I promise I'll be a good wife to you, Edwin. We'll talk later," she said and fled his office, almost running past his secretary. She walked swiftly out of the building and got into the buggy. When she looked up, Edwin was staring at her through the window and he blew her kisses. She waved back and tried not to shudder.

What kind of devil's bargain had she just made? However, if it would save Rio's life, it would be worth it. A nagging thought haunted her as she drove away. Could she trust the senator to keep his end of the bargain?

Behind her, Edwin smiled as he put the dueling pistols back in the bottom drawer of his desk. He wanted that beauty in his bed enough to promise her anything. However, he could never claim her completely as long as that low-class Mexican lived. Edwin might have her body, but that vaquero would have her heart and soul.

Well, maybe having her body would be enough. He thought of her lush curves and took a deep, trembling breath. He was sure he could love her enough and spoil her enough that she would finally submit to becoming his wife, especially if he became governor or even president. No woman could turn down the chance for such prominence and wealth. They would have a good life with a house full of children and he would give her anything her heart desired.

Just what was he to do about Rio Kelly? If the man lived, Edwin's life would always be in danger, but just how could he kill Rio and still have Turquoise after the promise he had made? It was indeed a problem, but there had to be a way. To possess that very special woman, to have her obediently submitting to him in his bed was well worth anything Edwin had to do to get her.

# Chapter 16

Turquoise drove her buggy to Rio's ranch. He was feeding calves out in front of the burned barn. Tip ran to meet her, his stubby tail wagging.

Rio looked up at her and frowned. "I thought I told you I didn't want to see you again until this is over Monday night."

She didn't answer him. Instead she said, "Aren't you going to ask me to get down?" She looked at him, loving him, thinking it was worth anything to save his life.

"*Perdone,* I forget my manners." He came to the buggy, his right hand still swollen and wrapped in a soiled bandage.

He put his hands on her slim waist and she saw the slightest wince in his dark eyes as he started to lift her.

"Never mind, I can get down alone." She brushed away his hands and got herself down quickly.

He scowled. "I keep forgetting I'm only half a man now."

"You're more of a man than most will ever be."

"Damn it, I'm crippled. Who knows if I'll ever be any good as a vaquero again."

She put her hand on his muscular arm. "Your hand will recover somewhat. It just takes time."

He shrugged. "Time I haven't got. Have you heard anything more from your guardian?"

"No." She shook her head. "Don't worry. He's the best with a pistol. I know he's taught some of the best guns in Texas."

Rio looked down at his swollen hand. "A lot of good that will do me."

"Rio, my darling"—she looked up at him—"you don't have to fight this duel. Why don't you just call it off?"

"Do you joke?" He turned on her, dark eyes fierce. "And be the laughingstock of every hombre in Texas? No, of course I can't."

"What do you care what others think?"

"Because I'm a man and in Texas, to be able to walk proud and straight, bend my knee to no one, that's important. First and last, I'm a Texan."

"You're stubborn, but I love you." She reached up to kiss his suntanned cheek. He tasted of salt and wind and wildness.

"And I do it because I love you," he whispered against her mouth. "If I don't kill him and get him out of our lives for good, we will always be looking over our shoulders, expecting him to turn up." He kissed her then, deep and fierce and possessive. She was this Texan's woman and nothing could ever change that.

Turquoise clung to him as the kiss deepened and he put his tongue deep in her mouth, touching the tip of his tongue against hers until all she could do was hold onto him while his grasp tightened and she could feel her breast crushed against his hard body.

"I need you," he whispered. "*Dios,* I never knew I could want a woman like I want you. You're a fire in my blood, Turquoise."

"And you in mine." She brought her fingertips up to touch his rugged face and despite her best efforts, tears came to her eyes and he kissed them away.

"Do not worry, sweet one," he said as he brushed the dark curls away from her face. "I'm not such a bad shot. I might kill him."

She was weeping because of the devil's bargain she had made with Edwin, but she dared not tell Rio. "If you only wound him—"

"If I only wound him, he will not be finished with me. No, I will have to kill him."

"And if he only wounds you—"

"He will not be satisfied with only wounding me," Rio said against her cheek. "He knows that only killing me will stop me from getting my revenge sooner or later. No, he will have to kill me to stop looking over his shoulder for the rest of his life."

"But if he misses and you miss," she insisted, "then the rules of the duel will be satisfied and you can both walk away."

He shook his head. "You may think so, all Austin may think so, but both he and I know that one of us has to die to end this thing."

"And it started because of me." She turned away. "I feel so guilty."

He caught her arm and pulled her to him, his left hand stroking her throat and then working its way down to the V of her breasts. "It might have happened anyway. The senator likes to see people bow before him and I was never one to bend my knee. I am a proud man, Turquoise, and if I die Monday night, I will die proudly."

She took a deep, shuddering breath as his fingers caressed her breast and then the dark circle of her nipple. Indeed this was a proud man and if he knew of the bargain she had made with Edwin not to kill him, he would hate her, never speak to her again. However, it was worth it to her to have him alive, even if she never saw him, never made love to him again. "You torture me with your fingers," she said with a sigh.

"But it is a sweet torture, no?" His fingers did not stop what they were doing.

She closed her eyes and let him stroke both her breasts intimately, possessively, as if they belonged to him without question.

"I wish I could know that someday, these would feed my sons," he whispered against her ear, "and I would give you many."

But that could not be, even if he survived Monday night, she knew, but she pushed that thought from her mind. She was going to exchange his life for sharing Edwin's bed, but that was not now and she didn't want to think past now. "Make love to me," she asked.

"That I can do," he said with a chuckle. "It's only my hand that is injured. Let's go up to the house."

She led her buggy horse as they walked up to the small adobe dwelling.

"This is not nearly good enough for a princess like you," he said as they tied up the horse and walked up the steps.

"Let me decide that," she answered, but her mind was in turmoil with what Rio had said. Yes, he was right; one man must kill the other or there was no end to this thing. Like two wild stallions fighting to possess a mare, it could not end without one of them dead or badly injured. Surely Edwin must know this, as did Rio. Why had she refused to see that, thinking that she could trust Edwin to miss his shot?

Inside the small adobe house, he reached to unbutton the bodice of her dress, then pull away the lace beneath. "I like to look at you," he said.

Instinctively, she covered her breasts with her hands but he caught them and pulled them away.

"Now your turn," he whispered and she reached up and

slowly unbuttoned the denim shirt that hid his big, muscular chest. It was brown with sun and scarred with cantina fights and barbed wire.

She ran her finger around the circle of his nipples and his nipples abruptly stood out and he groaned. She bent her head and kissed him there and he caught her dark head, tangling his fingers in her glossy curls, and held her face against his chest. "Bite me," he pleaded. "Bite me there."

She obliged and his feverish hands pulled at her clothes. "I would kill any man who tried to take you from me," he whispered. "That is why I will duel."

She felt her face go ashen as she suddenly saw an image of herself lying in Edwin's big bed with its silken sheets, lying there like a wax doll while he pumped and sweated and moaned over her small body, claiming the marital rights that would be his if they both kept their part of the bargain.

Rio didn't seem to notice. He was kissing her breasts and stroking her all over with his good hand and she forgot about Edwin and thought only of making love to Rio because it might be for the very last time.

He rolled over on his back and pulled her on top of him, reaching up to touch and caress her breasts. "Now you make love to me," he demanded.

She spread her thighs and mounted his big maleness and gasped as she felt that pulsating rod of flesh deep in her depths. "Oh, you feel so good."

He put his hands on her hips and brought her down on him hard.

"More," she gasped. "Deeper!"

He obliged and she rode him harder and faster until bare, sweating flesh slapped hard against bare, sweating flesh, slamming harder and faster in the rhythm of love until she reached a pinnacle of excitement just as he gasped and went rigid all over, holding her tight against him so that she could not escape from the hot flow of seed he was giving up to her.

After a long moment of clinging together they both collapsed, sweating and gasping for air.

"No man could ever give me that kind of pleasure," she gasped against his ear.

"I would kill any man who tried, and no man ever will, as long as I live and breathe," he promised.

*Monday,* she thought. *Monday, and I have made such a mess of this.* She rolled over to lay in the crook of his left arm and he brushed the black curls from her face and held her close. Had she really thought Rio would let Edwin possess her if Rio came through the duel unscathed?

"You are very quiet," he mused.

"I—I am only tired," she lied. "We should get dressed. Trace's train will be coming in soon."

"I'd rather make love to you again." He laughed.

"Can you think of nothing else?" She tried to sound light-hearted.

"With you? No." He sat up on the edge of the bed and began to hunt for his clothes.

She stood up on the floor by him and he reached out and slapped her lightly but possessively on the bottom. "Mine," he said. "No other man shall ever touch this."

He would be furious with her if he knew of her bargain and would never speak to her again, but if it would save his life, she would keep her promise. She imagined spending the rest of her life in Edwin's bed. She might survive his lovemaking if she pretended it was Rio who rode her.

"We've got to meet a train," she said and grabbed for her clothes.

"You weren't too worried about that train ten minutes ago."

"Ten minutes ago, I wasn't thinking of anything but getting a big stallion inside me," she answered truthfully, and she walked over to the wash basin and poured some water.

He came up behind her and put his arms around her, both of them still naked. "I try not to want you," he confessed. "I know you're out of my class, but I forget about all reason when I'm close to you." He kissed the back of her neck.

She could feel his big maleness against her hips as his hands went up to cup her breasts.

"I wish today would never end," she said, laying her head back against his massive chest. "I'm so happy in your arms."

"And I in yours." He reached for a washcloth and the bar of soap. "Now we must stop touching each other before we end up back in bed. Trace will be waiting in the train station and wondering where we are."

"Of course."

Quickly they both washed and dressed. Then they went outside and Rio said, "We can take the buggy to the station and bring Trace back here."

In minutes, they were on the way to the train with Rio driving and little Tip riding in the back and barking at passing horses. She glanced over at Rio's swollen right hand in its bandage. "Do you think you can shoot with your left hand?"

He looked down at the bandaged hand. "I reckon I'll have to try."

"Trying isn't good enough," she said with such emotion that he looked at her strangely.

"Sweet one," he said, "you are letting the tension get to you."

"How can I help it?" She burst into tears. "Someone is going to be killed and all you men act like it's some kind of athletic competition."

He put his arm around her. "That's what men do when they face death, my darling. They joke and make light of it or they fall silent and brood over it. Do you have no faith in my ability to shoot?"

"I just don't want to see anyone die."

He shrugged. "And you won't because you aren't coming to the duel. You'll meet Senora Durango's train and wait for me to return."

"And suppose I wait and wait and—"

"Then your guardian will bring you word. I would ask that you let my mother know what has happened. Sell my ranch and send the money to her at the convent."

"Of course I would do that."

"Then that's all I ask. Look, I see a train pulling in at the station. Perhaps that is the one with Senor Durango."

Sure enough, up ahead, a black locomotive was whistling and blowing smoke as it puffed into town. At least this would give her something else to think about. Turquoise pasted a smile on her face as they drove into the station and Rio got out to tie up the buggy, then came around to help her down.

They walked out onto the platform amid the crowd and waited for the train to grind to a halt amid a puff of acrid smoke and cinders. The conductor stepped down and put out a little stool, then turned to help the waiting passengers debark. First out came a drummer with his suitcases of samples, then an older couple, and finally Trace Durango stepped down. She thought the half Cheyenne landowner was still tall and handsome, although his black hair was streaked now with gray.

They went to meet him, the two men attempting to shake hands, and she saw how Trace frowned when he saw Rio's right hand. "How bad is it?"

Rio looked into his eyes. "Bad enough."

Turquoise hugged her guardian, feeling relief. "We knew if there was anyone who could teach him how to handle a pistol, it would be you."

Trace swore in Spanish under his breath and reached to pick up his small bag. "That damned Forester. I've been wantin' to kill him myself for years, but I guess this is the next best thing. How on earth did you end up challengin' him to a duel?"

"It's a long story, senor," Rio said, "a matter of honor."

Trace nodded. "*Si.* I can relate to a matter of honor."

"You men," she snapped. "I don't think honor is worth getting killed over."

"That's because you're a girl." Rio grinned. "If a man has no honor, he has nothing."

"Agreed," Trace said, "especially a Texan. "Now, we don't have a lot of time. Let us get right to it."

Turquoise swallowed the lump in her throat and followed the men to the buggy as they talked.

Once back at Rio's ranch, the two men loaded pistols and set up targets out by the small lake.

Trace said, "Hombre, unwrap that hand and let's see how bad it is."

"No!" Turquoise objected. "He's not going to be able to use it."

Rio ignored her and unwrapped the hand and tried to flex it. He grimaced with pain. Turquoise looked. The hand was swollen and discolored, the four-leaf clover barely visible on the purple bruising.

"*Dios.*" Trace sighed. "You're right, Turquoise, it hasn't had time to heal yet. It may eventually get better, but we're short on time. Well, Rio, I'll see what you can do with your left hand. How good with a pistol were you before?"

Rio shook his head. "Not good. I can handle a rifle like any Texas rancher should, but I've had no use for learning gunfighting."

"This isn't gunfightin', where speed matters." Trace frowned. "This is duelin'. What counts here are steady nerves. You'll both walk twenty paces and turn and aim.

Sometimes the one who is not the best shot with a pistol but has the best nerves, wins."

Turquoise looked at him. "Have you ever been involved in a duel before, Uncle Trace?"

He nodded. "As a second to my father many years ago when I was hardly more than a boy. He killed the other man."

"Senor Trace, I would be honored if you would be my second," Rio said.

"Of course I will. My only problem at this time is what to do about my family, who will be comin' in on the train from Philadelphia about sundown that night."

"Turquoise can meet the train," Rio said. "I don't want her at the duel anyway."

"You might at least let me make that choice," she bristled.

He gave her a stern look. "Please don't make this any worse than it is, sweet one."

She nodded and the men loaded pistols, and Trace showed Rio how to hold the gun with his left hand. "Now take careful aim," he cautioned. "Remember, with a Colt, you've got more bullets. With a dueling pistol, you only get one shot and you've got to make it count."

They practiced another hour.

Trace nodded encouragement. "You're improvin', Rio. Now remember, don't let your anger get the best of you. You have to be very cool and deadly in a duel."

"We're low on shells," Rio noted. "I'll go back down to the house and get more."

After they watched him walk away, Turquoise turned to Trace. "I never heard about a Durango duel. What was the old don fighting about?"

"A woman's honor," Trace said.

"A woman's honor doesn't seem worth killing a man over," she scoffed.

"I'd kill a man if he insulted my woman—any Texan would. In this case the woman was my mother," Trace said. "The man tried to seduce her and failed. Then he publicly called Velvet Eyes an 'Injun whore.'"

"Oh."

"So you see, the don had no choice but to kill him. There were other things leadin' up to it for many years and several generations. They had long been bitter enemies, but that was the final insult that put them beneath the big oaks by the river."

"I reckon men will always be men."

Trace nodded. "And what is this duel about?"

Turquoise shrugged. "A number of things."

"Men usually fight duels over two things: honor or women. I presume you are the woman?"

She felt her face flush. "I didn't think it would lead to this."

"Women never think it will lead to bloodshed, but they don't know how primitive a man can be when another male wants his woman."

"Uncle Trace, would you allow me to marry Edwin Forester?"

Trace's face hardened and he looked both shocked and bewildered. "What?"

"Don't ask." She looked at the ground and stubbed her toe in the dirt.

Trace sighed. "I don't know what you're up to. Very well, I'd like to say over my very dead body you'd marry into the Foresters, but if it were your choice, I would allow you to make it."

"Do you think Rio has a chance in hell Monday night?"

He didn't answer for a long moment. "I don't really know, Turquoise. He's not very good with a pistol, that's true, but I've got a couple of days to work with him. Sometimes miracles happen."

They both turned to watch Rio striding back with the bullets.

She asked, "So I should pray for a miracle?"

*"Si,"* Trace said, nodding, "or maybe make one happen."

Rio came back just then with the boxes of shells. "So what were you two talking about?"

"How well you're shootin'," Trace said with a grin, "and how I should give Turquoise a large dowry when she marries you."

"I've got to survive the duel first," Rio reminded him.

She couldn't stand to look him in the face. "It looks like you two have a long afternoon ahead of you," she said. "I think I'll go to the nearest church and light some candles and pray."

"You'd better pray to Saint Jude, the patron saint of hopeless causes," Rio suggested.

She shook her head. "No, I'll pray to the Virgin and all the saints and then I'll come back about sundown tonight to see how it's going, Uncle Trace."

He nodded and she got in the buggy and drove away, listening to the echoing pistol shots behind her.

Yes, she needed more than prayers; she needed a miracle. Now what could she do to make a miracle happen?

# Chapter 17

After she prayed, she went back to Rio's to watch the men shoot and to fix them some supper. Since the men wanted to go to bed and get an early start on their practice, she decided to return to Fern's ranch. Her friend and her father were sympathetic, but there wasn't much they could do to help. Mr. Lessup did say that he had organized some ranchers to help rebuild Rio's barn late next week. That is, if Rio survived Monday night. Turquoise spent a restless night, mostly praying for help and guidance.

In the morning, a huge bouquet of pink roses and a diamond bracelet arrived by messenger. The card read, "Looking forward to my life with you. Much love, Edwin."

Once she had loved the scent of roses, but now their sweet fragrance reminded her of funerals. She tore up the card and tossed the bracelet aside. Could she be sure Edwin would keep his end of the bargain? Not knowing what to do, she told Fern the details of everything that had happened.

Her friend was round-eyed. "My word. Will you go through with it? "

Turquoise shook her head and paced the floor. "I guess

I'll have to. But I don't know whether I can trust Edwin and Rio would be furious if he knew what I had done."

Fern bit her lip. "Is there any chance Rio might kill him in the duel?"

"There's always a chance, I guess." Turquoise put her hand to her throbbing head. But he's shooting left-handed and he said he wasn't much with a pistol to begin with."

"You said Senor Durango was helping him."

"That's true, but I doubt if he has enough time to really turn him into a marksman."

"You could go to the law," Fern suggested.

"And then they'd all be mad at me. Men are such proud creatures. Their honor means more than anything to them. We ladies are so much more practical. Besides, I reckon Edwin has the law in his pocket. The Foresters own everyone in Austin."

"Oh, Turquoise, what are you going to do?"

Turquoise wiped her eyes. "I'm not sure. I might have to take action myself."

Fern's eyes grew even rounder. "Like what?"

"Oh, I don't know." She paced up and down. "I might have to shoot Edwin myself."

"What? You could go to jail or get hung for that." Fern grabbed her arm, but Turquoise shook her off.

"Don't you think I know that? It would be worth it if it saves Rio's life." She reached for her shawl. "I think I'll go see how the shooting lessons are going."

"What shall I do?" Fern seemed to relish her part as co-conspirator.

Turquoise shook her head. "I'm afraid there's nothing you can do yet. I'll let you know later what's happening."

"Didn't you say Senor Durango's family is due in Monday?"

Turquoise nodded. "Around sundown. Couldn't come

at a worse time, I think. I've been assigned to meet her train because Uncle Trace will be at the duel."

"My word! You're not going to miss that?" Fern asked.

Turquoise turned at the door. "I don't know, but I think that's the men's plan. I want to be there and yet, I don't want to be there. May I borrow your buggy again?"

Fern nodded. "Anything I can do to help, I will."

Turquoise drove first to the state capitol and hurried into Edwin's office, ignoring his protesting clerk.

There were two other men in Edwin's office and all three gentlemen stood up as she entered.

"Ah, Senators Black and Willoby, I'd like you to meet Senorita Sanchez."

"Charmed," said the two plump, middle-aged men as they bowed.

"Pleased to meet you," she said and indicated with her eyes to Edwin that they needed to talk.

He frowned, but nodded to the two men. "Well, I suppose we can continue this discussion about the water legislation later since the legislature won't be back in session for a while, gentlemen."

"Of course." They hurried out, smiling at Turquoise.

"Now, dear"—Edwin lifted his lapel to his nose and sniffed the pink rosebud—"what can I do for you so early this fine morning? You know Tuesday's a holiday and I have some work to finish up."

She listened to the sound of an occasional firecracker outside the building. She had completely forgotten about the Fourth of July. "You're very calm, considering you're fighting a duel at sundown Monday."

"But that's just a sham, remember?" He walked over and put his arm around her but she stayed wooden and unresponsive. "Did you get my little gift this morning?"

"Yes." She stepped away from him. "It's extravagant."

"Oh, not by a long shot." He laughed. "You can expect more of the same once we are married."

"Edwin"—she turned toward him—"you are going to keep your promise and not shed any blood, aren't you?"

"Of course," he assured her. "I'll just shoot in his direction and hope he does the same. That ought to satisfy both our honors. I hear he's a lousy shot with a pistol."

"Who told you that?"

He scratched his head. "I don't remember. Anyway, things like that get around."

"I need to be going," she said. "I spent a rather sleepless night worrying about this."

He came over to her and kissed her forehead. "No need to, poor darling. Unless something goes terribly wrong and he jumps in front of my pistol, he'll walk away unscathed."

"Thank you, Edwin. I wouldn't want to begin our marriage with blood on your hands."

"Now you run along, my dear. Will you be at the duel?"

She shook her head. "I think I may be the only one in town who won't be. I'm scheduled to meet Senora Durango's train late that day."

"That's nice." He sounded absent, as if his mind was already on something else. "A duel isn't something that welcomes ladies. It's for men. I'll see you later this evening. Maybe we'll dine? There's a fine new restaurant in town."

"I—I don't think so." She decided not to tell him her guardian was in Austin. Town gossip would let him know that soon enough. She left his office, ignored the curious stare of his clerk, got in the buggy, and drove out to Rio's ranch.

Here and there along the way, she heard firecrackers echoing across the landscape. The boys of Austin were getting an early start to their celebrations.

As she drove through the ranch gates and back toward

the lake, she heard the sound of pistol fire and, as she neared, bits and snatches of conversation.

"No, Rio, hold the pistol steady."

"I'm trying. I'm not good with my left hand."

She drove up and reined in, watching Rio shoot as Tip came running to meet her.

"No, a little lower," Trace instructed. "Always aim for the body. It's a bigger target. Let's have none of this fancy stuff about tryin' to just wound him or knock the gun from his hand."

"It's hard for me to shoot at a man, even if it is that damned Forester," Rio argued.

"You better, if you want to walk away from this alive."

Now they seemed to notice Turquoise for the first time and turned toward her. "How's the practice going?" She tried to be bright and light-hearted.

She saw the two men exchange glances.

"Just fine," Rio said, but he didn't look at her.

"He's gettin' much better." Trace nodded, but she saw the doubt in his dark eyes.

Rio came to the buggy to help her down and she clung to him and abruptly began to cry.

"Now, now, let's have none of that," he murmured and gently stroked her hair. "I'm not dead yet and Trace is a good teacher."

"But you don't have enough time to learn," she said, sobbing.

Trace cleared his throat. "Uh, maybe I'd better walk down to the house and get some more ammunition," he muttered, "while you two finish your conversation."

She watched him walk away and turned back to Rio. "How are you doing, really?"

"Fine." He avoided her direct gaze. "Of course I'd feel better if we were using rifles. I'm damned good with a rifle, even if I had to shoot left-handed."

She looked at his bandaged hand, still swollen. "It's not better?"

"A little. It just needs time, that's all."

"Couldn't you postpone this duel?"

He snorted and turned away. "That sounds just like a woman. 'This isn't a convenient time, sir. Can we schedule it for another day?'"

She saw the dark circles under his eyes and felt the underlying tension in the man. "You didn't get much sleep last night, did you?"

"Did you?" He looked into her eyes and she ducked her head, afraid he could read what was there.

"No." She shook her head. "But maybe all is not lost. Maybe you're worried for nothing."

"What does that mean?" He grabbed her arm.

"Nothing. Maybe Edwin isn't as good a shot as you think, and maybe he'll miss."

"I doubt that. Everyone says he's an expert with dueling pistols."

"So you really feel you're going to your death?"

He nodded.

"Then don't go. Forget the damned duel." She was losing her temper with men and their honor.

He caught both her arms. "We've had this conversation before and you don't understand. I couldn't walk the streets of this town if I run."

She looked up at him, loving him, worried that there was so much angst and tension in his rugged face. She wanted to comfort him. "Just stop worrying about the senator killing you." She reached up to kiss him, but he caught her small face between his two big hands.

"Why, Turquoise? Why should I stop worrying?"

She was babbling in confusion, trying to look away, but he was holding her face, looking down into her eyes.

"I—I just think maybe he'll only make a gesture, that's all, or miss."

He didn't let go of her. "Now why would he do that?"

She tried to pull away from him. "I—I really don't know. Maybe I heard a rumor, that's all, that he doesn't plan to kill you."

"You're a poor liar, Turquoise. What is it you know?"

She struggled to pull away from him. "Nothing," but she didn't look at him.

He tightened his grip on her.

"Oh, you're hurting me!" She was fighting to get away from him, but his hands were strong on her arms.

"Turquoise, what is it you know?"

"Nothing." Her mouth was so dry, she was choking.

"You've made a deal," he guessed. "You've made some kind of deal with the devil."

"No." She tried to pull away. "He only said—"

"So you've talked to him?"

"No, yes, oh God, Rio, let go of me!"

"Not until you tell me what sort of scheme you've agreed to."

She shook her head and tried to look away, her eyes blinded by tears. "He—he won't kill you, he'll only take a shot and miss."

"I wouldn't trust him on a stack of Bibles. Why would he do that?"

She pulled away from him, tearing her sleeve in the process. "I—I don't know."

"You little bitch. You've promised him something, haven't you?" He moved toward her, dark eyes blazing.

She backed away defensively. "So what if I have? I'm not as proud as you. I'd do anything to save your life!"

"And you have no confidence in my ability to win?"

"You—you said yourself he was an excellent shot and you weren't—"

"But at least I'd go down with honor, not hiding behind a woman's skirts."

"You're a fool then and maybe I've made a devil's bargain, but I love you enough to do whatever it takes to stop him from killing you."

"Your body," he seethed. "You damned little whore, you've promised him your body."

She didn't say anything, only fled to her buggy. She drove out at a fast pace, whipping up the horse while he railed accusations after her.

God, now he hated her, but she couldn't help that. Yes, she'd made a devil's bargain, but if it saved Rio's life, it was worth it to spend a lifetime in Edwin's bed. That thought made her nauseous. She drove past Trace, who yelled at her, but she didn't stop. She kept driving until she realized she was back in town and the horse had slowed to a walk.

What was she to do? Rio was now furious with her, not appreciating her sacrifice. On the other hand, she wasn't sure she could trust Edwin to keep his word. What kind of action could she take now? She spent a sleepless weekend, barely talking to Fern and not going out to Rio's ranch. She couldn't face him, not knowing if he had told her guardian about her deal with Edwin Forester. All she could do was pray and pace and hope that Edwin would keep his part of the bargain if Rio didn't kill the senator.

Finally it was Monday. It had come in spite of all her prayers. Now she had finally decided what she must do. The weather felt sweltering as she dressed in a white eyelet dress and big hat. It was past noon and the July day was as hot as the firecrackers that exploded occasionally on the streets. She borrowed Fern's buggy, took her little reticule, and drove blindly, looking at shops and lampposts festooned with red, white, and blue crepe paper and ribbons. Tomorrow there would be a parade, picnics, and speeches and a band playing in the park as the country celebrated its hundredth birthday, but today, she was only concerned with what would happen at sundown under the big oaks by the river.

They might hang her for murder, but she had made her decision. Turquoise drove to a gunshop and reined in, got down, and tied up at the hitching rail. Clutching her reticule firmly, she went inside.

To the mustachioed proprietor, she said, "I'd like to see a gun, please."

He looked at her askance. Most women did not buy weapons. "A rifle? A gift for a gentleman, perhaps?"

"Uh, no." She shook her head. "It's for me."

He smiled and nodded. "Oh, protection. Good idea with all these drunken galoots celebrating the Fourth. All right, miss. How about a nice little Derringer? You can carry that in your purse and—"

"No, that's only good at very close range, isn't it?" She looked him squarely in the eye. "I think what I have in mind is a Colt revolver."

He scratched his head. "Uh, little lady, that's a pretty big pistol for a woman. Now a nice Derringer—"

"No, I think I want a Colt."

He sighed and shook his head. "It might knock you down when you try to shoot it," he said. "Have you ever shot a Colt before?"

She shook her head. "No, but I've shot a rifle a few times. Surely it can't be that much different."

He smiled suddenly. "Oh, you want to make some noise for the Fourth. Why don't you just buy a few firecrackers?" She shook her head.

He hesitated. "Do your menfolk know what you're up to?"

"I am an independent Texas woman," she snapped. "And I don't need any man's permission to buy a gun."

"All right." He seemed to shrug off responsibility. "I'll show you some, but I don't think you know—"

"Let me see some Colts," she demanded.

He was right; it was heavy. She hefted it in her hand and sighted down the barrel. "Yes, I think this will do. Now sell me some shells and load it for me, please."

He sighed and muttered something about stubborn females as he got a box of shells off the shelf. "Now here's how you load it, miss."

She watched him slip six shells in the barrel and click it in place. "Now is it fully loaded?"

"Yes, ma'am." He nodded. "Just be careful where you point it."

She hefted it in her small hand again, trying to imagine pulling the trigger and killing someone. Could she do it? "How much do I owe you?"

He told her and she paid him, then walked outside with the Colt. It was too big to fit into her reticule. Maybe she could hide it in the folds of her full white skirt. At least now, if Edwin didn't keep his part of their bargain, he wouldn't live to see the stars come out. Could she kill a man? She thought about it and gritted her teeth. If Edwin shot Rio, she could kill him with no more qualms than stepping on a bug.

She found a pasture with no one in sight and practiced for a couple of hours. It was late afternoon now as she drove back to Fern's ranch and hid the Colt under the buggy seat.

When she went inside, Fern demanded, "Where have you been? I've been worried to death about you."

Turquoise shook her head and walked into the kitchen for a drink of water. "You don't want to know."

"Are you going to do something desperate?"

Turquoise shrugged. "I really don't know. Rio is furious with me over the deal I've made, and I'm not at all sure I can trust Edwin, but I can't stand by and let him shoot down the only man I'll ever love."

"Oh, Turquoise, whatever you do, think about it. You could make a terrible mistake."

"I already have. Now I'm just trying to rectify the mess."

Fern sighed. "Nothing this exciting ever happens in my life. It's deadly dull."

"Be thankful for that." Turquoise sipped her water.

"But I mean, isn't it exciting to have men dueling over you? That handsome vaquero and a state senator—"

"Fern, somebody's probably going to die tonight and that's not exciting, it's nauseating."

"Oh, yes. You look pale. Don't you want something to eat?"

Turquoise shook her head. "I don't think I could eat a bite. I can't even breathe easy until this day is finished."

"What can I do to help?"

Turquoise turned and looked at the grandfather clock in the dining room. "I'd appreciate it if you'd take another buggy and meet Senora Durango and her children at the train."

"What'll I tell her?"

Turquoise shrugged. "I don't know. Maybe you can just stall her and keep her occupied until this thing is over."

"And what are you going to do?"

Turquoise took a deep, shuddering breath and realized the hand that held the tumbler of water was shaking. Was it shaking too much to hold a pistol?

"I'm going out to the dueling grounds."

"My word. Women won't be welcome out there. This is men's business," Fern objected.

"I said I'm going to the duel." She set the tumbler down with a bang and whirled to leave the house. As she got into the buggy, she thought again about the Colt revolver. Did she have the guts to use it? To save Rio's life, she would.

# Chapter 18

The sun was low on the horizon as Fern drove her buggy to meet the incoming train that was now pulling into the station with much soot and smoke.

She walked up and down the platform, watching for Senora Durango as the conductor began unloading the baggage. Then a beautiful blond woman holding the hands of two wiggling children, a boy and a girl, stepped off the train.

Fern took a deep breath. "Senora Durango?"

"Yes?" Cimarron looked up and down the platform. She was tired and impatient to head home. Now where was her family?

"Senora, you may not remember me, but I'm Turquoise's friend Fern."

"Of course." Cimarron smiled and nodded as she recognized the plump redhead. "Where is everyone?"

Fern started to shake and began to cry. "My word! It's all such a mess! Your husband is helping Rio learn to duel and—"

"Who?"

"Rio. The man Turquoise loves," Fern babbled. "He's got to fight a duel at sundown with Senator Forester."

"Why?" Cimarron blinked and held onto her two wiggling children.

"Because Senator Forester has him on a murder charge and he wants to marry Turquoise, and—"

"Who wants to marry Turquoise? Honestly, Fern, I'm having a difficult time understanding—"

"But Turquoise has promised to marry Senator Forester if he just won't kill Rio, and—"

"Senator Forester. Do you mean Edwin Forester?"

"Why, yes. He's mad for Turquoise, enough to kill—"

"Double damnation," Cimarron cursed. "This is a mess. He can't marry Turquoise."

"I know your two families have been feuding for years," Fern wept, "but he's determined to have her and . . . what's the matter, senora? You've turned pale."

"I—I'll be all right." Cimarron took a deep breath and straightened her shoulders, then let go of her children. The dark-headed boy and girl ran up and down the platform. yelling and playing. "When is this showdown supposed to happen?"

"At the old dueling grounds about sunset." Fern wiped her eyes.

"All right. I'll take charge now, Fern. Can you deal with my baggage and maybe take the kids across the street for some ice cream?"

"Well, of course, but—"

"No time to talk now." Cimarron dug in her reticule for some money. "Where can I find the senator?"

"Maybe at his capitol office if he hasn't already left. But why—"

"May I borrow your buggy?"

"Yes." Fern nodded. "It's the one out front with the paint horse. The buggy has yellow wheels."

Cimarron took off at a run. "You kids tell Fern about your trip and I'll be back later."

"But, Senora . . ." Fern yelled as she grabbed for the boy and girl, but Cimarron was running for the buggy. Then she looked down at the pair and sighed. "I'm Fern Lessup, Turquoise's friend."

The dark young boy smiled. "My name's Diego, but they call me Ace."

"And I'm Raven," said the beautiful little girl.

Fern took their hands in hers. "Well, you two tell me about your trip. Do you like strawberry or vanilla?"

Black-haired little Raven said, "There were lots of pretty clothes—"

"And big buildings," Ace interrupted. "And a man named Bell has invented something called a telephone."

Fern was too worried to listen but she nodded. "Let's go get some ice cream and you both can tell me everything you saw in Philadelphia."

Cimarron clambered into the buggy and whipped up the horse. She had to stop this duel before it was too late, so she had to find Edwin Forester. The capitol. Fern said he might be at his office at the state capitol. She could only pray she was in time as she took off in a cloud of dust down the street.

When she pulled up and jumped out, the lot looked fairly vacant. No doubt most legislators had already left for the summer. She hurried into the building, the empty granite hallways echoing under her shoes.

To a bored guard, she asked, "Senator Forester's office?"

He pointed down the hall. "He might still be there. He sometimes works late."

She could only hope. She almost ran down the hall and passed a small pimply faced man with wire-rimmed spectacles clearing off his desk. "Is the senator in?"

The little man looked annoyed. "We are just closing for the day, but—"

"Tell the senator I need to see him desperately."

"All right." The little man looked intrigued, but he didn't ask. He disappeared through a big door and in a moment, returned. "The senator is getting ready to leave for an important appointment. He says come back tomorrow."

"Tell him it's Senora Durango and he must see me."

The little man shrugged. "All right," he said irritably. "I don't think it will do you any good."

He got up again and went to the big door but as he opened it, Cimarron rushed past him and into the room.

"Senator Forester?"

The handsome man looked annoyed as he stood up. "I said I have no more time for appointments today—"

"But I must see you. I am Senora Durango."

For a moment, he only stared at her with those pale, cold eyes. "What is it you want?"

"We must talk." She strode over to his desk and sat down in front of it and looked him over. He was indeed a handsome man, possibly nearing forty, with just a touch of gray at the temples of his light hair. He wore an expensive, light gray suit with a pink rosebud in his buttonhole.

"I don't know why—"

"We must," she said again firmly and he sighed and waved the irritable little man out of the office.

"It's about the duel."

He frowned. "If you've come to plead for that Mexican's life," Forester snapped, "it will do you no good." He blew on the inked sheet of paper he'd been writing on. "The duel will go on as scheduled."

"It must not." She shook her head, looking at the shape of his face, so familiar, the unusual color of his eyes, and knew that what she'd been told was true. "I don't know anything about most of this. I've been away for several months."

"Then why . . . ?"

"What are you working on?" She asked, staring at the paper he was now folding.

"If it's any of your business, I am a very thorough man and I am updating my will. Another five minutes and you would have missed me."

She took a deep breath. "Senator, I have something I must tell you, a secret that only I know."

"Now why should I give a tinker's damn about—"

"Because it may change your actions today."

"Aha! I knew it! You think to dissuade me from—"

"It is my understanding that if you deliberately miss and not kill the vaquero, Turquoise has promised to marry you."

"Now how would you know that?" He sounded very annoyed. "I am in a hurry and you are stalling for time—"

"Senator, I must tell you my secret, and we will be the only two people in the world who know it, a fact that the old don himself whispered to me on his deathbed."

Edwin made a face. "The old Don Durango. There has always been bad blood between the families for many reasons." She nodded. "You may try to talk me out of marrying Turquoise, but I intend to have her if I have to fight every man in Texas. I have never met a woman who hypnotized me like she does. She intrigues me, completes me. This is the woman I have looked for all my life."

She stared at him, knowing what the old don had whispered to her as he lay on his deathbed was true. Trace and the priest had been out in the hall when she had come quietly into the room to say her good-byes to the dear old man. Now she felt very, very sorry for Edwin Forester. "Don't you realize why you love her so much? Are you blind? Haven't you guessed?"

"What are you hinting at?" he snarled. "I don't have time for—"

"Edwin"—she kept her voice low and gentle because she was about to destroy the man—"pour yourself a stiff drink and sit down. I have something to tell you and then you will decide what to do next."

He seemed to be mystified, but he got up and poured himself a large whiskey. "Would you like some sherry?"

She shook her head, waiting for him to sit down.

"You can say anything you wish"—Edwin nodded—"but I will have her. I'd just as soon be dead if I can't marry Turquoise, so you won't talk me out of it."

She motioned for him to sit down and he did, sipping his drink. Then she took a deep breath and told him what the old don had revealed with his dying breath.

Edwin Forester's pale eyes widened and then narrowed with rage and disbelief as the tumbler fell from his nerveless hand and crashed on the floor. "You lie!"

Cimarron held up her hand. "I swear on the Blessed Virgin that what I have told you is the truth. How could you have looked into her face and not realized it? Are you blinded by love?"

Her words seemed to sink in and for a long moment, the room was very quiet except for the ticking of the wall clock. Edwin's face went a pale, sick gray. "Oh my God."

For an eternity, he stared into blankness and said nothing. From outside came the crackle of a string of firecrackers and a small boy's laughter. Cimarron watched the long shadows creep across the room through the window. It would soon be sundown.

Edwin finally spoke and it was barely a whisper. "I—I was just making out my will as a precaution. I am a very cautious man."

"I know," Cimarron said and felt so very sorry for him.

"But I love her still," he argued as if that would change

everything. There were tears in his eyes. "I was planning to leave all my riches to her if I were killed."

Cimarron shook her head. "She probably wouldn't accept anything from you."

"Not even if she knew—"

"But she must never know. This is our secret," Cimarron reminded him.

"Yes, of course." He ran his hand across his chin and his hand shook visibly.

"I am going now." She stood up and walked toward the door, paused there, and looked back. He sat like a dead man, staring into the dusk of evening. He did not answer. "Edwin," she said softly, "for what it is worth, I feel very, very sorry for you. I deeply regret you had to find out. I intended to take the secret to my grave."

He laughed but there was no humor in his voice. "What is it they say? What goes around comes around and your sins will find you out?"

Tears came to her own eyes at the pain and tragedy in his face. All his money and power could not help him; maybe only God could. "I will pray for you," she whispered and went out.

She walked softly past the clerk's desk and he looked up and said, "Is the senator about ready to leave?"

"I don't know," she answered. "I really don't know. Give him a few minutes."

The clerk pulled out his pocket watch. "But we have someplace to be in less than thirty minutes."

"Maybe not," she said and went down the hall past the guard and out to the buggy. Once there, she broke into sobs and buried her face in her hands. She had done everything she knew to do. Now it was up to Senator Forester.

Back in his office, Edwin stared at the door for a long time, listening to the occasional firecracker from outside, then down at the papers on his desk. There were things to do. He stared at the will, unable to see the print because he was blinded by his own tears. The building was quiet, so very quiet that he could hear his big office clock tick. He had someplace he was supposed to be. Where was it? Oh, yes. He caught the slight scent of the pink rosebud in his lapel and stared down at it. The scent was faint and in the sweltering July air, the flower was beginning to wilt. It didn't matter. Nothing mattered now.

He tried to collect his thoughts and blinked again at the papers before him. After a moment, he wrote a short note, put it with the will, and stood up. With a shuddering sigh, he walked to the outer office. "Elmer, I need you to witness my signature."

"Aren't we in kind of a hurry?" Elmer blinked like an owl through his big spectacles.

Edwin ignored the question. "Get that building guard, too. I need two signatures to make this legal."

Elmer glanced at his watch as he stood up. "Can't this wait until tomorrow, sir?"

"No, it can't."

The clerk shrugged and went off down the hall, returning soon with the guard.

"Ah, Senator, and what is it you need this evening?" the guard asked with a laugh.

Edwin laughed, too, only he felt like shrieking. "Just need a couple of signatures to make this legal, that's all. You don't need to read it. I'm just going to sign it and you two sign as witnesses."

He signed it with a flourish and they signed right under his name. "Now," Edwin said, forcing himself to smile, "I'll just get a couple of things from my office and we'll close down for the evening."

"Are you gonna ride in the parade tomorrow, Senator?"

the guard asked. "I hear you're thinkin' of running for governor next term."

Governor. Once that had been important; now nothing was, nothing but a girl he loved with all his heart and soul. Ironic, really. He was rich and important, and powerful, but none of that meant anything now. "I'll be right out."

He went back into his office, took the will and the short note, put them in an envelope, sealed it, addressed it to his own lawyer, and laid it on his desk in plain sight. Then he reached into the bottom drawer for the dueling pistols. His hands trembled as he took them out and loaded them. One of them got a full load. The other, he shorted on the gunpowder. This one would not reach across forty paces to hit the target. However, no one would know that unless they were knowledgeable in handling pistols. He had to take that chance. He picked up the leather pistol case and went into the outer office. "All right, I'm ready now."

Elmer looked at his watch again. "We've barely got time to get there."

"Mmm," Edwin said and nodded to the guard and the three of them started down the hall to the big front doors.

"I will follow you out and lock up," the guard said. "See you tomorrow at the parade. You have got my vote, Senator. Why, I think you'd make a great president."

"Thank you," Edwin said and really looked at the man for the first time in all these years. The Irish cop was a human being with hopes and dreams and children. Edwin had always only thought of him as one vote in a ballot box. After all these years, he didn't even know the man's name. "I really appreciate it . . . ?"

"Mahoney," said the guard with a grin.

"Yes, Mahoney. I appreciate the way you've always checked my office and run little errands."

He noted that even Elmer's eyes widened. Edwin wasn't known for being grateful. He was a Forester, after all, and took privilege for granted. Anything the Foresters wanted, they got. But not this time. Not this time.

He and Elmer got in the buggy and Edwin held the dueling case and let his clerk drive. He glanced down and saw the pink rosebud in his buttonhole was wilting fast, but he couldn't do anything about that now. "I'll always love pink roses," he thought aloud.

"What?" Elmer glanced over as he drove.

"Never mind. Elmer, I've left an envelope on my desk addressed to my lawyer. If anything happens to me, you are to take it immediately to my lawyer tonight. Tonight, do you understand?"

The little clerk stared sideways at him as if to ask a question, but only nodded. "Yes, sir."

"Do you know anything about guns at all?"

"Well, no, sir, not a thing. But I'm honored to be your second, whatever that is."

Good. Elmer wouldn't realize that one pistol was short-loaded. Now if he could just keep anyone else from inspecting them. . . .

"You're awfully quiet, sir."

"Am I? Just deep in thought, I reckon, about that water legislation that will come before the Senate next term."

"Who was the beautiful blonde who just left your office?"

"God's avenging angel," Edwin whispered.

"What?" His expression said Elmer was worried about the senator's mental state.

"None of your business," Edwin snapped. "Just forget you ever saw her."

"Yes, sir."

Edwin realized that the man thought there was something shady, but he couldn't do anything about that now. He could never tell the secret, not to anyone.

* * *

It was not quite sundown when they arrived at the dueling grounds. A curious crowd of men had gathered in a circle to see this ritual that men had fought for a thousand years. He saw old Judge Wright come out of the crowd. The vaquero stepped forward, his mouth tight, his face pale with tension. Edwin noted his swollen hand was still bound up. Rio would have to shoot left-handed, which made him an easy target. Trace Durango stepped up behind the vaquero.

The judge looked around at the crowd and then at the two duelists. "Can this not be settled any other way?"

The vaquero took a deep breath. "I don't think so, senor."

"What about you, Forester?"

Edwin did not trust himself to speak. He only shook his head.

The judge sighed and straightened his shoulders. "Then the duel will proceed. Now, everyone gathered here knows that what's happening is illegal and could get us all arrested."

A murmur swept through the crowd of men, but no one made any attempt to leave.

"Very well," intoned the judge. "So when it is over, no matter the outcome, every man will keep his mouth shut to avoid prosecution and we will all scatter. This event must not end up in the newspapers."

Again no one made any move to leave.

Old Judge Wright motioned to both sides. "I will talk to the seconds." Edwin nodded to Elmer to go over and Trace Durango went to the judge's side and glared at Edwin.

It seemed like forever that the old judge instructed the seconds while the ring of witnesses whispered to each other. Edwin looked up at the sky. It was going to be a hot night, maybe with lots of fireflies and a glorious sunset.

Why had he never paid much attention to such lovely things before? Well, it didn't matter now.

The seconds were returning to opposite sides of the big circle.

Edwin watched the sun just setting on the rim of the hill country, throwing long shadows from the giant oak trees across the grass. The vaquero was down on one knee, evidently praying. The last rays of sun reflected off the crucifix around his neck. Now he crossed himself and stood up.

Edwin looked around. Why had he always been too busy to notice how beautiful this grove of trees and the river were? Why had he failed to appreciate so much in his lust for power and wealth? He had always been busy; so busy. And now it was all for naught. Man plans. God laughs.

"Does the challenger want to examine the pistols?" the old judge said.

Edwin held his breath. They must not discover he had tampered with them, because Trace Durango could spot that.

As Trace stepped forward and Edwin held out the pistols for his examination, abruptly Edwin noticed movement in the crowd and got a quick glimpse of a girl in a snow-white dress and big hat. Turquoise. What was she doing here? Edwin saw Turquoise's agonized face, pale with desperation and hatred as she stared toward him. Then he saw a glint of fading light on something in her hand.

"Look out!" Edwin yelled and people screamed and ran and ducked. All except Trace Durango, who raced across the circle and grabbed the girl, struggling with her.

"Give me that! Give me that gun, damn it!"

Edwin watched almost hypnotized as Trace struggled with Turquoise for the Colt now held high above her head.

"Let go of me! I'll kill him!" she screamed. "I'll kill him!"

But Trace had wrestled the gun from Turquoise's hand.

The sidelines were in confusion as he struggled to keep her from regaining the pistol while she shrieked and fought.

She had intended to kill him, Edwin realized as she looked toward him, hate in her turquoise eyes. She was planning on killing him because she didn't trust him not to shoot her love. And her love was the vaquero, not Edwin, with his wealth and big house and power. The cowboy had nothing, yet he had everything because he had Turquoise. Edwin blinked back tears as the judge shouted "The duel will continue!"

In the excitement, everyone had forgotten about examining the dueling pistols. While Trace struggled to control the girl, Edwin held the pair of pistols out to Rio. The challenger would get his choice; that was the rule.

Rio hesitated in choosing between the guns and Edwin held his breath, wondering what to do if Rio chose the wrong one. Edwin smiled to himself and offered the pistols again to Rio, who paused, then chose one.

Good, he had chosen the pistol Edwin intended him to take, and no one had inspected either one. Indeed, with Turquoise screaming and fighting in the background, no one had thought about anything but getting this event over with. It would be over soon enough, Edwin thought as he took the other pistol from the leather case, tossed the case aside, and stepped out into the middle of the circle.

"You will stand back to back," intoned the old judge. "Then as I count, you will each take twenty steps. At that point, you will turn and fire at will. Each pistol holds one shot. If no one is hit or only wounded, the deed is done and the seconds will deal with the injured. Do both of you understand?"

Both men murmured yes.

Edwin stood with his pistol cocked, his back against the big vaquero. Rio Kelly was a broad-shouldered, handsome man, he thought. Edwin couldn't defeat him except with guile and conniving. Rio had nothing, but Turquoise was willing to kill to protect him. She must love him very much.

"One," said the judge, and Edwin took a deep breath and stepped forward and heard the cowboy do the same.

"Two," shouted the judge, and Edwin took another step. He had a slight smile on his lips as he took step after step. It was all working out just the way he planned; not the way he wanted it to be, but the way it should be.

As he took the next step, he turned his head ever so slightly and looked at the tense, nervous faces watching the two men step off the distance. He glanced toward Elmer and gave him an encouraging nod. The young clerk looked like he might faint at any moment.

*I'm a rich, powerful man,* Edwin thought, *and yet I do not have one, no, not even one good friend to be my second. I had to use a hired clerk.* He suddenly envied Rio Kelly because he had at least one good friend, maybe more than one, and best of all, he had a woman who loved him, loved him enough to kill for him.

"Ten . . ."

Edwin took another step. Soon it was all going to be over and he was surprised at how calm he was. He turned his head again and looked at Turquoise, who was being held back by her guardian. Why had he been so blind that he had not seen? Well, it didn't matter now. *I love you,* he mouthed at her as he heard the judge's voice and took another step.

In response, she spit at him and tried to charge at him, but Trace Durango held onto her.

"Fifteen!" rang out the judge's voice.

Edwin tried to breathe a prayer, but it had been so long, he had forgotten how. He could feel sweat plastering his fine, hand-made shirt to his body, and smell the slight scent of the wilting rosebud. He should have taken off his gray suit jacket so he wouldn't be so hot.

He tried to collect his thoughts, but they whirled like a child's toy pinwheel. All he had repeating itself in his head like a children's sing-song nursery rhyme was: what-goes-around-comes-around-what-goes-around-comes-around-what-goes-around-comes-around-what . . .

"Eighteen!" shouted Judge Wright and it seemed to Edwin that he heard the silent circle of men take a collective breath.

"Nineteen!"

Edwin took another step and rethought the decision he had made. He still had a split second to change it. No, it was the right decision and he would make it again for her, for his darling Turquoise. He wanted her to be happy.

"Twenty! Fire at will!"

Edwin took a deep breath, turned, took aim, and fired.

# Chapter 19

"Twenty! Fire at will!"

Rio's heart pounded hard as he whirled and faced the senator. In that split second, he tried to aim with his awkward left hand, tried to remember everything Trace Durango had taught him. His pulse seemed to be pounding so fast, he barely heard the command to fire even as Turquoise screamed.

Turquoise struggled to break free of Trace Durango as both shots rang out simultaneously. For a split second, neither man moved and there was a collective sigh from the crowd as the acrid smoke hid both the duelers.

She saw Rio take one step forward and then the pistol dropped from his nerveless fingers and she screamed again, sure he was hit.

But at that instant, Edwin smiled at her, took two steps forward, then went down to his knees. A scarlet stain spurted suddenly, and he reached his hand up to his chest at the red color spreading quickly across the front of the light gray suit. Blood ran between his manicured fingers and he looked down at them as if he couldn't quite believe what he was seeing. Then Edwin reached out one bloody hand toward Turquoise and fell on his face in the grass.

"Something's wrong with one of the pistols!" Trace protested. "I heard a strange sound!"

The old judge tried to restore order and gestured the two seconds into the circle even as Turquoise broke free of Trace and ran into Rio's embrace. Rio took her in his arms and held her close, cradling her head against his chest. "It's over, sweet one, it's over."

Trace and Elmer stepped to examine Edwin Forester's body, Elmer's face white as milk. They turned the senator over and the crowd grew very quiet at the sight of all the carmine blood on the green grass, the senator's light gray coat and the pink rosebud now dripping bright red. Turquoise's sobbing was the only sound heard.

Trace stood up. "He's dead."

Elmer stumbled out of the ring, vomiting, as the judge stepped forward to pick up the two pistols, his wrinkled face a mask of disbelief.

In the background, men were whispering, "Edwin Forester was a crack shot. What happened?"

Trace said, "Something is wrong with one of those pistols. I could tell by the sound."

The old judge examined the pistols, then stared at Trace in astonishment as he handed them to him. "What?"

Trace examined them both and he was as astounded as Judge Wright. "Edwin's pistol was short-loaded. It didn't have enough gunpowder to go the distance."

A murmur of disapproval from the crowd of men. "Well, what do you think about that? The senator probably meant for the vaquero to get that pistol and Rio took the wrong one."

The judge walked over to Rio, who was holding onto the sobbing Turquoise. "Son, did you feel like the senator was trying to get you to choose a certain pistol?"

"Well, yes, I did," Rio admitted, "so I took the other one."

A man in the crowd yelled, "What a crook! Forester

thought the cowboy would take the short-loaded pistol and got confused over which one he had his own self."

The crowd murmured agreement and the judge sighed. "I reckon that's it, then. Not that it matters. One man is dead and that settles the duel. Will his second load the senator's body into his buggy and take him back to his house?"

"Me?" squeaked Elmer. "He's all bloody and anyway, I can't lift him."

The judge scowled at him. "Doesn't Mr. Forester have any friends in this crowd who will help?"

No one came forward.

"God damn it," Rio swore. "I'll help." He and Trace stepped forward and carefully lifted the dead man and laid him in the back of his buggy. Turquoise walked up and looked down at him. "Why, he's smiling. I reckon he thought he had the loaded pistol right up until he felt the bullet."

Rio looked down at the dead man. "You think that's it?"

"Why else could it be?" Turquoise asked.

Elmer got in the buggy seat.

"Wait a minute," said the judge. "You'd better take these to his mother." He handed Elmer the dueling pistols in their leather case. "I know these pistols have been in the family a long time, and she may want them, but you must not tell Harriet details about what happened here tonight or we'll all be in trouble."

"She'll want to know," the clerk said.

"Tell her at your own risk," the judge warned.

"Why do I have to face the Iron Lady?" Elmer whimpered.

"Just do it!" the judge thundered. Elmer snapped the whip and the buggy pulled away.

"Now we must all scatter," ordered the judge. "And not a one of us must breathe what's happened here tonight."

Men began melting away into the shadows.

Turquoise only had eyes for Rio. She embraced him a

long moment, loving him as she could never love another. "I thought you were going to be killed."

Rio kissed her forehead and stared down into her face. "You've forgotten," he whispered, "this isn't the end. I still have that murder charge hanging over my head. No doubt I'll be sent to prison or be hanged."

Trace strode over. "Not if I can hire the best lawyers in Texas."

Rio looked grave. "I've just killed one of the most important men in this state." He turned to watch the buggy disappearing up the road. "No doubt his mother will do her best to see me hanged."

Trace nodded. "Well, that's not today's worry. Let's get back to the hotel. I reckon I have an upset wife waitin' for me there. I'll explain what happened."

However, Cimarron ran into his arms when they arrived at the hotel. "I've been so worried about all of you."

Trace held her like he would never let her go and kissed her. "Darlin', everything's all right now, but there's a lot to tell you."

Cimarron looked anxiously at Turquoise. "I heard some of it from Fern. Are you all right, dear?"

Turquoise held onto Rio's arm to control her trembling and nodded. "I want you to meet the man I'm in love with."

Rio kissed Cimarron's hand. "So glad to meet you, senora."

"Where are the kids?" Trace looked around.

"Fern's got them up in our suite, playing games with them. It's too late to catch the train back home. Why don't we stay over for the Fourth?"

Trace grinned. "Darlin', there's a parade tomorrow. I'm sure the kids would love that."

"Good." Cimarron linked her arm with her husband's. "Then let's go in the hotel."

* * *

However, the next morning, Cimarron excused herself from the festivities, saying she wasn't feeling well. Turquoise was out at Rio's ranch, both of them still shaken up from yesterday's tragedy. Trace had taken the children to the parade and festivities. Now Cimarron dressed, called for a carriage, and had the driver take her to the Forester residence. As she passed the state capitol, she saw that the state flag was flying at half-staff in honor of the dead senator, but nothing could stop Texans from celebrating the Fourth of July. Around her, she heard firecrackers exploding and children laughing and in the distance, the echoing sounds of a parade.

The carriage passed a newsboy shouting, "Extra! Senator Dies! Extra!"

Cimarron signaled her driver to stop and get her a paper and read it as the carriage started up the winding road to the elegant Tarrytown.

"Senator Edwin Forester, of the important and well-known Forester family, was killed under mysterious circumstances yesterday evening. Sources said he died of a gunshot wound. Authorities have been unable to figure out what actually happened to the powerful legislator, who had been rumored to be planning on running for governor next term. . . ."

Cimarron sighed and laid the paper aside, dreading what she knew she must do this morning. There were many carriages out in front of the imposing Forester mansion and a black-ribboned wreath on the big front door. "Wait for me," she said to her driver. "I'll only be a few minutes."

There were other carriages there, no doubt people coming to offer condolences and to view the body.

When the Mexican butler conducted Cimarron into the entry hall, she noted somber people standing around in the parlor, where the body was laid out in a magnificent casket. There were flowers everywhere that seemed to override the scent of dust and furniture polish. It was sort of a decaying, sweet scent, like the whole house was rotting down along with its residents.

"Tell Mrs. Forester that Cimarron Durango is here to see her," she whispered to the butler.

He nodded and left, returning in a few minutes. "I'm sorry, but Mrs. Forester says she is not at home to you."

"She must see me," Cimarron insisted. "Tell her I have something I must tell her."

He disappeared into the library again and returned once more to shake his head. "Sorry."

"I must see her." Cimarron pushed past the butler and strode into the library with the butler protesting behind her.

Harriet Forester stood up, cold and distant in her black silk mourning dress. "How dare you come into my house with my dead son still not buried?"

"We must talk," Cimarron said, noting that the Iron Lady had once been a beauty, but now her iron-gray hair was turning white and her face was lined with sorrow.

"I will call the police and have you thrown out!"

"Hear me out first and then you do what you think best." Cimarron stood her ground.

"Very well, but I doubt you have anything to say that would interest me." She waved away the butler. "Jose, close the door behind you and see we are not disturbed."

The butler bowed out of the room and closed the door.

Mrs. Forester glared at her with those pale turquoise eyes. "You will understand if I do not offer you tea."

"I did not expect any. This is not a social call." Cimarron sat down on a small satin love seat.

From somewhere in the house drifted haunting laughter.

"My daughter Emily." Harriet made a motion with her jeweled hand.

"I understand," Cimarron replied softly. Even though she knew the Foresters did their best to hide their insane relative, most everyone in Texas knew about this girl who had been carried off by the Comanche and returned with a damaged mind.

"Well, what is it you want?" The Iron Lady paced up and down, her long black silk dress swishing in the silence.

"I am sorry about your son," Cimarron said.

"You'll be sorrier when I tell you I intend to begin an investigation into Edwin's death and send everyone involved to prison. His secretary told me some of what happened. Moreover, I'll send that dirty Mexican to the gallows."

"Mrs. Forester." Cimarron hesitated. "I'm not sure you'll want to do that when I tell you what I know."

"Don't try to talk me out of it." Mrs. Forester picked up a newspaper from a table and shook it in Cimarron's face. "Have you seen the papers? Some are saying that my dear boy fought an illegal duel, short-loaded that pistol, and got it himself by mistake. They have ruined his reputation."

Cimarron took a deep breath. "I don't think that's what happened at all."

"I don't understand it," Harriet murmured and walked over to the desk to pick up the leather case that held the pistols. "Edwin was an expert shot and very familiar with these guns. They've been in our family at least fifty years. My husband was killed by these very pistols and by your father-in-law."

Her expression turned ugly and for a moment, Cimarron thought the woman would hurl the case at her. She remembered then what she had been told, that years ago, the old Don Diego Durango had indeed fought a duel with the senior Forester and killed him for attempting to seduce and then insulting the don's beloved Cheyenne wife, the gentle beauty Velvet Eyes.

"Mrs. Forester, I don't think Edwin was confused and I do think he deliberately short-loaded the one pistol, but I also believe he intended to take that pistol himself."

"Why?" Mrs. Forester's pale turquoise eyes flashed sparks.

Cimarron took a deep breath. "I had a conversation with Edwin less than an hour before he died."

Harriet's eyebrows went up and she looked puzzled. "The guard did say a blond-haired woman visited Edwin's office just before he left for the duel. Why were you there?"

"What I told Edwin, I'm going to tell you now," Cimarron said. "And you must never breathe a word of it. It changed Edwin and I think it will change you."

"It will not!" Harriet snapped. "And another thing, I was given that copy of his will this morning by his lawyer, and he leaves all his wealth to that Mexican girl. I assure you I will fight it all the way to the Supreme Court. The vixen will not get one penny, if that's what she's after."

"No need to go to court," Cimarron said softly. "I'm sure Turquoise would not accept his money."

"Then why are you here?" Harriet paced up and down, her black silk dress rustling like dead leaves from a dying tree.

Cimarron took a deep breath. "I have come to tell you what I told Edwin yesterday afternoon in his office. It is a secret that the old don told me on his deathbed and I have kept it all these years."

"Humph!" the woman huffed. "I'm not inclined to keep a secret of the hated Durango clan."

"On the contrary, it is a secret of the Foresters—no, a secret of Edwin's that you must keep to protect his memory and your family from scandal."

Harriet Forester paused and stared at Cimarron. "What is this great secret?"

"Did you ever meet my ward?"

"Of course," Harriet snapped. "Edwin brought her to the house. Although I had a feeling I knew her and it made me uneasy somehow, Edwin was crazy for her. He was determined to marry her, come hell or high water."

"I told him yesterday why he could not marry Turquoise, even if he won the duel."

Harriet snorted. "Evidently you do not know the financial and political power of the Forester family. If my son was determined to have her, I would have moved heaven and earth to make it happen and the Durangos would not have been able to stop the marriage."

Cimarron sighed. This was going to be so difficult. "Harriet, do you remember a very pretty Mexican maid named Rosa you hired here more than twenty years ago?"

"Of course not. What has that got to do with anything?" Harriet paced up and down, her mourning dress rustling. "We've had dozens of pretty Mexican girls work in this house. I can't remember one Rosa from a Maria or a Carmelita. They're just hired help, after all."

"Edwin obviously took a real liking to this particular girl," Cimarron said.

"Edwin was always taking a liking to this maid or that," his mother said with a snort. "I was always having to fire them or ship them back to Mexico because Edwin helped himself to their charms like so much free candy. A lot of rich, spoiled young men do that."

"You threw this one out in the winter cold without a penny," Cimarron said. "My mother-in-law, Velvet Eyes, discovered Rosa starving on the streets and took her home to the Triple D as her personal maid."

"I don't see what all this talk of a Mexican slut has anything to do with—"

"Mrs. Forester, did you take a really close look at my ward?"

"Of course she was pretty, if that's what you're getting at," Harriet snapped. "I'll admit I've never seen Edwin so crazy about a girl before."

"Because Edwin loved himself so much and when he looked at her, it was like looking in a mirror," Cimarron said.

"What?" Harriet whirled.

"Did you not notice the girl has pale turquoise eyes? Did you not see the shape of her face, the way she moves? So like you?"

Harriet went suddenly pale. "What—what are you trying to tell me?"

"The same thing I told Edwin yesterday afternoon," Cimarron said softly. "No matter what, he couldn't marry Turquoise because she was his own daughter by Rosa."

Harriet collapsed on a chair, shaken. "My God! How dare you? You lie!"

"Do I?" Cimarron got up, walked over to the sideboard, poured a small sherry, brought it back, and placed it in Harriet's shaking hand. "You must have sensed there was something different, eerily familiar about her. Certainly Edwin did. Only neither of you realized that you were seeing a Forester."

Harriet sipped her drink and Cimarron saw the woman's hand shake.

For a long moment, there was no sound except the haunting laughter of the crazy daughter and the echo of fireworks from outside.

Finally Harriet said, "And what has all this to do with the duel?"

Cimarron sighed. "I have to tell you that I think when Edwin realized I was telling the truth, that the woman he adored he could not marry, he committed suicide."

"No, he wouldn't." She shook her gray head.

"He was rich and spoiled and had always had everything in the world his own way. The Forester money and power bought everything, but this was the one thing he wanted most and could not have. I think he deliberately short-loaded that pistol, made sure he got it himself, and walked out on that duel ground to be killed."

Harriet's face had gone pasty white and she said nothing

for a long moment. "Then in a way, he's a hero, not a villain, as the newspaper painted him."

"I suppose. But of course, you must never tell this. Neither Turquoise nor her beloved, Rio, know this and it would only bring more scandal to your family."

Outside in the distance, fireworks exploded and the silence in the library was deafening.

"I must go now." Cimarron stood up.

"Wait." Harriet held up a hand. "Are you telling me I have a granddaughter, the only grandchild I may ever have, and I must never acknowledge or have a relationship with her?"

Cimarron nodded. "It's part of the price you pay for Edwin's sin. Now I presume you will not probe into this duel any deeper?"

Harriet nodded and tears sprang to her turquoise eyes and ran down her cheeks. "My granddaughter will now marry the man who killed Edwin?"

"As Edwin knew she would. I think he was all right with that, you see."

"Yes." She looked suddenly very forlorn and old sitting in her chair, and the laughter from the crazy daughter drifted through the house again.

"I really must go." Cimarron walked to the door.

"Wait." Harriet came to her feet and held up a restraining hand. "If Edwin wanted her to have all his property, I would—"

"I told you she wouldn't accept it, and anyway, it would raise questions."

Harriet set her sherry on the desk. "But I can't bear to think of a Forester being poor. I—I think I should send a gift to her. Edwin would have wanted it."

"You know that would make her wonder, and the secret cannot come out," Cimarron protested.

"I can't even attend her wedding, can I?" Mrs. Forester wiped her eyes and looked humbled, a broken woman.

Cimarron shook her head. "I'm sorry. It would cause talk."

"My only grandchild," Harriet murmured, "marrying a poor man and living in poverty. All the dead Foresters would roll over in their graves. I'm sure this is not what Edwin wanted for his child."

"Well, we're giving the couple a herd of fine-blooded cattle and horses," Cimarron said, "so in a few years, if they can acquire some land—"

"He has no land?"

"Only fifty acres," Cimarron admitted. "We wanted to give him some of ours out near our place, but they want to stay in Austin."

Harriet paused, then smiled. "I have plenty of land. In fact, we own five thousand acres on the south side of the city through one of our New York companies."

Cimarron shook her head. "I told you, it would cause talk if you gave her anything—"

"But if she thought it came from her guardian and I transferred the land to the Durangos . . ."

"Are you sure you want to do this?" Cimarron paused with her hand on the doorknob.

Harriet nodded. "I think it is what her father would have wanted me to do. Yes, Edwin would be pleased." Tears came to her eyes again, those pale turquoise eyes that had been the telltale mark of all the Foresters for generations. "My most trusted lawyer will contact you."

"All right. Then we can make this work without Turquoise ever finding out the truth."

"Oh, there's a note that Edwin left. His lawyer gave me a copy and is waiting for my approval to release it to the courts. I told him I didn't understand it and to destroy it," Harriet said and walked to the desk.

"There's really no need—" Cimarron began.

"Yes, there's a note Edwin added with the will. It should

make my granddaughter very happy." She went over to the big desk and pulled out the folded paper, handing it to Cimarron. "I will tell my lawyer to release it to the proper authorities and the newspapers tomorrow after I bury my son."

Cimarron took the note, read it, and smiled. "Yes, this will make her and Rio very happy."

"I'm glad." Harriet smiled through her tears. "There has been so little happiness in this house. The Foresters were always about power and money and ruthless ambition. All it has done is make us the most hated family in Texas."

"I'm sure that's not true." Cimarron patted her shoulder gently.

"Oh, it's true." Harriet walked to open the library door and looked at the crowd filing past the coffin in the parlor. "All those people in there to pay their respects? They're not here because they liked Edwin. They are here because they fear not to come and some of them probably just want to make sure he is really dead. The Foresters have no real friends."

"I am so sorry," Cimarron said as she saw the tears run down the once-beautiful face.

"Not as sorry as I am," Harriet whispered. "I wish I could have you as a friend, but I know that would cause talk. We won't meet again, will we?"

"Not in this life." Cimarron shook her head.

"Then tell my granddaughter for me . . . No, you can't do that, can you?"

Cimarron shook her head. "I am so sorry; so sorry you had to find all this out this way."

She noticed then that the coffin was draped with pink roses and turned a curious look to Harriet.

Harriet shrugged. "His employee said Edwin requested them, but why, I'll never know."

"I don't suppose it matters now," Cimarron whispered. The scent of cloying, decaying flowers again mingled with the scent of dust and mold and furniture polish as she pulled her scarf up around her face, went out the door, down the hall, keeping her face turned away from those in the parlor. No one must ever know she had been here, except Trace. She would have to tell her husband everything.

It was all going to work out. She slipped outside, got in the carriage, and said to the driver, "Back to the hotel, please."

She went up to her room and wiped her eyes and washed her face. She was just dressing for dinner when Trace came in.

"Darlin', you missed a great parade."

"Oh, did I? Did the children enjoy themselves?"

"Yes. Turquoise and Rio are down in the dinin' room now havin' lunch with them. Oh, I think that pair are wantin' to get married later this month, as soon as he finds out if he's goin' to have to stand trial or not."

"Then we'll plan a wedding." She came into his arms and kissed him. "I've heard a rumor that something is about to break in that case."

"Oh?"

"Let's see what happens tomorrow." She smiled and kissed him again, remembering the note Edwin had added in with the will:

> *Rio Kelly is not guilty of murder. I myself hired some men to burn his barn and kill him, but he managed to shoot one of the attackers. It was self-defense. The men I forced to do this evil deed owed me money or I blackmailed them and I forced them to take part. I also had Rio attacked and beat up. Those thugs hang out at the Boxing Ring Saloon. Hamilton, the owner, was one of them. He hired the other two. I write this of my own free will and under no duress. Signed Edwin S. Forester, this day of July 3, 1876.*

"I've got something I must tell you and then we will never mention it again." Cimarron held Trace very close and kissed him. She only hoped Turquoise was as happy today as she was.

# Epilogue

Turquoise held onto Rio's hand tightly as they ran down the aisle and out onto the church steps, where their friends showered them with rice as the church bells rang joyously. "Oh, Rio, I'm so happy to finally be your bride!"

"Not as happy as I am, my beloved, to finally be your husband." He paused then and kissed her deeply as the crowds of well-wishers gathered around them, shouting congratulations. "I've sent my mother news of our wedding. I'm sure she will be so happy and pray for us."

"I'm sorry she could not attend," Turquoise whispered.

"My word!" Fern, her maid of honor, ran up to her. "I just hope my wedding next month is as lovely as this one!"

Turquoise hugged her. "It will be."

Cimarron and Trace walked up, all smiles.

"Well," said Cimarron, hanging onto her children, "Raven and Ace did pretty well as flower girl and ring bearer."

"They did a great job!" Turquoise squatted to hug the two dressed-up children.

"Is there cake yet?" Ace asked.

"No, silly." Raven whacked her brother. "That's at the big party. Don't boys know anything?"

Cimarron laughed. "Ladies don't hit their brothers. It was a great wedding, and now we'll have the biggest reception Austin ever saw, with everyone in town invited."

"It should be big." Trace laughed. "I've hired a band for the town plaza and there's enough food and beer for thousands."

He shook hands with the smiling Rio. "You're getting a beautiful girl. You two don't be strangers, *si?*"

Rio clapped him on the back. "We'll come out and visit your ranch often, I promise."

The children were already running around on the church lawn as Cimarron brushed back Turquoise's long white lace veil and hugged her. "Oh, by the way, we have a little extra gift for you."

"Another?" Turquoise's eyes widened. "You've given us so much already. Why, Night Spirit alone is worth a fortune."

"I think you'll like this." Cimarron handed her the envelope.

"What is this?" Turquoise opened the papers and read them, her eyes growing wide. "Oh, this is too much."

Trace shrugged. "We thought you could use it."

Turquoise turned and looked up at her love. "Rio, darling, the Durangos have just given us that five thousand acres next to your little ranch."

"What?" Rio took the papers from her hand in disbelief. "Why, we can't accept such a generous gift."

"But of course you can." Cimarron smiled. "It's not as if we don't already own half of Texas. We didn't need this little bit."

Turquoise hugged her. "All this time, I had no idea you had a New York company."

Cimarron shrugged and Turquoise saw her guardians exchange glances. "There's lots of things you don't know, my dear, but this is just an extra surprise for your wedding."

Turquoise nodded blissfully, already lost again in the dark eyes of her new husband. Then she noticed an ornate carriage stopped across the street from the church. In the carriage was an elegant, gray-haired woman all dressed in black. The woman looked familiar somehow. "Who is that?"

Cimarron turned and looked as the carriage pulled away and went slowly down the street. After a long moment, she said, "Hmm. Maybe just some old lady who was reliving memories of her own wedding or wishing she had a daughter or granddaughter to give a big wedding for."

"Poor thing," Turquoise murmured.

"Yes, poor thing," Cimarron echoed, "poor, poor thing."

Fern diverted their attention. "My word, Turquoise, you forgot to throw the bouquet."

Turquoise looked down at her armful of scarlet oleander blossoms. "I know some may think it was an odd choice for a bridal bouquet, but it has special significance for us." She winked at her bridegroom and he winked back.

"It's beautiful," Cimarron said.

"I'll throw it at the big reception tonight," Turquoise promised, "and Fern, you must be sure and catch it."

"Maybe you can throw it to one of those pitiful debutantes who'll show up uninvited and alone." Fern laughed. "I don't need it. I've already got my man, remember?" She put her arm through the bashful, lanky Luke's.

"We both do!" Turquoise reached up to kiss Rio again and he held onto her like he would never let her go.

"My darling Senora Kelly," he whispered, "I can hardly wait for the dancing and party to be over so I can hold you in my arms all night and kiss you again and again."

"Me too!" she agreed. "And for many more years to come, my vaquero!"

"See everyone at the reception!" she called. Then she

gathered up her yards of white lace skirt and they both ran for their fine open carriage under a shower of rice. Tip was sitting in back, all washed and groomed with ribbons around his neck. The little dog barked and barked, wagging his stubby tail. Silver Sippers and Peso were tied to the back of the carriage, flowers and ribbons woven into their manes and tails. They were placidly munching the fresh flowers strung all over the back of the vehicle, not caring they were destroying the decorations.

Rio lifted his bride in and the married couple drove away, looking forward to a deliriously happy future together forever in Texas.

Fans of western historical romances
won't want to miss
Georgina Gentry's first book
in her exciting new series,
THE TEXANS.
Read on for a sample of


DIABLO,


a Zebra paperback on sale now!

# Prologue

*The Texas Panhandle, Autumn, 1877*

He Not Worthy of a Name crouched with his knife, watching the big herd of longhorns grazing in the coming twilight. On the flat plains, there was nothing—not a hill, not a tree, only hundreds of fat longhorns munching the arid buffalo grass.

He was so weak and sick that he swayed a little, knowing that he would only get one chance to kill a steer. If he missed, the spooky animals would all turn and thunder away, bellowing a warning to the others. If he managed to bring one down, he would have to eat it raw, but he had been eating anything he could catch raw for weeks now, and he felt the Spirit of Death hovering over him. He had one chance to fill his shrunken belly, and if he missed killing a beef, he would fall to the ground and die because he was too far gone and too fevered to walk farther. He had seen only fourteen winters, but he did not expect to see another.

By the campfire, Trace Durango dismounted with a tired sigh and looked up at the fading sunset. As always, the wide Texas sky was splashed with purple, orange, and scarlet as the sun sank low to the west. "God, I'm wrung out like a dishrag. Cookie, you got any coffee?"

"Boss, don't I always?" The grizzled old man took a tin cup off the backboard of the chuck wagon and hobbled over to the big pot on the fire. "The boys about got all the strays rounded up?"

Trace accepted the cup gratefully and knelt by the fire as he fumbled in his denim shirt for his makin's. "Yep. Another day, we'll have them all headed south for the ranches before the Blue Northers blow in." Damn, that coffee was good. He sipped the strong, hot brew and rolled himself a cigarette.

In the distance, wafted on the cool wind, he heard a steer bellow a warning, and then another picked up the cry. The giant herd moved restlessly, stamping its hooves as other cattle took up the lowing. "Oh hell, don't tell me we've got a lobo or some coyotes sniffin' around the edge of the herd. They'll start a stampede." Irritably, he threw his coffee in the fire and stood up as Maverick, his half-Comanche adopted brother, rode up at a gallop.

"Trace, you hear that?" In the twilight, Maverick's eyes gleamed as gray as a gun barrel.

"*Si*, let's get out there and see what's upsettin' the steers." Trace swung up on his black stallion.

"I already sent some of the boys up to the north end of the herd, but figure they'll need backup if it's a pack of coyotes."

"Damn, and things had been goin' so well all day." Trace pulled his rifle out of the boot, checked to make sure it was loaded, then spurred his horse. "We don't need a stampede."

Trace, followed by Maverick, took off through the milling herd of lowing longhorns.

"Hey, boss!" One of the McBride cowboys rode toward

him. "You ain't gonna believe what we got cornered up on the north edge of the herd."

Trace hardly paused. "If it was coyotes, why didn't you just shoot them? You know how nervous these steers can get."

"We didn't know what to do with him, but none of us wanted to tangle with that big knife."

Trace reined in. "What the hell are you—?"

"You'll see. I told the boys to do nothin' 'til you got there."

Trace cantered past him, leading the trio now as they pushed through the milling cattle. He didn't know what was going on, but he was bone tired and not in the mood for games. They rode through the uneasy steers on this land that was as flat as a peso, heading into the twilight for the big group of riders circled on the far outskirts of the herd.

"What's going on, amigos?"

He swung off his stallion as the men made a path for him. What he faced took him a minute to take in, and even then, he didn't quite believe it.

A scrawny boy, probably not more than thirteen or fourteen, crouched in a defense mode behind a newly slaughtered steer. The boy wore nothing but a breechcloth, and his black hair was long. The fading light reflected off the bloody knife in his hand, and the boy's face was smeared with fresh blood. *Half-breed*, Trace thought, *like me*.

The boy was almost handsome until he turned his right side toward Trace and Trace got a good look at him. "Good God! What's going on here?"

He Not Worthy of a Name did not give ground, still gripping his knife. He had not gotten to eat much of the steer, only a few hurried raw bites, and now this white man would hang him. He knew by bitter experience that one did not kill the white man's cows without retribution. Well, he would go down fighting even though he was almost too sick to keep his balance.

"Boss," one of the McBride cowboys took off his hat and

wiped his forehead, "we just followed the noise, thinkin' it was a coyote, and here's what we found. What'll we do with him?"

Trace watched the boy, horrified and fascinated at the same time. The kid was so thin his ribs showed. He must not have eaten much in weeks, and the right side of his face . . . Trace shuddered. What was left of it was swollen, disfigured and burned.

Maverick whistled. "Looks like someone took a running iron to him."

"Who would do that to a kid?" Trace demanded and stepped forward.

The kid promptly waved his knife at Trace and took a shaky step backward.

"Some bastard who valued his cattle more than people, I reckon," one of the other cowboys muttered.

"Hey, Trace," Maverick said, "this is about like it was when you found me all those years ago. He's certainly a half-breed; let me see if I can talk to him." He stepped forward and said softly in Comanche, "We will not hurt you."

The boy looked puzzled, swayed on his feet, and brandished his knife.

"He didn't understand you," Trace said. "Let me try some Spanish or Cheyenne." He asked the boy his name in both languages, and the starving kid blinked and shook his head.

"Hell, this isn't doing any good," Trace said. He stepped toward the boy slowly, holding out his hand. "Give me the knife," he commanded. "We will help you."

"Watch out, brother," Maverick warned. "He looks desperate enough to kill you."

\* \* \*

He Not Worthy of a Name looked around at the circle of cowboys. He hadn't a chance against so many, but he would rather die fighting than hanging. He could speak a little English he had learned when the Sioux went to trade, but he did not trust these men. He might be a worthless half-breed slave, but he could die like a warrior and he would fight even though he was having a hard time staying conscious.

Trace watched him warily. The boy was near fainting, and he swayed on his feet. In the shape he seemed to be in, it was a wonder he was still alive. At that moment, Trace charged him suddenly, grabbing for the knife. The boy fought valiantly, but in his starving condition, he was no match for the big half-Spanish, half-Cheyenne cowboy. Even as Trace struggled with him, the boy lapsed into unconsciousness and collapsed.

"Hell," Trace threw the bloody knife away and swung the boy up in his arms. "This kid is all but dead. Maverick, ain't there a town about five or ten miles to the west? Ride in there and see if they've got a doctor."

Maverick wheeled his horse. "A doc ain't gonna like riding out here at night for an almost dead half-breed kid."

"Then persuade him," Trace snapped and lifted the limp boy up on his black horse and swung up behind him.

Then he turned to the crowd of curious cowboys. "You men see if you can quiet this herd, and Mac, you bring in some of that butchered steer. We'll all have steak tonight."

The men scattered, and Maverick galloped away into the coming night. Trace cradled the boy in his arms as he rode back through the milling herd to the campfire.

Cookie came out to meet him. "What you got there?"

Trace handed the boy down, then dismounted and turned

his horse over to one of the cowhands. "Some wild boy eating one of our steers raw. He's burning up with fever." He took the boy in his arms again and carried him over by the fire, laid him on a blanket. As the fire crackled, the boy opened his dark eyes, glanced at the fire, and evidently terrified, began to fight Trace.

He was no match for the big cowboy. "Take it easy," Trace whispered, "no one's gonna hurt you."

Whether he understood or not, the boy continued to fight while Trace held him down. "God, he's scared. Cookie, get him some water."

"No wonder," Cookie grumbled, limping toward the chuck wagon. "Looks like someone took a brandin' iron to his face." He brought Trace a tin cup of water and Trace held it out to the boy.

The boy hesitated and stopped fighting. Then slowly, he reached for the water and gulped it, most of it running down his chin from his shaking hand.

"Get him some more, Cookie." Trace handed the cup back to the other man and stared at the right side of the boy's face. "I'd say it was a running iron, not a regular branding iron."

"Rustlers?" Cookie hobbled over to refill the cup, brought it back, and handed it to the boy, who drank it in three gulps.

Trace shrugged. "Well, those are the ones who usually use a makeshift branding iron. Maybe he interrupted a gang of them changin' brands on someone else's cattle, and that's how they punished him."

"Sick bastards," Cookie grumbled.

The fevered boy looked around, leaning on his elbows. He tried to speak. "Texas?"

"What?" Trace asked, taken off guard.

"Texas?" The boy looked up at him with big brown eyes.

He would have been handsome if it weren't for the burnt, swollen right side of his face.

Trace nodded, puzzled. "Texas. *Si*, this is Texas."

The faintest ghost of a smile crossed the boy's mouth, and he sighed. "Texas," he whispered and nodded, then fainted.

Trace put his hand on the boy's forehead. "He's burning up with fever and so near dead, I don't know if we can save him or not."

Mac rode up just then with a haunch of the butchered steer. "Hey, Cookie, looks like we all eat good tonight."

"And here I was plannin' on giving you a special treat: beans," Cookie said wryly.

Trace examined the boy. "Cookie, see if you can get some broth boilin' for the kid, and Mac, go get me a fresh bucket of water from the spring. If we can't get his fever down, he won't make it 'til the doc gets here."

Cookie paused and looked at the boy's feet. "Oh, hell, Trace, look at his feet. They're raw and bloody. He must have walked a hundred miles."

"Or maybe more," Trace said, shaking his head. "I reckon killin' a steer and eating it raw was his last effort to stay alive. Why do you think Texas was so important to him?"

The others shook their heads, and Cookie took the beef from Mac, began to cut it in chunks.

Trace took the boy's chin in his hand and gently turned the head so he could see the right side of his face. It was swollen and, in places, burned black. "Somebody tortured this kid. I wish I could get my hands on that bastard."

Mac had gone for the water and now returned to the fire. "You think he's from around here?"

Trace shook his head and began to wet the blanket the boy was wrapped in. "Don't think so. He didn't understand either Comanche or Cheyenne. Must be from farther north, maybe Colorado."

"Ute?" Mac squatted by the fire and poured himself a cup of coffee.

"Who knows?" Trace shrugged. "From the looks of the soles of his feet, he may have walked several hundred miles. He might even have started with a horse and, when it gave out, began walkin'. Wish I knew why Texas was so important to him."

Cookie got a pot of broth boiling and then began frying steak and making biscuits. The scent brought most of the Triple D and the Maverick-McBride ranch hands in to dismount by the fire.

"Whose turn is it to ride night herd?" Trace asked.

"Ted and Bill," a tanned cowboy said as he dismounted and strode over to stare at the unconscious boy. "God, he looks almost starved to death. What are you gonna do with him, Trace?"

Trace sighed and pushed his Stetson back. "Well, I reckon I'll take him home until I find out where he belongs. Cimarron will bring him through if nobody else can. You know how she is with all the hurt critters the kids bring in."

The others nodded agreement.

Cookie said, "Suppose he don't belong nowheres?"

"Well, then," Trace reached to pour himself a cup of coffee. "I reckon we might keep him. That's what we did with Maverick years ago, and it worked out okay."

The boy barely stirred as Trace tried to clean his burned, swollen cheek. Then old Cookie squatted and spooned broth in between his lips. "He's in pretty bad shape, Trace; he may not make it."

\* \* \*

He Not Worthy of a Name heard the man's voice deep, deep in his soul as he felt the life-giving broth run down his throat. So they weren't going to torture him yet for killing the white man's cow. They would wait until someone named Maverick returned. It didn't matter. He was too weak to fight anymore and he had made it to Texas. That had been his goal all these long, hungry moons and now he was here. He could die now.

Trace stared down into the boy's sweating face. "He's running a terrible fever. Didn't I see some willow trees over at the stream?"

A cowboy behind him said, "Yep, I saw 'em."

"Go peel the bark off some of them, and Cookie, you get ready to boil that. It's an old Indian remedy."

It was long past dark when Maverick returned with a cranky old doctor on a thin horse.

"If you'd told me how far it was, I wouldn't have come." He dismounted and reached for his black bag.

Maverick spat to one side. "You would have come if I'd had to throw you across your saddle."

The grizzled doctor rubbed his mustache and squatted by the fireside, staring at the boy. "You dragged me away from my dinner for a boy who's almost dead, and an Injun at that?"

Trace frowned. "Do you know who I am?" His tone had a warning edge to it.

"Uh, well, no, I reckon not."

"Trace Durango of the Triple D ranch."

The older man swallowed hard. Everyone knew the Triple D empire that covered hundreds of thousands of acres. "Oh, sorry, Señor Durango, I didn't realize—"

"Now see what you can do for this boy. There's gold in it for you if you save him."

The greedy old man's eyes lit up, and he reached for his bag in a hurry. "I'll see what I can do, but I can't promise anything. My God, what happened to his face? He looks like a monster!"

Trace shrugged. "We don't know for sure; maybe someone took a brandin' iron to it."

The doctor opened up his bag, took out some carbonic acid, and wiped the area around the swollen wounds. "Some back East got this new theory about something called germs, say you can kill 'em by disinfecting the area."

"We've been spoonin' willow bark water down his throat to bring his fever down," Cookie offered.

"Old Injun hogwash," the doctor snorted. "Don't think it's worth a damn."

"It works." Trace frowned.

The crew gathered around to watch silently as the old man cleaned the wound. "It's swollen up some, and he'll always be as ugly as hell. Too bad; looks like he was once handsome." He pulled down the blanket and looked the boy over, then turned him on his side. "This kid is almost starved to death, and he's got old scars on his back."

"Oh?" Trace stared at the boy's back, nodded. "He's been treated bad, maybe over a number of years. Take a look at his feet."

The doc squinted and frowned. "Good God, how far has he walked?"

Trace shook his head. "We don't know. We found him trying to eat a steer raw. He don't speak Spanish, Cheyenne, or Comanche, so he has to be from farther north, I reckon, or maybe west."

The doc shuddered as he cleaned and put medicine on the boy's soles, then leaned back and sighed. "Reckon I've done all I can for him. He needs food and rest, and even then he may not make it."

Trace stood up. "If I can get him home to my wife, she'll take care of him; she's the one who doctors all our cowboys and critters. Stay for supper, doc—we're having steak and biscuits."

"Sounds good," the old man grinned for the first time.

Later, Trace sent the man on his way with a very generous fee. Then he watched Cookie spooning broth into the boy's mouth. The Indian kid was barely conscious.

"Well, Maverick," he said with a sigh, "If I head back to the ranch with the kid, can you take over here?"

"You know I will, Trace. We'll move these steers farther south before the weather turns frosty."

The next morning, Trace fashioned a travois behind his black horse, which shied nervously as the men put the semiconscious boy in the blankets. "It'll take me a few days to get home, but I know where the water holes are along the way, and I can kill enough game to keep us fed."

"You watch out for that kid," Cookie warned, rubbing his chin with a flour-dusted hand, "I think he'd try to kill you if he got a chance."

"He's in no shape to kill anybody," Trace said as he mounted up, "but he's game enough to try. I'll see you boys back at the ranch in a few days. Adios."

Cimarron glanced out the window of the big white hacienda and saw her husband dismounting in front of the courtyard fountain. "Trace!" She flew out the door and into his arms. "Honey, what are you doing home early?"

"Hi, darlin', he kissed the tip of her nose. "Nothing wrong. I just brought in a half-breed kid we found up in the Panhandle."

She stared at the boy on the travois. "Oh, the poor thing!"

Trace watched her hurry to the half-conscious boy. She might be older than the first time he saw her in 1864, but to him, this yellow-haired wife had only grown more beautiful. "Oh, Trace, double damnation, what happened to him?"

Trace shook his head. "It's a long story, and we may never know all of it. I figure if anyone can help him, you can."

Cimarron turned and ran toward the house, shouting for vaqueros and the house servants. "Come quickly! *Muy pronto!* We have a very sick boy to help!"

Cimarron planned to put the boy in a bedroom of the big hacienda, but Trace wanted him put in the bunkhouse. "Darlin', I know you aren't thinking about this, but this kid could be dangerous. We don't know a thing about him."

"He's hurt—that's all I need to know. All right, we'll put him in the servant's quarters at the back of the house."

"Okay, I give up. See if Maria can cook up something he can eat. He may try to get away, but he won't get far with those feet. He's too weak to stand anyway."

Over the next several weeks, the boy improved. At first, Cimarron knew he was terrified, but he seemed to gradually realize no one would hurt him. The roundup crew was back at the ranchero by the time the boy was hobbling around the floor. His face was healing, but the right side would always be so scarred and twisted that little children backed away when they saw him and ran to their mothers who crossed themselves and muttered prayers. Cimarron had all the mirrors removed from the house so that he would not see his disfigured reflection.

The weather was spitting snow the day that he limped across the room toward a chair and the man who had saved him came in and shut the door. He Not Worthy of a Name backed away. He had no weapon to defend himself now if the white cowboys were going to torture him.

Trace smiled and gestured him into the chair. "Are you

feeling well?" he asked in English, feeling foolish because
he did not know what tongue the boy spoke.

The boy nodded.

"What is your name?" Trace asked.

The boy had not spoken for a long time and it was hard
to mouth the words. "I am called He Not Worthy of a
Name. I have not earned one."

"Do you want me to give you a name?" Trace leaned
back in a chair and reached into his shirt for a cigarillo.
"You can be a Durango."

The boy shook his head, watching Trace's hands. "I must
earn my own."

"All right then." Trace searched his pocket for a match,
and when he struck it, he saw the fright in the boy's dark
eyes as he shied away.

Trace noted the terror and, remembering the boy's
burned face, shook out the match. "We will not hurt you,"
he whispered.

The boy did not look as if he believed him.

"What tribe are you?" Trace leaned back in his chair.

"Santee Dakota."

Trace snorted in disbelief. "That tribe is hundreds of
miles north of here."

The boy only looked at him.

"All right then." Trace decided not to pursue that. "The
servants say you scream at night in your sleep."

The boy flushed and looked away.

"It is all right," Trace assured him. "We all have night-
mares now and then. Are you afraid?"

The boy hesitated. Evidently, he was ashamed to admit
his fear.

"If you are afraid, I can teach you to handle a pistol; then
no one will hurt you."

The boy smiled for the first time. "You—you would
do that?"

"*Si.*" Trace nodded. "How old are you? Do you know?"

The boy's face furrowed. "I—I think fourteen winter counts."

"Would you like to stay here at my ranch?"

"Is this Texas?" The boy looked out the window.

"Yes, this is Texas," Trace assured him, wondering why it was so important to him.

"Texas." The boy smiled. "Yes. I got here. I did not think I would."

Trace waited, but the boy did not elaborate. "Are you good with horses?"

The boy nodded.

"Fine." Trace leaned back in his chair. "You can move into the bunkhouse and be part of my crew. I will pay you to help with chores and care for horses."

"Pay?" The boy looked puzzled.

"*Si.*" Trace nodded. "You know, you work and I give you money for it."

"I have never been paid to work. I was a slave to an old Santee woman."

*Dios!* What all had happened to this boy in his short life?

"Well, now you will be paid. When you feel like it, you can come eat with the other cowboys."

The boy evidently did not believe him. "You—you are not going to torture me for killing your cow?"

Trace shook his head. "Is that what happened to you before?"

Terror crossed the boy's face as he seemed to remember something, but he did not answer. There was something very dark and terrible in his past, Trace thought, something the boy might never tell—maybe something more terrible than the branding.

"All right then," Trace stood up. "When you feel like it, we will begin lessons with the pistol, and I will show you around the ranch. This is a good place. Ask Maverick when he comes to visit. I found him as I found you. You can have a good future here in Texas." Trace went out and closed the door.

He Not Worthy of a Name stared after him. He could not believe everything the man had said, but then this was Texas. Hadn't his friends told him how wonderful it was before they died?


Over the winter, Trace taught the boy to handle a gun and allowed him to take care of the ranch's prize quarter horses.

One day in the early spring, he watched the boy through the window. "Cimarron," he mused, "this kid has an amazing talent for horses and pistols. I think he's better than I am."

"That's saying a lot, honey." She leaned over to kiss him. Trace Durango might be getting a little gray in his hair, but he still had a reputation as the best gun in Texas. "Don't you think we should give him a name?"

"I tried," Trace shrugged and sipped his coffee, "but he says he must earn his own name. Until then, we all just call him 'kid.'"

They watched their young children, Ace and Raven, run across the yard toward the boy. "Hey, kid," Ace yelled, "you want to saddle up and ride today?"

The boy nodded.

Cimarron smiled. "And you warned me he was dangerous. Our children love him."

"We still don't know a damned thing about him," Trace said. "But he does seem to have a special way with children and animals."

"Well, I don't care. If he wants to stay on the Triple D the rest of his life, we can always use a good hand."

Trace nodded. "I told him that. I also told him I have a few thousand acres over in the Big Bend country I'd sell him cheap if he ever wants to go out on his own. There're lots of wild horses there. He could make a good livin' catchin' and breakin' them, and he wouldn't have people staring at him all the time."

Cimarron's eyes misted. "It would be lonely for him without a woman."

"*Si*, but look at him, darlin'. He looks like a monster. Can you imagine any woman lovin' him?"

"A special woman," Cimarron whispered, "a woman who loves him for his heart, not his looks."

Trace shook his head as they watched the boy saddle up three horses. "It would take a special woman all right, but I'm afraid he won't find her."

"I'm going to teach him to read and write," Cimarron said. "If he's lonely, he can always lose himself in a book."

Trace grinned at her, loving her more than ever. "Darlin', whatever you want to do."

And so she taught the mysterious boy along with her own children and the children of the vaqueros. There was something very sad and angry about him that she was unable to fathom. It had to be worse than just mistreatment, she thought, but he would never let anyone get close to him. He was a loner—an angry loner.

One warm spring day, she happened to be looking out the front windows toward the big fountain with its pool of water. The kid, passing by, stopped to stare at the fountain, then looked into the pool.

Cimarron wanted to run out and stop him, but he was already staring at his reflection, first in disbelief, then in horror as he backed away. Since she had taken down all the mirrors, he must not have realized how he looked, and now the terrible reality had sunk in and there was nothing she or anyone could do to protect him from that. She ran out the French doors onto the veranda.

"It's all right," she reassured him and tried to put her arm around him, but he shook his head and backed away, tears gathering in his eyes. Then he turned and ran into the barn, where he hid.

She told Trace what had happened.

"Leave him alone," he said. "The kid will have to learn to live with it, painful as that might be. I don't think there's anything we can do except be kind to him."

One day she was reading her little class a book of fairy tales when the kid interrupted suddenly, evidently disturbed. "Why is it the beautiful yellow-haired princess always kisses the beast or the frog and he becomes a handsome prince? Couldn't she love him if he were not handsome?"

Cimarron winced. Why had she not remembered the boy's disfigurement? "Of course she could," she answered softly, "if she were the right kind of girl—a kind, caring one."

"I don't want to hear any more of those." He turned over his chair as he ran out, slamming the door behind him. It was weeks before he came quietly into her class again, but she read the class no more fairy tales.

Events at the ranch went along quietly for the next few months as the half-breed boy grew tall and lithe. Then one late summer morning, Trace found a note on the veranda table as he sat down for breakfast.

Cimarron came outside, saw Trace's ashen face. "What's the matter?"

He offered her the note. "The kid has left."

"What?" She took the note from his hand. She had taught the boy to read and write, and here in his simple handwriting, he was thanking them and moving on. "But why? He's still just a boy, and we gave him a good home." She began to cry.

"I think I've always known he wouldn't stay," Trace sighed. "He's as restless as a wild mustang, and we never really knew much about him. I think he has unfinished business somewhere in his past, something terrible, more terrible than brandin', and maybe he can't rest until he takes care of it."

"How could anything be more horrible than that?"

Trace shook his head. "I don't know; I reckon no one does but him."

"But how will he live?" she whispered and crumpled the note. "And what will I tell the children?"

"I've taught him well, maybe too well," Trace sighed. "In a year or so, he'll probably be the best gun in Texas, better than me or even Maverick. There're plenty who would pay a top gunfighter to do their dirty work. I hear they're looking for hired guns in Lincoln County, New Mexico. There's talk of a range war there."

"A gunfighter." Cimarron sank back in her chair. "They never live very long; there's always a better, faster gun."

"I know, and to think I taught him. He was a strange, moody kid, with a terrible life before I found him. He never did tell us much, and now I reckon we never will know his secrets."

"Maybe he'll come back to us someday, and he'll find a girl and be happy," Cimarron said doubtfully.

"Not likely. You think any girl could love a man with a face like a monster?" Trace rolled a cigarette. "Maybe we'll never know what happened to him. I shouldn't have taught him to handle a gun."

"He wanted that badly, and he was so afraid, and full of so much rage," she reminded him.

"And he never got a name," Trace mused. "Maybe he'll finally 'earn' one. It seemed important to him. With that scarred face, if there's news of him, people will remember, and the tales will travel all across Texas."

Cimarron ducked her head and blinked back the tears. Gunfighters didn't live long, everyone knew that. No doubt he'd die in the middle of a dusty street somewhere far away. She closed her eyes and said prayers for the strange, maimed kid and hoped he would find happiness, or whatever it was he was seeking.

# Chapter 1

*On a northbound train to Wyoming, early April 1892*

Diablo paused between the swaying cars, looking through the door to see who was inside before he entered. No gunfighter worth his bullets would enter an area without checking out the lay of the land, especially since this car was full of Texas gunfighters, all hired killers like himself.

He had come a long way since Trace Durango had found him fifteen years ago when he was a Santee slave known as He Not Worthy of a Name. Well, he had earned a name now, and when men heard it, they turned pale and backed down from the big, half-breed gunfighter with the scarred face. He dressed all in black, from his Stetson down to his soft, knee-high moccasins. The superstitious peasants along the Rio Grande had given him the name: Diablo, the devil. It suited him just fine.

Now finally he was headed north to take care of unfinished business. He had waited a long, long time for this, and all these years he had been planning and perfecting his aim. Though the Wyoming Stock Growers Association was paying exorbitant money to bring this trainload of killers north, the money did not interest Diablo. What interested him was vengeance, and now, finally, he would have it. He was no longer the small and weak half-breed slave. No, now he had a name and was respected and feared throughout the West. Diablo had gained a reputation as a fast, deadly gunman.

Trace Durango had done well in teaching him to use a Colt, and he had used it time and time again in range wars and saloon showdowns. His gun was for hire, and he had fought side by side with men like Billy the Kid. Billy had been dead more than ten years now. Many of the others were dead too, before they reached middle age. In the end, that would probably be his fate, but for now, all that mattered was finishing his business with four men. His biggest fear was that they might now be dead and no longer able to face a showdown.

Diablo swung open the door and stood there watching the others inside. The shades had been ordered drawn, and the light in the swaying car was dim. Most of the men turned to stare at him, unsmiling, cigar smoke swirling above their heads. They did not nod a welcome, and he had expected none. These were hired pistoleros like himself, Texas gunfighters, on a special train to Wyoming where a range war was about to start. An hombre named Frank Canton had come down to hire twenty-five of the best, offering great pay and bonuses for every rustler and nester killed.

The train swayed, and the tracks made a rhythmic click-clack as conversation in the car ceased. All the men were looking at him, but he stared only at the men in the first row of seats. Diablo liked to have his back against the wall. The two men withered under his frown and hurriedly got up and retreated down the car. Diablo took the space they had vacated as if it were his right.

"Who in the hell is that half-breed?" The growling voice drifted toward him.

"Shh! Be quiet, Buck; that's Diablo. You don't want to make him mad."

"The Diablo?" Now he sounded impressed.

"There's only one," said the other.

"He don't look like so much."

"You challenge him, you'll find out."

"Maybe I'll just do that when we hit Wyoming."

Diablo sighed, pulled his black Stetson down over his eyes, and leaned back against the scarlet horsehair cushions, then opened the shade, stared out the window at the passing landscape. Quickly he averted his eyes, not wanting to see the reflection of his scarred face, and closed the shade again.

He probably didn't look like much to the others, who sported noisy, big spurs, fancy silver conchos and pistols, and boots of the best leathers in bright colors. Diablo dressed in the color of the night, and he wore moccasins, the better to move silently against an enemy without them knowing he was coming. Silver conchos and pistols had a way of reflecting light that an enemy could see for a long way. He not only moved silently, but his appearance was as black as a thunderstorm, with no bit of reflected light to give him away.

Now he stuck a slender cigarillo between his lips, but he did not light it. He never lit them. The flash of a match or the slightest scent of tobacco smoke would also give a man away, and he had learned from the Santee Sioux that he must move as silently as a spirit—kill and be gone. No wonder the Mexicans averted their eyes and crossed themselves as he rode past.


Hours later, Diablo decided he would have a drink and moved toward the club car. Balancing lightly in his moccasins as the train rumbled and click-clacked along the rails, he was acutely aware of each man he passed, sensing whether each was a threat or not. One or two eyed him, hands fidgeting nervously, as if thinking of being the one who killed the infamous Diablo, but each seemed to think twice and let him pass unchallenged.

In the club car, five men hunched over a table playing cards. Diablo paused in the doorway, looking them over. Then slowly the conversation ceased as each turned to look at him.

"Good God, look at his face!" the big, unshaven one muttered. He had red hair, and freckles showed through the balding spots.

"Be quiet, Buck," warned a pudgy one with missing teeth, and a greasy ponytail of brown hair. "You want to die before you ever get to Wyoming?"

"But he looks like a monster."

Nobody else said anything, waiting to see if the newcomer would take offense, but Diablo pretended he had not heard the remark. If he killed or challenged everyone who commented on his scarred face, his six gun would never be in its holster. Instead, he walked softly to the small bar and addressed the black waiter. "Beer."

He felt the gaze of the others on his back, but he ignored them.

"Hey," the one called Buck asked, "you got a big rattlesnake hatband and rattles on that Stetson. You kill it yourself?"

Diablo nodded as he took his beer and moved across the scarlet carpet to a comfortable chair with its back against a wall and sat down. Play at the poker table seemed suspended.

"Hell," snorted a short man in a derby hat, "it ain't no big thing to kill a giant rattler. Anyone can shoot them."

Diablo drilled him with his hard stare. "I didn't shoot it. When it struck at me, I put my foot on its head and killed it with my knife."

The man with the ponytail raised his bushy eyebrows, and the light reflected off the silver conchos on his leather vest. "Man has to be fast as greased lightnin' to kill a snake that way."

Diablo didn't answer, and he knew they all stared at his rattler hatband with the dozen rattles still attached. Now he took out a fresh cigarillo, stuck it in his mouth, and gazed out the window.

"Hey, half-breed, you need a light?" The one called Buck half rose from his chair, his voice challenging. He wore big spurs, and when he moved, they rattled like the tin pans on a peddler's cart.

The others tried to shush him.

Diablo was in no mood to kill someone today. He merely looked at the challenger, dark eyes glowering, and the man sat down suddenly.

"Well, boys," Buck huffed, his dirty, freckled hands as nervous as his unshaven face, "let's get this game goin', shall we?"

Diablo watched the country gliding past the train windows for a long moment. They were only hours from Wyoming, and he was weary of the long trip. He reached for a newspaper on the nearby table. Cimarron Durango had taught him to read, and that made up for his loneliness. The others raised their heads and watched him as if astounded that a gunfighter was reading, then returned to their poker game.

Sunny sat between her father and Hurd Kruger as Hurd drove the buggy along the dusty road toward the train station in the town of Casper. Early spring flowers now bloomed along the way and in the fields where hundreds of cattle grazed.

"Thank you, Mr. Kruger, for inviting me along," she said politely, looking up at him. He was a big, beefy man with yellow teeth that he sucked constantly. His hair and mustache were coal black, and when he sweated, little drops of dye ran down the sides of his ruddy face.

"Now, Sunny, dear, you ought to at least call me Hurd. I'm not really your uncle."

The way he looked at her made her feel uneasy. He'd been looking at her that way ever since she'd gone into her teens, and now that she was eighteen, he looked at her that way more and more often. She brushed a blond wisp back under her pale blue bonnet. "All right," she agreed and looked over at her father. Swen Sorrenson did not look pleased.

"Hurd, I still don't think much of this idea," he said, his Danish accent still strong after all these years.

"Now, Swen, we've been through this before, and anyway, we shouldn't discuss this in front of our Sunny, should we?"

It upset her that her father seemed uneasy. Her mother had died giving birth to her, and Sunny felt obliged and guilty about Dad's loss. If it hadn't been for his obligations in raising a daughter in this rough land, he might have re-married or even returned to Denmark. He had always seemed frail and ill suited to this wild wilderness.

"Uncle Hurd, I mean Hurd, why are we going to town?" she asked.

"Business. The Stock Growers Association business. You know I am the president. But don't you worry your pretty little head about that, Sunny—you can go shoppin' while your dad and I tend to it."

That didn't account for the unhappy look in Swen's pale blue eyes, but she decided not to ask any more questions. A trip to a big town was a rare treat for a ranch girl.

They were approaching the town, and her excitement built. In the distance, she heard the distinctive wail of a train whistle. "Oh, a train! Who do you suppose is coming in?"

Her father started to say something, then closed his mouth.

"Some men," Hurd said, sucking his teeth, "part of the cattlemen's business."

They came into town on the main road and headed toward the train station. Others were gathering, too. The arrival of a train in this small, isolated town was big news.

They pulled into the station, and Hurd got down and tied the horse to the hitching rail. Then he came around to help Sunny out of the buggy, but her father got there first.

Hurd frowned. "Now, Sunny, dear, you go along and shop. Your dad and I and some of the other members will meet the train."

"But it's so exciting!" she protested, shaking the dust from her pale blue cotton dress and readjusting her skewed bonnet, "I want to see who's getting off."

"Next year," Swen said to her with a smile, "maybe you will ride the train to Boston and go to college."

Hurd frowned. "Aw, don't put such high-falutin' ideas in her head, Swen. Maybe she'll want to get married instead. There ain't much need for a ranch wife to get an education."

Swen looked like he might disagree, but instead, pulled his Stetson down over his sparse hair as pale as Sunny's and turned toward the station.

The crowd of curious onlookers was growing on the platform as the trio joined them. In the distance, Sunny could see the smoke from the engine and hear the whistle as it chugged toward the town.

"Casper! Coming into Casper!" The conductor walked up and down the aisle and into the next car, "Casper next stop!"

On the sidewalk near the station, Sunny Sorrenson smiled at her father. "Oh, Dad, I never saw a train up close!"

"Yes, dear," Swen smiled back at her with eyes as blue as hers. "Hurd's been expecting it."

"Yep, this is a special train." Hurd walked toward them, smiling. "Now we'll get some action."

"What's going on?" Sunny smiled up at him. She was petite next to the big man.

"Now, sweetheart, never mind," Hurd paused in sucking his yellow teeth and nodded. "It's just cattle business—nothing to worry your pretty little head about."

"All right, Uncle Hurd." She saw a slight look of worry pass over her father's tanned face. He didn't often disagree with Hurd Kruger, their neighbor from the big K Bar ranch, especially since Hurd held the mortgage on their small spread and had been extra nice to them.

The train pulled into the station, puffing and blowing acrid smoke. People started gathering on the platform. The train arrival was always a big event in town. The three of them walked to the station in time to see the conductor step down and begin unloading baggage. After a moment, the passengers began to disembark. They were all men—tough-looking, weathered men, all wearing gun belts. The newcomers looked over the crowd, not smiling, then strode to the stock car, started unloading horses.

Sunny shielded her pale eyes from the sun. "Look at all those cowboys. Do you think they'll be able to find work here? I thought there were plenty in the area."

"Uh," her father cleared his throat, "Hurd brought them in."

"Be quiet, Swen," the other man snapped; then he smiled at her and said, "Now, Sunny, dear, why don't you run along and do some shopping? We men have things to discuss."

There was something wrong here, but she wasn't quite sure what it was. There must be almost twenty-five or thirty of these tough-looking cowboys milling about on the platform, gathering up their carpetbags and unloading their horses.

A tall, straight man with a mustache got off the train and strode over to them, smiling. "Well, Mr. Kruger, I brought them. Handpicked them, too, twenty-five or so of the best from Texas."

"Shut up, Canton," Hurd said, glancing at her. "We'll talk later."

She felt the men were withholding something because of her, but she was always obedient, as was expected of a young lady, so she walked away down the platform as Canton, Dad, and Hurd went to meet some of those men. They gathered and began to talk as she looked up at the train.

Then one final man stepped into the doorway of the railcar, looking about as if checking out the landscape. He caught her attention because he was so different than the others—taller and darker. He was dressed all in black, his Stetson pulled low over his dark face, and he wore moccasins instead of boots. From here, she could see the left side of his face, and he was handsome, with dark eyes and just wisps of very black hair showing beneath his hat. A *half-breed*, she thought. Unlike the others, he wore no silver conchos or spurs, and his pistol and gun belt were very plain and worn low and tied down. This was no ordinary cowboy, she realized with a sudden interest.

At that point, he turned his face toward her, and she took a deep breath and stepped backward in shock. While the left side of his face was handsome, the right side was scarred and twisted. "Oh, dear Lord," she whispered, trying not to stare but unable to take her eyes off the stranger.

He seemed to sense her horror, and he winced and turned quickly away so that his right side was hidden again.

* * *

Diablo watched her from the car step. He was almost hypnotized by the girl. She was certainly not yet twenty, and small. Her blue dress accentuated her eyes, which were as pale as a Texas sky, and her hair was lighter than corn silk. The tight waist accentuated her tiny body, and she was fragile and delicate, almost too delicate to be in this cold, harsh country. He had never seen anything like her before. He found himself staring at her full, pink lips, and without thinking, he turned his head to get a better look.

Too late he saw her hand go to her mouth and the way she stepped backward in dismay. Diablo turned his face away, too aware that his scarred face had frightened her, and the old anger arose in him. He would always have this effect on women, always. The fact made him angry with the beautiful, petite girl, although he knew it was not her fault.

Two men walked up to join the girl, not looking at Diablo. The older one had wispy hair, almost snow blond, and eyes as pale as the girl's. The other was middle-aged, perhaps in his forties with a small potbelly, and hair and mustache dyed too black to hide the gray.

Diablo's hand went to his pistol as the old memories flooded back. Then he forced himself to concentrate and not think of that long-ago day. He would pick the day and time, and this was not it. He grabbed his carpetbag and stepped back into the shadows of the car door so the men would not see him. He stared at the girl again, thinking he had never seen anything so fragile and beautiful. He wanted her as a man wants a woman, but was angry because she had recoiled from him. What could he expect? Didn't women always shrink back from his ugly face? And yet, he always hoped there would be one who wouldn't. Sunny, yes, that was what they had called her, and that was a good name for her. This girl was a magnificent princess; she could have any man she wanted, and she would not want him. He sighed and turned his attention again to the men congregating on the platform.

The man called Canton had joined the other two, and everyone's attention was on the crowd of gunfighters as they gathered around.

Diablo heard the big man say something to the girl about going shopping. She nodded, but Diablo saw that she was still staring back at him in a sort of horrid fascination.

"But Uncle Hurd, what about you and Dad?" the girl asked.

"We've got Stock Growers Association business to tend to. Now don't worry your pretty little head—you just run on, and we'll meet up with you later in the day. Here," the big man reached into his pocket, "here's some extra money to spend."

The older man objected. "But Hurd, I give her money all ready."

"So I give her some more. I've got plenty to spoil her."

The girl tried not to accept it. "Oh, Uncle Hurd, it's too much—"

"Nonsense. Now you run along and buy yourself something nice to wear at the party I might give soon."

The girl took the money, hugged both the two men, and left. Diablo's gaze followed her until she disappeared down the brick sidewalk and past the station. Then he watched the two men she had accompanied, and a terrible rage built in him as he remembered something too horrible to be voiced.

After fifteen years, he had returned as he had always promised himself he would. He cared nothing for the cattlemen's war. Diablo had come to Wyoming for one reason and for one reason only: he had come to torture and kill certain men, and one of them was one of the two men the girl had embraced.

# To My Readers

Yes, the mass hanging of the mostly Irish deserters of the St. Patrick's battalion during the Mexican-American War actually happened. The rebellion of almost six hundred soldiers was something the army managed to keep secret for more than one hundred years, but the scandal finally came out. It is our government's largest official execution in North America. However, as I've told you before in my earlier book, *Diablo,* it is not the largest mass execution within the United States' borders. That doubtful honor goes to the hanging of the Santee Sioux after an uprising known as Little Crow's War in Minnesota in 1862.

How many were hanged in the army rebellion? Figures vary, but it appears to be somewhere between forty and sixty. Why did the soldiers revolt? Some say it was because they were new immigrants, mostly Catholic, who had to deal with strict Protestant army officers. Others say it was because Mexico offered any soldier who joined up with them 320 free acres of land and Mexican citizenship. Some of those hanged were not even American citizens yet, so there is some question as to whether our government could legally punish them. Some soldiers were not hanged, but were given fifty lashes on their bare backs and branded on the cheek with the letter "D" for deserter. This was the fate of the revolt's leader, John Riley. The Saint Patrick's Brigade is still revered in Mexico today, with a monument to them in Mexico City.

For more information on this subject, I suggest the movie *One Man's Hero,* starring Tom Berenger. Look for Prince Albert of Monaco (yes, movie star Grace Kelly's son) in a cameo scene. In the credits, he's listed under his mother's maiden name.

Interesting reference books are: *The Shamrock and the Sword: The St. Patrick's Battalion in the U.S.-Mexican War,* by Robert Miller, OU Press, Norman, Oklahoma; *Rogue's March: John Riley and the St. Patrick's Battalion, 1846–48,* by Peter F. Stevens, published by Potomac Books Inc., Dulles, Virginia. Finally, if your local library has the Time-Life Old West series, the volume entitled *The Mexican War* is very readable.

Dueling used to be a way for gentlemen to solve their disagreements. It was so popular in Texas in the 1830s that a law was passed forbidding it. Of course, the most famous duel in American history is Alexander Hamilton versus Aaron Burr in 1804. The pistols belonged to Hamilton and his son had been killed with those very pistols in an earlier duel. These pistols still exist and today are in a bank vault in New York City. When they were closely examined in 1976, it was discovered they had trick "hair" triggers that could cause them to shoot prematurely.

If some of the characters in Rio seem familiar, the Durango family has appeared in a number of my stories. Turquoise and Edwin Forester first appeared in *Cheyenne Princess.* If you have already read that book, you were not surprised at the shocking ending to the story you have just read.

So what will I write about next? I'm going to continue the Texan series. *Diablo* was about a gunfighter, *Rio* about a vaquero. Next, we are going to cover Colton Prescott, a lieutenant in the U.S. Army in Texas. The army was attempting to hold off the Comanche Indians who were ravaging that state's western borders in the 1850s, before the beginning of the Civil War.

Colt is a true Texan and a career soldier; tall, with black hair and bright green eyes. When he was young, he lived among the Comanche for five years and knows their ways.

How does this story fit into the panorama of the Old West? Colt was a small boy on the 1830s wagon train along with Texanna, the beauty who was carried off by the Cheyenne. Texanna became the mother of Iron Knife and Cimarron, who both had their own stories earlier.

Now grown up, Colt is engaged to the major's beautiful and arrogant daughter, Olivia, who has inherited a great fortune from her mother's family. She wants her daddy to promote Colt so she can marry him and take him back to a civilized life in Washington, D.C., where they can live comfortably in rich society.

Then the army rescues Hannah Brownley, a yellow-haired woman who has been held captive by the Comanche for three years, and she comes with a small half-breed son. She is an outcast and certainly her husband, who has already married again, doesn't want her back since she has been used by a savage and won't give up her Indian son.

Hannah doesn't seem to fit in anywhere, especially at the fort with Olivia and the officers' wives and daughters, who are horrified she didn't kill herself rather than share a savage's blankets. All the soldiers think of Hannah as a whore and try to sleep with her, but she resists their advances.

As the weeks pass, it's more and more evident that she might as well go back to the Comanches because she fits in nowhere and no one knows what to do with this hapless girl. However, her brave and indomitable spirit appeals to Colt and her small, outcast son tugs at his heartstrings. Is he willing to fight a Comanche chief to keep her and turn his back on his promising military future? Torn between his rich, beautiful fiancée and the ragged outcast, Hannah, which will Colt choose?

Our next book of the Texas series probably will be out in early 2012. Look for *Colt: The Texans.*

For those who keep asking how the stories all fit together, here it is. Remember the books are not written in chronological order. If you want to read them in chronological order, go by the date the story begins. Thus, *Warrior's Honor* (1857) was the first in the series, although it was the twentieth printed.

The Panorama of the Old West

1. *Cheyenne Captive* (1858)
   Iron Knife and Summer Van Schuyler, the Boston socialite

2. *Cheyenne Princess* (1864)
   Cimarron (Iron Knife's sister) and Trace Durango

3. *Comanche Cowboy* (1874)
   Cayenne McBride and Maverick Durango (Trace's adopted brother)

4. *Bandit's Embrace* (1873)
   Bandit and Amethyst Durango (a Mexican cousin to the Texas Durangos)

5. *Nevada Nights* (1860)
   Dallas Durango (Trace's sister) and Quint Randolph

6. *Quicksilver Passion* (1860)
   Silver Jones and Cherokee Evans (a friend of Quint Randolph

7. *Cheyenne Caress* (1869)
   Luci and Johnny Ace (son of Bear's Eyes, Iron Knife's Pawnee enemy)

8. *Apache Caress* (1886)
   Sierra Forester and Cholla (the Forester family are old enemies of the Durangos)

 9. *Christmas Rendezvous* (1889)
    Ginny Malone (Sassy Malone's cousin) and Hawk

10. *Sioux Slave* (1864)
    Kimi and Rand (Randolph) Erikson (a cousin on
    his mother's side to Quint Randolph)

11. *Half-Breed's Bride* (1865)
    Sassy Malone and Hunter (Sassy used to work
    as a maid in Summer Van Schuyler's mansion)

12. *Nevada Dawn* (1887)
    Cherish Blassingame and Nevada Randolph
    (Quint and Dallas's son), a sequel to *Nevada
    Nights*

13. *Cheyenne Splendor* (1864)
    Summer, Iron Knife, and their children (a sequel
    to *Cheyenne Captive*)

14. *Song of the Warrior* (1877)
    Willow and Bear (Iron Knife once saved this
    Nez Perce warrior's life)

15. *Timeless Warrior* (1873)
    Blossom Murdock and Terry (brother of Pawnee
    scout Johnny Ace)

16. *Warrior's Prize* (1879)
    Wannie and Keso (the children adopted by
    Cherokee Evans and his wife, Silver), a sequel to
    *Quicksilver Passion*

17. *Cheyenne Song* (1878)
    Glory Halstead and Two Arrows (Iron Knife's
    cousin)

18. *Eternal Outlaw* (1892)
    Angie Newland and Johnny Logan (Johnny was
    in prison with Nevada Randolph)

19. *Apache Tears* (1881)
    Libbie Winters and Cougar (Cholla's fellow
    scout and friend)

20. *Warrior's Honor* (1857)
    Talako and Lusa (a schoolmate of Summer Van
    Schuyler)

21. *Warrior's Heart* (1862)
    Rider (a gunfighter taught by Trace Durango)
    and Emma Trent (the girl raped by Angry Wolf
    in *Cheyenne Splendor*)

22. *To Tame a Savage* (1868)
    Austin Shaw (Summer Van Schuyler's former
    fiancé) and Wiwila; also their son Colt and
    Samantha McGregor

23. *To Tame a Texan* (1885)
    Ace Durango (son of Cimarron and Trace
    Durango) and Lynnie McBride (younger sister
    of Cayenne McBride)

24. *To Tame a Rebel* (1861)
    Yellow Jacket and Twilight Dumont, Jim Eagle
    and April Grant (both men are scouts and friends
    of Talako)

25. *To Tempt a Texan* (1889)
    Blackie O'Neal and Lacey Van Schuyler (one of
    the twin daughters of Iron Knife and Summer
    Van Schuyler)

26. *To Tease a Texan* (1890)
    Larado and Lark Van Schuyler (Lacey's twin
    sister)

27. *My Heroes Have Always Been Cowboys* (1893)
    Henrietta Jenkins and Comanche Jones (a cowboy
    from Trace Durango's Triple D ranch)

You may write me at: Box 162, Edmond, OK 73083, or
see my new website at: georginagentrybooks.com. If you
would like to buy some of my past novels, many book-
stores carry them or can order them. You can also find
some of them online at www.kensingtonbooks.com. This
long, continuing series began in 1987, so it is very difficult
to find the earliest books. Perhaps Kensington will reprint
them eventually.

*Via con Dios,*
Georgina Gentry